...rri Flowers is an award-winn... **LIBRARIES**
...er, mystery and romance fic...uired ...
...-dimensional protagonists, riveting plots, unexpected
...s and turns, and heart-pounding climaxes. With an
...rtise in true crime, serial killers and characterising
...gerous offenders, he is perfectly suited for the
...s & Boon Heroes series. Chemistry and conflict
...veen the hero and heroine, attention to detail and
...orporating the very latest advances in criminal
...estigations are the cornerstones of his romantic
...pense fiction. Discover more on popular social networks
...l Wikipedia.

...w *York Times* and *USA Today* bestselling, award-winning
...thor **Lisa Childs** has written more than eighty-five
...ovels. Published in twenty countries, she's also appeared
...n the *Publishers Weekly*, Barnes & Noble and Nielsen
...op 100 bestseller lists. Lisa writes contemporary
...omance, romantic suspense, paranormal and women's
...ction. She's a wife, mum, bonus mum, avid reader and
...ess avid runner. Readers can reach her through Facebook
...r her website, lisachilds.com

SPECIAL AGENT WITNESS

R. BARRI FLOWERS

PROTECTING COLTON'S SECRET DAUGHTERS

LISA CHILDS

MILLS & BOON

First Published in Great Britain 2023
by Mills & Boon, an imprint of HarperCollins*Publishers* Ltd
1 London Bridge Street, London, SE1 9GF

www.harpercollins.co.uk

HarperCollins*Publishers*
Macken House, 39/40 Mayor Street Upper,
Dublin 1, D01 C9W8, Ireland

Special Agent Witness © 2023 R. Barri Flowers
Protecting Colton's Secret Daughters © 2023 Harlequin Enterprises ULC.

Special thanks and acknowledgement are given to Lisa Childs for her contribution to *The Coltons of New York* series.

ISBN: 978-0-263-30742-9

SPECIAL AGENT
WITNESS

R. BARRI FLOWERS

In memory of my beloved mother, Marjah Aljean, a devoted lifetime fan of Mills & Boon romances, who inspired me to do my very best in finding success in my personal and professional lives. To H. Loraine, the true love of my life, whose support has been unwavering through the many years together; and to the loyal fans of my romance, mystery, suspense and thriller fiction published over the years. Lastly, a nod goes out to my wonderful editors, Allison Lyons and Denise Zaza, for the opportunity to lend my literary voice and creative spirit to the Mills & Boon Heroes line.

Prologue

Homeland Security Investigations Special Agent Rosamund Santiago was on an undercover assignment with her HSI partner, Special Agent Johnnie Langford, in Dallas, Texas. They were on their way to an important make-or-break meeting this evening. *We can't afford any slipups*, she thought, as they headed south. If things went as planned, after a six-month investigation, they would soon put a major human trafficking, sex trafficking, and money laundering operation out of commission. In this undertaking, they were working in conjunction with the U.S. Immigration and Customs Enforcement, Federal Bureau of Investigation, North Texas Trafficking Task Force, and the Dallas Police Department. The primary target and ringleader of the criminal enterprise was a man named Simon Griswold, who pretended to be a reputable businessman, importing antique and contemporary furniture from Mexico and South America. In fact, this was nothing more than a facade for his real mission, which was the human trafficking and sexual exploitation of noncitizens and vulnerable American women and minors, enriching himself and his operatives in the process.

For Rosamund, as important as taking down human traffickers and other criminals was for her career, it was also personal. As a thirty-two-year-old Latina, born and raised in El Paso, Texas, she had witnessed firsthand as a girl the smuggling of humans against their will across the Rio Grande and U.S.–Mexico border, and the even greater cruelties that often awaited them in the states they were dispersed to. She knew then that she wanted to do something to stop this when she was old enough and the opportunity presented itself. It did, once she had completed her Master of Arts degree in Criminology and Criminal Justice from the University of Texas at Arlington and went to work for the Department of Homeland Security's Center for Countering Human Trafficking seven years ago. With literally tens of thousands of human trafficking cases documented in Texas every year, ranging from child trafficking and domestic servitude, to forced prostitution and sexual exploitation, to human smuggling and labor trafficking, Rosamund admittedly had her hands full.

With such a workload, it didn't give her time for a meaningful social life, much less the opportunity to have a serious romance. But this didn't mean she did not long for both at some point. Who wouldn't? As for a love life, she had to believe that if the right person came along, she would know it, and everything else would fall into place. Wouldn't it?

"How you doing over there?" Langford asked as he drove them to the destination in the black Ford Explorer. Part of their work together was their undercover life, posing as an unmarried couple who had gotten comfortable building a lucrative business as human traffickers. In truth, thirty-five-year-old Langford, a ten-year veteran with the Department of Homeland Security, was happily married to a lovely woman named Katie and was the father of two cute and energetic little boys. And the only real involvement between her and Langford was their shared desire to make the world a better place in the small way they could contribute to that happening.

Rosamund realized she had been silent in her reverie. Or feeling slightly tense, as always, whenever an operation was about to go down. She eyed him from the passenger seat. African American, he was as fit as she was, four inches taller at six feet, and had short black hair styled in waves and a line-up cut. His brown eyes were deeper than her own, which were a softer hazel. She forced a smile and said convincingly, "I'm good. Just want this to go without a hitch." She knew they would be meeting Simon Griswold alone, hoping to catch him in a moment of weakness and get just enough additional evidence to what they had already accumulated to make an arrest. At which time, they would really lay the hammer to him in the hopes of breaking up the entire human trafficking ring.

"It will," Langford assured her. "Griswold has no reason to believe this is anything other than business as usual. Whatever he gives us to hang himself, we'll take. And if he has brought any trafficked victims along for the ride, we'll make sure they're taken care of without blowing our cover."

"Okay." She smiled again, realizing this sense of dread she was feeling was nothing more than wanting to get this over with, as always. Griswold was supposed to give them the time and place for the arrival of a tractor trailer that was being used to smuggle noncitizens into the country. Rosamund and Langford would pretend to aid in getting them fake identifications and otherwise helping with integrating them into society and introducing them to would-be exploiters of the trafficked victims. In reality, these were fellow HSI and ICE agents removing them from harm's way.

But should there be any hiccups, there were other investigators on standby, ready and able to come to their assistance, when and if they gave the signal. Beyond that, Rosamund knew she and Langford were armed with Sig Sauer P320-XTEN 10-millimeter striker-fired pistols and wearing ballistic vests. Then there was the fact that she had recently taken up Thai boxing as a means for self-defense and as a combat sport. So, really, what was there to worry about?

They arrived at the Bricks Motel on Appolane Road and parked in the lot. Langford said with a quiet sigh, "Let's get this over with."

"I'm ready," she said calmly and flipped her curly black ponytail for effect. They exited the vehicle and approached Room 110. As they did so, Rosamund got an uneasy feeling. *Something's not quite right*, she thought. The parking lot was lowly lit and there were a few other cars in the lot. She did note the familiar metallic gray BMW iX parked in front of the room. Once they neared it, the driver's-side door opened and the man they were meeting stepped out.

Simon Griswold was forty years old and just under

six feet tall with a medium build. He was wearing a dark suit with dark shoes. His salt-and-pepper hair was styled in a pompadour fade. "You're late," he said brusquely.

"Traffic," Langford told him tonelessly.

"In fact, we're actually ten minutes early," Rosamund said, suspecting Griswold was simply pushing their buttons for whatever reason.

"Why don't we go inside?" he said tersely, his blue eyes landing on her briefly.

As they followed him to the door, she again had the sense that something wasn't right. She wondered if they should abort the meeting. But before she could act on this and alert Langford, the door was opened and Langford went inside, along with Griswold. The moment she stepped through the door and Griswold shut it behind her, Rosamund saw he was holding a gun. It looked like a .357 Magnum revolver. The weapon was pointed at Langford, who said angrily, "What is this?"

"You tell me," Griswold responded gruffly. "I don't like doing business with feds."

Langford looked uncomfortable. "I don't know where you got your intel, but it's wrong."

"I don't think so," the human trafficker spat. Before Langford could go for his weapon, Griswold shot him point-blank in the head. She watched with horror as her partner fell to the floor, feeling both helpless and shaken to the core in that moment.

Then out of the corner of her eye, Rosamund spotted movement. A tall and stocky bald-headed man had come out of the bathroom. She turned to see him reach for something inside his leather jacket. A gun. *He plans to kill me too, unless I can beat him to the draw*, she told herself. Instinctively, she pulled out her own weapon and immediately fired at the man, twice, putting him down. She turned back to Griswold to see he had lined her up in his sights for the kill before she could aim her gun at him.

"Goodbye, Special Agent Santiago," he said with a sneer.

As her life flashed before her eyes, Rosamund couldn't see any way out of this. No future to look forward to. No romance with a loving man waiting in the wings. But as she stood there, expecting to be shot in the head like Langford, she saw that Griswold's gun had apparently jammed. As Griswold muttered an expletive, Rosamund realized she now had the upper hand. But before she could use it, Griswold charged her, dislodging the gun from her hand as the two went down.

"I'll kill you with my bare hands," he said.

But as he tried to wrap his thick hands around her neck, Rosamund felt just as confident in her ability to take him in hand-to-hand combat. *I have to fight back or die trying*, she told herself. Relying on quick movements she had learned in her Thai boxing classes, Rosamund slammed both fists into Griswold's temples as hard as she could and then smashed a fist solidly into the top of his bulbous nose, breaking it and rendering him unconscious as he slumped beside her on the hard tile floor.

After quickly handcuffing the man, Rosamund scurried over to her seriously wounded partner and gasped. It didn't take much to realize that Johnnie Langford was gone.

THREE DAYS LATER, Rosamund attended the funeral of Homeland Security Investigations Special Agent Langford, who was laid to rest in a cemetery in his hometown of Beaumont, Texas. His beautiful widow, Katie Langford, was overcome with emotion as the pastor paid tribute to the slain investigator at the graveside service. Standing on opposite sides of her were Katie's sons, Johnnie Jr. and Desmond, ages seven and five, respectively. Both reminded Rosamund of her fallen partner. She couldn't imagine what they must be going through, having lost their dad before ever having enough time to truly get to know him as a father, man, and someone who gave his life fighting crime and victimization.

Rosamund felt both grateful and uneasy that his killer had failed to take her out. Instead, she had turned the tables on him and stopped him from his lethal mission. But even with that victory, she realized there was still much work to be done to destroy the human trafficking operation that had resulted in so much suffering and exploitation. Until she was able to finish the job by testifying against the trafficker, Rosamund knew that Johnnie Langford would never be able to rest in peace.

Chapter One

Rosamund sat on a plush armchair in the large office of the HSI Dallas Field Office special agent in charge Harold Paxton, the fortysomething former Bureau of Alcohol, Tobacco, Firearms and Explosives deputy special agent in charge of the field office in Albuquerque, New Mexico. She informed Paxton that she believed there was a mole in the organization who had caused the death of her partner, Johnnie Langford, at the hands of reputed human trafficker Simon Griswold.

She knew Griswold was now in federal custody and faced a slew of charges, including murder and attempted murder, human smuggling, and the sexual exploitation of women and children. She also knew someone had tipped off Griswold that they were undercover agents, which had cost Langford his life. Rosamund felt it was only by sheer luck, or something akin to a gun malfunctioning miracle, that she had survived Griswold's attempt to silence her for good. It had failed, but she was still reeling from the way things had gone down. Rosamund glanced at her new partner, Virginia Flannery, who was sitting beside her. Virginia was the same age as Rosamund, tall, slender, and attractive, with aquamarine eyes and light blonde hair styled in a feathered pixie. Rosamund imagined she could have chosen any occupation and been successful, with a degree in computing and linguistics from Yale University. Instead, she preferred a career in law enforcement and had been with the DHS for nearly a decade. Though saddened at having lost her partner, Rosamund felt fortunate that his replacement was someone she believed Johnnie would have approved of.

She turned to Harold Paxton, who stood behind his desk wearing a gray suit on a husky frame. He had short red hair and a horseshoe-shaped hairline. Gold-flecked green eyes with bags beneath looked back at her pensively. Next to him was Monroe Cortez, U.S. Marshal for the Northern District of Texas. In his early fifties, he was tall and lean, with short gray hair tapered on the sides and brown eyes behind oval glasses.

"You were right, Agent Santiago," Paxton said with a sigh. "We do seem to have a problem in our midst that needs to be dealt with."

That's an understatement, Rosamund mused. She batted her curly lashes. "With all due respect, Sir, that 'problem' has compromised our entire investigation and got Johnnie Langford killed. It needs more than merely being dealt with." Immediately, Rosamund wished she could take it back, fearing she had overstepped her bounds. She glanced at Virginia, who offered a tiny supportive smile.

"I couldn't agree more," he said levelly. "Losing Langford has affected all of us, up and down the chain. Whoever ratted him out will be discovered and prosecuted to the full extent of the law." Paxton's brow furrowed. "The work you two put in cannot be overstated in nailing those involved in the sordid business of human trafficking. And cannot be further jeopardized by having someone come after you too. Your testimony key in successfully prosecuting Simon Griswold. It will have a ripple effect on his entire operation."

"I'm aware of that," she told him, feeling the pressure of needing to stay alive. "And I will certainly take any necessary steps to ensure my safety."

"Unfortunately, we'll need to go further than that," he said. "Since Griswold is desperate to keep you from testifying, making you a sitting duck is simply not an option."

Rosamund swallowed. "So, what are you saying? Round-the-clock protection?" She tried to imagine having to wine and dine security at her place while essentially giving up her privacy. But wasn't that preferable to being killed?

"We'll be placing you in the federal witness security program," Paxton stated with a straight face.

"What?" For a moment, Rosamund thought she misunderstood him.

Then he reiterated it. "We need to keep you out of harm's way till Griswold goes to trial in a few months. I know this may seem extreme, but—"

She interrupted him, "Witness security program, really?" The thought of what that could entail unnerved Rosamund. "Can't you assign marshals or even a secret service detail to protect me?" She glanced at Monroe Cortez, who remained impassive.

"We intend to do the former. Not so much the latter."

Paxton rubbed his jutting chin for a beat. "In this instance, even that is insufficient for protecting you."

Rosamund sensed there was more to this. "What aren't you telling me?" *Or will I need to figure it out myself?* she thought uneasily.

He paused again, his forehead wrinkled. "We have good reason to believe that Simon Griswold put a hit out on you."

"What?" she said, chilled at the notion.

"According to one of our informants, Griswold has hired an unidentified professional assassin to take you out," Paxton told her bluntly. "Griswold figures that with you out of the way, he walks. He has a good point. Your testimony and corroborating evidence are enough to put him away for life. But if you die, with Langford no longer around to testify in court, the case against Griswold could very well fall apart. It's a chance we're not willing to take." He flashed his eyes at Cortez. "This is where the U.S. Marshals Service comes in. Till we go to trial, under the WITSEC, they'll be relocating you, and providing a new identity and authentic credentials to that effect. U.S. Marshal Cortez will coordinate this and brief you accordingly."

"I'll be happy to answer any questions you have, Agent Santiago," Cortez spoke up.

Indeed, Rosamund did have more questions than she could get out at once, unsure precisely how this would work. But one question in particular came to mind. "When exactly will this go into effect?"

"It already has," Cortez responded matter-of-factly.

"From this point on, your life is no longer your own, per se." Cortez looked at Paxton for help.

"You won't be able to go back to your apartment," Paxton advised her. "It's too dangerous. Agent Flannery will drop by, accompanied by deputy marshals, to collect a few personal items and clothing and that's it. You'll need to hand over your cell phone and laptop, along with any other devices that have information that can identify or track you and possibly lead a hired killer to your whereabouts."

Virginia touched her shoulder. "I'll be sure to keep my intrusion into your personal space as minimal as possible," she uttered sympathetically. "And it will be just as you left it upon your return."

"Thank you," Rosamund acknowledged, knowing she was only doing her job.

"Sorry our newfound partnership will be short-lived," Virginia said. "But we can pick up where we left off once the threat has been neutralized and Simon Griswold and his cronies have been put away in federal prison for the rest of their lives."

Rosamund nodded. *Griswold deserves nothing less after his coldblooded murder of Johnnie*, she thought. Same for his partners in the crimes involved within human trafficking. She looked forward to coming out of this on the other end and resuming her career as an HSI special agent. That was, assuming she was successful in hiding from Griswold's hired assassin. The fact that he was willing to take this to such extremes made it clear that he feared what she knew and would say in court to take him down. She had to abide by the rules if she was to successfully testify against Griswold and re-claim her life.

As if to hammer down those sentiments and sense of urgency, Paxton, with his thick brows knitted, said, "I don't think I need to tell you, Agent Santiago, just how important it is for you and the DHS's Center for Countering Human Trafficking, along with the other agencies involved, to keep you alive and able to do your job as laid out."

"I'm able and willing to do what's necessary, Sir," Rosamund made clear, in spite of some concerns about making the needed adjustments that came with a new life. How could she not acquiesce, considering the alternative? "You can count on me to cooperate fully."

For the first time since she'd come into his office, Harold Paxton flashed a smile. "I was hoping you'd say that." He glanced at Cortez. "Well, let's get this over with, and in no time flat Simon Griswold will pay the price for all his illegal activities and then we can all go about our business of enforcing the law against other lowlifes like him."

Rosamund grinned in an act of cooperation, even while feeling butterflies in her stomach in taking on a new and unexpected challenge in her career.

ROSAMUND HAD BEEN temporarily relocated to Weconta Falls, a small, picturesque waterfront town tucked away in Northern California, not too far from the San Francisco Bay Area. Admittedly, this was the type of place Rosamund could have imagined retiring to, with its peaceful environment, abundance of Douglas fir, Western hemlock, and tanoak evergreen trees, and parks, and running trails. Problem was that her desired retirement was years, if not decades, away. Rosamund would have preferred to be back on the job, trying to do her part to put away the bad guys. Such as Simon Griswold. But she needed to lay low until such time when her testimony could wipe the smugness off his face, even as he awaited trial.

In the interim, she was now Tisha González. Rosamund had chosen the name as a combination of her beloved late grandmother's middle name and the last name of a childhood friend, Maria, before she married and took her husband's surname. Rosamund felt the new name had a nice ring to it, even if she lived for the day when she no longer needed to use it. But for the time being, she would do whatever was asked of her if it meant staying alive.

That included not drawing undue attention to herself, while still trying to fit into her new surroundings. Presently, she was at the Creek Crust Townhouses complex on Fenella Street, where she had been provided an end unit on a dead-end street.

"Well, here it is," voiced her handler, Leah Redfield. The deputy U.S. marshal was in her midthirties and well-proportioned on a five-foot-nine frame. She had short red hair in a pixie bob cut and blue eyes. This was her fifth year on the job and second as a divorcée. "Probably not what you were used to, huh?"

Rosamund sized up the downstairs. Fully furnished with contemporary furniture, it was pleasant enough with a separate living room, dining room, den, and kitchen, with engineered hardwood flooring and faux wood blinds on bay windows. *I'll make it livable*, she told herself. But still, she already missed her spacious split-level loft, with its floor-to-ceiling fiberglass windows, vinyl plank floors, and bamboo furniture. "It's fine," she told the handler, committed to trying to make the most of it.

"Why don't we take a look upstairs," Leah said.

Rosamund followed her up the staircase and found two bedrooms similar in size and with furnishings matching those downstairs. Again, not her taste, but it would have to do for as long as she was a resident of Weconta Falls. And who knew how long that would last. They went back to the main floor and Rosamund noted the door off the kitchen. She asked, "Where does that lead to?"

"Actually, I was just about to show you." Leah opened the door. "It's a direct access to the garage. And your car."

"Really?" Rosamund stepped into the garage, curious. In her other life, she had recently purchased a Subaru Forester Sport. She eyed the silver vehicle.

"It's a Hyundai Elantra," Leah told her. "Comes with GPS to help you get around more easily. Keys are inside."

"Hmm...okay." Rosamund was ready to take it for a test drive, but that would have to come later, as they went back inside the townhouse.

"There's a security system," Leah said. "It's a pretty safe area, so there shouldn't be any problems, generally speaking."

"Good." Rosamund nodded, while thinking that an assassin was past the point of generally speaking, should he or she ever find her location before the trial. So a security system was an important part of her safety. Along with her firearm, one of the few things she had been allowed to keep in her new life as a means for self-defense.

"Using the program's vast resources and connections

with a temp agency, we were able to find you a job as a waitress at a restaurant in town," Leah was saying. "I looked at your file and saw that you did some waitressing in college. So this should be a piece of cake for you and save the trouble of looking for something yourself."

Rosamund frowned. "I'm still drawing my salary, but not able to access it, of course," she pointed out, which was the least her employers could have done for an involuntary reassignment until it was over. In the meantime, before this went into effect, she was able to draw out some cash from her savings that had been tucked away for a rainy day, which this certainly qualified as.

"That's great you're still getting paid. Not all persons under witness protection are afforded that luxury." Leah smoothed a thin brow. "But it's important for you to give the guise, if nothing else, of fitting in with a normal life so as not to stand out. Working in a job that doesn't draw much attention is part of that process."

"I understand," Rosamund relented. "Don't mean to be difficult." Or maybe venting a little made her feel better about the situation. She forced a grin. "When do I start?" She hoped the waitressing all came back to her in a snap.

"Tomorrow," her handler said. "All you need to do is show up. The sooner you get acclimated, the better."

Rosamund nodded. "Juggling dishes and drinks, here I come," she joked.

Leah chuckled. "Well, I'll let you get settled in."

"All right." She walked her to the door, while Rosamund wondered what the future had in store for her as she navigated this new life under an assumed name.

"Oh, I almost forgot." Leah turned around and pulled

out a cell phone from her leather jacket. "This is for you."
She handed it to Rosamund. "It's a secure line and you'll
always be able to reach me whenever you need to. I'm
sure it goes without saying that you're not to use it to
contact family, friends, colleagues, you get the picture.
Anyone from your former life who has even an inkling
of your whereabouts could put you in danger, along with
themselves."

"Got it." Rosamund clutched the cell phone to her
chest. One of the most painful things in leaving Dallas
was not even being able to call her parents and younger
sister to say goodbye. But those were the rules of WIT-
SEC, along with temporarily removing access to credit
cards, bank accounts, social networks, and any other
traceable means for someone out to kill her. She was
more than up to the task, having no desire to jeopardize
the safety of anyone she cared about.

Leah smiled. "Then I'll be on my way." She gave her
a supportive look. "Good luck with this."

Rosamund smiled back. "Thanks." She saw her out
and peeked through the window as Leah got into her official vehicle, a red Buick Encore, and drove off. Alone
for the first time since all this started, Rosamund got
the measure of the place she would be calling home for
the foreseeable future. She ended up in the en suite of
the primary bedroom. Glancing at her reflection in the
mirror above a soapstone countertop, she took note of
the new hairstyle. Her previously mid-back-length curly
dark hair, cut in a U-shaped blunt style, was now medium
length in a layered lob. She liked it, but it would still take
some getting used to. It hadn't been a prerequisite of the

program, but more of a precautionary move to make her appearance that much different than before. What hadn't changed was having a complexion that made it unnecessary to wear much, if any, makeup. *Hopefully, I'll fit right in with the surroundings and new job*, she told herself. As though she had much of a choice. Not when it came down to that in order to stay alive.

THE HITMAN WONDERED where the pretty Homeland Security Investigations special agent was hiding. Rosamund Santiago had seemingly vanished into thin air. At least that was what Special Agent in Charge Harold Paxton would have one believe. In coordinating with U.S. Marshal Monroe Cortez, they had put Rosamund in the federal Witness Security Program and relocated her somewhere across the United States, other than Dallas, believing she would be safe from harm. Long enough to testify against the hitman's employer, Simon Griswold. Well, think and think again. That would not happen. As far as the assassin was concerned, the question was not if, but when he would fulfill the hit on the target for which he was being paid handsomely.

He was sure it would be sooner than later. Rosamund Santiago may be living under a different name to try to escape her all but certain fate, but he was undeterred. The hitman was methodical in tracking down those slated for death. His very reputation depended upon finishing every job he started. That meant following every lead and turning over any stones that would point him in the right direction. *Enjoy hiding out, Agent Santiago, for as long as you can*, the hitman thought, feeling the adrenaline rush that came with the hunt before the kill. When it was over, Rosamund Santiago would be dead like her late HSI partner, Johnnie Langford. And with this, the case against Griswold would go away.

DETECTIVE RUSSELL LYNLEY sat in the well-worn tufted armchair at his equally weathered wooden desk inside the small office at the Weconta Falls Police Department. The office had been passed along to him eight months ago by his predecessor, Fritz Kowalski, who retired the day he reached sixty-five, while still able to go out on his own terms. Russell only wished he could say he'd taken the job under his own terms. Instead, his life and times had been more or less dictated by family heritage and misfortune. None of which he had been able to have much control over, if not for lack of trying.

His parents, Taylor and Caroline Lynley, had both been involved in the criminal justice system in Oklahoma, where Russell was born and raised. While his father had a career in law enforcement with the Oklahoma City Police Department, rising to the rank of chief of police, his mother left her mark as an Oklahoma County District Court criminal judge. When they weren't dispensing justice, his parents were raising four children, including one adopted. Like Russell, all would end up following their parents' footsteps into law enforcement.

Russell was the third oldest sibling, behind Scott and Madison, and just ahead of Annette. After graduating from the University of Oklahoma with a Master of Science in Criminal Justice, Russell chose to go Scott's route in joining the FBI, becoming a special agent. Two years ago, he had been based in St. Louis, Missouri, enjoying the good life with his college sweetheart turned wife, Victoria, and their seven-year-old daughter, Daisy. Then unimaginable disaster struck. A brazen daytime home invasion left his wife and daughter dead, devastating Russell. Though the culprits were apprehended, tried, and convicted, before being sent to prison for the rest of their disgusting lives, the violent victimization left its mark on his life, coming so soon after the death of Russell's parents two years earlier in a car crash. Losing Victoria and Daisy had shaken his faith in human nature and the laws of morality.

Feeling empty and disillusioned, Russell quit his job with the Bureau. In spite of the support of his siblings, who had always been there for him, it simply wasn't enough. Wanting to seek a new direction in his life, he landed a job with the Weconta Falls PD as a senior detective and had settled, more or less, into a life in the small town in Northern California. While he wouldn't go so far as to say it was a crime-free atmosphere—there were the occasional murders, attempted murders, and other crimes of violence—much of the criminal activity was nonviolent or juveniles stirring up trouble to escape boredom. All in all, it was a nice respite from the big city crime and its consequences that he had left behind.

Though he would always carry with him the treasured memory of his wife and daughter, Russell had reached the stage where he was at least open to pursuing a new relationship, should it come knocking on his door and the pieces fit. Until such time, he was content to roll with the punches in simply fitting in and enjoying the things he did in his personal life, such as jogging, working out, reading, and relaxing to the sounds of jazz standards.

Russell was finishing up some paperwork on an investigation into an overnight shooting between feuding neighbors, leaving one with a non-life-threatening gunshot wound to the leg and the other in jail, when Detective Ike Wainright and Detective Gloria Choi stepped into his office. The two were partners and probably the ones Russell felt closest to on the force. Like him, both were in their early thirties. Ike was African American, an inch taller than Russell's six-foot-two height, a bit leaner, and had sable eyes and dark hair worn in mini dreads. Gloria was Korean American, a few inches shorter than six feet, slender, with long black hair pulled tight into a ballerina bun, and brown eyes.

"What's up, you two?" Russell asked, knowing they had been investigating a drug deal gone sour.

"We arrested the suspect," Gloria said. "Turns out the drug dealer was a twenty-seven-year-old unwed mother of three."

"Claims she only wanted to sell a small amount of fentanyl to pay the bills," Ike said.

"Did you believe her?" Russell asked, not that any excuse was justifiable for distributing illicit drugs into the community.

"Not really," he responded. "If she'd had her way, we'd be trying to locate more than a small amount of fentanyl, along with the meth and cocaine she possessed. But her buyer turned out to be a church deacon, who not only stiffed her, but turned the illegal drugs over to the authorities."

Russell grinned. "Good for him—and all of us, wanting to keep drugs off the street."

"Amen to that." Gloria chuckled.

A FEW MINUTES LATER, Russell left the building driving his official vehicle, a blue Dodge Charger SRT. While on duty, he was armed with a Glock 26 9-millimeter pistol, which he kept in a shoulder holster. He drove to a clothing store in the Weconta Falls Shopping Center on Tolton Way and took the statement of a clerk for an alleged shoplifting. Afterward, since he was in the area, Russell stopped by one of his favorite places to get a cup of coffee, Shailene's Grill, a block away on Liverwood Street.

He had just taken a seat by the window when he laid his solid gray eyes upon the gorgeous, dark-haired waitress waiting to take his order. The name tag on her beige café uniform identified her as Tisha. Giving her the once-over, he saw that she was appealingly small and around five foot eight. Her mid-length raven hair was in an attractive French roll updo. She had a square face and high cheekbones, pretty brown eyes that twinkled, perhaps even without her being aware, and a delicate nose. *Just the type of woman I could see myself with*, he thought, knowing full well he was putting the cart ahead of the horse. Not that the waitress was horselike in any way, shape, or form.

"If you need a few more minutes," she said impatiently, one hand on a narrow hip, "I can come back."

Russell colored, realizing he had been staring, a habit he usually tried to avoid, other than when interrogating suspects. He was fairly sure she wasn't a criminal in disguise. Yet, he sensed there was something more to the lady than taking orders for gawking men like him. "Actually, Tisha," he said smoothly, "I think I'll just have coffee, black."

She managed a smile and replied evenly, "One black coffee coming up." And with that, she left him wanting to know a lot more about her.

Chapter Two

In spite of her best efforts to the contrary, Rosamund couldn't help but check out the good-looking customer in what was her second full week as a waitress at Shailene's Grill. She guessed he was in his early thirties with black hair in a high and tight cut. He had deep gray eyes that she imagined a person could get lost in. An oblong face featured a broad nose, wide mouth, and a pleasing five o'clock shadow. Tall, with a solid build, he wore a business casual tan linen blazer over a navy cotton shirt, steel-colored khaki pants, and brown loafers.

Rosamund found herself trying to picture his lot in life. Businessman. Educator. Law enforcement. She wondered if he was married. Or had children. Not that it mattered. Knowing her time there was temporary, she wasn't exactly in a position to seek out someone to build a relationship with. On the other hand, as this was her current location and there was no one waiting back in Dallas for her return, she supposed there was nothing wrong with keeping an open mind. After all, wasn't that part of the requirements for the witness protection experience, to acclimate oneself to the community, as though one of its own? Except for the fact that, while in Weconta Falls, she was no longer Rosamund Santiago but Tisha González, she reminded herself. How long could she keep up the pretense before slipping?

Her eyes crinkled at the man who had just ordered black coffee, and she realized she'd been staring. "I'll just get that for you," she said quickly.

He flashed her an amused smile. "Take your time, but not too long."

She nodded, not wanting to keep him waiting any longer than necessary. Padding across the laminate flooring in comfortable slip-on flats, she put in another customer's order with Shailene McEnany, the fifty-two-year-old do-everything co-owner of the grill, before heading to the coffee station and starting another pot. Shailene, a breast cancer survivor, had bought the place a decade ago with her husband, Everett, and she was put in charge while he divided time between the grill and being a member of the Army Reserve.

"Keep it moving, Tisha!" Shailene yelled. With a medium build, her rose-blond hair was in an A-line cut. Her blue eyes widened behind contacts as she said, "There are other customers waiting."

"I'm on it," she told her and went about taking other orders in what had suddenly become a busy afternoon, before making her way back to the black-coffee hunk. "Here you are," Tisha said sweetly.

He tasted it. "Good."

She smiled. "I'll pass that along to Shailene."

A grin played on his lips. "I'm Russell, by the way. Russell Lynley."

"Tisha," she told him, even though he already saw the name on her name tag. "Tisha González."

"I know this may sound like a cliché or a line, but I haven't seen you around here, Tisha González."

"Yeah, that definitely sounds like a line." She couldn't help but chuckle. "As it is, I've only been working here for a couple of weeks, so…"

"Well, that explains it, as it's probably been that long since I last came in," he said, and laughed. "Anyway, nice meeting you, Tisha."

"You too, Russell." She found herself wishing they could talk more, as he seemed like he could be interesting, but duty called. "Have to get back to work. Shailene has no tolerance for slackers."

"I understand." He grinned at her. "Hope to see you around."

Almost sounds like he means it, Rosamund mused, but left it at that as she knew nothing about him and couldn't be too careful right now. She grinned back and went on her way. She had just delivered a stack of pancakes and a grilled cheese melt to a table and taken another order, when she was stopped in her tracks by another waitress.

Tracy Sheridan was a few years older and on her second marriage, with four kids between them. She was about Tisha's size. Her short, thin hair was brown with blonde highlights and parted to the side. Tisha felt comfortable with her as a work friend, almost on the same level as her friendship with Johnnie Langford. "Looks like someone has eyes for you," Tracy teased her.

"Who?" Tisha asked innocently, though in following

the flight of Tracy's blue eyes, Rosamund guessed who she was referring to.

"The coffee drinker. Who else?"

Tisha glanced over her shoulder, while trying not to make it too obvious they were talking about him. It didn't seem to work, as Russell already seemed homed in on her and, with amusement, lifted his cup, as if in a mock toast. She looked away quickly, blushing, but curious about him nonetheless. "Do you know him?"

"Not personally," Tracy answered. "Maybe if I weren't already madly in love with my Milburn. Anyway, that's Detective Russell Lynley."

"As in police detective?" Tisha asked.

"Yeah. He joined the Weconta Falls Police Department about seven or eight months ago."

"Hmm...interesting." Rosamund had considered he might be law enforcement by the way he carried himself. Her instincts had proven to be correct. "Does he have a family or...?"

"Used to," Tracy said. "I heard he lost his wife and daughter. Don't know how. But apparently, he moved to Weconta Falls alone. I've never seen him in here with anyone, other than other detectives. So, I'd have to assume he's single. Especially by the way he's been checking you out."

"Oh, stop it," Tisha protested lightheartedly.

"I'm just saying." Tracy chuckled. "Don't know your relationship status, but if you're looking for someone, he might be a great place to start."

"I'm not looking for anyone," she said flatly, as though trying to convince herself of this. She hadn't been for a while now. And even if she was, it probably wasn't really a good idea to be interested in someone in law enforcement, like she was. Only she wasn't in law enforcement at the moment, consigned by circumstances to being a waitress while a hired killer was trying to hunt her down. Maybe it wouldn't be so bad getting to know Russell Lynley better, if he was truly interested in her, and see what came of it, if only on a temporary basis. When Tisha turned to look his way, she was disappointed to see that he was gone.

AFTER THE WORKDAY ENDED, Russell arrived at his single-story, three-bedroom, mid-century modern home on Drapmore Drive in a wooded area of Weconta Falls, still thinking about the attractive waitress named Tisha. Though only a few words had passed between them, there was something about her, beyond appearance, that captured his fancy. He hadn't quite figured out just what that was yet. Maybe tomorrow he would find an excuse to visit the grill again and see if they could talk longer than a minute or two. Maybe if she was single and available, she would even be amenable to going out with him. Or was his loneliness starting to play with his head? This was the first time anyone had gotten his attention even remotely since losing his wife.

Russell walked through the house he had purchased six months ago, attracted to its location as well as the blending of old with contemporary style, which suited him. It had an open concept with wood plank flooring in the living room and picture windows for natural lighting, a U-shaped modern kitchen with porcelain tile, and more

than enough space for him to stretch out. He had outfit-
ted the place with mid-century furniture and added a few
modern accent pieces along the way. Still, he imagined
it could probably use a woman's touch to feel more like
home, but he'd learned to be content if he was to make
this work, living so far from home.

In a corner of the living room, Russell kept a stack
of classic jazz vinyl records his parents had left behind,
along with a modern wireless record player. He pulled out
a Billie Holiday album and set it to play on the turntable,
then went into the kitchen, where he grabbed a beer from
the stainless steel refrigerator. He sat down on a gray
armchair and listened to the music while going over the
events of the day, including meeting the new waitress at
Shailene's Grill.

AFTER SPENDING THE next morning in court, testifying
against a man charged with domestic violence, Russell
headed to the grill, expecting to get another black coffee and more conversation with Tisha. He even sat at
the same table as a sort of good luck charm. Only it was
Tracy who came to take his order. "What can I get for
you today, Detective Lynley?"

"I was hoping Tisha might be around." He spoke candidly.

"This is her day off," she told him. "Sorry."

Russell frowned. "So am I, but that's the way it goes."

Tracy smiled. "She'll be in tomorrow. But I would be
happy to get you whatever you need."

He couldn't help but grin at the effort. Part of him
wanted to ask her about Tisha, such as where she was

from, if she was actually new in town, if she was single, and how she felt about dating a police detective. Stuff like that. But smartly, he realized that the best way to get answers was to ask Tisha himself. "I'll have black coffee," he told Tracy.

She cracked a placating smile. "Coming right up."

Later in the day, while driving around, Russell learned there was a disturbance at Weconta Falls Park. Apparently, some teenagers had been reported as harassing park goers. In Russell's mind, this was the first step toward the kids ruining their lives through escalating crimes that went into adulthood and gave them little opportunity to change the course before it was too late. He headed to the park and hoped to arrive before someone did something that couldn't be undone.

Tisha welcomed a day off to recharge her batteries. With Weconta Falls Park and its excellent running trails not too far from her townhouse, it was a great place to unwind. Jogging was one way she liked to do this. Though wary that a possible hired killer could be lurking about like a thief in the night, waiting for the chance to strike, Tisha had to believe she had been safely relocated. Protected and far from Simon Griswold's reach. As such, she was determined not to allow him to enjoy a moral victory of sorts by having her petrified at her own shadow. She still needed to have a life. Even if that life was away from work, family, and friends. She simply had to make the most of her situation until Griswold's trial and, presumably, conviction, at which point Tisha looked forward to reclaiming her life. She wondered, though, just what she would be going back to, with no one to come home to and cuddle up with at night. Would it really be enough to continue on with life as it was? Hadn't Johnnie's death proven, if nothing else, just how short and totally unpredictable life truly was?

Tisha ran down the well-worn path through a grove of ash trees and came into a clearing, when seemingly out of nowhere, she found herself surrounded by two, three, no actually, four persons. All looked like teenagers. Three male, one female. What were they up to?

"Hey, what do we have here?" said a tall and lean male with big blue eyes and a two-tone quiff haircut. He seemed to be the leader of the pack.

"No one you want to mess with," Tisha warned him. She did have pepper spray in the side pocket of her running shorts but didn't think it would be necessary to use. Not to mention her Thai boxing skills. Hopefully, it wouldn't come to that. The last thing she needed was to draw any undue attention to herself.

He sneered at her. "You sure about that, lady?"

"She's pretty," said the lone female, who was chewing gum and looked to be barely in her teens, with green eyes and rainbow hair in an edgy style with the sides shaved.

"Yeah, real pretty," said an African American teen, who was tall and lanky, and had dark eyes and black hair in a high flattop fade.

"I just want to finish my run," Tisha told them in a calm tone, smoothing her short ponytail. "I don't want any trouble."

"So don't cause any," said the other member of the

pack, who was Asian and stocky, with brown eyes and curly brown hair in a brushed-up style.

Tisha frowned. "Go pick on someone else."

"Or what?" the leader of the group challenged her. "You're going to beat us up?"

While she weighed her options, having no desire to hurt any of them, but in no mood to be intimidated, Tisha heard a strong male voice that had a ring of familiarity state, "Maybe she won't, but I just might…" Tisha turned and saw Detective Lynley approach them. Where had he come from? He had a dour look on his face. "Heard some punks were stirring up trouble in the park," he said. "Thought I'd check it out for myself."

The leader suddenly seemed to shrink in Russell's presence, as though recognizing him, and uttered meekly, "We were just playing around."

"Yeah, right." Russell got up in his face. "Not cool to bully people simply trying to enjoy what the park is supposed to offer. You're lucky I don't arrest you and your friends on the spot and make an example of you for other idiots who like to play with fire but aren't prepared to face the consequences. I'll let you go with a warning this time. If it happens again, you'll all end up in jail. Not a nice place to be. Trust me. Now get the hell out of here!"

Tisha watched with amazement as the four scattered like scared rabbits. She faced the handsome detective, who asked, "Are you okay?"

"I'm fine." She met his eyes. "Thanks for your help, but I think I would have been able to defuse the situation on my own," Tisha told him stubbornly, though she was actually flattered that the detective had come to her rescue. She wondered what other damsels in distress he had saved lately.

He cocked a brow. "I'm sure you would have," he said apologetically. "Guess I should have mentioned yesterday that I work for the Weconta Falls PD. As such, after taking the call that some teens were harassing park goers, it was my duty to intervene—in case things got out of hand. Besides, I happen to know the father of the one I spoke to, who's a neighbor of mine. Whenever I can, I try to divert youths from entering the juvenile justice system, not to mention the criminal justice system, before they overstep and suffer the consequences that could last a lifetime."

"That's admirable, Detective," Tisha had to admit, knowing that she generally felt the same when she could use her own law enforcement skills and powers of persuasion to help at-risk youth avoid a life of crime and tragedy back in Texas. Sometimes it worked. Other times it didn't. "Hope it works. I'd hate to see them try that on someone else who might be packing. Or otherwise hit them back where it hurts."

"I couldn't agree more," Russell said evenly, studying her. "Kids will be kids, unfortunately. Sometimes they're misguided in trying to escape the doldrums of their lives. We'll see what happens. Or not." He was thoughtful. "I went by the grill today, hoping to see you there, but was told it was your day off."

"Yes, I actually do get one every now and then," Tisha quipped. She imagined that Tracy was only too happy to fill him in on the story of her life. At least as much as she knew. Fortunately, it wasn't very much, under the circumstances.

Russell laughed. "Same here."

"I'm working tomorrow," she told him, though suspecting he already knew this.

"Cool. But since I have you here, before I let you get back to what you were doing, maybe I could buy you dinner sometime, away from Shailene's Grill. Tonight, perhaps. Or whenever. If you're open to that type of thing..."

Rosamund sensed that he was fishing to see if she was single and available. She was, of course. But was it a good idea to even get semi-involved with a local, knowing that her real life was elsewhere? "Dinner sounds nice," she said, ignoring her previous thought. Maybe it was a good idea to have a police detective in town as an ally. Even if it went nowhere when all was said and done. Who said they couldn't be short-term friends? "I'll be free on Friday night." That was two days from now, giving her more time to get her stories straight in keeping up the necessary persona that had been created for her.

Russell smiled. "Friday, it is. Shall I pick you up or..."

"I'll meet you at the restaurant," Tisha tossed out quickly. She wasn't quite ready to share her address or cell phone number with him, even if she believed she could trust the detective. Right now, the rules of the game dictated that she needed to remain cautious about information she shared. Aside from the basics, most info was on a need-to-know basis. She was pretty sure that Russell didn't need to know things that might arouse his curiosity, causing him to pry and endangering her life in the process.

"No problem," he said. "What type of food do you like?"

"All types," she responded, knowing she was pretty much open to anything that wasn't too off the charts.

"Italian?"

"That works."

"Good. There's a great Italian restaurant on Kroper Lane called Italy's Corner."

"Sounds good," Tisha told him, grinning. They agreed to meet there Friday at six. Afterward, she resumed her run and found herself looking forward to her first date since arriving in Weconta Falls.

Chapter Three

Italy's Corner seemed like a great place for a first date to Russell. Or maybe it wasn't so much a date, per se, but getting to know each other better. At least that was what he hoped to get out of wining and dining Tisha González, who was not only hot as hell, but seemingly ready to rumble with some teenagers threatening her, whether harmless or not. This caused Russell to believe she was someone who was used to fighting her own battles. Was this a reflection of her upbringing? Or had she been a victim of bullying or another form of aggressive behavior that had toughened her up?

Russell couldn't help but think about Tisha's preference to drive herself to the restaurant rather than be picked up by him, the gentlemanly way. He wondered if she'd had trust issues with men in the past. Or was she merely erring on the side of caution, in case things between them took a bad turn? He would make sure the latter wasn't the case. As for the former, winning her trust was something he was happy to work on, if she let him.

When Tisha showed up right on time, she didn't disappoint in the least, wearing a body-hugging floral sheath dress and wedge sandals. Her hair was down and she looked great. "You look nice," he greeted her, downplaying just how much in his eyes.

"Thanks." Tisha blushed. "You too."

Russell grinned, taking the compliment in stride. He was wearing a plaid sport coat, with a peach-colored button-down shirt, brown chino pants, and boat shoes. The truth was, he was used to being viewed as good-looking, as was the case for all his siblings. Since arriving in Weconta Falls, more than one woman had made a pass at him. Though flattered, he had kept them at arm's length, not ready to start dating again. At least till now. They were seated at a table and had ordered white wine while perusing the menus.

"What do you recommend?" Tisha asked, as if he were an authority on the offerings.

In fact, Russell had only been there once before. But he was happy to share what he had then. "How about the chicken pietro and a combination salad?"

She smiled. "Works for me."

"Same here."

After the wine came and they ordered the food, Russell asked casually, "Are you from around here, Tisha?" He assumed she hadn't actually been living in Weconta Falls all this time. Though not tiny by any stretch of the imagination, it was still small enough that he would most certainly have noticed the striking woman at some point, had she been around.

She kept a straight face when responding equably, "No, I'm from back east."

"New York?" he asked curiously.

"Rhode Island. Cranston."

He had been there once on assignment for the Bureau. Small world. Would have been even smaller had they somehow crossed paths. "Long ways from home," he told her.

"Yeah," she concurred.

"How did you wind up in Weconta Falls?" It seemed a reasonable question to him.

She paused thoughtfully while sipping wine. "Things weren't going my way back home. I needed a change of pace. Made my way to San Francisco, where I had visited once. But that didn't do it for me." Another taste of the drink. "I was passing through Weconta Falls and, somehow, it clicked as a seemingly nice place to live."

"It is." Russell sipped his own wine, while pondering what things hadn't gone her way that caused her to want to relocate. A bad relationship, perhaps? Or something else? He gazed at her, interest piqued. "Thinking of settling into the town, are you?"

"Not so sure about that," she hesitated. "There may be some opportunities to pursue elsewhere. Right now, I'm just taking it one day at a time and seeing if this is where I truly belong."

"I see." Russell felt slightly disappointed that she might not stick around long enough to get to know. On the other hand, he admired her being candid about where things stood in her life, which he had to respect. Maybe the more she experienced life in Weconta Falls, the more she might want to stay.

After the food arrived, Tisha turned the tables on him, asking, "So, how long have you been in law enforcement?"

"Seven years," he answered pensively.

Her gaze held his. "And you've spent all of it working for the Weconta Falls Police Department?"

"Not quite." Russell sat back, holding his fork. "I was a special agent with the FBI for five years."

"Really?" Tisha reacted as though the notion took her totally by surprise, but recovered while continuing to eat.

"Yes. Up until eight months ago, I was working out of the Bureau's St. Louis Field Office."

"What happened?" Her voice soft.

"I turned in my resignation." He took a ragged breath. "Two years ago, my wife and daughter were killed during a home invasion."

"I'm so sorry, Russell." Tisha's eyes widened with sadness, but not necessarily shock. He considered that someone at the grill, such as Tracy, may have mentioned their deaths to her. If so, Tisha was tactful enough to let him tell her about it in his own words.

"It was horrible," he voiced, which had to have gone without saying, but he did so anyway. "The home invaders destroyed my life as I knew it then, and damn near my spirit. We caught them and they'll die in prison." Russell sighed. "Anyway, I needed to get away from everything that reminded me in a sad way of Victoria, my late wife, and our seven-year-old daughter, Daisy. So, I moved on and found work with the Weconta Falls PD. Not exactly bustling with serious criminal activity, taking nothing away from teenage troublemakers, but it's keeping me busy and has given me a new focus that I can live with for now." In so saying, Russell had to wonder if he was prepared to stay put any more than she was. Maybe someday he would re-up with the Bureau. Or find some other law enforcement career that could challenge him. But for the time being, Weconta Falls was where he wanted to be.

"I'm glad you've found a way to process your pain and stay in law enforcement," Tisha told him, forking some salad.

"So am I." Russell sliced the knife into his tender chicken. He was happy to feel enough of a connection with Tisha to share a part of his past that he hadn't very often since leaving St. Louis. Just as he was glad to learn more about her. Still, he sensed there were other things she was keeping to herself. "What's your relationship status these days, if you don't mind my asking?" He assumed there was no one in the immediate picture since she wasn't wearing a ring and was having dinner with him.

"I don't mind," she stated without prelude. "I'm single. Never been married and no children." She paused. "Guess I've just never taken the time to go down that road. The fact that the right man has never come along to sweep me off my feet probably has something to do with that," she added with a defensive chuckle.

"Usually does." Russell grinned softly. He definitely wasn't holding it against her that she wasn't divorced, with children often caught in the crossfire of a broken home. While his parents had stayed the course in loving matrimony and parenthood till the day they died, he knew firsthand this wasn't always the case. Better for Tisha to have held off for the right man at the right time for love and a family. Russell considered that such person could even be him, if both stuck around town long enough to give things between them a decent shot to blossom.

After the meal, he walked Tisha to her car and Russell found himself eager to maintain the momentum he sensed was happening. "Hope we can do this again soon."

"Me too." Her eyes lifted to his. "I just don't want to rush into anything."

"No pressure," he insisted, even if a tad disappointed that she seemed to be holding back for reasons he hadn't quite figured out yet. "We can move at your pace. All I know is that I like you and spending time with you, though it hasn't been very much up to this point."

"I feel the same way," Tisha said genuinely. As Russell relished her words, she cupped his cheeks and planted a kiss on his mouth. Her lips were amazingly soft and tantalizing enough that, were it up to him, they could have kissed the evening away. But after maybe a full minute of their mouths testing the waters of compatibility, she broke the lip-lock and said breathlessly, "Thanks for the dinner and company, Russell. Night."

He thanked her and then watched as she got in the car and drove off. Savoring the taste of her lips on his, Russell headed to his own personal vehicle, a white Jeep Grand Wagoneer, feeling that things might finally be starting to look up after losing Victoria and Daisy. Yet he sensed there were still layers to uncover with Tisha, in spite of her ability to apparently downplay things, which in its own way made her even more compelling to get to know.

IS THIS REALLY *my best move, getting involved with a local detective?* Rosamund questioned, as she headed home.

Her lips were still tingling from the kiss she had initiated, which had been reciprocated in kind. There were clearly sparks between them. She supposed this had been the case to some degree from the moment they met, even if she had tried not to see it for obvious reasons. He seemed like a nice guy but may be looking for love in the wrong place at the wrong time. Was he truly over his beloved wife, dying so tragically? Or merely on the rebound?

I'm not interested in a rebound relationship, Rosamund told herself, nearing the townhouse complex. And she doubted that Russell would be much interested in her, if he knew she was not really a waitress named Tisha González but a special agent with the Department of Homeland Security, forced to hide her true identity while being pursued by a hired killer. Would he still see her as girlfriend material if he knew that, like him, she was in law enforcement in her real life and, as such, would always be in potential danger when on missions, undercover or not. Apart from being forced to lie to him, could Russell handle being with someone who, at least in theory, could end up dead and buried if Simon Griswold were to have his way?

It wouldn't be fair to put him through that, Rosamund believed, as she parked the car in the garage and headed toward her mailbox. Would it? Or perhaps she wasn't giving the detective enough credit for being open-minded and flexible when it came to understanding and going with the flow. Whatever that might be. After grabbing the mostly junk mail, she headed across the asphalt and was stopped in her tracks when she heard what sounded like rustling in the bushes. Though the parking lot was reasonably well lit, there were still dark places where, she imagined, a potential killer could be hiding.

There was the noise again. It seemed to be coming from a cluster of medium-sized juniper shrubs nearby. They were certainly thick enough and high enough to hide a human being, Tisha believed. Her first thought was that the hired killer had found her and planned to go on the attack. She did not have her firearm, believing it was smarter not to carry it everywhere in what was supposed to be a relatively low threat location. She did have the pepper spray, but feared it would be insufficient to stop a determined assassin.

She heard the sound again, only louder, as if to get her attention, if that hadn't been the case before. Just when she was about to demand the person reveal him-or herself, and while whipping out her cell phone to call for assistance, and at the same time considering making a run for it to her open garage door, Tisha watched in shocked relief as a raccoon burst through the shrubs and scampered across the pavement toward another set of junipers.

Taking no chances of further surprises, she raced into the garage, where she quickly pushed the button to lower the door, and then went inside the residence. She placed the code into the security system and then reset it to protect herself from any potential intruders. After sucking in a deep breath, she went into the kitchen and poured herself a glass of red wine. She tasted it and then had to laugh. *Guess I got carried away out there*, she told herself. The boogeyman turned out to be nothing more than a raccoon who was probably as startled by her as the other way around. Still, it reinforced just how freaked out she was at the potential for danger around every corner, so long as a hired assassin was intent on hunting her down like an animal.

Tisha drank some more wine while kicking her shoes off. At least she had found a sexy new friend, who happened to be a police detective and seemed more than capable of taking care of himself. Even if she was forced to draw the line at how much she could share with him about herself, she liked his company and he seemed to like hers. The fact that they both had experienced real tragedy made Tisha feel close to Russell. It also concerned her that neither may be ready to jump headfirst into something both might regret.

Her thoughts turned to the absence of family and friends in her life. And even her new partner, Virginia Flannery, who understandably had to be kept out of the loop for her own safety. It was easily the hardest part of being in the program. No goodbyes. Just gone like that, leaving others to explain for her. She didn't dare go against the rules and try to sneak a call or two, only to have it blow up in her face, with Griswold's hired gun getting the bead on her as a result. *No, I can't make this easy for him*, Rosamund thought, as she headed out of the kitchen, turned off the lights, and went up the stairs for a nice hot bath before going to bed. She needed to see this through and stay under the radar until it was time to come up for air and do her part to put Simon Griswold away for good.

THE HITMAN HAD seized on some intel that suggested the target, Rosamund Santiago, may have fled to California.

This, of course, would need to be double, even triple checked, so as not to waste his time. After all, time was money, and he aimed to keep as much of it as possible for the day when he would not need to silence people for his rich and powerful clients. As it now stood, his inside source believed that the U.S. Marshals Service pattern of relocation of witnesses tended to ship them out to certain areas of the country relative to the original point of departure. Seemed as though California was the preferred location for Texans needing to be relocated. But where in California might the as-good-as-dead HSI special agent be hiding? And what name was she going by? When would he figure it out?

The hitman laughed at the thought of the agent squirming in knowing he was coming after her and would never stop. Until she was dead, like her late partner, Langford. The assassin wondered if the woman who shattered Simon Griswold's nose in multiple places, affecting his breathing and making him hate her all the more, would put up a fight against him as well. *Bring it on*, he thought. It was a fight she would lose. Over and over again. Unlike Griswold, the hitman never played by the rules. Except for his own. That meant his only objective was to get the job done, no matter who stood in his way. That included the target herself.

Rosamund Santiago may or may not be able to sleep at night. But she would know no rest for as long as she was alive. He would see to it. When he located her, she would never see him coming. Not till it was too late and she had breathed her last breath. Only then would the hitman be able to present to his employer the necessary proof that the mark had been eliminated. And thus, the biggest impediment to Griswold's future in continuing his lucrative business of human trafficking.

The hitman set his sights on gathering more intel and strategizing, before the time came that he would meet face-to-face with his prey. With the expected result of another job well done for him. At her expense as a dead woman.

Chapter Four

Russell was in his office, bright and early as usual to start his day, making himself comfortable at his desk. There always seemed to be paperwork, interviewing witnesses, taking phone calls related to investigations, or department meetings that kept him on his toes. Not to mention the incidents that brought him to the scene of crimes and required his investigative abilities be put to good use. Though none of these things taxed his brain like when he was thrust into high-profile cases with the Bureau, he was sure this was where he was meant to be at the moment. Especially where it concerned meeting Tisha. He'd had a mostly sleepless night just thinking about her and the tender—well, maybe a little passionate—kiss they shared after he walked her to her car after dinner last night. Maybe he was getting carried away in thinking that one kiss and a meal could be the start of something special between them. She did say she wanted to take things slowly. He needed to abide by that and let this play out at her own pace. But did that mean she would object to his dropping by the grill this afternoon for a cup of coffee, just to see her again?

That train of thought was interrupted when Russell's cell phone rang. He lifted it off his desk and saw that the caller requesting a video chat was his brother, Scott. Four years his senior, Scott was the oldest of the Lynley siblings and currently a special agent with the FBI, based at the Bureau's Louisville, Kentucky, Field Office. He had been trying unsuccessfully to get Russell to rejoin the Bureau ever since he left. Was this yet another attempt in that regard? Or was something else happening in the family that he needed to know about?

Russell accepted the chat invitation and watched his brother's handsome face appear on the screen. "Hey," he said to him in a friendly tone.

"Hey." Scott grinned sidelong. Like him, his brother had their father's gray eyes and prominent features on an oblong face. His thick black hair was in a comb-over pomp style with an edge up and low fade. "Hope I didn't catch you at a bad time?"

"That depends," Russell half joked. "Was just finishing up some paperwork on a break-in. What's up?"

"Nothing nefarious," he assured him. "Just had a little free time on my hands after wrapping up a major investigation into a decades-old homicide that had ties to a current methamphetamine trafficking network and thought I'd check in on my little brother. How are you doing?"

"Congrats on solving the cold case," Russell told him, knowing this was his brother's area of expertise. "Me, I'm good." He sat back. "Keeping busy."

"So, you're not getting bored with small-town police work?"

Russell chuckled. *Here we go*, he thought. Subtle, if

not direct, insults about his job. "Not at all," he told him. "As a detective, I'm kept in the loop for most of what goes on around here. While it may lack the serial killer, mass murderer, terrorist, or even drug-trafficking vibe I left behind, it's what I need at this time in my life."

Scott scratched his jaw. "I hear you, man. Seriously. You're entitled to grieve in any way you see fit." He paused. "I just think that leaving the Bureau as a coping mechanism was the wrong move."

"It was more than just a coping mechanism," Russell said. "I needed a change of pace. I found that here. I'm happy with my decision." At least for the most part. He saw no reason to second-guess decisions that seemed right at the time. He decided to throw his brother an olive branch, if only to keep the peace, but be candid. "I'm not closing the door on the Bureau," he promised him. "If I find myself burned out as a police detective, I'd certainly be open to returning to the FBI, if they'd have me."

Scott flashed his teeth. "You'll always be welcomed back into the fold, bro, if I have any say in the matter. Whenever you're ready to return."

"Thanks for having my back," Russell told him with a crooked grin.

"All of us have your back, Russell," Scott insisted. "That's what siblings are for."

"Works both ways." Russell knew he would always be there for them, as their parents would have expected. They spoke for a few more minutes, catching up on the latest family gossip, before hanging up.

Afterward, Russell finished what he was doing and conversed with some of the other detectives before heading out for lunch. He was eager to see Tisha again. The moment he stepped inside Shailene's Grill, his wish came true as there she was, busy at work. Russell wondered if she even noticed him as he took the same table he had sat at the first time he laid eyes on her. And once again, she was a lovely sight for sore eyes, uniform and all.

When Russell shook off another waitress, her spunkiness aside, making it clear who he was waiting for, he wasn't disappointed in the slightest as Tisha walked over with a big smile on her face. "Well, look who dropped in."

He laughed. "Hey, stranger."

She feigned disappointment. "Forgot me already, huh?"

"Not on your life," he told her seriously.

"Just testing you." Tisha chuckled. "Especially since you chose to bypass another waitress for me and any tip you might have left her."

Russell chuckled too. "You're worth it," he insisted.

"We'll see about that." She blushed with a little discomfort, he sensed. "So, let's see...coffee, black, right?"

"Yes, that's right. But I also thought I'd have lunch today since I have some extra time on my hands." *That I get to spend in your presence*, Russell mused. He lifted the menu. "Do you recommend anything in particular for a hungry camper?"

"Hmm... If you're not in a hurry, I would go with the Shailene Special, which includes a nice-sized turkey club, fries, a glass of lemonade, and a slice of homemade apple pie," Tisha said.

"Sounds tasty," he had to admit. "I'll go with the Shailene Special."

"Coming right up," she said.

"Cool." Russell flashed a smile, holding back on what he wanted to ask her till she returned with the lunch. He watched as she sashayed away and couldn't help but wonder if she had been waitressing before moving to Weconta Falls. Or was she taking a different direction occupationally, like him? Something told him it was the latter, though he had no idea how she made a living in Cranston. He supposed she would get around to telling him when ready, were that the case.

By the time the meal arrived a few minutes after the coffee, Russell had gathered his courage to continue his pursuit of the lovely Tisha González, while being careful not to crowd her. "Here you go," she uttered, setting the plate down, along with the lemonade.

"Looks great," he told her. "Can't wait to dig in."

Tisha laughed. "Hope you're not disappointed."

"Never." At least not where she was concerned. Russell would reserve judgment for the meal.

"Good." She grinned. "Then I'll let you dig in."

"Before you go, Tisha," he said, meeting her eyes, "while we're in the spirit of good, if not great, food, I was wondering if you'd like to come over to my house for dinner tonight. I'm pretty good in the kitchen. Learned how to get around in there from my mother, who managed to keep four hungry kids and a hungrier husband satisfied."

Tisha hesitated. "That sounds wonderful about your mom."

"It's only dinner and conversation," Russell threw out reassuringly. "No pressure, remember?"

Her features relaxed on that note. "I'd love to come over for dinner," she said.

He considered the come over bit, rather than his picking her up, his preference in an old-fashioned style of dating. But he didn't want to pressure her into anything that made her feel uncomfortable. "Cool."

Tisha flipped to an empty page on her pad and asked straightforwardly, "What's your address?"

Russell gave it to her while wondering how long it would take to exchange phone numbers. Or was there a reason why she was hesitant to give him her number? "How does seven sound?"

"Sounds good," she told him. "See you then. Now, I'd better get back to work before Shailene cans me for fraternizing with a customer too long."

He grinned. "We certainly wouldn't want that. I'll see you at seven."

Tisha smiled back at him and walked off. Russell dove into the lunch, while already counting the minutes when both of their workdays were through and they could have their second date, more or less.

ROSAMUND ONCE AGAIN second-guessed herself for accepting another date with Russell. Was she playing with fire by allowing herself to get closer to the detective, who knew her only under an alias? If one thing led to another, would she only be setting herself up for more hurt in her life, once the truth came out and whatever was between them ended up going nowhere? Didn't Russell deserve someone who would stick around for a while, at the very least? As opposed to only being in town till it was time for her to testify, before resuming the life she left behind?

But he did say it was just dinner and conversation,

right? Did he mean it? If so, what harm was there in that? Russell seemed to need a shoulder to lean on and so did she. Friends perhaps with short-term benefits might not be such a bad thing. If it was, she would feel it. Instead, Tisha felt just the opposite. It somehow felt right to be spending time with him, even with the future full of uncertainty where she was concerned.

Rosamund mulled over these thoughts as she went about feeding hungry customers on a busy afternoon. She glanced occasionally at Russell, offering him a smile whenever she could squeeze it in, but making sure she didn't neglect her duties, having little time to spare. In spite of a serious departure from her life as an HSI special agent, Tisha had surprised herself somewhat in quickly getting the hang of waitressing again. It was almost like she was back in college. At least she had an occupation to fall back on, should the Department of Homeland Security no longer have a need for her.

When she glanced again at Russell, Tisha saw that his table was empty. Already she missed seeing his handsome face, but knew it wouldn't be long before they got together at his place.

"He left you a generous tip," Tracy pointed out. "You must be doing something right," she joked.

"It's all in the wrist action," Tisha joked back. "Good service usually makes for good tips."

"True enough." She laughed. "But something tells me the detective wouldn't care if you were the world's worst waitress," she said. "As long as you're open to giving him a shot. Are you?"

I hate to be put on the spot like that, Rosamund told

herself. She recovered and answered candidly, "Yes, I think so. We're having dinner tonight at his house."

"Oh, really?" Tracy beamed. "You go, girl!"

"Try not to read too much into it," she felt the need to say. "We're not rushing into anything."

"Nor should you," Tracy insisted. "I made the mistake of doing that the first time around. Took a second before I knew what I was doing." She giggled. "When you're ready to roll, you'll know it. Trust me. And if he turns out to be a dud, you'll know that too. But I'm not seeing that in the detective, who seems like a stand-up guy you can count on."

Rosamund felt that too with Russell. She just wasn't as sure the same was true in reverse, considering her present circumstances. "Right now, we'd best concentrate on catering to the needs of those waiting to be served," she reminded Tracy, who agreed as they fanned out.

After taking another order, Tisha saw that a woman was now seated at the table previously occupied by Russell. Only when she gave her a soft smile did Rosamund realize it was her handler with WITSEC, Deputy U.S. Marshal Leah Redfield. Though they spoke regularly over the phone, Tisha had only seen her periodically, with Leah believing the threat level for her current location as a hidden witness was low, thereby not necessitating 24/7 surveillance.

Tisha walked over to her and pretended she was just another hungry patron. "Hi there," she said coolly.

"Hi, Tisha," Leah said unevenly. "Can you get away for a few minutes to my car?"

Rosamund sensed that something was wrong but knew

this wasn't the place to elaborate. But she also couldn't just walk off the job, and doubted Leah would want that either, seeing that it was through the deputy marshal that she got the job. "I go on break in fifteen minutes," she told her.

"That's fine," Leah said.

"In the meantime, do you want something to drink?" Tisha thought to ask.

"Yes, coffee with cream would be great."

A minute later, Tisha brought the coffee to her and Leah paid for it. "I can get some work done on my cell phone while I'm waiting," she said.

When her break came, Tisha walked with Leah to her car, as the handler asked casually, "So, how have you been doing?"

"Good," Tisha told her. "I'm adjusting to my surroundings."

"Great." Leah looked at her. "Making any friends?"

"A few." Rosamund could think of one person in particular, Russell, who she considered a friend. Two, when she counted Tracy. Then there was an elderly next-door neighbor named Marlo Monaghan who Tisha had become friendly with, and who reminded Tisha of her beloved grandmother.

"Good to hear," Leah remarked. "Blending in is important as part of this new life."

Rosamund didn't disagree, in spite of longing for the best parts of her old life, which she anticipated returning to at some point. They reached the vehicle and got inside. Only then did Tisha ask in anticipation, "What's happening?"

Leah remained composed as she responded, "There's been a development..."

"What kind of development?" Rosamund could think of any number of developments. Had the threat to her safety been identified and neutralized? Would she be able to get back to her life sooner than anticipated? Had Simon Griswold upped the ante in wanting her dead?

"Through exhaustive efforts, we've been able to identify the hired killer," Leah said stiffly.

Tisha cocked a brow with expectancy. "Who is it?"

"His name is Arnold Nishimoto," she said. Leah opened her laptop and pulled up an image, passing it to Tisha to see. "Nishimoto's a thirty-six-year-old Japanese assassin out of Hawaii. He's been linked to at least a dozen murders, with hits put out by organized crime syndicates, drug traffickers, foreign governments, and, in this instance, a human trafficker currently awaiting trial, Simon Griswold."

Tisha's pulse skipped a beat as she studied her would-be assassin. Arnold Nishimoto had coal eyes, a round face, and short black hair in a fade cut. At a glance, he seemed like an average person and not a paid hitman. She imagined that false facade was what made him apparently so successful and in demand by desperate criminals who wanted someone out of the way. "Sounds like a scary person," Tisha remarked uneasily.

"He is," Leah said flatly. "Unfortunately, he's proven to be rather elusive. Right now, we have no idea where he is, but we're using all the resources available to locate and apprehend him."

Though that gave her some comfort, Rosamund felt

even more anxiety in being able to put a name and face to the person who wanted her dead. "Do you think he has any idea as to my location?" she asked the handler bluntly. "Or name change?"

Leah sighed. "It's highly unlikely," she stressed. "We go through extraordinary efforts to move witnesses to a location where they will not be easily found. And only a small group of people in the U.S. Marshals Service have knowledge of this. Including the new name you've been assigned. So, relax. Arnold Nishimoto has no idea where you are. I'm only passing along to you this new intel, which I'll email you, so you're kept abreast of the latest news relative to your being in the program."

"Thanks for letting me know," Tisha told her gratefully, realizing she was overreacting to the idea of an increased threat level now that she knew who was after her.

"It's my job." Leah closed the laptop. "Though you should carry on with your life here as normal as possible, it's still important that you remain vigilant to any and all potential threats to your safety—to be on the safe side," she said, in what Rosamund believed was supposed to be a comforting voice.

But what Tisha actually picked up on was that, despite downplaying the threat, it had made it even more real to her. Meaning she would be that much more stressed while awaiting either the capture of the assassin, Arnold Nishimoto, or the trial of his employer, Simon Griswold. Neither one gave her much comfort at the moment, as Tisha felt the need to look over her shoulder at every corner for anyone who might be coming after her.

Chapter Five

Russell was admittedly excited about the opportunity to cook for a woman for really the first time since he came to Weconta Falls. Not counting the barbecue he'd hosted for his police department colleagues during the summer. As it was, Tisha was the first person he actually wanted to try to impress in the kitchen since Victoria died. Moreover, he liked the idea of spending some alone time with her, as opposed to a restaurant or other public setting. Even if it didn't lead to intimacy, which he certainly wasn't opposed to, he respected her boundaries. If she felt like the connection needed to progress further, he was all in.

For now, let's just work on her palate, Russell told himself, wearing a linen kitchen apron as he prepared veal parmigiana, sautéed mushrooms, and chopped salad. He made some oatmeal cookies for dessert, in case she was still hungry after the meal. There was wine and beer to drink, as well as water, coffee, and tea. In spite of being a little jittery at playing host, he was ready to go. If he played his cards right, Russell imagined that Tisha would be inviting him over to her place in no time flat.

When she arrived, he could tell Tisha was a bit nervous herself. He wasn't sure if it was the company or something else. He tried to make her feel at home. "Thanks for coming."

She smiled. "Thanks for inviting me."

"The food's nearly ready."

"Smells delicious," Tisha said, dressed casually but with enough style to get his attention. He had little doubt that were he to ever get her naked, she would be even more amazing.

Russell grinned. "I think I'll put on some music."

"Sounds good."

He went over to the record player. "Ever seen one of these before?" he half joked.

"I have a time or two." She laughed. "My parents actually owned a few turntables over the years. But I thought they'd gone the way of the dinosaur," she teased him.

"Then I suppose I'm a Tyrannosaurus rex." Russell chuckled. "My parents left me and my siblings with a stack of vinyl records. Between my brother and two sisters, I was the only one who chose to keep and play them. Fortunately, they still have some retro record players around."

"That is so cool," Tisha insisted genuinely.

"Do you like jazz?"

"Love it. Especially Sarah Vaughan, Antônio Carlos Jobim, Ella Fitzgerald, Billie Holiday, and Frank Sinatra."

"Great." Russell pulled out a Sarah Vaughan album and put it on. The fact that Tisha was into jazz was yet another feather in her cap, as far as he was concerned. "I can give you the grand tour."

"Okay." Tisha looked around. "I'm liking what I see so far."

"Then you should like the rest," Russell told her.

When they got to the primary bedroom, he wondered if it might be too forward to go in just yet. But she did so on her own. She surveyed the mid-century furnishings, including a king-size platform bed with duvet cover and a barrel chair.

"Nice," Tisha said. "Very nice."

"Glad you think so." Russell had no problem lingering in there, but decided not to push it. "Well, the food should be ready now."

"Good, I'm starving." Tisha laughed. "Never mind that I spent much of my day inside a restaurant."

He grinned. "I won't hold that against you if you don't criticize my cooking."

She chuckled again. "Deal."

Russell admired her good-natured style that was a good fit for his own. Tisha helped him put the food and drinks on the beveled top of the dining room table with boomerang-style legs, before they sat across from one another in upholstered side chairs. The conversation seemed to flow freely as they discussed some of their favorite pastimes, with Russell telling her that he too loved to jog as part of his workout regimen. He proposed they might run together sometime, which Tisha agreed to.

"So, tell me about your family." Russell was curious to get to know more about her background. "Any brothers or sisters?"

Tisha moved the food around her plate. "My parents are semiretired, living the good life in Florida," she said.

"And I have one younger sister, Gabby. She's married to a doctor and has two children. They live in Nebraska."

"Your family's spread out across the country, like mine," he remarked, cutting into the veal parmigiana. "Makes it easy to rack up the flier miles."

"Very true." She smiled thoughtfully. "Did you grow up in Missouri?"

"Actually, I'm originally from Oklahoma."

"Do your parents still live there?" Tisha asked, forking a mushroom.

Russell reacted to the question in bringing a painful memory to the surface as he tasted his wine. "They were killed in a car accident four years ago," he lamented.

Her brow creased. "Oh, that's terrible," she gulped.

"Yeah." He twisted his lips sadly. "They never saw the other driver coming. No chance to say goodbye properly."

"I'm sorry, Russell." Tisha reached across the table and touched his hand. "I'm sure they knew how much you loved them. Even if you were unable to express it at the end."

"You're right," he said. They had expressed this sentiment often enough while still alive to appreciate it. Russell gazed down at Tisha's hand. Her fingers were soft. He liked the way they felt touching his skin. He met her eyes musingly. "Have you ever lost anyone you were close to?"

Tisha paused, played with her food, and then looked at him before responding. "Yeah. I lost my grandmother ten years ago, but it still hurts, as we were pretty close." She took a breath. "I also lost a good friend recently. He left behind a wife and two children." She paused again.

"Sometimes life sucks, but you do what you need to do to carry on."

"Sorry for your losses," Russell told her sincerely, realizing that he wasn't the only one who had to carry and process such pain. "And yes, we have to find a way to adjust accordingly, if we're not going to let it drive us crazy."

"True." She flashed him a tender smile. "So, how about a couple of those oatmeal cookies for dessert?"

He grinned and stood. "Sure. Oatmeal cookies, it is."

Minutes later, they had eaten some cookies, before moving over to the square-arm sofa in the living room with their wine goblets. Russell was playing an Ella Fitzgerald album. "So, what else would you like to tell me about yourself?" he asked her, sensing there was still more that Tisha was holding back on. Not that he needed to know her life story, any more than she needed to know his, from top to bottom.

Tisha sipped her wine ponderingly. "Nothing much to tell, really," she seemed to dodge the question. Or was he looking for something that wasn't there? Then she said, as if a lightbulb went off in her head, "Actually, I've always had a fantasy about writing crime novels someday. Don't ask me why. Maybe it's the culture we live in that just makes me think I could sanitize the worst of it and create some memorable characters mixed with mystery and intrigue."

Russell chuckled. "Sounds like it could be interesting," he said, then sipped his wine. "I say go for it. With my background in law enforcement, I'd be happy to serve

as an advisor, if you like, in terms of giving verisimili-
tude to the plot."

"I'd love that," Tisha said. "If I ever do plunge into
the world of fiction writing, I'll definitely take you up
on that."

"Good." He smiled, believing this might be a sign that
there was some type of future for them to build upon. It
gave him an opening to put forth another question he was
curious about. "Have you always waitressed for a living?"

Her lashes fluttered. "Do you have something against
waitresses?"

"Not at all," he stressed, hating for her to get the wrong
idea. "I have nothing but respect for waitresses or any
other jobs where the employees have to put up with sometimes difficult patrons. Also, I used to be a dishwasher
and maintenance man on campus, while paying my way
through college, so I'm never one to judge. Just wondering if you ever pursued or were into other occupations,
in getting to know you better."

Tisha smiled. "Yes, I have worked other jobs," she
said easily. "In fact, before I moved to Weconta Falls, I
was a manager at a department store. But the economy
being as it is, they started laying people off, including
me. I took the opportunity to go in a different direction,
literally. The waitressing gig is only a temporary thing,"
Tisha stressed. "I don't see myself waiting tables for the
rest of my life, trust me."

"I do trust you," Russell told her, more than he had
anyone in a while insofar as in a dating capacity. "But for
the record, whether you choose to be a waitress or any-

thing else, it's fine by me. I'm just happy to have been fortunate enough to make your acquaintance."

She blushed. "I feel the same way about you."

"Good to know." Now he was the one blushing.

They listened to the music for a bit, before moving in for a kiss. The kiss made Russell realize just what he was missing in terms of an intimate connection since Victoria's death. He was eager to see where things could go between them. After a while, Tisha pulled away and touched her swollen lips, then said, "As nice as that was, I think I'd better head home now."

Russell thought immediately about her wish not to rush into anything. He certainly wanted more, but would not push her out of her comfort zone. "Okay."

They got to their feet and Tisha said, "Thanks for dinner. I'll have to return the favor sometime."

"Whenever you like, I'll be there," he assured her with a smile. Russell thought this was a good time to see if he could get something more from Tisha as an indication that they were progressing in this relationship. "Can I have your phone number?"

She blinked thoughtfully. "Hand me your cell phone." He did and she added her name and number to his contacts. Returning the phone to him, Tisha warned lightheartedly, "Don't share it with anyone. Otherwise, I'll have to kill you."

Russell laughed. "Duly noted. I won't share it with another living soul."

"Good." Tisha smiled at him. "Walk me out?"

"Of course."

It was a warm evening and the stars were out. They

took note of the latter admiringly, shared one more kiss, and Russell saw Tisha off. He headed back inside, believing they had turned a corner in whatever came next for them.

DID I BLOW IT? Rosamund asked herself as she drove to her townhouse, still feeling the strong sensations from Russell's kiss. Had she overstepped in opening up perhaps too much with him? What if this prompted him to do some digging and he somehow figured out she was lying about some rather important issues in her life? Would he think less of her? Or have even more respect for what she was doing, for all the right reasons?

On the opposite side of the spectrum, Rosamund felt almost certain she could trust him. If so, why shouldn't she share more with him when she had no one else to lean on, outside of official channels? Giving him her phone number was the least she could do as a normal means of communication. She also knew that it would not reveal anything about her real life that would imperil her safety. But she now had his number as well, as he'd sent her a sweet goodnight text. Having someone locally that she could reach out to, if needed, was important to Tisha. The fact that Russell worked for the Weconta Falls Police Department didn't hurt matters any. She considered that his own boss, Diane O'Shea, the chief of police, was privy to her being in town under the federal program, having been informed by the U.S. Marshals Service and Department of Homeland Security as both a courtesy and as sensitive information in an ongoing federal criminal investigation. But O'Shea was not obliged to share this information with other members of the department, unless absolutely necessary. Much like the predicament Rosamund found herself in where it concerned Russell. She could only hope that once she revealed her true identity and the life she left behind, he would not take the secrets she'd kept personally, and would understand why it had been necessary. How it might impact their relationship, or the possibilities thereof, was another matter they would need to talk about at the appropriate time. Assuming things went much further between them.

Once inside the townhouse, Tisha locked the door and activated the security system. The thought that Simon Griswold's hired assassin, Arnold Nishimoto, could track her down unnerved Tisha. She had to be careful not to become complacent. Or let down her guard, with the threat real, as long as she was seen as a crucial witness in the federal case against Griswold.

She showered and went to bed, allowing her mind to relax somewhat in thinking about Russell and what he was starting to mean to her as a boyfriend or even husband in a potential relationship. Would he be open to a long-distance involvement? Would she? Could they get past her being two different people, while still maintaining one heart?

THE FOLLOWING MORNING, while having coffee in the breakfast nook, Tisha received a call in a secure communication from the HSI Dallas Field Office special agent in charge, Harold Paxton.

"I understand that Deputy Marshal Redfield brought

you up to speed yesterday on the killer hired by Simon Griswold," Paxton said in the video chat.

Tisha nodded. "Yes," she said solemnly. "I know that a man named Arnold Nishimoto is gunning for me and has a long track record of killing people." The thought turned her stomach. "And that he apparently never quits till he achieves his objective."

"Neither do we," the special agent in charge argued. "We're hell-bent on finding this guy, no matter how good he is at keeping a low profile, before he can find you."

Tisha cocked a brow. "Can he find me?" she had to ask. "Isn't that the point of my being in WITSEC instead of being well protected by armed marshals or the DHS in Dallas while maintaining my job as an agent—to keep me safe and secure?"

"That's exactly the point," Paxton said sternly. "We need you alive to help put Griswold away for the rest of his life. Along with some of his underlings. Better safe than sorry, as it related to putting you in witness protection versus subjecting you to armed guards for months. We've taken all the necessary precautions to ensure that your location remains top secret. That means Arnold Nishimoto is not going to discover your whereabouts."

Tisha sighed. "That's good to know." The thought that he could show up around any corner and mow her down or murder her in another fashion didn't sit well with her. How could it? "It's bad enough that Griswold ended Johnnie's life well before it should have been his time to go. The last thing we need is for him to succeed in silencing me too, so Griswold can continue trafficking human beings for hard labor, sexual exploitation, and trafficking of illegal drugs."

"I understand how you feel," Paxton insisted. "We won't let anything happen to you, Agent Santiago." He paused and Rosamund realized he had erred in using her real name that in turn could cause her to mistakenly refer to it, jeopardizing her safety. "Just continue living your life as Tisha González for the time being and you'll be fine," he said, correcting himself.

Tisha forced a smile. She had been venting to her boss, though he had tried to reassure her that the only thing to fear right now was fear itself, as the saying went. "Thanks, I will," she told him.

"So, how's it going there anyway?" Paxton asked.

"It's going." Tisha sipped her coffee, which was now cold. "Doing my best to make my life here workable." She thought about Russell. He played a big part in making Weconta Falls more than just a temporary place of refuge. Leaving it—and him—behind was something she wasn't looking forward to. Even while at the same time, she longed to get back to her real life, .

"Good to hear." Paxton sighed. "If there's any more news to share, you'll get it from me, your handler, or even the police chief there, if warranted."

"Thank you," Tisha said, while wondering if Diane O'Shea could wind up spilling the beans to Russell before she had a chance to do so.

After hanging up, Tisha made plans for the rest of her day. She wasn't scheduled for work till the afternoon shift. This would give her time to go for a run and maybe do a bit of shopping. She was thinking it might be time to invite Russell over for dinner, as she had intimated to him last night. He seemed more than amenable to the idea. Though cooking was not necessarily her strong suit, in spite of her mother being a great cook and her father too. But Rosamund was sure she could put something together that reflected her Hispanic heritage and would satisfy Russell. If not in the kitchen, then maybe elsewhere.

Chapter Six

Russell did fifty pushups to get his morning started and fifty more to get the blood pumping. Honestly, he was feeling pretty light on his feet these days, thanks to Tisha González showing up in town at just the right time, giving him a whole new reason for being there himself. He liked the trajectory of where things seemed to be headed with them. If he had his way, they would speed this up and get to the bedroom part of getting to know one another. But since she seemed to be hesitant about taking it to the next level, he would abide by her wishes, happy to have a shot with the beautiful waitress.

After the workout was done, Russell took a call from his adopted sister, Annette. She was only three months younger than him and the sibling he felt closest to. His parents had already decided they wanted to add another member to the family and taken the steps to make that happen when they realized his mother was pregnant. Russell was happy they had gone through with the adoption of the biracial girl, as he couldn't imagine what life would have been like if he hadn't had Annette to play with and confide in over the years.

He watched as she appeared on the video screen. Annette, now a Dabs County sheriff's detective in Indiana, was an attractive woman with pretty brown-green eyes and long wavy brunette hair parted in the middle with bangs that were chin length. "Hey, you," she said spiritedly.

He grinned. "Hey, Annette."

"What are you up to?"

"Same old, same old," he claimed, while knowing there was something different in his life these days. "How about you?"

She frowned. "We're dealing with a double homicide here," she told him. "A man and woman were found shot to death in a vehicle. Not sure if it's drug-related, intimate or jealousy type of crime, or something else."

Russell wrinkled his nose. "Sounds like you've got a real doozy on your hands."

"Tell me about it." Annette gazed at him. "Anything out of the ordinary on the crime front in your neck of the woods, Detective Lynley?"

"Nothing like that, thank goodness," he told her. "Just the usual alcohol and drug offenses, delinquent acts, a hit-and-run here and there, and the occasional violent crime."

She chuckled. "Sounds like I should transfer there as a detective, while also keeping an eye on you."

Russell laughed. "You're welcome anytime. I'd love to have my kid sister around to hang out with."

"Kid sister? Hey, we're practically the same age," she joked.

"True." He grinned back at her. "Scott and Madison will certainly agree that, as the youngest, we both had to take our lumps from them. Maybe one too many," he added lightheartedly.

"That's for sure." Annette laughed. "But we got them back too," she reminded him.

"Yeah, there was that." Russell chuckled, then waited a beat. "So, I've met someone."

"Oh, really?" She narrowed her eyes with interest. "Tell me more."

"Her name is Tisha," he said. "We met at the restaurant where she works and hit it off." He was happy to share this with Annette, even when Russell wasn't sure where the future lay with Tisha. Only that he hoped there was something there to build upon.

"I'm happy for you," Annette gushed. "It's about time you put yourself back out there."

"Yeah, I've heard that from Madison and Scott," Russell admitted, as if that was news to Annette. "Hasn't been easy to let go of Victoria, who was the first love of my life."

"I know. That should never have happened. But Victoria would want you to be happy."

"You're right." He couldn't deny that, nor could he fight any longer the notion of being happy. Even though he was a widower, he was still young enough to start over.

Annette attempted to lift the mood. "Can't wait to meet Tisha."

"I hope you get that chance." Russell grinned noncommittally. "We'll see where it goes."

"Well, I have another call to make," Annette told him. "Speak soon."

"You bet," he agreed, and ended the video chat.

Russell took a quick shower and got ready for work. He still had Tisha on his mind as he left the house and wondered when they might get together again.

TISHA WENT JOGGING in Weconta Falls Park. Mindful of her previous run there and the encounter with some teens looking for trouble, she took a different route this time, hoping to avoid a repeat just in case they hadn't gotten the message Russell tried to impart to them. Thankfully, she had no one impeding her way or otherwise challenging her right to jog peacefully. Not that she would mind having Russell show up again to come to her rescue, even if unneeded. He did say he was a jogger too, didn't he?

But her romantic interest was nowhere to be found. Tisha wondered just how much they could make a go of it once she spilled the beans on her true identity. Would Russell really be game to date a Homeland Security Investigations special agent? Would he ever consider rejoining the FBI if it meant being able to have a relationship closer to her world? Or would this be expecting too much of someone who left the big city and its association with the loss of his wife and daughter in favor of the slower pace and less stress of a small-town police force?

As she ran down the meandering trail, flanked by Western hemlocks, Rosamund's thoughts turned to her deadly pursuer, Arnold Nishimoto. In spite of the assurances of Leah and Harold Paxton that there was little to be worried about where it concerned Nishimoto, Tisha was taking no chances that he could discover her whereabouts and come after her. Were that the case, she needed to be ready. She was. Apart from pepper spray, she carried a mini stun gun in the side pocket of her sweatpants. Moreover, not even trusting that to stop a certified killer in his tracks, Rosamund kept her Sig Sauer P320-XTEN 10-millimeter pistol in an ankle holster for concealed carry. If Nishimoto expected her to be an easy mark, he had better think twice.

By the time Tisha came out of the park to jog back to her townhouse, she had relaxed, believing there was no current threat to her safety. As she ran along the sidewalk parallel to Pragten Road, she decided to invite Russell over for dinner tonight. Based on their previous meals, she had some idea of what he liked to dine on. Or should she pick something interesting to cook and surprise him? While grappling with food choices, Tisha heard the sound of a young female child. She seemed to be crying out in resistance to something. Or someone.

When Tisha turned her head, she saw a girl, six or seven, with long braided blond hair, being dragged against her will by a tall, thirtysomething, thickset man with dark hair in a cowlick messy cut and a Hollywood-style beard. He was dressed in black clothing and intent upon putting the screaming little girl into the open door of a gray Range Rover Evoque SUV. Tisha heard wailing from elsewhere. She looked to her right and saw a thirtysomething, thin woman with a blondish, red-cropped pixie haircut racing frantically down the sidewalk, but too far away from the child abductor, while the woman pleaded for someone to stop the stranger from taking her daughter.

For an instant, Rosamund thought about not getting involved, having no desire to expose herself when trying to maintain anonymity in the face of a real threat against her own life. But as she was the last thing standing between the child kidnapper and his getting away with his prey, possibly to never see the child alive again, Rosamund knew she had to spring into action. The thought of what this monster could do to the girl once he had her alone, including use her for sex trafficking, caused Tisha to shudder, while steeling her resolve. She immediately removed her firearm from its holster and raced toward the perp and frightened child, while yelling at the kidnapper, "Let her go!"

At first, he ignored Tisha, still determined to get the girl into the SUV. But as Tisha neared the two, she repeated her demand vociferously, "I said, let her go!"

The man turned toward Tisha and glared at her, while still clutching the girl, and said defiantly, "Or what?"

She was now just a couple of feet away from the culprit and his captive. Aiming the gun directly at the kidnapper's face, inches above the child he was holding, Tisha made her intentions crystal clear. "Or I will shoot you," she snapped. "And I'm a very good shot. Now, for the last time, let the girl go!"

As the man took a moment to weigh his options, he seemed to think better than to test her and released the girl, who ran into the arms of her joyous mother. He planted his dark eyes on Tisha, who told him before he could even think about coming after her or making a run for it, "On your knees!"

"I don't think so," he spat, grimacing.

In a normal situation in the course of her occupation in law enforcement, Rosamund might have shot him for

threatening her life by his presence and the fact that he
had reached into his pocket for possibly a gun. But in
this instance, knowing that by doing so she would only
be inviting even more scrutiny upon herself, she did the
next best thing to mitigate her exposure as much as possible. Before he could pull out a weapon, with lightning
speed she put her gun away and whipped out her stun
gun and placed it on his neck. When he fell to the ground
in agony, his muscles involuntarily contracting, she was
able to disarm him. Afterward, her nerves frayed and
once again holding him at gunpoint, Rosamund called
Russell to report the crime, while hoping against hope
that the local media wouldn't make a story out of it. With
her caught in the middle for all the world to see. Or one
dangerous hitman, in particular.

RUSSELL WAS IN the office of Police Chief Diane O'Shea.
The forty-one-year-old petite and attractive divorcée and
former police chief of the police department in Redwood
City, California, sat in an ergonomic executive chair
across from him at her U-shaped mahogany desk. She
had been appointed to the position last year and seemed
to Russell to thrive in the job and was unafraid of having
to make tough choices. He listened as she vented about
the latest proposed budget cuts that the city council had
voted on. According to the chief, this would lead to a
freeze in hiring new officers, waning employee morale,
and limiting the tools to fight crime. He had heard it all
before, even on the federal level. As far as Russell was
concerned, one had to play the hand dealt and act accordingly. Of course, he didn't tell this to his boss.

Instead, he listened and, once she was through, moved on to the reason he had come to see her in the first place. "This probably comes at a bad time," Russell indicated, "but I was thinking that it might be a good time to step up patrols around schools in town."

Diane, who wore her long brunette hair in a chignon bun, batted blue eyes at him. "Really?"

"We've had reports of increased drug activity on and outside school campuses," he explained. "The greater the police presence, the greater the deterrence in drug dealing and use."

"I take your point." She leaned back in her chair thoughtfully. "I'll see what I can do."

He smiled, taking that as a victory of sorts. "Thank you." Russell's cell phone rang. He was going to ignore it, but when he removed it from the pocket of his pants, he saw that the caller was Tisha. Curious as to why she was calling him during work hours, he gazed at the police chief and asked, "Do you mind?"

"Not at all." Diane grinned at him. "We were done. And I need to check my own messages." She lifted her cell phone from the desk.

Russell took Tisha's call. "Hey."

"I just stopped a creep from abducting a child," she said tensely. "Since I'm currently holding him at gunpoint, you might want to get over here. Now!"

He got the location from her and said, "On my way."

"What's going on?" Diane asked after he disconnected.

Russell was already on his feet when he informed her, "There's been an attempted child abduction. I need to go."

She nodded. "Keep me posted."

"Will do." He left her office and informed other detectives about the incident before heading out. As he drove, Russell considered how and why Tisha happened to be in possession of a firearm.

ROSAMUND HAD BRACED herself for the questions she might be asked in effectively making a citizen's arrest and detaining the suspect till the police arrived. She couldn't shy away from doing the right thing when confronted with a child abduction situation. Even at the risk of exposing herself for a hitman to discover. Now she needed to try to minimize the damage, if possible, by maintaining her cover as Tisha González, a Good Samaritan who just happened to be in the right place at the right time. And hope that Russell bought it, even if she hated having to lie to him. But with the case against Simon Griswold still hanging in the balance and her testimony paramount to convicting him of human trafficking and related offenses, what other choice did she have?

By the time Russell showed up, other law enforcement had arrived after a 911 call from a neighbor, taken Tisha's statement, and had the suspect in custody. He was now handcuffed in the back of a squad car, while his firearm—which Tisha recognized as a 9-millimeter Luger semiautomatic handgun—and vehicle were confiscated as evidence and part of a crime scene.

"Are you okay?" Russell asked as he put a hand on Tisha's shoulder, causing her to feel the sensation of his gentle touch.

"Yes, I'm fine," she told him, even if shaken up by the crime and what it could potentially mean for her own safety. They were inside his official vehicle, not too far from the two-story Craftsman-style home where Suzette Haskell and her seven-year-old daughter, Deena, the girl who Tisha saved from being abducted, lived. She was now safe and sound, which gave Tisha a good feeling, knowing just how much worse things could have been for the girl and her mother. As for herself, Rosamund had managed to avoid any interaction with the local press thus far, putting her true identity at risk.

"Okay." Russell lifted his hand from her shoulder. "Now walk me through exactly what happened."

Tisha told him how she was in the cooling down stage of jogging when she came onto Pragten Road and witnessed the brazen attempted abduction by the suspect, prompting her to take matters into her own hands. "I wasn't going to let him take her," she insisted unapologetically.

"I'm glad you were able to stop him," Russell told her. "But it was still dangerous to take on an armed criminal. He could've killed you."

"Coulda, woulda, shoulda." Tisha rolled her eyes, though not meaning to be flippant about this. "The way I saw it, that little girl's entire life was on the line. In that moment, I wasn't thinking about myself so much as the real fear that she would end up sexually assaulted, sex trafficked, murdered—or all of the above. I just reacted on impulse like anyone else probably would have in my shoes."

Russell glanced at her ankle where Tisha had replaced her weapon in the holster. "How often have you been carrying a loaded firearm while jogging, or otherwise?"

She expected this question to come up sooner or later. Rosamund knew she had to tread carefully, while hoping not to arouse his suspicion any more than was already the case. "Since I ran into trouble, no pun intended, with bad guys back in Cranston," she said, which had some truth in it, though under a different context. "I didn't want to become another victim in yesterday's news."

"Do you have a permit to carry a concealed weapon?" he asked, gazing at her.

"Yes, I made sure of that after moving to California." It was something Rosamund knew was part of the setup in her relocation under a new identity, while maintaining her right and need to be able to defend herself from a known threat. "Between the gun, a stun gun, and pepper spray, which I also happen to carry, I used the stun gun to subdue the suspect," she disclosed. "I just want to feel safe. Even in a relatively peaceful place like Weconta Falls." She met his eyes intently. "Evidently, there are bad people who wish to do really bad things, even here."

Russell turned away. "Yeah, there is that reality," he conceded. "At least there's one less bad guy on the streets of Weconta Falls, thanks to you. Hopefully, he won't be able to make bail and see freedom again anytime soon."

I'm keeping my fingers crossed that he stays behind bars, Rosamund thought, knowing that was where child abductors belonged. "What do you know about the suspect?" she asked casually.

Russell didn't appear to give much thought to the question, which was legitimate enough even for a waitress to ask, under the circumstances. "His name is Paul Skinner," he responded. "Thirty-seven years old, he has a record for child sex crimes, as well as other criminality. Apparently, he spotted the girl playing in the front yard, lured her over to him, and then grabbed her."

"Thank goodness it went no further than that," Tisha stated, knowing that even the attempted abduction would likely be enough to trigger nightmares and maybe require therapy for the victim.

"Yeah." Russell waited a beat. "We may need you to come to the station in the coming days to make a formal statement as to what you saw and did, if that's all right?"

Tisha smiled softly. "Yes, of course," she said levelly. "Whatever you need me to do."

She was not eager to give herself more exposure for something unrelated to the crimes perpetrated by Simon Griswold. But Rosamund wasn't about to give Russell more reasons to want to dig into her past by rejecting his request. Even if she had been assured that her true identity would be tough, if not impossible, to crack while under the program.

"Good." He grinned sideways. "Can I drive you home?"

"Yes, please do." If she might have been hesitant for him to do that before, Tisha was more than happy to have him know where she was currently staying now. Not only was it a smart idea that he was aware of her location right now, but it was a good segue to what she had in mind for them this evening. "In fact, before this nasty business of attempted child abduction occurred, I was planning to invite you over for dinner tonight. If you didn't have any other plans," she threw out, just to cover herself and any disappointment should he turn her down.

"No other plans," Russell stated without hesitation.

"After I complete the investigation for today, which might be a bit later than my usual end of workday, I'd love to come for dinner."

"Since I'll be working the afternoon shift at Shailene's Grill, that should be perfect," Tisha said.

He grinned. "Then it's a date."

"A date it is." She was happy to see they were on the same page on that front, deciding there was no way around it, they were dating. Even if not everything was out on the table where it concerned the details of her other life, though it was getting harder and harder to keep this from someone Rosamund had begun to develop feelings for. But coming clean prematurely could do more harm than good, she feared, while placing her security, and potentially his, in jeopardy.

Chapter Seven

Russell couldn't belzieve that Tisha had singlehandedly stopped a would-be child snatcher in his tracks. When combining that courageous effort with her willingness to take on a bunch of teen bullies at the park, and being comfortable with a firearm, it was obvious there was more to the gorgeous waitress than met the eye. But what? She mentioned having trouble with bad guys in Cranston. What kind of trouble? Had this forced her hand in readiness to be able to defend herself and others in harm's way?

No matter how he sliced it, Russell was sure that there was a backstory to Tisha and how she wound up in Weconta Falls. Perhaps she would divulge some of it tonight at her place. Or if not, then soon, the more she got comfortable with him and knew he was someone she could trust. For his part, Russell resisted for now the temptation to pry into her history, believing that to do so might undermine whatever was building between them. He knew intuitively that she was definitely not a bad person and, as such, he could deal with anything else. What he also knew was that he was falling for Tisha and he had to trust her as much as he wanted her to trust him.

He sat at his desk, reviewing the information they had on Paul Skinner. It irked Russell, the thought that Skinner had been preying on children in Weconta Falls. How many had he already victimized? Were any reported missing of late? Had they really gotten so lucky as to stop a child kidnapping in progress the first time around for Skinner since his last stint behind bars?

I'll even take being serendipitous if it means saving a minor from the victimization brought about by the likes of Paul Skinner and others who perpetrated such heinous acts, Russell thought. He was still pondering this when Detective Gloria Choi came into the office with news.

"We have information that Paul Skinner may have been hanging around Loraina Elementary School the other day, before he tried to abduct the Haskell child," she said. "A car matching the description of Skinner's Range Rover Evoque was seen parked outside the school. There's even a report that someone may have tried to lure a girl going to school into the SUV."

"The pattern fits." Russell bristled, knowing that child sex offenders went from place to place in an attempt to snatch a child with the best chance to succeed in the disgusting endeavor. "We need to see if there were any other victims."

"We're looking into it." Gloria touched the fabric of her one-button crepe blazer. "And also whether or not the attempted abduction could be part of a larger network of human traffickers."

"Good." He hated to think that human and sex trafficking was going on in Weconta Falls. But anything was possible. Especially when crime syndicates and criminal gangs knew no boundaries when it came to potential targets and locations for sexual exploitation. As such, why not Weconta Falls as a place for this type of activity?

"It's fortunate that Tisha González happened along when she did to prevent Skinner from carrying out his plan," Gloria remarked.

"Very true," Russell had to admit.

"Maybe we need to recruit her to come work for the Weconta Falls PD."

"Good luck with that," he said thoughtfully, even if it seemed like Tisha did have what it took to be a great law enforcement officer, starting with courage. Would she ever consider such, which would be a big departure from her previous occupations? "According to Chief O'Shea, budget cuts are coming, including a freeze on hiring in the department."

Gloria frowned. "That's too bad. We can always use more good people for the job."

"You'll get no argument from me there." Even so, Russell wondered just how much longer he would be cut out for detective work there, when part of him still longed to return to his previous job with the Bureau. Or was that simply a reflection of growing homesick?

"Didn't think so," she said with a chuckle.

"In the meantime, we'll just keep doing what we're doing and not get too distracted with decisions outside of our control," he told her, of which Gloria concurred.

AT WORK, TISHA was still rattled about the near abduction of a girl by a man who apparently saw an opportunity to grab her for his own deviant purposes. *What if*

I hadn't come along and been in the right place at the right time to come to her rescue? Rosamund asked herself, as she juggled a hot plate with a BBQ beef brisket sandwich and fries and another plate with a garden salad and fish sandwich. She didn't even want to think about what that child might have had to endure had the perp succeeded in his brazen plan to take her. Tisha considered as well the horror the girl's mother experienced in watching the crime take place before her very eyes. She was surely second-guessing herself for letting her daughter out of her sight for even a second, while probably vowing to never let it happen again. If only that could be the case for all children preyed upon by sex offenders and traffickers. Rosamund knew all too well that prevention was only half the story. Arresting and prosecuting those who had succeeded in committing such offenses was the other half.

Tisha served the hungry customers, knowing that most had no experience being a victim of criminals of one sort or another. She hoped that would always be true. After taking the order for an elderly African American couple, Tisha looked toward the table where Russell normally sat. It was occupied by a burly, bald-headed man instead. She frowned but understood that Russell wouldn't be showing up today, as he had to investigate the attempted child snatching and build the case against the perp. Tisha looked forward to having dinner with the detective tonight. She hoped it would go well, even against the backdrop of the unsettling crime she had witnessed and immersed herself in, likely against the advice of her marshal handler, Leah Redfield.

THAT EVENING, RUSSELL had showered, trimmed the hair on his face, and changed clothing before heading over to Tisha's place. He stopped off at a store first and grabbed a bottle of red wine for his contribution to the dinner. He wasn't sure what Tisha had in mind beyond that, but he was certainly open for spending time with her in any way she saw fit.

"Hey," she uttered in a pleasant voice after opening the door.

"Hey." He flashed a grin as he stepped inside. "Brought wine."

"Thanks." Tisha took the bottle. "This will go great with the meal."

Russell smiled again. "Good."

"You clean up nicely," she told him, scanning his clothing.

"You too," he had to say, though unable to keep himself from recalling how sexy she looked in the purple sports bra and tight black yoga pants she wore earlier with running shoes.

She blushed. "Thank you."

He scanned the downstairs for his first opportunity to check out her townhouse, noting the interesting layout and modern furnishings. "I like your place."

"It's not really my style," Tisha told him candidly. "But I needed something on kind of short notice and this was on the market, so here I am."

"I see." Russell wondered about the needing on short notice comment, as well as what her previous place looked like in Cranston. It only added to the mysteries of her life he still hoped to unfold.

"The food's ready," she said, heading toward the kitchen. "Hope you like Mexican?"

"Yeah, I love it." He looked at her, wondering if some recipes had been passed down to Tisha by her parents or grandparents. "Can I help with anything?"

"I've got it covered," Tisha insisted. "Relax."

Russell nodded. "All right."

Soon, they were sitting at a round solid wood dining table on white bouclé dining chairs, eating grilled chicken quesadillas with steak fajita salad and guacamole dip.

"It's delicious," Russell said, marveling over the food.

"Glad you like it," Tisha said, grinning, as she dabbed a napkin to a corner of her mouth.

He brought her up-to-date on the investigation of attempted child snatcher Paul Skinner, and the likelihood that Deena Haskell wasn't the first one Skinner went after. "We think he may have been targeting girls at local schools," Russell informed her, "including Deena."

Tisha's brow creased. "Not surprised," she said. "He fits the profile."

Russell agreed, though curious about how she had reached this conclusion. Had she encountered child abductors before? Or was it merely guesswork considering the suspect's characteristics? "Yeah, seems that way. Glad we got him before he was able to fully execute his game plan."

"Yes, that is a relief," Tisha said musingly, and bit into her chicken quesadilla. "Hope he's put away for a long time."

"Me too." Russell stuck a fork into his fajita salad and

hinted that they were exploring if there could be a wider network of child abductors in Weconta Falls.

She lifted a brow. "You think they could be trafficking girls here?"

"Doesn't seem likely," he contended realistically. "My guess is that Skinner acted alone. But, given the nature of the crime, we need to assure those within the community that this isn't a bigger problem that needs to be addressed."

"Makes sense," she said pensively, and sipped her wine. He noted that Tisha pivoted away from talk about child abductions to more personal things like family. "So, do you get to see your siblings often?"

"Truthfully, not as often as I'd like," Russell confessed, lifting his wineglass. "Between living in different states and everyone being busy with their respective careers and social lives, it hasn't left us much time to get together." He knew that moving to California had put him even farther away from the others, making it that much harder to see one another. But it also gave everyone a good excuse to visit his neck of the woods whenever they wanted. "How about you? Do you see much of your parents or sister?"

"I wish I could say I do," she said, a catch to her voice. "But I too haven't made the effort of late to bridge the gap between us." Tisha paused. "Hopefully soon I'll make the time to pay them all a visit."

"Or maybe invite them to visit you in Weconta Falls," Russell suggested. He assumed there was no bad blood between them or other impediments to visiting her.

"Yes, that's a thought, once I'm more settled in," she said, sipping more wine.

Russell wished he could get into her head, see what she was hiding from him. Or would that be too intrusive when he needed to trust his own instincts that whatever was in Tisha's past that brought her to Weconta Falls, he was grateful for her presence in his life. When it was time to get to the unknown aspects of her history, Russell was sure Tisha would share this part of her with him. Until then, he needed to take her for who she was. She meant more to him than anyone had in some time.

While caught up in his reverie, Russell had barely noticed that Tisha had stood up and reached out to take his hand. He allowed her to and got to his feet, whereby she started to kiss him. He kissed her back, pulling her into his arms, as their bodies molded together through the clothing.

"I like kissing you," Tisha murmured, while their mouths were locked.

"I feel the same way about kissing you," he told her candidly, and they went back to making out like teenagers. Or perhaps newlyweds.

"I want you to make love to me, Russell," Tisha urged after they had made their way into the living room between hot kisses. "I think you want that too."

"Definitely," he gasped. With his erection dying to come out in full force, Russell fought hard to maintain self-control, while knowing this was what they both needed from each other. Anything else could wait. "Let me make love to you, Tisha."

"Please do," she pressed, and led him silently up the winding staircase, down a short hall, and into the primary bedroom. At a glance, Russell saw a room with contemporary furnishings and an overhead wood ceiling fan with a light. He homed in on the white oak storage bed with a textured teal coverlet and fluffy pillows atop. Returning his ravenous gaze to Tisha, Russell uttered, "I'm eager to try your bed out for size."

"Be my guest," she challenged him enticingly. "So long as I'm in it with you."

"Wouldn't have it any other way," he insisted, and gave her another passionate kiss, before pulling back and watching keenly as she removed the spaghetti straps of her watermelon-colored tiered wrap dress from her shoulders. She allowed it to fall to the floor, then kicked off her slide mules. Russell took in her amazing body as Tisha removed her underwear and stood before him. "You're beautiful," he said, with her perfect breasts and the right proportions from head to toe. He wondered if she possibly knew just how gorgeous and sexy she was.

"Show me your body," she demanded, and he proceeded to shed his smoke-colored herringbone shirt, exposing his upper body. He dug into the pocket of his navy trousers and removed the condom he brought, having anticipated he might need it tonight. He tossed it on the bed and removed his Oxford shoes. Then came the pants and underwear. They were now both naked and at each other's disposal. "You are incredibly perfect," Tisha gushed.

Flattered but more enamored with her attributes, Russell cupped her high cheeks and laid another solid kiss on her ready mouth, before scooping her into his arms and carrying her to the bed. Tearing open the condom, he put it on and joined her atop the coverlet. They went right into foreplay, bringing each other joy through their mouths and hands. Russell resisted going further, wanting to pleasure Tisha first, above his own needs.

When she apparently could not stand it anymore, Tisha cried out, "Please, Russell, don't make me wait any longer. Let's come together. Make love to me. Now!"

With this directive, Russell felt it was time to let loose. He positioned himself between her legs and entered her. As a primordial craving erupted inside, he made love to her, getting back as much as he gave, and then some. Their climaxes came quickly while exchanging passionate kisses. Afterward, they caught their breath and Russell knew Tisha was everything he could have imagined and more. Was this the beginning of what it felt like to fall in love again? Or was it too soon to even think that way, with some uncertainties Russell sensed were still swirling around them?

"YOU WERE INCREDIBLE," Russell whispered in her ear as if someone else might overhear him.

"So were you!" Tisha boldly stated as they lay side by side. She was still feeling aroused after climaxing with Russell simultaneously. The sense of urgency she had experienced in wanting to make love to him that night both frightened and excited her. The sexual chemistry between them from practically the beginning had finally caught up to her and, clearly, based on his bodily response, he was just as ready to take that next step.

"We make a great couple," he declared enthusiastically, while massaging her foot.

"You think so, do you?" Her voice was playful as Tisha

enjoyed the massage, his long fingers magical in caressing her toes and heel.

"Absolutely. Or at least we have the makings of a great couple, if we allow ourselves to explore this and all its potential."

She felt a tingle at the suggestion. He had proven to be as skilled a lover as Rosamund had imagined and had given her another reason for wanting to be in Weconta Falls. If only to see through what they had started in what could become the incredible romance that had been missing in her life for so long. But was it realistic to think that this could actually go somewhere once her truth emerged? How would they do this? Was he ready to get to know the real her, beyond the real parts she had already shared?

Once Simon Griswold's trial had come and gone, Rosamund wondered if the feelings she had developed for Russell would sustain when she was no longer under a cloud of uncertainty and danger about the future. Wasn't it desirable and incumbent upon her to meet him halfway, if he still wanted her, and allow nature to take its course?

"There are things you don't know about me, Russell," Tisha hesitated to say, feeling she owed him at least that much.

"And you'll fill me in whenever you're comfortable doing so," he said understandingly. "I won't rush you."

"Okay." She left it at that for now, knowing that revealing her secrets might change everything for better or worse. Breaking further rules of the federal Witness Security Program might not only endanger his life even more, but could draw Russell into unwanted territory.

Hadn't he left the FBI to escape the pressures he felt after losing his wife and daughter? Would it be fair to expect him to become ensconced in her own drama, Rosamund wondered.

She felt Russell's protective arms wrap around her, pulling them close in a warm snuggle and show of support.

SO, ROSAMUND SANTIAGO was now going by the name Tisha González, Arnold Nishimoto thought, as he gazed at the image of the special agent on his laptop while sitting in the front seat of the black Porsche Panamera Platinum Edition he was renting. No doubt she had altered her appearance somewhat from the official DHS picture. Perhaps she had changed the color or shortened the length of her hair. Maybe she wore contacts to change the color of her eyes. Or wore more or less makeup to disguise her true self.

Nishimoto had been sent the information from a source within the HSI that told him what he needed to know to get the bead on the fed's key witness in the human trafficking case against Simon Griswold. To that end, Nishimoto flipped to another image and set of info on the laptop that had his attention.

Leah Redfield was the deputy U.S. marshal assigned to Rosamund Santiago aka Tisha González. Nishimoto studied the good-looking deputy marshal. He saw that she was currently operating in a Northern California town called Weconta Falls. Did this mean that Tisha was there too? Or a nearby town, where Redfield could easily come to the aid of the special agent and protected witness? He

scheme of things. She believed it was unlikely the hired assassin would be smart enough or lucky enough to tie a small-town act of heroism to the HSI special agent and witness he was tracking.

That's good enough for me, Rosamund told herself, feeling relieved. She had been so preoccupied with her thoughts that she nearly spilled the caramel macchiato and chai latte drinks she was holding on a tray as she and Tracy came face-to-face.

"Hey," Tracy said, taking a breath, as she managed to hold onto a plate with biscuits and gravy, alongside bacon and scrambled eggs. "If you wanted to switch orders, all you had to do was ask," she quipped.

"Funny." Tisha laughed. "I figured practically bumping into each other was a good way to demonstrate dexterity in this business."

"Good one," she said with a chuckle. "I'll have to remember that. You can fill me in later on how things went with Detective Lynley last night," Tracy teased. "Right now, there's someone at his table other than him who needs a menu once your hands are free."

"Got it." Tisha didn't mind being bossed around a bit by the more experienced waitress who served as the assistant manager whenever Shailene wasn't there, which was the case today as she had a doctor's appointment.

After setting down the drinks, Tisha turned to the table where Russell liked to sit. She expected he might show up at lunchtime. If so, hopefully she wouldn't blush too much for all to see when thinking about their lovemaking last night. But sitting at the table was a tall, thin man in his midforties with two-toned hair color of medium-length, worn in a faux-hawk style, and a patchy beard. He wore a green crewneck T-shirt, relaxed tapered jeans, and black tennis shoes.

"How are you this morning?" Tisha asked him in a friendly tone, handing him a menu.

He ignored the question and stared at her with close-set blue eyes. "Are you Tisha González?"

Tisha's heart skipped a beat. Who was he and what did he want? The fact that he hadn't referred to her as Rosamund Santiago gave her hope that he wasn't working for Simon Griswold. Or with Arnold Nishimoto. Not that this gave her much comfort. She was feeling at a decided disadvantage. "Who's asking?" Tisha thought it best to use the direct approach.

"Name's Freddie Hildebrand," he said matter-of-factly. "I'm a writer for the *Weconta Falls Journal*. I'd like to ask you about the attempted child abduction yesterday on Pragten Road."

"I don't know anything about that," she claimed.

He jutted his chin. "According to a reliable source with the Weconta Falls PD, a Tisha González intervened while armed with a gun to stop Paul Skinner from abducting the little girl." Freddie looked at her. "I did a little digging and discovered a Tisha González worked here as a waitress. So here I am."

Tisha was furious that someone at the police department had decided to share her personal information with the press. She was quite sure it wasn't Russell. That left one of the other detectives or officers she spoke to. Her first thought was to deny she was the person the journalist was looking for. But Tisha was certain he wouldn't buy it, thereby putting even more unwanted attention on her. So she decided her best course of action was to get this over with and try to minimize the damage. Then it occurred to her that he might not be who he claimed. Mindful that his motives could be anything but pure, if not deadly, she asked him pointedly, "How do I know you really work for the *Weconta Falls Journal*?"

"That's a fair question," he said, and pulled his credentials from the pocket of his jeans. "Here's my ID."

Tisha studied it and decided it looked official enough. Still, she remained wary. "I'm a very private person, not looking for attention," she told him in a straightforward voice. "If you're looking for a story, you won't find it here."

"I just have a few questions," he persisted, "and then I'll get out of your hair."

She sighed. "As you can see, it's crazy in here, so I don't really have time for this."

Freddie picked up the menu. "How about if I order something?"

You don't give up, do you? Rosamund mused, her patience waning. "What would you like?"

"A Belgian waffle sounds good. And coffee with cream."

"I'll put the order in," she said. "Then you have two minutes, but no picture of me for your article. As I said, I value my privacy and have no wish to show my face and become the story. Are we clear?"

"Yeah." He flashed a grin, displaying dingy teeth. "Deal."

After clearing it with Tracy, Tisha brought the waffle

and coffee and sat across from him. "So, what would you like to know?" she asked tensely.

Freddie spread hot butter across the waffle and covered it with syrup. "How were you so courageous in taking on an armed child kidnapper in broad daylight?"

"I only did what any law-abiding citizen would do," Tisha said, seeking to downplay it, "when faced with that situation. It was really no big deal."

"Most would say it was a very big deal," he argued. "If you hadn't come along when you did, the outcome for that kid might have been a lot different."

Tisha didn't doubt that one bit, imagining what she would have gone through had it been her own daughter targeted by a child snatcher. "I'm just glad I could help her," she said evenly.

"Yeah, about that..." Freddie dug his fork into the waffle. "Do you normally carry a concealed weapon?"

He favored her with a curious look, and Tisha could almost see the wheels turning as he wondered if there was more to her simple life than it appeared. She had to keep him at bay. "I like to when I'm out running, for self-defense," she told him smoothly. "I usually feel safe but know that there are those who might target women or children by themselves." She drew a breath. "Sometimes having a gun is the only way to get past the danger."

He nodded. "Sure worked this time for one little victim."

"Yes," Tisha said simply. "Well, I have to get back to work." She rose. "Enjoy the rest of your meal."

"Thanks, I will." Freddie smiled. "And thanks for stepping up and stopping that creep. Not everyone would have gotten involved."

Tisha acknowledged this much. "Just did what I had to." She walked away, while hoping this would be the end of it as far as drawing attention.

Tracy came up to her and asked, curiosity dotting her face, "So, what was that all about?"

Meeting her gaze, Tisha answered as honestly as she could without blowing her cover. "Nipping a potential problem in the bud." She left it at that while moving on to another table.

RUSSELL SAT IN his office and placed a video call on the laptop with his sister, Madison. A year and a half older, Madison was a U.S. law enforcement park ranger, working in the state parks system of North Carolina. Her attractive face appeared, which reminded him of their mother, including the bold turquoise eyes. Madison's blond hair was stylish in a shaggy wolf cut with curly bangs. "Hey," he greeted her, smiling.

"Hey, Russell." She smiled back, showing her straight, white teeth. "Nice surprise."

"Been meaning to call," Russell said guiltily, knowing she reached out more often than he did.

"It's cool, really," she assured him. "I'll take calls from my brothers and sister whenever I can, short of visits both ways."

"We'll have to try to get together for Christmas." He recalled the holiday was always a family favorite when their parents were still alive. It was even more fulfilling when Victoria and Daisy were still in the picture.

"I'd love that," Madison said. She ran a finger across a thin brow. "I'm sure Scott and Annette feel the same." She waited a beat. "So, would you be bringing the new lady in your life?"

Russell smiled, knowing he had yet to spill the beans to her, though not deliberately. "New lady?" he played along.

"Annette mentioned you had started seeing someone," Madison said. "I think she said her name was Tisha?"

"Yeah, that's right." Russell grinned, thinking about the amazing night they spent together and the endless possibilities that suddenly presented themselves for the future as a consequence. "We're not quite at the point of making plans for Christmas this year, but things do seem to be looking up for me in the romance category."

Madison's face lit. "That's wonderful. Can't say the same, but I'm always optimistic."

"You should be," he reassured her, knowing about the recent breakup with her boyfriend. "You're a great catch. There's someone out there for you, sis."

"Always nice to have my siblings there, even if from afar, to feed my ego," she uttered, chuckling. "We'll see what happens. In the meantime, it's ranger business as usual." Russell listened as she talked about her latest case involving suspected gang activity and drug abuse. "Seems like it's becoming a real problem around here of late," Madison complained.

"It's becoming a problem everywhere." He thought about the drug activity at schools in Weconta Falls, with a likely gang component. Not to mention the child abductor arrestee suspected of targeting local schoolchildren and the broader possibility that child sex trafficking could be an issue that bore further investigation. It was all the more reason that the police chief needed to step up in increasing patrols and surveillance in and around schools.

"I'm sure," his sister concurred with a frown.

Just as he was about to mention how Tisha had rescued a girl from victimization, giving him another reason to admire her strength in character, Russell was interrupted when Detective Ike Wainright knocked on his door and then opened it, stepping inside. The look on his face told Russell that something was up.

"I can come back in a bit," Ike uttered.

"Stay," Russell ordered. He gazed at Madison on the screen and said, "Sorry to have to cut this short."

"It's fine," she told him with a smile. "We both have things to do."

He grinned at her. "Talk to you soon."

"Promise?"

"Yeah, definitely."

"I'll hold you to that," Madison stated. "Later."

Russell waved goodbye to her and ended the video chat. He turned to Ike and asked attentively, "What's up?"

"Something interesting," he said nebulously, and walked toward the desk, plopping down on an armless vinyl guest chair. "Ballistics ran the 9-millimeter Luger semiautomatic handgun that Paul Skinner had in his possession during the attempted kidnapping of the girl."

"And...?" Russell peered at him keenly.

"Well, initially, nothing came up. Then the firearm and the ammo in it was entered into the ATF's National Integrated Ballistic Information Network," Ike pointed out, running a large hand across his mouth. "We got a hit. A confirmed match was made between the weapon and shell casings collected at a crime scene earlier this year in Atlanta, Georgia. The ballistic markings on the casings linked them to bullets that were in a gun used to kill a man named Earl Cummings at a party store, during an armed robbery."

Russell cocked a brow. "No kidding," he said.

"Turns out that those bullets matched test fired bullets taken from Skinner's gun where the barrel has a right-hand twist and five lands and grooves," Ike said, rubbing his chin.

"So, the weapon Skinner had was used to commit murder," Russell said.

"Yeah, that's about the size of it. What we don't know yet is whether Skinner committed the armed robbery," the detective stated. "Or if he ended up with the firearm after the fact. We're trying to see if Skinner lines up with the robbery suspect surveillance video recorded at the time."

"If so, that would certainly help put him away for a very long time." Russell leaned forward. "Even if he didn't commit the robbery, we've got him dead to rights on the attempted child abduction. Along with possession of an illegal firearm." As far as Russell was concerned, if convicted on both counts, that would ensure Paul Skinner spent years behind bars. This would certainly be something Tisha would take solace in, given her heroics in taking the perp down. And if Skinner was responsible in any way for the death of a man during an armed robbery, he deserved to be held fully accountable for that as well.

HALF AN HOUR LATER, Russell got a call about a woman found dead in a vehicle under suspicious circumstances. He headed to the scene, a warehouse district in downtown Weconta Falls, the attempted child abductor and possible armed robber and killer Paul Skinner still on his mind. Russell hated to think of what else the suspect may have been into. At least they had him in custody, thanks to quick and decisive action by Tisha, who deserved a medal, as far as he was concerned. That was on top of the fact that she was great in bed and great girlfriend material. He imagined she would make an even better wife and mother, were things to continue to progress between them.

When he arrived at his destination on Breckton Street, Russell got out and mentally prepared himself for whatever might present itself in this latest investigation. The decedent's car, a red Buick Encore, was parked haphazardly outside a building under construction. Detective Gloria Choi approached Russell. "So, what do we have?" he asked.

"A white female is dead, the apparent victim of a self-inflicted gunshot wound to the head." Gloria creased her brow. "An elderly married couple, Edward and Ruth Davidson, were walking their dog when they spotted the irregularly parked vehicle and grew suspicious enough to check it out. That's when they discovered the victim in the front seat and called 911. I checked for a pulse." She shook her head forlornly to indicate there wasn't one.

Russell walked up to the car on the driver's side. The door was already open. He eyed the decedent, who was slumped over the steering wheel. She was slender and looked to be in her thirties, with red hair in a pixie bob. There was blood on her beige twill blazer and dark cigarette jeans worn with pointed toe booties. On the floor of the car was what looked to be a Glock 27 .40 S&W caliber pistol.

Donning a pair of nitrile gloves, Russell carefully reached over the decedent to the leather bag on the seat and dug out her wallet. He lifted an ID and raised a brow when stating uncomfortably, "The victim's name is Leah Redfield. She's a deputy U.S. marshal."

"Hmm..." Gloria moaned. "Why would a deputy U.S. marshal take her own life?"

"Good question," Russell said. The Crime Scene Investigation Unit arrived, as was standard procedure in what Russell saw as a suspicious death. The medical examiner, Doctor Jessalyn Zegler, also arrived. A petite woman in her early forties, she had mid-length brown hair worn in space buns and blue eyes behind gray browline glasses. After a preliminary examination of the victim, Dr. Zegler said somberly, "The decedent likely died from what appears to be a self-inflicted gunshot wound to the right side of the head, causing massive damage inside."

Russell grimaced at the thought. "Any indication that drugs might have been involved in her death?" He considered depression or the stress of her job for the U.S. Marshals Service, similar to other types of pressure-packed roles in law enforcement, as possibly playing a role in the suicide. Assuming it was a suicide, which troubled him somewhat. Most of those in federal law enforcement, he believed, were thick-skinned, even amid adversity. At least where it concerned taking one's own life.

Had Redfield gone against the grain? Or was it made to look like it?

"I certainly wouldn't rule out the presence of alcohol or drugs in the victim's system that may have contributed to her death," the medical examiner replied. "We'll know more once the toxicology report comes in."

As the body bag was headed to the morgue, Gloria said to Russell with a catch in her voice, "I've got something interesting you might want to see, Lynley..."

He turned away from surveying the surroundings, while wondering why the deputy marshal would choose this location to off herself, to find Gloria holding in gloved hands an evidence bag containing the deputy marshal's cell phone. "What is it?"

"Seems like Leah Redfield made a number of calls recently to one number," Gloria began. "It belongs to Tisha González."

A brow shot up as Russell said with shock, "Tisha?"

"Right. The very same Tisha González who saved the day in stopping Paul Skinner from abducting a seven-year-old girl." Gloria batted her lashes. "Looks like there's more to unpack with this Tisha than at first glance."

He was inclined to agree, as Russell couldn't help but think that the woman he'd made love to last night, and again in the wee hours of the morning, had some explaining to do. He wondered if it would change the nature of everything he thought they had going for them.

Chapter Nine

Tisha was happy to be home after a busy day on her feet at Shailene's Grill. She had forgotten over the years just how exhausting it could be, waiting on hungry and demanding customers at a restaurant. She thought about talking to the writer, Freddie Hildebrand, about preventing a child snatching. Though she could do without the attention and was still perturbed that someone from the police department had leaked her information to a member of the press, Tisha hoped the article might actually do some good in putting the spotlight on the dangers of child abductions, even in small-town America, the warning signs, and how everyone needs to get involved to one degree or another in order to prevent this from happening as much as possible.

Tisha had removed her shoes and liked the feel of the hardwood flooring on her bare feet. She imagined them being massaged by Russell, as he had last night. Might there be a repeat tonight? Or would it be better to tone things down a bit till more things were out in the open between them?

When she heard a car drive up, Tisha peeked out the

blinds. She smiled when she saw it was Russell. Had he texted her to say he was coming and she missed it? Would he suggest having dinner at his place? Hers? Or a restaurant other than Shailene's Grill, knowing she spent enough time there not to want to use it as the setting for a date.

I'm open to whatever he has in mind, Rosamund told herself. And whatever came later. She opened the door before he could ring the bell. Grinning at him, she said, "Hey."

Russell was stone-faced in responding flatly, "We need to talk."

Tisha didn't particularly like his tone. What was going on with him? Did he have a change of heart about them before she got the chance to disclose the secrets she kept? Or did he have secrets of his own to reveal? "Come in," she told him. Only after he had whisked past her and she followed him into the living room did Tisha meet his un-blinking eyes. "What do you want to talk about?"

"Leah Redfield," Russell said tonelessly.

Rosamund reacted to the name of her handler. What did he know about Leah? Had she confided in him about her situation? Should she even acknowledge knowing Leah Redfield? "What about Leah?" she asked tenta-tively.

He folded his arms. "She was found dead in her car," he said sharply.

"What?" Rosamund's voice shook. "How?"

"An apparent single self-inflicted gunshot wound to the head. There was a firearm found in her car."

"Oh, no." She put a hand to her mouth, disbelieving that Leah would have killed herself. Could she have?

"Your name and number were on speed dial on the deputy marshal's cell phone," Russell pointed out, making it clear he was aware of Leah's profession. If not her current mission. He peered at Rosamund. "Before I jump to any wrong conclusions, is there something you want to tell me…?"

"Yes, a few things." Rosamund's shoulders slumped. Under the circumstances, she didn't see how she could possibly remain silent about who she was. Not with him. "Where do I start?"

He sat down on an upholstered corner accent chair as he implored her patiently, "How about the nature of your relationship to Leah Redfield?"

Rosamund, her legs suddenly feeling wobbly, sat on the round-armed loveseat. She sucked in a deep breath, before saying candidly, "Leah is my handler with the U.S. Marshals Service."

"Really?" Russell adjusted his frame contemplatively. "Go on…"

"I'm in the federal Witness Security Program," she told him. "But not as a typical civilian witness. I work for the U.S. Department of Homeland Security's Center for Countering Human Trafficking as a Homeland Security Investigations special agent." Rosamund paused, while giving him a moment to digest this. "My real name is Rosamund Santiago. Last month, I was working undercover with my partner, Johnnie Langford, on a human smuggling, sex trafficking, and money laundering ring operation out of Dallas, Texas. We were ambushed." She sighed as this was where it got hard. "I witnessed Johnnie get executed right before my eyes by the organization's ringleader, Simon Griswold. He tried to kill me as well and would have, had his gun not jammed. I managed to take out one of his cronies and get the jump on Griswold till help arrived."

"Sorry you had to go through that," Russell lamented. "And that your partner lost his life."

"Unfortunately, it gets worse." She twisted her mouth. "Griswold put a hit out on me to stop me from testifying at his trial on murder, attempted murder, and human smuggling charges, among others."

"So, they took you out of the field and put you into the WITSEC till Griswold goes on trial?" Russell ascertained.

"Yes, that's about the size of it," Rosamund confirmed. "I was given the moniker Tisha González, planted in Weconta Falls, and given a job as a waitress at Shailene's Grill. My only intention was to lay low till I needed to come out of hiding." She paused, gazing at him. "I never expected to meet you...and make a real connection."

"Was it really real?" He flashed her a doubtful look. "Or part of a convincing alias as Tisha González till it was time for you to pull up stakes and go back to your real life as Rosamund Santiago?"

Rosamund's nostrils flared. "That's not fair!" she snapped, even if part of her understood his skepticism. "Some things can't be faked. Not this. What we have... had...was real, no matter what name I was forced to go by."

"Dammit, you should have told me." His voice lowered. "Trusted me."

"I do trust you," Rosamund said honestly, but still needed to push back. "As an HSI special agent and chief witness against a major human smuggling operation, I was bound by certain rules of the game. Being a former FBI agent, you should know this. There could be no exceptions to the rule, not even you. Otherwise, I would risk not only endangering myself, but anyone else brought into the fold." Did he not get that? Surely he realized that this was bigger than the two of them?

Russell sighed raggedly. "You're right," he conceded. "You did what you were supposed to. I had no right to expect you to break the rules. Not even for me."

Rosamund was glad he acknowledged this. But that hadn't stopped her from wanting to do just that, more than once. "I tried to tell you last night," she uttered, "but you insisted there was no rush. To go at my own pace." She met his eyes. "Did you mean it? Or was that simply pillow talk in the afterglow of lovemaking?"

"I meant it." He held her gaze. "Whatever was going on with you, I never wanted to pressure you into filling me in before being ready to do so. Now I understand why you were holding back. I don't fault you for that."

Again, she felt relieved to hear this. Did it mean they could still have a future, once this was over? "Thank you," she said, pressing her palms together. "Just so you know, though, the U.S. Marshals Service did inform your police chief, Diane O'Shea, of my presence in town and alias under the WITSEC. So, it wasn't as if there were no active lines of communication between the DHS, USMS, and Weconta Falls Police Department in coordinating this effort."

Russell ran a hand along his jawline. "You played it by the book and that's the way it's supposed to be. Sorry if I made you think otherwise."

"Maybe I would have felt the same way, had the situation been reversed," Rosamund admitted, picturing it in her head. "I'm glad it's out in the open now." She frowned, while wondering how this would affect them moving forward. "I just hate that it had to happen with the death of Leah."

He leaned forward thoughtfully. "About that...did she seem suicidal to you?"

"Not really." Rosamund considered this. "I know she was divorced and hadn't seemed to be able to get the ex totally out of her system, but I didn't see her as being suicidal. She seemed to love her job." Which made Rosamund all the more uncomfortable with her handler's untimely death.

"Do you know if she used drugs?" Russell asked.

"We only met a few times and I never saw her take even an aspirin, much less any illicit drugs," Rosamund said. *Not that Leah couldn't have hidden this, as did many substance abusers*, she thought. Still, she had to give the handler the benefit of the doubt. "I think Leah was clean," she said point-blank.

"We'll see what the toxicology report reveals," he said. "In the meantime, the U.S. Marshals Service has been notified of Redfield's death. I'm sure a replacement handler for you is already in the works."

"I would hope so." Rosamund gripped the arm of the

loveseat more than intended, while wondering if she had been made by the hitman, with Leah being a mere casualty in his way.

As if reading her mind, Russell asked, "What have you been told about the hired killer?"

"His name is Arnold Nishimoto," she responded, ill at ease. "He's based out of Honolulu, Hawaii, but apparently travels the world as a highly paid assassin. The feds are trying to determine his whereabouts and take him into custody."

"Hmm..." Russell uttered cynically.

"I can send you the info I have on him," Rosamund volunteered. "Nishimoto supposedly has no idea where I am. Or my new name, Tisha González." She paused. "But with the strange death of Leah Redfield, I'm not sure what to think."

"Neither am I." Russell chewed on his lower lip. He hit her with a soft gaze. "My brother, Scott, is an FBI agent. I'll ask him to see what the Bureau has on Nishimoto that might be of assistance. In the meantime, maybe you should stay at my place while we try to figure this out."

While she welcomed his show of support, Rosamund didn't want to make any sudden moves till she spoke with Harold Paxton, the special agent in charge of the HSI Dallas Field Office, as well as Monroe Cortez, the U.S. Marshal for the Northern District of Texas. The worst thing she could do was jump the gun and endanger Russell's life in the process. No matter his good intentions. She cared about him too much for that. "Thanks, but I should be safe staying here right now." She tried to sound convincing. "The townhouse has a security system, a good vantage point of anyone coming or going, and is where I'm supposed to be. Besides that," Rosamund reminded him, "I have a loaded weapon and am quite good at using it, if necessary." She also knew that she had her Thai boxing skills as another means of self-defense. Not that any of this necessarily ensured her safety from a determined assassin, but she needed to keep a positive approach for herself and Russell.

"All right," he acquiesced. "What about work? As a waitress, I mean? In light of what's happened to your handler, will you continue to work at Shailene's Grill?"

Rosamund supposed it was a reasonable question. "I intend to keep things going as they are, until told otherwise by the powers that be," she told him straightforwardly. "A normal existence is part of the program, unless there's a direct threat to that."

He nodded. "Just checking. Makes sense on some level."

A thought occurred to her. "On that note, I do have a bone to pick with your department."

"What would that be?"

"Apparently, someone there leaked my fake name to a writer for the *Weconta Falls Journal*," she told him. "He's doing a piece about the attempted child abduction and was able to track me down at the restaurant for an interview. While I gave in and did it, under the condition that no photograph of me was to be used, I wasn't happy that my private info as a Good Samaritan had been exposed, given that I'm trying my best to keep a low profile for what you now know are obvious reasons."

"Sorry about the leak of your assumed name," Russell

said. "I'll look into it. Of course, if Arnold Nishimoto's none the wiser that you're going by Tisha González these days, it shouldn't be a problem."

"Hopefully not," Rosamund agreed, while reserving judgment.

Russell stood. "I have to go."

"Okay." Rosamund got to her feet as well. She moved toward him and wanted to give him a kiss, but didn't dare. She didn't want to make things worse between them by making assumptions that he still wanted to be involved with her. Or, for that matter, whether that would even be possible once her time as a witness in protection was over and done with.

Russell gave her a peck on the cheek and said tenderly, "Just be careful, and if you sense any danger whatsoever…"

"I'll let you know," she promised, grateful to know that at least he still had her back. What she wasn't sure of was if she still had his heart.

She saw him out, then locked the door and wondered uneasily what came next in what was turning out to be a potentially deadly game of cat and mouse.

RUSSELL WANTED TO kick himself for acting like a bratty teenager who had been left hanging at the prom by the prettiest girl in school. Well, maybe that was getting carried away with his reaction upon learning that Tisha González, the gorgeous waitress he had started to fall in love with, was actually Rosamund Santiago, a Homeland Security Investigations special agent and in the federal program. It was less about the fact that she had intentionally misled him, given that Rosamund had no choice really, but that he had failed to discover this on his own as a former FBI agent who was usually quite perceptive in unraveling clues that presented themselves. *Maybe I didn't want to know that Tisha was anything other than what or whom she pretended to be*, Russell told himself, as he drove back to the police department. Maybe it was safer for him to wear blinders so he wouldn't be hurt again, as he was when he lost his wife and daughter.

But didn't hurt come with the territory of living? Would he ever be able to truly steel himself from the pain of things being out of his control? He had to believe that there really was something there between him and Tisha or Rosamund. She had as much as told him so. He didn't believe for one minute that the way they were together in and out of bed was just for show. Rosamund had been put into a nearly impossible situation after watching her partner die and being left to fend for both of them against a human smuggler. Obviously, the DHS felt her testimony was critical to putting away Simon Griswold. So much so that, rather than risk her being killed after Griswold had put a hit out on her by having her continue her normal duties as an HSI special agent, they took the unusual step for someone in her position and placed her in witness protection. In which case, they hoped to keep Rosamund alive long enough to testify against Griswold.

She had never asked to be temporarily relocated to Weconta Falls and pursued by a lonely police detective who found her attractive. Rosamund must have seen something in him that made her want to get to know him as much as he sought to get to know her. They clicked, pure and simple. Having a different name to go by and different circumstances coming to light wouldn't change that. The fact that, as Tisha, she risked life and limb by exposing herself to prevent a little girl from being abducted by a known child sex offender told Russell all he needed to know about Rosamund.

He owed it to her and himself not to bail at a time when Rosamund's life was in danger, with her being pursued by a hired killer who may have found his target. Once her safety had been assured and the business of testifying in court against a trafficker was over, they could decide where to go with their own relationship. If there was anywhere to go. He needed to be realistic about this, his own desires notwithstanding. They had both established themselves in their chosen professions in different parts of the country. He couldn't expect Rosamund to walk away from the life she had built and he wouldn't expect that she would ask the same of him. Russell knew that, no matter what, he would have to respect whatever happened. For now, the focus needed to be on doing what it took to keep a hitman from carrying out his assignment. To Russell, the idea of watching another person he had fallen in love with die before her time was unthinkable. Not as long as he was still breathing and determined to prevent that from happening.

Chapter Ten

After Russell left, Rosamund's cell phone rang. She saw that the caller was U.S. Marshal Monroe Cortez. She took the call nervously, as this was their first contact since she entered the federal program. "I gather you've heard that Deputy U.S. Marshal Leah Redfield is dead," he voiced somberly.

"Yes," Rosamund responded, as she stood in the kitchen. She felt saddened that another person in law enforcement she had gotten to know somewhat was a victim of fatal gunfire. "They think she committed suicide."

"That appears to be the case," the marshal acknowledged. "Though, an investigation is still pending."

"Why would Leah take her own life?" Rosamund questioned. "She seemed happy."

"We can't ever truly know what's going on inside a person's head, can we?" he said flatly. "Maybe Deputy Marshal Redfield was battling depression or other demons that she was able to successfully conceal outwardly. Till she couldn't any longer."

Rosamund wondered if the pressure of being her handler had been too much for Leah. But if that were so, wouldn't she have been able to pick up on it during their communication? "Maybe Simon Griswold's hired killer, Arnold Nishimoto, got to Leah?"

Cortez cleared his throat. "There's no indication that Nishimoto has discovered your whereabouts," the marshal insisted. "He's likely unaware that we're onto him and pursuing every lead in bringing him to justice. We think you're still safe for now."

Rosamund wasn't convinced that the assassin hadn't somehow made his way to Weconta Falls against all odds. After all, wasn't that the nature of this beast, eluding capture while successfully going after his own prey? "Will I get a new handler?"

"Yes, that's why I'm calling," he said, "along with reassuring you that the tragic loss of Deputy Marshal Redfield does not mean we'd shirk our responsibilities in protecting an important witness. Assigned to take her place as your handler is Deputy U.S. Marshal Patrick McDermott. I'm sending you his photograph now."

"Okay." Rosamund received the picture, studying her new handler. Patrick McDermott was in his midforties and biracial with curly dark brown hair in a low skin fade cut and deep sable eyes.

"McDermott is a fifteen-year veteran of the U.S. Marshals Service, based in San Francisco," Cortez said. "He has lots of experience in these types of assignments and will be setting up a meeting with you in the morning. Meanwhile, to be on the safe side, we've arranged for the Weconta Falls Police Department to keep an officer outside the townhouse and at your workplace for your protection till then. If need be, we'll relocate you to a different area to ensure your safety till Griswold's trial."

"All right." She welcomed the officer's presence but, truthfully, would have preferred to have Russell on hand, if anyone. But Rosamund wasn't sure he felt the same way, in spite of their seeming to have gotten past the strain that came from her true identity being revealed. As it was, she was prepared to defend herself from a known enemy if need be.

"Any questions?" Cortez asked.

Rosamund had none at the moment that hadn't already been addressed. What queries she did have would be addressed with Harold Paxton. And then she would go from there in an effort to stay one step ahead of danger.

WHEN RUSSELL WALKED into Diane O'Shea's office, the chief of police was clearly expecting him. "Sit down, Lynley," she ordered in a controlled tone of voice. He complied, taking a seat, while she leaned against a corner of her desk. "I understand that you and Choi are looking into the death of Deputy U.S. Marshal Leah Redfield."

"Yeah," he told her. "The medical examiner views it as a probable suicide."

"But you don't?" Diane seemed to pick up on this.

"It looks that way," Russell conceded. "But I have reason to believe that she could have been murdered. At the very least, the timing of Redfield's death is more than a little suspicious, considering she was the handler for a federal witness in a human trafficking case." He wondered if the chief would come clean on her knowledge of this.

Diane arched a brow. "You know about that?"

Russell met her eyes. "Yeah," he admitted. "I know that Tisha González, a waitress at Shailene's Grill, is actually Homeland Security Investigations Special Agent Rosamund Santiago, who's been put in the federal Witness Security Program while awaiting her testimony in the trial of suspected human trafficker Simon Griswold."

"But how?" Diane looked perplexed.

"In the days leading up to her death, Redfield made several phone calls to Tisha," he pointed out. "I recognized the name..." Russell considered whether or not it was a good idea to fess up on his involvement with Rosamund and how this might play with the police chief in moving forward when it came to keeping the witness safe. "Full disclosure," he said, deciding to lay it out. "I've been seeing the waitress whom I knew as Tisha González up until today. She brought me up to speed on her true identity, Rosamund Santiago, HSI special agent, and what was going on with respect to her association with Deputy U.S. Marshal Redfield and laying low in Weconta Falls till it was time to reemerge to testify against the reputed human trafficker." He paused. "Rosamund also told me that you were privy to her presence in our town."

"As the chief of police, of course I was," Diane acknowledged. "I called you in here to brief you after learning about the death of Deputy Marshal Redfield."

Russell frowned. "You might have given me a heads-up on the particulars before now." He realized she wasn't obligated to do so, but he would have liked to know they had a federal witness there to help protect. Never mind the fact that had he known Tisha, the waitress, was an alias for a DHS special agent, it could have changed the trajectory of their relationship. For better or worse.

"That wasn't really my call," the chief said, defending herself. "The U.S. Marshals Service was in charge of the process and didn't necessarily want us stepping on any toes by having too many feet in the game, so to speak. And the witness did not appear to be in imminent danger, as I was told, to necessitate a greater role in protecting her, beyond having a patrol car drive by her place every now and then. Besides, you had your hands full, Lynley, and didn't need any distractions."

Russell couldn't very well push back from that assessment, seeing that she was right. It wouldn't have been the norm to have him involved in protecting a federal witness. Of course, there was still twenty-twenty hindsight considering his relationship—if there was still one— with Rosamund. "I understand," he said respectfully. "So, where do things stand now in keeping Special Agent Santiago out of harm's way?"

Diane scratched the side of her nose. "A new deputy marshal will be sent in to be her handler," she replied. "In the meantime, at the request of the USMS, we've assigned an officer, Kevin Wilkinson, ten-year veteran of the Weconta Falls Police Department, to keep an eye on her."

"With Agent Santiago being targeted by a hitman, I'd like to be an extra pair of eyes in ensuring her safety while she's in our jurisdiction." Russell knew he was asking a lot of the chief, with a staff shortage and obvious conflict of interest, but he wasn't going to sit back and let an assassin have his way in taking out Rosamund.

Diane pursed her lips. "Getting romantically involved

with a federal witness is never a good idea," she cautioned. "Even worse is interfering with a WITSEC underway."

"I know." He furrowed his brow. "But it is what it is. I need to do this," he insisted.

She held his firm gaze. "I strongly advise against butting heads with the USMS, as it seems as though they've got this." The chief sighed. "However, seeing that it was unplanned on your part to connect with Agent Santiago in the way you have, do what you need to while holding the line in representing the department in this assignment. Beyond that, what you do off duty to help keep Agent Santiago safe is up to you. Just be smart about it."

Russell grinned. "Thanks, Chief." She did have his back and, for that, he owed her one.

Diane nodded. "Good luck," she said, leaving it to him to interpret her meaning.

He went to his office, closed the door, and sat at his desk. The first thing Russell found himself doing was getting on his laptop to get a better read on Rosamund Santiago, for who she really was, as opposed to what he had been led to believe. In doing a general search for federal employees, he found her profile. Age thirty-two. Single. Born in El Paso, Texas. Attended the University of Texas at Arlington, where she received a Bachelor's degree in Interdisciplinary Studies and a Master's degree in Criminology and Criminal Justice. She went to work afterward for the Department of Homeland Security's Center for Countering Human Trafficking. Within this context, Rosamund became a Homeland Security Investigations special agent, receiving commendations for her efforts in taking down human traffickers and their networks.

All in all, Russell couldn't help but be impressed by the special agent. Obviously, she was doing something good with her life that she should be proud of. He once felt that way when he was with the Bureau. Till faced with the type of tragedy he wouldn't wish upon his worst enemy, causing him to retreat.

He brought up an article on the human trafficking operation she was involved in that took the life of her partner, Special Agent Johnnie Langford. Rosamund barely survived. Russell winced at the thought of not having the opportunity to meet Tisha, aka Rosamund, were it not for the unlikelihood of a gun jamming. He had to believe they met for a reason. One he couldn't ignore. As though it were fated that they take this journey and find a way to build upon it.

He opened the file that Rosamund sent on Arnold Nishimoto, the creep Griswold hired to finish the job he started. It was pretty much as she had laid out. Nishimoto was a successful killer for hire and authorities had been unable to bring him in, making him all the more a threat to Rosamund and others who wound up in his crosshairs.

Russell reached out to his brother, Scott, for a video chat. Momentarily, he appeared on the screen.

"Hey," Scott said.

"Hey." Russell jutted his chin. "Got a sec?"

"Yeah." His brother flashed him a worried look. "What's up?"

"I need a favor."

"Okay," Scott said. "How can I help?"

"I need whatever the Bureau has on Arnold Nishimoto," Russell told him.

"Hmm...the name does ring a bell." Scott gazed at him. "Who is he?"

"Nishimoto's a hired killer," he informed his brother. "I'll send you a file the USMS put together on him."

"All right," Scott said. "Why your interest in Nishimoto? Is someone there being targeted by him?"

"Yeah, I'm afraid so." Russell creased his brow as he described the situation with Rosamund and her predicament, knowing that he could trust Scott. He didn't leave out the fact that he was sweet on the special agent, even while still coming to grips with her true identity versus the one he first knew her as.

"Wow!" Scott's eyes widened. "Annette and Madison mentioned that you were seeing someone. Figured you'd get around to telling me sooner or later. But this puts your love life in an entirely different light."

"Tell me about it," Russell muttered, while thinking that anything worthwhile was worth fighting for. The way he saw it, Rosamund definitely fit into that category. "Needless to say, before I can see if there's legs to this relationship, I have to make sure Rosamund lives to testify against her partner's killer, Simon Griswold."

"I hear you," Scott said evenly. "I'll see what I can dig up on Nishimoto and see if the Bureau's intel is any different than the USMS file on the killer."

"Thanks, Scott."

"Anytime," he insisted.

After Russell ended the conversation, there was a knock on the door and Gloria Choi came in. "So, what did you find out about the connection between Deputy Marshal Leah Redfield and Tisha González, who's being called a Good Samaritan around here for preventing a child abduction?"

Though Russell wanted to satisfy her curiosity, while eliminating anything that could place Tisha in a bad light with the detective where it concerned Redfield, he knew he wouldn't be able to reveal that Rosamund was in WITSEC. Not just yet. As a delicate situation where any leak to the wrong person in the department could put Rosamund in danger, Russell had to keep this to himself. He considered that someone in the department had leaked her alias to a writer, which in and of itself was a no-no that could have placed Tisha in peril. Not that he believed for one minute that Gloria was a threat to Rosamund in any way. Or unable to play by the rules of witness protection. But with Redfield's death under mysterious circumstances and a chance that Nishimoto may have been responsible and was in town gunning for Rosamund, it wasn't a good idea to put her at further risk by exposing her. If the chief chose to expand those in the know, he would deal with it then. For now, Russell only wanted to manage the situation as best he could.

"Redfield and Tisha were acquaintances," he told the detective with a straight face. "They both liked to jog and did so together sometimes. Tisha was broken up over Redfield's death."

"I see." Gloria regarded him contemplatively. "Does she have any idea why Redfield would kill herself?"

Russell pondered the question, before answering candidly, "Tisha didn't see Redfield as suicidal. I'm not sure I do either."

"Hmm…then you're talking about a faked suicide," she said. "Or the murder of a deputy marshal?"

Knowing what he did, he said bluntly, "I think it's a distinct possibility."

"And one more headache for us to deal with," Gloria moaned. "Along with the feds who, if it turns out to be true, will undoubtedly want to take the lead on this investigation."

"I'm guessing they already have," Russell argued, knowing from his work with the Bureau that any deaths, no matter the circumstances, needed to be investigated from within the federal agency involved for their own satisfaction as to when, how, and why a death occurred.

ROSAMUND SAT ON the sofa with the laptop on her legs as she contacted Harold Paxton for a video chat. She wondered if, with Leah's death, he would want to move her. If so, what would that do to her chances of making things work with Russell? Could they come back from the distrust he may feel now regarding her motivations for becoming intimate with him? Could he not see that her actions in becoming close to him were as real as anything she had ever felt in her life? Or would convincing Russell that she was falling in love with him be an uphill battle? That was further complicated by her agreeing to testify against Simon Griswold, which had brought her to Weconta Falls and Russell in the first place.

When Paxton appeared on screen, he had a dour look on his face. "Hey," he started equably, "I just got off the phone with Monroe Cortez. He briefed me on the tragic death of Leah Redfield. I'm sorry you've had to deal with this, on top of everything else."

"Me too." Rosamund took a soft breath and thought about Russell having come into her life as a result of being put in witness protection. "I'm having a hard time believing that Leah took her own life," she told him frankly. "I fear that something more ominous than that may be at work here."

"I understand how you feel," Paxton indicated. "We're cooperating with the U.S. Marshals Service in doing everything possible to get to the bottom of it. But as things now stand, the sentiments are that this was a suicide caused by job stress and financial woes, as Redfield was apparently heavily in debt. These things were overlooked when she was assigned to be your handler. Cortez has assured me that her replacement, Patrick McDermott, is rock solid and has an exemplary record with the USMS."

Rosamund felt somewhat relieved to hear this, but doubts about Leah's death still lingered. "What's the status on Arnold Nishimoto?"

Paxton rubbed his nose. "Still no sign of him. We have federal agents and marshals searching far and wide. He's likely onto us and may be in disguise, while seeking to elude capture. Hopefully, it won't be long before we get him, one way or the other."

Rosamund wasn't convinced that the hitman would be apprehended anytime soon. She sensed that he was bent on carrying out his assignment, based on previous successes as a hired killer. "Is it possible that Arnold Nishimoto got to Leah, in trying to get to me, making it seem like she committed suicide?"

"We have no indication that Nishimoto is in California," the special agent in charge asserted. "Much less, has discovered you're hidden away in Weconta Falls. Of course, if it's determined that Deputy Marshal Redfield was murdered, then that would change everything. We'd get you out of there in a hurry."

"Only to have Nishimoto follow me elsewhere," Rosamund surmised cynically, "determined to finish the job."

"That's not going to happen." Paxton frowned. "We need you to stay strong. Your testimony is of utmost importance in Simon Griswold's trial, to make sure he pays for the murder of Johnnie Langford, attempting to murder you, along with the human trafficking charges. If you feel unsafe there, I'll make arrangements with the USMS to relocate you elsewhere as soon as possible. Just say the word."

I don't really want to leave here, Rosamund told herself. At least not before the trial, giving her the time to try to make things right between her and Russell. Assuming they still had a future to work toward. She hoped with all her heart that was the case. But first, she had to survive the nightmare of being pursued like an animal by an assassin. "I'll stick it out here till the trial, which should be as safe as the next place," she contended. "A police officer has been posted outside the townhouse. And I believe that other members of the Weconta Falls PD are looking out for me as well." Especially Russell. Rosamund was sure that, in spite of the recent strain on their relationship, he still cared about her.

"Good," Paxton said, cracking a grin. "You'll get through this, Agent Santiago."

Rosamund nodded, wanting to believe it, and then asked, "Any news on the mole within the organization?"

He shook his head. "Nothing I can share at the moment," he said. "I can assure you, though, that we're doing everything we can to expose the individual and hold them accountable."

"All right." She wondered what he might be holding back from her, if anything. The idea that whoever was responsible for setting up Johnnie to be murdered, and nearly costing her own life as well, riled Rosamund. She could only hope the DHS and HSI Dallas Field Office would get to the bottom of it and that there would be justice.

An hour later, Rosamund echoed the same sentiments over the phone to Russell, who called to check on her. "I'm sure they'll discover who the mole is," he said. "The federal law enforcement agencies are usually pretty good at this type of thing when dealing with the ultimate in betrayal."

"You're right," she said, knowing that traitors within the DHS would not be tolerated, with the success of future missions at stake. She was sitting on the sofa, legs curled beneath her, happy to hear his voice, even if the tension between them was still evident.

"I sent my brother the file on Arnold Nishimoto," Russell informed her. "If the Bureau has anything more on him that might help to track Nishimoto down, Scott will let me know."

"Thanks. It's no fun having a hired killer bent on taking you out," Rosamund voiced humorlessly.

"I know. I can only imagine how difficult it must be to have to deal with this. But Nishimoto will fail," Russell insisted.

"I wonder how many of his other victims were told the same thing," she questioned, "before he finished them off?"

"That's a fair point." He sighed. "Now that I know what's going on, I'll do everything in my power to ensure your safety while you're in Weconta Falls. Even beyond. The chief is backing me on this. That includes the presence of Officer Kevin Wilkinson outside your door, over and beyond the arrival of your new handler, and greater coordination with the U.S. Marshals Service. I'll also be available whenever you need me. If Nishimoto is somehow able to learn your location and foolish enough to show his face in town, we'll be ready for him."

"Thank you." Rosamund felt better about the situation, even though she was still concerned that Leah's death may not have been self-inflicted. She considered that the deputy marshal could have been targeted by someone other than Arnold Nishimoto, for whatever reason.

"Just doing my job," Russell suggested. Abruptly, he changed course, admitting, "It's more than a job. Whether you're Tisha González or Rosamund Santiago, I still care about you and want to see where we can go with this. Assuming you feel the same way, now that your cards have been laid out on the table and I know who you are and why you're here."

"I do feel the same way, Russell," she made clear. "I

just think we need to dial things back a bit till we see how this plays out with the trial and what comes after." It pained her to have to say that, especially knowing the way she felt about him, but Rosamund didn't want to set up any false expectations for either of them. Russell deserved to be with someone who could fit into the life he'd made for himself in Weconta Falls. Whether with her or another woman. She just wasn't sure if that could be her with the life she had established elsewhere.

"I agree," he told her without prelude. "You're under enough pressure as it is without my adding to it by making demands on your time or expectations for the future. Let's concentrate on keeping you alive for now. Anything else will work itself out."

"Okay." Rosamund felt relieved that he was so understanding. And at the same time, was willing to keep the door open for a future that she hoped to still have with him. Wherever that might take them. She said good-night, while wondering if she would actually be able to sleep at all, given the twists and turns the day had taken.

ARNOLD NISHIMOTO SAT in a wide barrel chair in a cheap motel room on the edge of town. He was holding an iPad Air and reading an article on the webpage of the *Weconta Falls Journal*. It was written by Freddie Hildebrand, who talked about a Good Samaritan waitress named Tisha González, who singlehandedly took down a would-be child abductor, Paul Skinner. The brazen risk to her own life to save another was admirable to Nishimoto. He hated creeps who went after children and hoped Skinner rotted away in prison. Unfortunately, that act of courage wasn't enough to save Tisha González, otherwise known as Rosamund Santiago, special agent for Homeland Security Investigations. Moreover, she was the fed's star witness in a case against Simon Griswold and, as such, needed to be eliminated.

That was just what Nishimoto planned to do to Rosamund Santiago, put her out to pasture permanently, as he was paid to do. Now that he knew where she worked and lived, the rest would be a mere formality. "Gotcha now, Tisha," he said out loud, and then laughed at the thought.

He skimmed more of the article, then set the iPad on a wooden table and grabbed a can of beer. Drinking a generous amount, Nishimoto thought about the deputy marshal who had served as the special agent's handler. He had managed to track her down and forced her to drive to a construction zone where the crew had gone home for the day. Using Redfield's own gun, he had shot her to death and made it look like a suicide, bolstered by the fentanyl he had given her.

Soon, Nishimoto planned to make quick work in disposing of Rosamund Santiago. Then he could make his exit from Weconta Falls as effortlessly as he had arrived in town. *Enjoy the short time you have left, Tisha González*, Nishimoto told himself, as he finished off the beer.

Chapter Eleven

The next morning, Rosamund was already dressed for her shift at the restaurant later in the day when she welcomed inside the townhouse Deputy U.S. Marshal Patrick McDermott. Before entering, he had to be cleared by Officer Wilkinson, a forty-year-old, thickly built and sandy-haired family man, who Rosamund learned had three kids and two dogs, to enter. Still, McDermott flashed his identification all the same, so she felt comfortable in having him as her new handler. He was tall with a solid build, and he wore a navy suit and cap toe, lace-up black shoes.

"Sorry to have to be here under these circumstances," he remarked lamentably. "Deputy Marshal Redfield was a great member of the team, a friend, and a good person."

"Yes, she was," Rosamund agreed, from what little she knew of her. "I too am sorry for what happened to her." She paused, realizing this was as awkward for him as it was for her. Not only was she outside her comfort zone, having been temporarily relocated from her normal habitat, but just as she was starting to form a rapport with Leah, the handler was gone. Had she really taken

her own life? "Would you like a cup of coffee?" Rosamund asked the deputy marshal.

"Sure, I'd love one," McDermott told her.

"Same here." She smiled at him, wondering if he would
last as her handler. Or would she end up being sent packing again and need a new handler to work with? After
making the two cups of coffee and adding cream and
sugar to McDermott's cup at his request, Rosamund
handed it to him and they sat in the dining room. "So,
how did you end up becoming a U.S. marshal?" she asked
casually.

"To make a long story short," he said, "I started off
being a deputy recruiting officer and worked my way into
a full-time job as a deputy U.S. marshal. I wanted to play
a larger role in the U.S. Marshals Service, be it protecting witnesses, such as yourself, or dealing with prisoners, or tracking down fugitives." He sipped the coffee.
"I've read your file."

"Hope you weren't too bored," she quipped, tasting
the coffee.

"Quite the opposite." He grinned momentarily, then
became serious. "Sorry to hear about your partner, Johnnie Langford. Seems like as HSI special agents, together
you played a big role in breaking up human and sex trafficking rings in Texas."

"We did the best we could," Rosamund said modestly,
while thinking about the very high price Johnnie paid in
trying to do his part in the process. "Honestly, sometimes
it feels like an uphill battle."

"But usually worth it in the end, right?"

"Yes, I suppose." She sipped more coffee pensively.

"I'm sure you're eager to get past being in the Witness Security Program," McDermott stated, "so you can get on with your life?"

Rosamund offered a weak smile in response, knowing there were mixed feelings on that score. She definitely was keen on putting WITSEC behind her, but wasn't nearly as eager to have to leave what she had started with Russell behind. How could she ever return to a life that was void of romance and the person who could be in her corner away from the job? "So, how will this work as my new handler?" she asked, knowing that he wasn't a local and likely wasn't expected to shadow her 24/7, so long as a viable and immediate threat to her safety had not been firmly established as a witness in protection.

"I'll be renting a place nearby," McDermott explained. "You'll have my number and I'll be in regular communication with you. I'll also work closely with the Weconta Falls Police Department should trouble arise, with Police Chief Diane O'Shea entirely cooperative. And Detective Russell Lynley being made available as additional backup, in case he's needed to keep you safe or thwart an attack."

"Sounds good." Rosamund resisted a smile as she thought of Russell going from a detective she was dating to someone offering protection to her from a hitman. In both instances, she felt fortunate to have Russell play a bigger role in her life, on and off the job. Even if it could only be short-lived, once she was no longer in the program.

After McDermott left in a metallic silver Lincoln Corsair Reserve, Rosamund notified the officer on duty that she was headed to work, knowing he would follow and make sure no one else was following. She wondered if Russell would stop by for coffee or lunch. Or had the routine taken a hit, now that he knew waitressing was not her primary occupation but just a stopgap measure till she could reestablish her occupation in law enforcement.

"THE SERIAL NUMBER of the Glock 27 pistol that was used to kill Deputy U.S. Marshal Leah Redfield was confirmed to be Redfield's official firearm as a member of the USMS," Ike Wainright told Russell, after Ike had come from the Weconta Falls PD Crime Lab.

Russell wasn't particularly surprised with this forensic finding, considering where the weapon was found relative to the cause of death. Still, he had to ask, "And what about the slug removed from Redfield's head?"

Ike creased his brow. "Forensics found it to be a match for the shell casing found on the floor of Redfield's vehicle," he said. "The bullet itself was a match for a test fired bullet from the deputy marshal's gun and both bullets came through the same gun's barrel with a left-hand twist and four lands and grooves. In other words, Redfield was killed with her own weapon and, based on the trajectory and proximity, it still appears to have been self-inflicted."

"Maybe," Russell muttered, knowing that appearances could be deceiving. Especially if someone had good reason to deceive them. Such as Arnold Nishimoto, in spite of having no evidence that he was in town and had been able to take out the experienced deputy marshal as a means to more easily be able to go after Rosamund. "We need to check out the surveillance footage in the area where Redfield's car was found. I know that warehouse was under construction, meaning there likely wasn't a security system in place yet. But other cameras may be able to tell us if any other cars came or left around the same time. Or, for that matter, may even show if anyone was in the vehicle with the deputy marshal at the time she supposedly shot herself to death."

"Worth a try," Ike agreed. "Maybe a long shot, but if Redfield didn't kill herself, someone sure wants us to believe that and, thereby, to get away with murder."

Russell nodded. "Let's see what we come up with." He went into his office and found a preliminary toxicology report on Leah Redfield on his desk. As he read it, he saw that the deputy U.S. marshal had a high concentration of fentanyl in her system. The report implied that it may have been contributory to her death. This was troubling to him, as random drug testing administered to federal employees would have likely detected drug use if she had been using fentanyl prior to this, not to mention abusing it. As such, Russell had to wonder if the drug had been given to Redfield against her will, as a prelude to murdering her.

This brought him back to the notion that Redfield could have been targeted. Russell admitted that it would take some getting used to for him to refer to Tisha now as Rosamund, her real name. But he was prepared to do that, if it meant separating the waitress from an HSI special agent whose testimony would help bring down a human trafficking ring. As for their personal relationship, he was also up to allowing that to play out, hopefully for the better.

His cell phone buzzed and Russell removed it from the back pocket of his trousers. The caller was from his brother, Scott. After sitting at his desk, Russell connected with him. "Hey."

"Got some news on Arnold Nishimoto," Scott said.

"Okay." Russell adjusted in the seat with expectation.

"Did some digging around and learned that, apart from his given name, Nishimoto is also known to use two aliases in evading authorities. Aaron Kamekona and Lyle Satoshige. I'm guessing he could be using any of the three right now, including multiple passports and fake IDs to that effect."

"Hmm…" Russell made a mental note of this new development. "Send me those names," he requested. "I'll see if any of them show up with any rental car companies between here and San Francisco, local hotels and motels, and the like."

"You think Nishimoto is in Weconta Falls?"

"Not necessarily," Russell responded. "That would mean he was able to break through the U.S. Marshals Service barriers in safeguarding the new identity and location of witnesses." He drew a breath. "On the other hand, as a paid and ruthless assassin, Nishimoto will likely do whatever it takes to locate his target and complete the mission. As such, we can't afford to minimize the risk he poses to Rosamund's safety."

"I can see you really care for her," Scott told him.

"Yeah, I do," he responded without preamble. More than he had cared for anyone since losing Victoria. He didn't take that lightly, no matter how he and Rosamund got to this point. "Beyond that, I care about law and order and keeping all residents of Weconta Falls, even temporary ones, safe from known enemies and real threats."

"I hear you," his brother said. "Whatever more I can do to help, let me know."

"I will, Scott, and thanks," Russell said sincerely.

"Anytime."

"Later." After ending the call, Russell got back on his feet to head over to Shailene's Grill, where he knew Rosamund was back at work as her waitressing alter ego, Tisha.

"ARE YOU READY to order?" Rosamund asked the thirty-something, bald-headed Asian man, who wore cat-eye glasses.

He gave her a soft grin. "Yes," he said. "I'll go with the green tea and avocado toast."

"Sounds good." She smiled at him. "Coming right up."

"Thanks." He met her eyes briefly, then turned to his cell phone that seemed to have some messages.

Rosamund put in the order and then went to wait on other patrons of Shailene's Grill. She admittedly felt a little weird still operating as Tisha González, now that the truth about who she was had been revealed. At least to Russell. She wondered if he would treat her differently now. Would their romantic involvement survive? Or would this new reality be too much of a hurdle to overcome for both of them? *I'll just have to see where it goes with us*, Rosamund told herself, as she delivered the order of avocado toast and green tea to the gentleman, who seemed grateful, as if she had done something special.

When the bell over the door rang to indicate someone new had entered, Rosamund turned to look, hoping it was Russell. She felt disappointed when she saw that instead it was a group of loud teenagers, recognizing them as the ones who had accosted her at the park. They sat around a table and the female glanced her way, but didn't seem to recognize her. Rosamund watched as Tracy went to take their orders. *I hope they haven't harassed anyone else in the park*, Rosamund thought, unsure just how much Russell had left an impression on them about going down the wrong path. She commended him nevertheless for feeling they were worth trying to reform before it was too late. It was yet another reason why she had fallen for the man and didn't want to lose what they had. She hoped he felt the same way at the end of the day.

When the bell over the door rang a few minutes later, Rosamund's eyes lit up when she saw that, this time, it was Russell. She eagerly headed his way, even as she felt butterflies in her stomach for what could be on his mind.

RUSSELL'S HEART SKIPPED a beat as he laid eyes on Rosamund, still looking great as a waitress, but with what looked to be a new level of confidence with his knowledge of her real occupation that rivaled his days with the FBI. If not more impressive and certainly just as important in the continuous fight against criminality. He took the last remaining table near the window, which wasn't his usual one. He barely noticed the Asian man leaving the restaurant, but did home in on the teens, remembering them from their run-in with Rosamund at Weconta Falls Park. He wondered if she noticed them. How could she not, given they were making noise, looking for attention. When they saw him, the group toned down the sounds, not willing to try his patience. Fortunately, for the most part, they seemed to have limited their misbehavior of late to normal teenage pranks and otherwise harmless activities.

"Hey," Rosamund came up to him, offering a nice smile, as if it was just another day of flirtations between them. He was game in doing his part in maintaining the facade, while believing in his heart that much of what existed between them was real.

"Hey," he told her. "Can we talk?"

"Sure. Give me five minutes to get someone to cover for me."

"All right." He watched her walk away and Russell found himself amazed at just how well Rosamund, as Tisha, had managed to fit in at Shailene's Grill. Though he knew some people who had been successfully placed in WITSEC, he had never been able to put himself in their shoes. Till now. Or at least somewhat in picturing everything Rosamund had given up in entering the program, including the loss of her HSI partner. Could she reenter her real life without missing a beat, while leaving the short-term life established in Weconta Falls behind? Including the bond they had formed?

Russell realized that his own relocation to the town had not been so different. He had turned his back on the life he had before, albeit with more of a choice in the matter, unable to cope fully with losing his wife and daughter.

Could he go back, leaving behind the new relationships he had forged in Weconta Falls with his colleagues and some friends?

"Coffee, black," Rosamund said, interrupting his musings.

"Thanks." He grinned crookedly, as she sat across from him. "Has everything gone all right for you today?" He needed to know.

"Yes, thus far." She studied him. "Did you have reason to believe otherwise?"

Russell tasted the steaming coffee. "We were able to confirm that Leah Redfield was killed with her own weapon," he reported in a low voice. "And the preliminary toxicology report indicates that she had a high level of fentanyl in her body at the time of death."

Rosamund frowned. "Leah couldn't have been a drug addict," she whispered confidently.

"I tend to agree with you there. Yet the fentanyl was in her system, leaving me to believe, when combined with the alleged suicide, the deputy marshal's death may have been staged."

"By whom?" She locked eyes with him. "You think Arnold Nishimoto could be behind Leah's death?"

Russell sipped more coffee. He hated to go down this road, but there was no sugarcoating his concern that the very assassin who had forced her to go into hiding could well have found her. "I learned from the FBI that Nishimoto has two aliases they know of that he uses, leaving me to believe it's at least possible that he has learned of your location and killed your handler in the process of trying to gather more information on your identity and whereabouts."

Rosamund put a trembling hand to her mouth. "Nishimoto here…in Weconta Falls?"

Russell reached out and touched her hand comfortingly. "There's been no positive confirmation of that yet," he stressed. "The odds are still in your favor that Nishimoto is completely in the dark as to your whereabouts and that Leah Redfield could well have taken her own life and been abusing fentanyl surreptitiously. We're checking to see if Nishimoto has accessed anything locally, such as accommodations, under his own name or one of his fake monikers. He may also have changed his appearance. Have you noticed anyone in here asking questions or otherwise acting suspicious?"

"Not really," she said contemplatively, "if I don't count the teenagers over there from the park. But they are who they are and, apparently, proud of it." Rosamund wrinkled her nose.

"I think they learned their lesson," Russell contended, though not in any way seeking to justify their delinquent behavior.

"There was this one guy…" She turned her head to a table that was now empty.

"What about him?" Russell asked curiously.

"Well, there was nothing in particular," she muttered, "except that I hadn't seen him in here before."

"What did he look like?"

She described an Asian male in his thirties and baldheaded, wearing glasses. "I suppose that could have been Arnold Nishimoto," she speculated. "Or just an inno-

cent man who happened in here for green tea and avocado toast."

"Hmm…" Russell sipped his coffee, lost in thought.
Could Nishimoto have been brazen enough to hide in
plain view in order to check out his target in advance of
the kill? "Maybe security video will show him and how
he got here."

Her lashes fluttered. "And if that was Nishimoto?"

"Then he's even more dangerous than ever." Russell
pulled no punches in this regard. "Either way, if it's all the
same to you, I seriously think you should move into my
house for now. There's plenty of room. I can clear it with
your handler and the DHS, but it's more isolated, secure,
and less desirable a place for Nishimoto to go after you."

"Yes, of course, I'll stay with you," Rosamund gave
in meekly. "Better safe than sorry, right?"

"Absolutely," he concurred. "I'll arrange for Officer
Wilkinson to accompany you back to the townhouse to
pick up some things, make sure you aren't being followed,
and bring you to my place." He took out his house key and
handed it to her. "I keep a spare in my car. With any luck,
it'll all turn out to be a false alarm and you can carry on
with your life here for as long as you need to." Which, in
his mind, would be long enough for them to continue to
build a solid rapport that could force them to make some
hard choices when the time was right.

"Okay." Rosamund stood up. "Have to get back to
my day job," she quipped, showing she still had a sense
of humor, even in the midst of danger and uncertainty.

"I better do the same," Russell told her, finishing

off the coffee and rising. He grinned. "Thanks for the chat, Tisha."

She made a face playfully and walked away. He would send someone later to check out the surveillance video from the restaurant, so as not to risk blowing Rosamund's cover, just yet.

Outside, Russell scanned the area, wondering if the suspect might still be lurking around. He saw no one. He glanced across the street at the apartment building, noting people coming and going normally, but no sign of someone fitting the description of the man. *Maybe I'm grasping at straws here*, Russell told himself. Or maybe Tisha's customer truly was Arnold Nishimoto in disguise.

Russell conferred briefly with Officer Kevin Wilkinson. He was seated in his squad car outside the restaurant, but close enough to act if Rosamund gave him the prearranged sign to say she was in trouble. After making sure they were on the same page, Russell headed back to the department, having a whole new reason for returning to his FBI roots as a small-town detective, trying to keep a special lady safe from a deadly hunter.

ARNOLD NISHIMOTO WAS pleased with himself for being right under the dainty little nose of his next target, Homeland Security Investigations Special Agent Rosamund Santiago, as she masqueraded as small-town waitress Tisha González. If only she had a clue that the mildmannered man she was serving green tea and avocado toast was really far more interested in sizing her up for what would be her last full day on earth. She foolishly believed she was safe and sound in Weconta Falls, out of his reach under the protection of the U.S. Marshals Service and local police department. It was this overconfidence and lack of appreciation of his skills and determination that would lead to the special agent's untimely demise.

Only then could he collect on the balance of the substantial payment Simon Griswold was willing to dole out to see Rosamund Santiago dead. Climbing behind the wheel of his latest rental car, a blue Mitsubishi Outlander Sport SE, Nishimoto cracked a devious smile as the perfect plan of action started to take shape in his mind. The special agent would never see it coming before her life ended. By the time her protectors tried to come to her aide, they would be left scratching their collective heads as she paid the ultimate price for getting on the wrong side of the human trafficker Griswold.

As he drove off and past Shailene's Grill, Nishimoto grinned again and muttered satisfyingly, "See you soon, Agent Santiago. Very soon."

Chapter Twelve

When he arrived home, Russell gave Officer Wilkinson the rest of the evening off. Unsure how awkward it might be having Rosamund there in a whole new light, Russell was surprised when he stepped inside and heard music. She was playing a Frank Sinatra album on the turntable. Even more surprising was that Rosamund had made them dinner and seemed perfectly relaxed. "If I'm going to possibly be here for a while, I figured I may as well contribute," she explained. "Starting with some good music and learning my way around the kitchen. I combined some of your leftovers with ingredients I picked up at the supermarket for homemade chicken stew and cranberry bread."

"Great choice in music." He grinned appreciatively. "As for the food, it smells delicious, Rosamund," he said, beginning to feel at ease referring to her by her real name.

"Hopefully, that will be matched by the taste," she teased with a chuckle.

"I'm sure it will be." Frankly, nothing surprised Russell anymore about the special agent who seemed more than capable of doing anything she set her mind to. Minutes later, he had washed up and they were seated at the dining room table, eating. "It's good," he told her, as expected, after tasting the chicken stew.

Rosamund blushed. "I just want to carry my own weight while I'm sharing this space with you."

"Your weight is perfect for your size," Russell couldn't help but say. It was but one of her many qualities that captured his fancy. He smiled. "But I'm sure you already know that."

"I do what I need to for maintaining a proper weight and staying in shape," she said coolly. "Which obviously applies to you as well."

"I try," he said, flattered, and bit off a chunk of cranberry bread.

"Any more news on Arnold Nishimoto?" Rosamund looked worried as she lifted a spoonful of chicken stew to her mouth.

"Nothing yet." Russell wished he could say differently. "No indication that Nishimoto is in Weconta Falls. We're still studying surveillance videos and using face recognition software to try to determine if he's anywhere in the vicinity."

"Good luck with that." She wrinkled her nose. "The man's made a career out of eluding the authorities. No telling what he's got up his sleeve to try to silence me. Including possibly taking out Leah as a warning sign."

Russell didn't disagree with her, as far as the hired killer's capabilities. But he wasn't about to allow Rosamund to believe it was hopeless to stop Nishimoto from ultimately carrying out the hit. "Redfield's death may or may not be a matter of foul play," he stated, using a napkin to wipe the corner of his mouth. "That's yet to be determined, notwithstanding the medical examiner making it a probable suicide. Either way, between the USMS, DHS, and the Weconta Falls PD, myself included, we'll make sure nothing stops you from testifying at Simon Griswold's trial."

"Okay." Rosamund sighed. "I'll just be glad when it's over."

"It will be, soon enough," Russell told her. "I promise." He wondered if being over meant them too. The notion that she would simply walk out of his life for good didn't sit well with him. He lifted a glass of water and took a sip, figuring this might be a good time to address a related issue on his mind in an attempt to get to know more about the real her. "So, I get that you needed a new identity and back story while in WITSEC, but was there at least a grain of truth about your family dynamics?"

"Actually, more than a grain." She shifted in the side chair uncomfortably while meeting his eyes. "My parents really are semiretired in Florida," she said candidly. "They moved to the Keys from Texas a few years ago and seem to be happy. My younger sister, Gabby, is married to an allergist and has two children, Zach and Nina. Only they live in Ohio instead of Nebraska."

"I see." He was glad to know she wasn't too far off about the family she was forced to be apart from. "Any real relation to Cranston, Rhode Island?" he asked curiously.

"My college roommate is from Cranston," Rosamund responded. "I spent spring break there with her once and it was the first place I could think of when asked to choose a new location that I was from. I figured it was unlikely that Griswold or his hired killer would ever make the connection."

Russell smiled. "I think you're right about that."

She smiled back and he remembered that it was one of her qualities that attracted him. And the list went on. He could only hope that what drew them together didn't somehow end up pulling them apart.

ROSAMUND KNEW SHE had a good thing—make that great thing—with Russell Lynley. She didn't want to throw that away, no matter how things turned out with the trial and afterward. Didn't she and Russell owe it to themselves to see if they could get beyond their separate lives and work toward a life that could bring them together? She felt heartened by his offer to put her up while a hired assassin remained at large and possibly aware of her location and new identity. Apart from the fact that Russell had gone over and beyond the call of duty as a Weconta Falls detective, Rosamund sensed that his feelings for her had not changed, in spite of having to adjust to her being someone other than waitress Tisha González. Just as she felt the same for him as before. He was someone who tugged at her heartstrings in ways she had never experienced before.

When they slow danced in his living room to the mellow voice of Tony Bennett, Rosamund gave in to her desire to want to be with Russell, pushing aside any reservations that what they had wasn't real. They ended up in his bedroom, where they comforted each other through the night. Their lovemaking was all-consuming, energetic, and just what she needed to occupy her thoughts, instead of the nagging fears that Arnold Nishimoto had the jump on her and would soon make his presence felt.

IN THE MORNING, Russell quietly slipped from Rosamund's grasp. If it were up to him, he'd stay in bed with her around the clock. She had come to mean that much to him. So much so that he may have let it slip out during sex that he loved her. Or maybe the words were in his head, but no less true. They had time to sort out what that meant and where she stood later. Right now, he needed to stay on top of the law enforcement efforts to keep Rosamund protected from the contract killer.

Russell thought Rosamund looked like a beautiful angel while asleep in his bed. He hoped this could last forever, but would gladly take one day at a time. He got dressed and, in the living room, called Officer Wilkinson to resume his official guard duty of Rosamund. Then Russell called Deputy Marshal Patrick McDermott to update him.

"I'll swing by Shailene's Grill when Rosamund goes to work," McDermott said, "and spell Officer Wilkinson. If anything seems out of sorts, I'll get the cavalry there, pronto."

"Sounds good," Russell told him. "Heard anything on the investigation by the USMS into the death of Leah Redfield?" It had now become a joint operation to look into the suspicious passing of one of their own, with suicide seeming less and less likely, given the red flags that made it questionable in the minds of some, himself included. Particularly the threat that Redfield posed as

Rosamund's handler to an assassin fixated on making sure Rosamund didn't live long enough to testify against Simon Griswold.

"Only that a memorial service will be held for Leah this weekend in her hometown of Citrus Heights, California," the deputy marshal announced. "As for her death, no one who knew her believes she would end it all like that. Not when she had so much to live for."

Russell lowered his chin. "I was thinking the same thing." The trick now was to prove their case, while at the same time confronting whoever might have killed Redfield. And temporarily, at least, left Rosamund vulnerable to attack.

THE SURVEILLANCE FOOTAGE of what appeared to be Leah Redfield's red Buick Encore was taken from a nearby building as the deputy marshal drove toward the spot on Breckton Street where her vehicle was found, close to the estimated time of death. "That definitely looks like Redfield's car," Russell remarked, sitting before the laptop on his desk, with Gloria hovering over his shoulder.

"It does," she agreed. "Home in on the license plate."

He did just that and, as expected, they were able to quickly establish that it was indeed Deputy Marshal Redfield's official vehicle with the USMS. "There appears to be two occupants in the car," Russell noted. He zoomed in on the still image, studying it.

"Redfield's the driver," Gloria ascertained. "The individual in the passenger seat is male. Can you get a better shot of him?"

"Yeah, I think so." Russell brought the image closer.

Though somewhat grainy, it still gave a reasonable picture of a bald man who looked to be in his thirties and could have been Asian.

"Does he look familiar?" Gloria asked.

Russell immediately thought of the person who Rosamund had described from Shailene's Grill. The car occupant fit the description. But he didn't exactly look like the photo of Arnold Nishimoto in the file of the wanted hitman. Had he changed his appearance?

"Maybe," Russell said vaguely. Not willing to tip his hand quite yet. "If this guy murdered Redfield and fled the scene of the crime, he obviously didn't leave in her car. So how did he get away?"

"In another vehicle?" Gloria deduced. "Maybe he forced Redfield to that location, having already determined there were no security cameras in a new construction zone, killed her with her own gun, and made his escape."

It made sense to Russell, considering the circumstances and Redfield found shot to death, with no one else in sight. "Let's see what cars passed in the opposite direction shortly after Redfield's vehicle drove by." He fast-forwarded the video footage till he saw a single car driving by, less than five minutes after Redfield had driven in the opposite direction.

Gloria asked, her voice lifted an octave, "You think that could be him?"

"Let's have a look." Russell rewound to get a closer look at the vehicle and driver. It was a dark blue Mitsubishi Outlander Sport SE. Zooming in on the driver, it was almost certainly the same man who had been in

Redfield's car. "I think we may be on to something," he told her.

"I think you're right," she agreed. "Home in on the vehicle's license plate and we'll see who the car belongs to." After Russell did that, Gloria took down the info and said, "Back in a sec."

After she left the office, Russell pulled up the surveillance video he requested showing the parking lot at Shailene's Grill yesterday. He was able to find footage of a man who fit the description Rosamund gave of the Asian customer, leaving the restaurant in the right time frame. Comparing the image with that of the man seen driving with Deputy Marshal Redfield and the man driving a different vehicle alone, it seemed like a match to Russell. Could this be Arnold Nishimoto, hidden in plain view?

Opening the file on Nishimoto, Russell looked at his photograph and compared it with the others. It appeared to be the same man. But what if he was wrong? He accessed the facial recognition software the Weconta Falls Police Department used, along with the Departments of Justice and Homeland Security, to help identify and track down known and unknown offenders. After supplying information, it came up with an apparent hit to indicate a strong probability that Arnold Nishimoto was the suspect in question and likely had murdered Leah Redfield to get at Rosamund.

Gloria came back into the office and said, an edge to her tone, "Turns out the car is registered to a rental car company in Oakland, California. It was rented to a man named Lyle Satoshige."

"Lyle Satoshige is an alias for reputed hitman Arnold Nishimoto," Russell stated with a sinking feeling in the pit of his stomach.

Gloria hoisted a brow. "Why would this Nishimoto kill the deputy marshal?"

After sucking in a deep breath, Russell looked her in the eye and said, "Because she was standing in the way of his real target, Homeland Security Investigations Special Agent Rosamund Santiago." Russell knew it was time to let the detective in on the situation, sure that Diane O'Shea would agree, given the gravity of where things stood. "You know her as the Good Samaritan waitress, Tisha González."

As Gloria's mouth dropped open in stunned silence, Russell filled her in on the need-to-know basis details of Rosamund's protection under the U.S. Witness Security Program and planned testimony against Simon Griswold. Afterward, Russell turned his attention and sense of urgency to determining Nishimoto's base of operations, sensing that every second counted in preventing him from carrying out his mission.

AS USUAL FOR ROSAMUND, there was a steady stream of hungry and thirsty customers in the morning rush at Shailene's Grill. Even Shailene McEnany herself, the co-owner, was in on the action, filling in where she was needed. In this case, it was as a waitress, substituting for Tracy, who had to take one of her children to see the doctor for an ear infection. "Hope you don't abandon me too, Tisha," Shailene whined, half seriously, as they crossed paths with dueling plates of steaming stacks of buttermilk pancakes.

Rosamund had to remember her moniker, seeing that she had gone back to her real name partly, now that Russell was privy to it and slipped up himself a time or two. She wondered how long it would be before she was able to return to who she was full-time. Or was that even possible at this point? Especially when her heart belonged in Weconta Falls, so long as Russell remained there. "Wouldn't dream of it," she told Shailene with a straight face, knowing full well it was a promise she couldn't keep. But she still needed to play the part and stick with it for as long as was needed in the scheme of things.

"Good to hear." Shailene looked relieved. "Now why don't we deliver these hotcakes before they're no longer hot."

"Right." Rosamund chuckled. She took the order to the table and was about to go to another, when her cell phone chimed. She slipped it out of the front pocket of her uniform and saw a text message from Deputy Marshal Patrick McDermott that chilled her:

Detective Lynley has informed me that Arnold Nishimoto is the man you saw yesterday at restaurant. Could even be inside right now. Stay alert, but don't tip your hand. I'm on my way in.

Nishimoto found me? Rosamund thought in near panic, after wanting to believe she had safely evaded the hired killer by moving to Weconta Falls. She couldn't understand how this could have happened. She wondered if the mole within the DHS or HSI was responsible for passing along her whereabouts to Arnold Nishimoto.

Rosamund gulped as her eyes darted around furtively in search of the hitman, who had shaved his head to disguise his appearance and deadly intentions. She did not see him at first glance or even second, which concerned as much as relieved her. Had she missed him? Was he in disguise? Was it his plan to try to kill her in a crowded restaurant? She doubted that a skilled assassin would put himself in such a position to be identified and possibly tripped up before making an escape. No, he was biding his time. Waiting for the right moment to finish her off. But when exactly was that?

As she assessed the situation and imminent danger, Rosamund's first instincts were to reach for the Sig Sauer pistol she had taken recently to keeping in her ankle holster, while hoping to never have to use it. Especially in a packed restaurant. But she needed to keep a cool head and not make any sudden moves that could give Nishimoto the upper hand. Assuming he didn't already have it.

"Get a move on, Tisha!" Shailene yelled at her. "The food won't serve itself!"

"All right." Rosamund did as she was told, preferring the stress and strain of waitressing to dodging a tenacious hitman. She went about her job for now, while waiting for Deputy Marshal McDermott's instructions on how to proceed.

Chapter Thirteen

Russell was wearing a ballistic vest and holding his firearm, as he and other armed members of the Weconta Falls PD converged upon the Weconta Falls Motel, Room 157, on Yerdlyn Road, on the outskirts of town. It was where Arnold Nishimoto was believed to be staying, using the name Lyle Satoshige. The U.S. Marshals Service and Department of Homeland Security were notified of what Russell believed was a strong indication that the assassin they were looking for was in Weconta Falls.

In spite of no sign of Nishimoto's rented Mitsubishi Outlander, they weren't taking any chances that he could still be inside the room. Short of that, they needed to know if he left any clues of what he was up to. Russell gave the nod and the door to the room was unlocked with a key supplied by the manager of the motel. Storming inside, they found it was unoccupied, with the bed unmade and a half-eaten pizza left on a wooden table, along with an empty can of beer. With no clothes or luggage present, it was clear the hitman had no plans of returning. This was troubling to Russell, telling him that Nishimoto was very likely in the process of executing his plans to go after Rosamund.

"He left something," Ike said, having been apprised of the situation by the chief and Russell.

"What do you have there?" Russell asked, noting that Ike had pulled something out of the wastebasket.

"Looks like a diagram of an apartment building," he replied.

Russell put his gun away and looked at it. He recognized it as the five-story building directly across the street from Shailene's Grill. Why would that be of interest to Nishimoto? Then it hit Russell. The hitman intended to use it as a staging area to launch a deadly attack on Rosamund. *I have to warn her*, Russell told himself, his heart racing at the thought of Nishimoto gunning her down.

"It's an apartment building on Liverwood Street," Russell told Ike. "Shailene's Grill, where Rosamund is working as a waitress, is on the other side of the street. Nishimoto is planning to assassinate her there."

Ike frowned. "I'll get all available units to the area and we'll stop him from succeeding in his plan."

Russell nodded and said, "I'm heading over there." He then instructed Ike to update the DHS and USMS on the situation, before Russell raced to his car. Inside, he phoned McDermott, counting on him to protect Rosamund, as was his job. Though she was armed, Russell knew she was at a disadvantage in her current role, with her would-be killer having no such restraints.

In the end, Russell believed it was up to him to stop Nishimoto from succeeding with the hit, while hoping it wasn't already too late.

Arnold Nishimoto scaled the stairs to the roof of the apartment building. He walked onto the roof and made his way to the front of the building and crouched low to avoid detection. He gazed across the street at Shailene's Grill. The place itself had floor-to-ceiling windows that were perfect for what he had planned for the fed's witness against Simon Griswold.

Nishimoto stepped away from the ledge and unzipped his fabric rifle case. He removed the parts of a Nosler M21 rifle and began to assemble it. Once done, he took a haphazard 360-degree peek through the scope, before moving back to the ledge. Positioning himself, he took aim at the windows of the restaurant, knowing that at any moment Rosamund Santiago would be serving a customer sitting by the window. It was then that Nishimoto would finish her off and report to his client, Simon Griswold, that the work was done and it was time to be paid in full.

Show your pretty face, Rosamund, and this will be over, the hitman mused, feeling antsy for some reason, as though there was reason to be concerned that his target might somehow slip away from him.

"Change of plans," McDermott told Rosamund, as he ushered her to a corner, away from others. "We have reason to believe that Nishimoto is somewhere in the apartment building across the street, likely armed with a high-powered rifle, with plans to open fire at any time."

Feeling the heat of the moment, she assessed this frightening news and gazed at the deputy marshal. "Can you stop him?" She hated to think that Nishimoto could somehow escape and be free to go after other targets in the future.

"We're certainly going to try." McDermott spoke in earnest. "But in the meantime, we need to protect you. Is there a back exit?"

"Yes, but I can't just leave like that," Rosamund protested. "We're super busy and already short staffed as it is."

His brow furrowed. "I understand your concern here, but that's not really your problem," he argued. "It's staying alive till you're called upon to testify in a major human trafficking case. My job is to make sure you survive an attempt to keep you from testifying. We need to get you out of here, Special Agent Santiago." His voice dropped an octave. "I'm afraid this isn't up for debate."

Rosamund knew he was right and she had to comply. As much as she felt loyal to Shailene and had bonded with Tracy, her first and foremost obligation was to herself and the DHS's Center for Countering Human Trafficking. She owed it to the memory of her late partner, Johnnie Langford, not to lose sight of why she was waitressing at the restaurant, instead of doing her real job fighting human smuggling, sexual exploitation of women and children, and the like. Beyond that, she wanted to get past this and see where things might go between her and Russell. None of that would matter if the hit Simon Griswold put out on her was allowed to succeed.

"Okay," she told the deputy marshal. "But I need to tell Shailene I'm leaving. I owe her that much."

"All right." McDermott nodded. "Make it quick. The

longer this goes on in making yourself a target, the more dangerous Nishimoto will be. For you, as well as others."

Rosamund received the message, loud and clear. She quickly tracked down her temporary boss, who frowned at her, as though sensing something was up.

"What's going on?" Shailene asked.

"I have to leave," Rosamund responded straightforwardly. "I know the timing is terrible, but I'm in trouble."

"What kind of trouble?" she pressed.

After a moment or two, Rosamund looked her in the eye and said, thoughtful, "I'm a federal government witness in a human trafficking case. I'll explain more later. Right now, someone is trying to kill me." She looked toward Patrick McDermott. "That's a deputy U.S. marshal, here to keep me safe—and everyone in this restaurant. So, I need to go now, through the back door."

Shailene nodded understandingly. "Do what you need to do, Tisha." She paused, as if realizing that was not her real name. "Wouldn't want anything bad to happen to you. We'll hold the fort, somehow."

"Thanks, Shailene." Rosamund gave her a tiny, grateful smile and a quick hug, before hustling along with McDermott toward the back exit. In the process, she could only wonder if this was a move that Nishimoto had anticipated, possibly leaving them as lambs to be slaughtered by the hired killer.

Rosamund followed McDermott out the back door. He had removed from a shoulder holster his Glock 27 pistol. Following suit, in needing to feel useful in her own self-defense, she grabbed the Sig Sauer pistol from her ankle holster, while knowing that her cover life had been compromised. Staying low, while fearing she could be a sitting duck for Nishimoto, Rosamund peeled her eyes in every direction, wanting to at least give herself a fighting chance at surviving, should McDermott be taken out.

"No sign of him back here," the deputy marshal remarked.

"Not yet," she warned, realizing the merciless hitman could still have more than one trick up his sleeve.

"Stay down and close to the building," McDermott ordered. "I'm parked right around the corner and out of view of the apartment building."

"I hear you." Rosamund kept her voice to barely more than a whisper, for fear that Nishimoto may have planted listening devices in order to trap her. Or stay one step ahead of them.

Following closely behind McDermott, she made her way behind the back of the restaurant and other small businesses, before they came upon McDermott's Lincoln Corsair Reserve. "Get in," he said brusquely.

She quickly climbed into the passenger seat, after which McDermott closed the door, and raced to the driver's side, getting in and starting the car. "Let's get you out of here, before Nishimoto figures out that you're nowhere to be found at the restaurant and comes after you at Lynley's place."

"Okay." As they sped off on a side street, Rosamund felt relieved that she had stalled, at least temporarily, Griswold's hired assassin from carrying out the hit. But would that put Nishimoto off, angering him? Just as unsettling for her was the thought that he could accidentally or intentionally kill someone else in his quest and coldheartedness. And where was Russell in all of this? Was he prepared to go toe to toe with a bona fide killer? Or would Russell allow those responsible for her safety to do the heavy lifting in going after Nishimoto?

All she could do was wait.

RUSSELL SPOTTED THE dark blue Mitsubishi Outlander Sport SE that Arnold Nishimoto was renting, using the alias Lyle Satoshige, parked on the street in front of the Liverwood Apartments. No one was inside. Russell only had to take one look to see that someone was on the roof of the apartment building across from Shailene's Grill. He saw just enough of the high-powered rifle to know that it was the hitman. Nishimoto's intention was to murder Rosamund through the window of the restaurant. No doubt the gunman had an escape route mapped out.

Sighing, Russell took solace in the knowledge that Rosamund had already vacated the restaurant under the protection of Deputy Marshal McDermott and been whisked off to the relatively safe location of Russell's own residence, awaiting word on how this went. Though he didn't believe that Nishimoto planned to kill patrons randomly, he didn't doubt that the hitman wouldn't hesitate to do so in going after Rosamund, viewing them as collateral damage.

Well, I won't let you harm a soul, least of all, Rosamund, Russell thought, while scaling the staircase to the roof of the apartment building. He knew that other law enforcement was en route and an effort was underway to quietly evacuate people from the area to be on the safe side. But he wasn't about to give Nishimoto an opportunity to escape the net and have Rosamund continuing to look over her shoulder, wondering when he would strike on behalf of his client.

Before opening the door that would take him to the rooftop, Russell removed his Glock 26 9-millimeter pistol from the belt holster, knowing it was loaded and ready to use. But he also knew he was dealing with a very dangerous man who had killed many people for hire, and quite possibly would prefer to go down swinging. If he went down at all.

I can't allow myself to worry about that, Russell told himself, willing to risk a gun battle that wouldn't necessarily go his way. This has to end now, if things between him and Rosamund were to have any real chance to prosper. He sucked in a deep breath and twisted the doorknob quietly. There was squeaking as the door opened and he stepped into the afternoon sunlight. To his left was an open and empty rifle case. To the right was the hired gun, dressed in black, down on one knee, and staring through the scope of a rifle that was perched on the ledge and aimed at Shailene's Grill below.

Russell took a few steps toward the perp, who surprisingly failed to hear him coming, so focused was he on nailing his prey. When close enough to serve his own purposes, Russell inhaled and stated in a deep voice, "Police! Arnold Nishimoto, drop the weapon. Now!"

Nishimoto, who was clearly startled, was defiant and wordless as he swung the rifle around to point it at Russell. But Russell never gave the hitman a chance to get off the first shot. He fired once, hitting Nishimoto squarely in the chin, and again, this one going into his left shoulder. Even as he went down like a sack of potatoes, the rifle flying from his outstretched hands, Nishimoto still appeared to reach for a handgun inside the waist of his pants. Russell recognized the weapon as a 38 S&W Special +P revolver. He kicked it away and placed the perp in handcuffs as Nishimoto fought to remain conscious.

When other law enforcement and paramedics arrived, Russell stepped aside and let them take over. Though he knew he would be put on administrative leave, pending a routine investigation into the shooting, Russell expected it to be fully justified in bringing down an armed and dangerous hired killer, while saving Rosamund's life as a result.

WHILE MCDERMOTT STOOD watch outside, Rosamund sat at the dining room table with her laptop and contacted Harold Paxton for a video chat. She needed to know what he thought about Simon Griswold's hitman, Arnold Nishimoto, having found her and what came next. When the special agent in charge's face appeared, he looked distressed, which wasn't surprising to Rosamund. "I suppose you've heard the latest news," she said.

"I know Nishimoto's been spotted in Weconta Falls," Paxton acknowledged grimly. "How the hell he managed to locate you is beyond me. The U.S. Marshals Service was supposed to be on top of providing you with a secure location till the trial."

Rosamund didn't disagree. "I'm sure they've done their best," she defended the USMS. "These things tend to happen sometimes."

"Shouldn't have happened this time, though," he barked.

"Maybe the mole within the organization is responsible for Nishimoto showing up," Rosamund suggested, knowing they had yet to identify the person and hold them accountable.

"That's highly unlikely," Paxton insisted. "Whoever has been leaking information would not have access to the USMS and WITSEC. If there is an inside job here, it would have to come from someone working within the U.S. Marshals Service. But that too is a stretch. My guess is that Arnold Nishimoto, an experienced hitman, likely used his skills to follow every lead and was somehow able to put two and two together in order to discover your whereabouts, in spite of the precautions taken to the contrary."

"So, what do we do about it?" Her tone was apprehensive. "How do we play this?"

"Right now, we do nothing to shake the apple cart, if you will," Paxton said with a direct look. "As I've been told, it appears that the locals have Nishimoto within their sights, with the feds closing in fast. My guess is that the threat he poses will soon be eradicated. If so, your status should remain the same and there will be no need to act."

Rosamund arched a brow. "And what if Nishimoto should remain on the loose and after me?" she asked, feeling ill at ease, knowing she couldn't remain there and feel comfortable about it.

"Then we'll reassess," the special agent in charge told her calmly. "Just know that your safety is our top priority within the DHS, Agent Santiago. We'll do whatever we need to do to stop Simon Griswold from silencing you before his trial begins. Let this play out and you'll get through it."

"All right." After they disconnected, in spite of his reassurances, Rosamund found herself still on pins and needles as she waited at Russell's house for word of what had happened after her pursuer attempted to kill her at Shailene's Grill. Had Arnold Nishimoto gotten away, prepared to wait for another day to track her down and complete his? Now that he had discovered her location and uncovered her identity, would she need to be renamed and moved to another safe space? If so, what would happen with her and Russell? She couldn't really expect him to follow her across the country, when he was content with his current life in Weconta Falls. Could she? Beyond that, if she was still to be a marked woman, would it be fair to him to be caught up in it? The one thing she would never want to see was Russell harmed and then have to live with it herself.

When he came through the door with Patrick McDermott, Russell looked exhausted, but otherwise unharmed. "Hey," he said to her, as she stood in the living room.

Rosamund responded in kind, "Hey." She tried to read his face but couldn't. "Tell me what happened with Nishimoto."

Russell ran a hand across his mouth, glanced at McDermott and then back to her, before announcing candidly, "The threat has been neutralized. Arnold Nishimoto is dead."

McDermott looked at Rosamund. "We were able to turn the tables on the hired killer," he said matter-of-factly.

"Yeah." Russell nodded. He faced Rosamund and said,

"Nishimoto perched himself atop the apartment building across the street from Shailene's Grill. There, he intended to shoot you through the window when the opportunity presented itself. Which, of course, never materialized."

"Thank goodness, he didn't succeed," Rosamund stated deeply. She would never have forgiven herself had the hitman killed innocent people in the restaurant because of her.

Russell twisted his lips. "We believe that Nishimoto murdered Leah Redfield and tried to make it appear to be suicide."

Rosamund flinched at the thought, glancing at McDermott and back. "All to get to me?" she asked guiltily.

"None of this falls on you," Russell told her. "Like all of us in law enforcement, Redfield assumed the risks of being assigned as your handler. Undoubtedly, Nishimoto got the jump on her, but chances are the DNA taken from Redfield's car will likely match Nishimoto's DNA as circumstantial evidence, to go with surveillance video, to link him to the crime."

"In the process, Leah didn't come away empty-handed per se, in what I believe was her intention at the end to somehow assist us in nailing her killer," McDermott said.

"Griswold's secret weapon in trying to squelch your testimony against him has failed," Russell told her. "You're safe now."

Rosamund fluttered her lashes, grateful to hear this and happy that, even in the midst of a no-win situation, Leah had managed to find a way through getting the assassin to leave behind DNA evidence to push back against Nishimoto's strategy. Still, Rosamund remained uneasy.

Would Griswold simply throw in the towel? Or try again to silence her? "Am I really safe?" she had to ask.

Russell met her gaze. "Yes, if I have anything to do with it," he assured her. "I won't let Griswold get to you. If he gets another hired gun, we'll deal with it and Griswold will fail again." He eyed McDermott. "We're all on the same team here, with the same objective—to keep you alive and well for your important role in taking down a human trafficking operation."

"Absolutely." The deputy marshal nodded in agreement. He grinned at her. "I'll leave you two alone and confer with my superiors on what the next move should be."

Rosamund smiled thinly. "Thanks for being there, Patrick," she said to him, as he had insisted that she refer to him by his first name.

"Just doing my job," he told her simply, and left.

Once they were alone, Russell held Rosamund's shoulders and reiterated, "It's going to be okay."

"I want to believe that," she uttered, looking into his eyes, while feeling his warmth.

"You should," he asserted and waited a beat. "Why don't I pour us some wine?"

"Okay." After they moved to the living room, Rosamund took a sip of wine and said, "Nishimoto must have been tipped off by someone on the inside about my whereabouts. Much like Simon Griswold knew about the undercover operation into his human trafficking organization, resulting in Johnnie's death. How else would Nishimoto have tracked me down?"

"You may be right," Russell agreed. "If so, between

the DHS, HSI, and USMS, they'll have to figure it out, hopefully before Griswold goes to trial. But it's also possible that as a cutthroat and highly experienced assassin, Arnold Nishimoto was able to use all his skills and resources to discover your whereabouts all on his own. Either way, we stopped him from carrying out the hit."

"But will Griswold hire someone else to take Nishimoto's place?" She narrowed her eyes with speculation.

Russell came closer. "If so, we'll be ready to react to whatever comes our way," he said flatly.

"Oh, really?" Rosamund considered this. "You have your own life to live, Russell. Not to mention your duties with the Weconta Falls PD. I can't expect you to always be at my beck and call."

"Maybe I want to be," he countered boldly. "You mean enough to me to want to fight the good fight by your side. And as for my work as a police detective, I'm currently on administrative leave, pending the investigation into Nishimoto's death. While I'm confident of being cleared of any wrongdoing, it means I have some extra time on my hands to get to know the real you better, Rosamund Santiago. If that's all right with you?"

Rosamund could hardly say otherwise, wanting that as much as he did. "Yes, it's more than all right," she told him, forgetting about any hesitations on moving full steam ahead with their relationship. "I'd like that."

Russell smiled. "I was hoping you'd feel that way." He sealed the deal with a kiss that she happily joined in on.

Chapter Fourteen

"I think we both know this isn't where I belong," Russell told the police chief, as they sat in her office. It was exactly a month since the day he took out hired killer Arnold Nishimoto and two weeks since Russell was cleared of any wrongdoing. But it served as a wake-up call that his skills could be put to better use elsewhere. Not to mention, he needed to be closer to his long-distance girlfriend Rosamund Santiago, who was back in Dallas preparing for her testimony in the murder and human trafficking trial of Simon Griswold. Though she was supposed to be safeguarded by the DHS and HSI, Russell was still concerned that someone within those agencies may try to harm her. He believed the only way he would feel secure in her safety right now was if he was there by her side till this ordeal was over.

Diane O'Shea ran a hand through her hair. "I'd be lying if I said I expected you to stick around forever, Lynley," she admitted from the other side of her desk. "You obviously have too much going for you to want to remain a small-town detective, even at the senior level."

"Glad you understand." He had thought she might put

up more of a fight to hang on to him. But it was better this way.

"I suppose you're headed back to the Bureau?"

"Probably." Though he hadn't made any definitive plans, it made the most sense to Russell. There still had to be an opening in the right place and, of course, a willingness on the part of the Bureau to take him back after his abrupt departure less than a year ago.

"Well, good luck to you," she voiced sincerely. "We'll miss you around here, but do what's best for you."

I intend to, Russell thought. "Thank you," he said. "I appreciate that you understand my situation."

Diane smiled. "But just so you know, if you ever get tired of big city crime and headaches, there will always be a place for you here."

He grinned. "I'll remember that."

Russell took a little time to say goodbye to his fellow detectives. "I'll miss you guys," he told Gloria and Ike, in particular, and meant it. They had become his family away from home.

"Yeah, right." Gloria rolled her eyes good-humoredly. "The moment you walk out that door, it'll be as though we never existed."

Ike was more envious when he said, "Maybe my time will come to pull up stakes and try something else."

"You never know," Russell told him. He smiled at Gloria. "I'll keep in touch, so I'll be sure to never forget you."

She smiled back. "Counting on that."

Once he was in his office, Russell packed his things and then opened his laptop for a video chat with Annette, the first of his siblings to hear the news of his official departure from the local PD.

Her eyes lit up. "You're just full of surprises," she teased him. "First your waitress girlfriend turns out to be a hotshot DHS special agent. Now you're looking for work again. What gives?"

He chuckled. "Well, what's life without a few twists and turns to keep things interesting?"

"Good point." She laughed. "So, when do I finally get to meet Rosamund face-to-face?"

Russell had already introduced her to all of his siblings and even a close cousin, Gavin Lynley, a special agent for the Mississippi Department of Corrections, Corrections Investigation Division, through a Zoom chat. In turn, he had gotten to meet by video Rosamund's parents, Julio and Theresa Santiago, and sister, Gabby. He looked forward to them all getting together in person one day. "Sometime after she testifies in the human trafficking case next week," he promised.

"Wonderful," Annette exclaimed. "Can't wait."

"Same here," he told her. After they disconnected, Russell checked in with Madison for a few minutes, got the scoop on her latest case and personal life; then called Scott, filling him in on the latest details of his life, before saying, "I think I want back in with the Bureau. Know anyone who can put in a good word or two for me?"

Scott laughed. "I think I may know someone who has a little pull in that regard."

"Good." Russell thought about syncing his work and private life with Rosamund, excited to be around her much more often.

"Welcome back to the Bureau," his brother voiced, perhaps prematurely. Russell liked hearing it all the same.

"I'll believe it when I see it," he half joked, fairly confident his former employer knew what he brought to the FBI's table. But for now, his only thought was to be in Dallas with Rosamund when she needed him most.

"You've got this, Rosamund," Special Agent Virginia Flannery, her new partner, said confidently.

"Oh, you think so, do you?" Rosamund said playfully. They were standing inside the Earle Cabell Federal Building on Commerce Street in Downtown Dallas, where she was to prep once more for the trial in a few days. With the threat to her safety diminished somewhat with the death of Arnold Nishimoto and Griswold's reach to access funds cut off, Rosamund had returned home, resuming her real identity. Deputy U.S. Marshal Holly Kendall shadowed her every move. The thirty-eight-year-old African American single mother was tall and slender, with dark brown eyes and long hair in wavy brunette dreadlocks. Virginia was there to back up Holly, if need be.

Though Rosamund was happy to be back in her element as an HSI special agent, she missed not seeing Russell every day, in spite of their daily video chats when not with each other. They had agreed to try a long-distance romance, while striving to close the gap, one way or the other, in furthering their relationship. For her part, Rosamund remained open to being anywhere that could allow them to grow, while maintaining their careers. She knew that Russell's roots and siblings in law enforcement would keep him in the business, wherever his career took him; whereas her own dedication to stopping the scourge of human trafficking was important to her. Maybe she would be able to transfer to the Homeland Security Investigations San Francisco Field Office. Rosamund was determined to keep all options on the table, in the name of love and the chance at lasting happiness.

"I have confidence that you'll do just fine on the witness stand in nailing Simon Griswold," Virginia asserted. "Shouldn't take much to convince the assistant U.S. attorney for the Northern District of Texas, Laura Gibson-Norcross, of that."

"Hmm..." Rosamund smiled at her. "We shall see."

"I'll be out here when you're through," Holly said, after they had taken the elevator up to the third floor to the assistant U.S. attorney's office.

"Me too," Virginia added. "Unless I need to step away for a bit, with other duties still expected of me."

"Not a problem," Rosamund said, sure that Holly was more than up to the job, along with being able to defend herself, when push came to shove. Besides that, she knew Russell was flying in tomorrow, wanting to be there to offer his full support for the trial, and even serve as her bodyguard till then, if necessary.

When she stepped inside the office, Assistant U.S. Attorney Laura Gibson-Norcross greeted her, along with Harold Paxton. "Nice to see you again, Agent Santiago," she said with a pleasant smile, sticking out her hand.

"You too," Rosamund told her, smiling back as she took in the attractive fortysomething attorney, with short, fine blond hair in a piecey style and close-set green eyes.

She was wearing a tailored periwinkle skirt suit and black pumps. Rosamund shook her hand.

"Special Agent Santiago," Paxton said, and put forth a large hand, which she shook too.

"Agent Paxton," she said, never feeling comfortable calling him Harold, as he had given her permission to do.

"Why don't we all have a seat," Laura said, extending her thin arm toward a set of upholstered task chairs around a cherry conference table near a wall with windows. Once they were seated, she clasped her hands and spoke candidly, "I think we can all agree that human trafficking and its components, human smuggling, sexual exploitation, and slavery, have no place in our state. It's imperative that we use everything at our disposal to stop this from happening." She eyed Rosamund. "Your testimony against Simon Griswold is key to putting a serious dent in this criminality in and around Dallas, while sending a clear message to other human traffickers that this won't be tolerated here and offenders will be prosecuted to the fullest extent of the law."

Rosamund nodded solemnly. "I'm happy to do my part in the fight against human trafficking in Texas," she stressed.

"You've gone well beyond the call of duty, Agent Santiago," Paxton told her. "After the ordeal you've been put through, including the tragic death of our fallen agent Johnnie Langford, and surviving not one, but two assassination attempts, I'd say you've earned your stripes within Homeland Security Investigations, and then some."

"Thank you, Sir," Rosamund said. She quickly got over the praise, though, knowing that any HSI or DHS special agents would do the same thing while performing their duties, and told the special agent in charge as much. She added humbly, "The important thing, as Assistant U.S. Attorney Gibson-Norcross indicated, is that we have to go after the human traffickers with everything we've got, so women, children, and even men can stop being illegally brought across the border or coerced into forced labor, commercial sexual exploitation, and other forms of involuntary actions."

Laura nodded appreciatively. "Well said, Agent Santiago. You're definitely a real asset to DHS and its Center for Countering Human Trafficking." She smiled, glancing briefly at Paxton, before saying, "Now, let's go over your testimony in the trial of Simon Griswold."

Rosamund didn't hold back in responding in detail to everything she knew about Griswold's human trafficking organization, including recruitment methods, pressure tactics, relocating, drugging, and sexually exploiting those impacted, and even committing murder as part of keeping members and trafficking victims in line. When it was over, both Laura and Paxton agreed that she was ready to testify against Griswold and that testimony, combined with hard evidence against the trafficker, would all but certainly lead to a conviction and the dismantling of his network.

On the way back to Rosamund's house, Holly Kendall asked her, "So, how did it go in there?"

"As well as could be expected," she responded, looking at the deputy marshal, who was behind the wheel of a blue Subaru Outback Wilderness. Driving behind them was Virginia in her white Ford Escape Hybrid. "I'm all set for the trial," Rosamund declared.

Holly grinned. "Well, good for you."

"Once this is over, I hope we can still hang out together sometime." Like Leah Redfield and Patrick McDermott before her, Rosamund liked having Holly around.

"Of course," Holly responded enthusiastically. "I'd like that too."

"Cool." Rosamund smiled, and imagined that, along with Virginia, the three could have some girls' nights out. Of course, she was more interested in spending as much time with Russell as their schedules allowed. Neither of them had spoken about tying the knot. For her part, Rosamund knew she loved him and wanted that. She suspected Russell felt the same, but both wanted to wait till after the trial to decide where they wanted to live before making any other plans.

They arrived at Rosamund's two-bedroom, split-level loft condominium on Mockingbird Lane, where Rosamund had lived for more than a year before the relocation to witness protection. It was in a recently renovated warehouse and had a fitness center and twenty-four-hour security patrol. The loft had vaulted ceilings, vinyl plank flooring, a gourmet kitchen with an open concept, and floor-to-ceiling fiberglass windows that offered amazing views of the city, with the loft's proximity to Uptown Dallas. She had filled it with bamboo furnishings and felt the loft was a good fit for a single woman. But with Russell now in her life, Rosamund wondered if it would suffice for them as a couple, should they decide to live together in the city.

That thought was put on hold as she enjoyed a glass of white wine with Holly and Virginia, while standing around the quartz countertop island in the kitchen. They talked about their lives, ups and downs, and future prospects. When Virginia's cell phone rang, she answered, listened, and then said grimly, "I'm on my way."

"What is it?" Rosamund asked uneasily.

"A search warrant has been issued for the home of a person suspected of possessing child pornography." Virginia furrowed her brow. "They want me in on it, so I have to go." She paused. "Hate to leave you high and dry, Rosamund."

"I'll be fine," she responded. "Holly is still here, and I wouldn't be surprised if more marshals showed up between now and the trial date. So go."

Holly eyed Virginia and echoed the sentiments. "I have a job to do and won't let anything happen to Rosamund to prevent her from testifying."

"I get it." Virginia made a face. "It's just like you two to gang up on me."

Rosamund chuckled. "I'll see you when I see you," she said, as she ushered her to the door.

No sooner had she settled down on the bamboo sectional with Holly, when the doorbell rang. Rosamund wondered if it was Russell, who wasn't supposed to arrive till the next day. She'd also given him a key. Maybe Virginia was back already, no longer needed for the mission.

"I'll go check it out," Holly said guardedly. "Stay here."

Rosamund remained seated and watched as the deputy marshal looked through the peephole before recognizing the visitor. "It's your boss," she said, and opened the door.

Harold Paxton came inside, looking flustered. "There's been a breach in security," he told them, and gazed at Rosamund. "We need to get you to a safe house till we can make sure this has been resolved satisfactorily."

"Okay." Rosamund stood up, feeling this must be serious, as it was the first time she had been visited in person by the special agent in charge of the HSI Dallas Field Office.

"I'll call it in," Holly said.

"No time for that," he insisted. "We need to go. Now! We'll take my car, as Simon Griswold's operatives will be looking for your official vehicle, Deputy Marshal Kendall."

Rosamund barely had time to grab her cell phone before leaving with Paxton and Holly. Inadvertently left behind was Rosamund's Sig Sauer striker-fired pistol.

Chapter Fifteen

After arriving at the Dallas Fort Worth International Airport, Russell grabbed his charcoal carry-on spinner luggage from the overhead compartment in first class and went to the rental car office to rent a Nissan Rogue. He called Rosamund to surprise her that he decided to come in a day early and should be at her place shortly. Moreover, he wanted to remind her that once he put his house up for sale shortly, they would never need to be apart again if he had anything to do with it. When she didn't pick up, he left her a text message to that effect. Though he had no reason in particular to believe there was anything to be concerned about, warning bells went off in Russell's head. Something wasn't right. Call it a gut feeling or a greater sense of dread that everything seemed to be going almost too well since Rosamund returned to Dallas. Not that he wasn't happy this was the case. But what if it was a false read, meant for people like him to let down their guard, so Rosamund could be prevented from testifying against Simon Griswold with little to no resistance? Just because Arnold Nishimoto was no longer in the picture didn't make Griswold any less dangerous in his desperation to keep from spending the rest of his life in prison.

Am I overreacting? Russell had to ask himself as he got on the road. Maybe his deep love for Rosamund and strong desire to give her the type of great life she deserved as his wife and mother of their future children was clouding his judgment. Or maybe his instincts were spot on. Wasn't there still an unnamed mole at the DHS or HSI? What if this person was gunning for Rosamund and found a way to get to her on behalf of Griswold or in conjunction with him?

When he got to her loft, Russell let himself in, hoping to find Rosamund there with the armed deputy marshal to protect her. And maybe Rosamund's partner, Virginia Flannery. Instead, the place was empty. He noted empty wineglasses in the kitchen. But nothing seemed out of order. Where was she?

Russell texted her again with no response. This left him even more alarmed. He tried calling Virginia, who answered right away. "Hi," she said spiritedly.

"I'm here at Rosamund's loft and she's nowhere to be found," he stated. "Not picking up when I call her or responding to texts. Do you know where she is?"

"Hmm…" Virginia sounded baffled. "When I left a little while ago, she and Holly, the deputy marshal, were still there."

"Did Rosamund mention anywhere that she planned to go?"

"Not that I can recall. I just assumed she was going to stay there for the evening." She paused. "You think something may have happened to her?"

Russell stiffened. "You tell me."

"Why don't I call Holly and see what she has to say," Virginia suggested.

"Please do," he urged her. "And send me Holly's cell phone number while you're at it."

After texting him the number and putting him on hold for a moment, Virginia came back on and said, "She's not picking up either."

Trying to remain calm, Russell asked her suspiciously, "So, why aren't you with them?"

"I was sent on another assignment," she explained.

"By whom?"

"Harold Paxton, the special agent in charge of the Dallas Field Office."

Russell mused about that. Why would Paxton want to take Rosamund's partner off helping to safeguard her this close to the trial of Simon Griswold? What was up with that? Was it a deliberate plan on his part to reduce the number of people present at the loft to Rosamund and Holly, thereby leaving Rosamund more vulnerable? "Did Paxton offer to add more agents or marshals to Rosamund's security detail?"

"No," she admitted. "I think he thought Holly would be enough security for now—at least till the day of the trial." Virginia took a breath. "What are you thinking?"

"That Rosamund may be in trouble and, if so, Paxton's involved," Russell said, making his feelings clear.

"He wouldn't hurt her," she insisted. "Harold's the special agent in charge, for crying out loud. Why would he want to stop Rosamund from testifying?"

"That's a good question." Russell jutted his chin

pensively. "When I have an answer, I'll let you know. Meanwhile, I'd appreciate it if this conversation stays between us for the time being." He sensed that she could be trusted, even if placing Paxton on a proverbial pedestal.

"Of course," Virginia agreed, and added, "I'm coming over there."

"Good," he said. "If Rosamund shows up, let me know."

"Where are you going?"

"To have a look around." Russell disconnected. He left the condo and headed down to a lobby area, where he noted the security cameras. He needed to see under what circumstances Rosamund had left and if it was of her own accord. Making his way to a small office on the property, Russell acted with authority, despite currently being between jobs, when he requested to the twenty-something woman on duty that he take a look at the surveillance footage.

Batting brown eyes, Mary Heard flipped back her long and layered ginger-colored hair before playing the video. When she came to the part where Rosamund showed up, Russell asked Mary to stop. He noted that Rosamund was next to Holly. A man was behind them, but clearly with them.

"Let's zoom in on the man there," Russell directed.

"Okay."

He recognized him as Harold Paxton, Rosamund's boss and the special agent in charge, as Russell had made a point of familiarizing himself somewhat with those in her inner circle with the HSI. Where was Paxton taking Rosamund and why? Was there a threat to her safety that he hadn't bothered to inform Virginia of? Or did he have something more ominous in mind in sending Rosamund's partner off to another assignment?

Russell left the office and got on the phone with his brother, Scott. "Rosamund's missing," he told him, recognizing that his suspicions were unsubstantiated at this point.

"Missing?" Scott repeated. "Explain?"

Russell filled him in, coming back to Harold Paxton. "I need you to see if there have been any red flags there, be it professionally or personally."

"I'll check him out," Scott promised. "But there could be a perfectly reasonable explanation as to why Rosamund's not responding to your calls or texts," he cautioned.

"I know," Russell allowed. "But my instincts are telling me otherwise." And in this case, that was something he couldn't afford to ignore. Not when Rosamund's very survival could well be on the line.

ROSAMUND WAS IN the front passenger seat as Paxton drove his maroon Chrysler Pacifica Pinnacle to a single-story farmhouse on Jamaica Street in the Southeast Dallas section of the city. It was at the end of a street lined with dogwood trees. She felt a bit uneasy about the situation and naked without her duty weapon, but counted on the special agent in charge and Holly, who was in the back seat, to keep her safe till more help arrived.

They exited the vehicle, with Paxton leading the way. While approaching the house, he said in a calm voice, "Nothing will happen to you here."

While she wanted to believe that, there was a coldness in his green eyes that made Rosamund wonder if there was something he was keeping from them. She glanced at Holly, who also seemed to have reservations. The moment they stepped inside the living room and onto the red oak hardwood flooring, Rosamund noted the space was sparsely furnished. The room was somewhat dark and the teal curtains were drawn on all the windows.

It was only when she looked into a corner did Rosamund notice what appeared to be a body lying on the floor. In a matter of seconds, she was able to assess that it was a slender adult male of short stature with dark hair in a mohawk fade style and a short, boxed beard. He was wearing faded jeans, a jersey T-shirt, and dark sneakers. Gasping, she turned on Paxton, just as Holly was saying with an edge to her voice, "What happened to him?"

Paxton was now holding in a gloved hand a gun—in what looked to Rosamund to be a compact 9-millimeter piece—and aimed it at them. "He's dead," the special agent in charge replied brusquely. "He is—or was—my informant, Leo Neuman. I killed him. Right after he killed you, Deputy Marshal." Before Holly could remove her firearm from the belly band holster inside her flare-leg pants, Paxton shot her in the chest. Instinctively, she put a hand to the spot where the bullet entered, before losing consciousness and falling onto her back. With lightning speed, he raced over to her and grabbed her Glock 27 pistol and faced Rosamund, before she could make a move. "Don't even think about it," he warned her, pointing his gun at her. "Not unless you're ready to die too…"

Rosamund weighed her options, which were little to

none, without having her own firearm. She wanted to go to Holly's aide, hoping she could somehow hold on. But Paxton was clearly not interested in helping someone he had just shot in cold blood.

"Actually," Paxton said with a wry chuckle, "you should already be dead, Agent Santiago. Right alongside your late partner, Langford."

Rosamund's eyes widened. "What?"

"That's right, you should also be dead and buried, had Simon Griswold been more competent in his ability to shoot you when he had the chance. But his gun had to lock at the worst possible time for him." Paxton grimaced. "Griswold certainly can't blame me for his current predicament. I handed you and Langford to him on a silver platter. It was up to Griswold to finish you both off."

"You're the mole?" Rosamund's voice cracked. How could this be?

"You got me," Paxton confessed brashly.

She glared at him. "Why?" she asked pointedly, while trying to wrap her mind around the notion that her boss could be a crook and killer, all wrapped in one.

"Griswold paid me handsomely to look the other way," he contended. "I needed the money for various reasons. But I also needed to make the efforts to go after Griswold and his human trafficking organization seem believable. So, I sent you and Langford in undercover, hoping you would do little more than scratch the surface to go after a few underlings. But you got too close and Griswold needed to know about it. Or it would ruin the good thing we had going between us."

"Does that mean it was you who also exposed me to

Griswold's hitman, Arnold Nishimoto?" she asked, still in shock.

"Right again." Paxton laughed, while still aiming the gun at her, his hand steady. "It was Griswold's idea to put a hit out on you. I went along with it because I didn't want your testimony to blow back on me and my career with the DHS. Though the U.S. Marshals Service was a tough nut to crack in giving you a new identity and place to live that was not directly accessible to me apart from phone communication, I was finally able to pin it down and give Nishimoto everything he needed to finish you off once and for all. But, like Griswold, he failed, leaving me to clean up his mess before this goes to trial and the assistant U.S. attorney puts you on the stand to tell everything you know about Simon Griswold. After that, it wouldn't take long before Laura figured out my role and came after me. I can't allow that."

Rosamund was almost speechless. He had betrayed his office in the HSI and his integrity as a human being. And for what? Profit and greed. Now he had blood on his hands and Paxton fully intended to get them bloodier by killing her. And he was in a good enough position that he just might be able to pull it off, Rosamund feared.

"Your phone?" Paxton demanded, holding out one hand, while keeping the gun on her with the other. "Toss it over. And don't try anything funny, Agent Santiago. Or I'll kill you on the spot!"

Though it pained Rosamund to obey his command by giving up her one lifeline, with Paxton having her at a serious disadvantage, she had no choice but to comply. She could only hope that by keeping it turned on throughout this ordeal, there was still time for her location to be tracked. She slid the phone from the back pocket of her pants, then tossed it on the floor near him.

Paxton then stomped on the phone till it broke. He chuckled wickedly. "Afraid no one can come to your rescue now."

Rosamund was of the same mind, but refused to give in to what seemed like an inevitable fate.

"THERE ARE NO red flags, per se," Scott told him, as Russell listened to him over the speakerphone, while driving around the city.

"Tell me more about the per se," he said intently.

"Well, there were rumors when Paxton was the deputy special agent in charge of the field office in Albuquerque that he had a problem with gambling and had accrued debts in relation to that. But this was never proven, so he kept his career going."

"If he was a gambling addict and maybe still is, that would open the door to Paxton seeking out ways to fund his habit," Russell put forth. "Including aligning himself with the likes of Simon Griswold."

"Certainly can't rule it out," Scott said, "even if that would be taking things to the extreme, if Paxton were to risk everything for essentially nothing."

"Isn't that always the case for desperate people?" Russell pursed his lips. "Paxton was clearly in a position to finger Rosamund and Langford in a deal with the devil. When it only resulted in eliminating half the problem, Paxton could also have ratted out Rosamund to Nishimoto to keep Rosamund from breaking up the profitable party. I'm just saying." He could barely believe this was possible himself. But it made sense on another level. And Russell knew that bad people came from all walks of life. Including possibly within the ranks of the U.S. Department of Homeland Security.

"You'll find her," his brother said quietly.

"Yeah." Russell wanted to believe that with all his heart. Anything less would be unthinkable. He saw that his cell phone was buzzing, and that it was Virginia. "I have another call I need to take," he told Scott.

"Okay." He waited a beat. "Keep me posted."

"I will." Russell disconnected and put Virginia on the line. "Is Rosamund there?" He hoped that all his worry and condemning Harold Paxton was much ado about nothing.

"Afraid not," Virginia replied soberly. "But I think I know where she is."

"Where?" He crossed over an intersection.

"A safe house we use sometimes when working with informants," she said. "I'd almost forgotten that I installed a GPS tracker on Rosamund's cell phone at her request. I checked and it shows her phone was at that address. Till it went dead."

Russell tensed in considering that last part. Why would her phone go dead? Was it off? Or disabled by someone who wanted to make it unusable? He told her that Rosamund and Holly left the loft with Paxton and asked what he already knew the answer to, "Does he regularly deal with witnesses directly in this way?"

"Not that I've seen," Virginia admitted.

"Didn't think so. I think he targeted Rosamund and sent you in another direction to buy himself some time."

"Maybe Harold saw a security threat and acted upon it, knowing how vital a witness Rosamund is?" she suggested.

"Maybe, but my gut is telling me otherwise." Russell sucked in a deep breath. "What's the address to the safe house?"

She gave it and said, "I'm heading over there too."

"Whatever you do, don't let Paxton know we're coming," Russell stressed. "If he gets wind of it, there's no telling what he might do if desperate enough."

"Got it."

"You might want to call for backup and an ambulance, in case someone's hurt," he told her, fearful that Paxton might already have harmed Rosamund or Holly.

"Will do," Virginia said.

He disconnected and used the car's navigation system to guide him to the safe house. He put on the speed, knowing that every second counted, if he were to get there in time to save the woman he loved.

"So, what, you plan to shoot me and try to pin it on the person over there?" Rosamund glanced at the dead man in the corner.

Paxton grinned as he kept the gun on her. "Actually, the way this is going to work, Agent Santiago, is that my dead informant shot you and Deputy Marshal Kendall with this gun, having done so in betraying me in some misguided attempt to help out an innocent Simon Griswold. I then had no choice but to shoot the informant,

Leo Neuman, with my official firearm in my own self-defense." He laughed at the absurdity of it all.

"You're not going to be able to get away with this," Rosamund told him, if only to buy some extra time, knowing it was running out fast.

"I already have," Paxton bragged. "You see, once this is over, I'll be able to sell the DHS and the assistant U.S. attorney on what went down, much to their chagrin, but believable nonetheless. With you dead, the case against Griswold falls apart and we get to go back to a mutually profitable arrangement." He chortled. "Nice working with you, Agent Santiago, but all good things must come to an end. At least for you. No lucky gun jamming this time around to save you, I'm afraid."

With nowhere left to turn and nothing to lose at this point, Rosamund lunged at Paxton, catching him off guard just long enough to grab his wrist and twist it violently, before he could shoot her. The gun flew out of his hand. As he howled like a wounded animal, Paxton was able to recover enough to use his other fist to slam it hard into her cheek, causing Rosamund to see stars.

"You've got guts, Agent Santiago, I'll give you that," Paxton voiced, ignoring his own pain. "But this is still only going to end one way."

"Maybe not the way you think," Rosamund retorted, as he swung another fist at her face, which she dodged and then went to some Thai boxing moves. She hit his face squarely between the eyes, grabbed his waist and rammed a knee solidly into his groin, then smashed a fist into his thick neck. Though he groaned with discomfort, Paxton used his greater size and strength to lift her off the floor and throw her against the wall. Rosamund grimaced from the pain and tried to clear her head, as she sensed that he was ready to move in for the kill. Was she still up for a fight for survival? Or had he already won the battle?

Chapter Sixteen

When he entered the house, Russell wasn't sure what to expect. All he knew was that if Rosamund was still alive, he would make sure she stayed that way. He noted right away an unidentified male and the deputy marshal Holly Kendall on the floor. Neither were moving and both appeared to have been shot.

Russell turned to his left and saw Rosamund against a wall and Harold Paxton ready to charge at her like a raging bull. By the looks of him, he had taken some punishment. But not enough to bring him to his knees. Russell was not about to let him hurt her any more than he may already have. Before Paxton could reach Rosamund, Russell caught up to him and grabbed his arm, swinging him around to face him. "I'd like to get in on the action, Paxton," Russell told him.

Paxton yelled an expletive and went into fight mode. Russell was more than happy to mix it up, as he went to town on the special agent in charge. Heavy blows to both cheeks and chin were thrown by Russell as Paxton flailed away, mostly at air, before he went down in a heap, passing out cold.

After putting handcuffs on Paxton, Russell went over to Rosamund and held her shoulders. "Are you okay?" he asked gingerly.

"I'll live," she told him honestly, but winced to let him know she was experiencing some aches and pains.

He nodded. "Glad to hear that."

"Holly…" Rosamund's voice cracked as she raced over to the deputy marshal. She was still unconscious and bleeding from the gunshot wound. Rosamund put a hand to her neck and detected a faint pulse. "She's alive!"

"Help is on the way," Russell told her, lifting Rosamund up.

She met his eyes. "I was afraid I'd never see you again."

"That was never going to happen," he insisted in a soothing tone. He hid his own fear that he might have lost her.

"How did you find me?" she asked curiously. "Especially since you weren't even supposed to arrive in Dallas till tomorrow."

"Virginia was able to track your location through the GPS tracker on your phone," Russell explained, "giving me something to work with." He added, "As for being in town, I decided to come a day sooner." He'd tell her about his employment status later.

Rosamund smiled gratefully. "Good thing."

"So, what happened here with Paxton?" Russell asked anxiously.

She drew a breath, glancing at the knocked-out special agent in charge. "He was in cahoots with Simon Griswold," she explained. "Paxton was the mole in the DHS by way of the HSI. He wanted both me and Johnnie dead so we wouldn't spoil the arrangement Paxton had with Griswold, who paid him blood money to bypass any serious investigation into Griswold's human trafficking enterprise. When I survived, Paxton worked with Griswold to take the hit out on me. Paxton fed Arnold Nishimoto the information on my whereabouts to finish the job and prevent me from testifying."

"And when that failed, Paxton went after you himself," Russell muttered, his brow creased with anger.

"Yes," Rosamund said with dismay. "He killed his informant and shot Holly, intending to set up the informant for our deaths, so Paxton could get Griswold off the hook."

"But it blew up in his face," Russell said.

"Looks that way."

As they mulled that over, Virginia showed up and embraced Rosamund. "You're alive!" she uttered happily.

"No thanks to him." Rosamund eyed their boss, who was still unconscious. "He tried to kill me...and Holly..."

Virginia frowned sullenly, glancing at the gravely injured deputy marshal. "The ambulance should be here any minute now."

"Good," Rosamund said, "I can only hope that Holly will pull through."

Paramedics arrived and Holly was stabilized, before being taken to the hospital, still alive. Soon the safe house was crawling with law enforcement and crime scene investigators, while Harold Paxton, battered and bruised, was placed under arrest on a slew of charges.

"It's over now," Russell said comfortingly, wrapping Rosamund in his arms as they stood outside.

"Not quite," she reminded him. "There's still my testimony that's needed to put Simon Griswold away for life."

"True." Russell took a breath. "And Harold Paxton will be joining him behind bars for a very long time," he stated confidently. "It's been rumored that Paxton had a gambling problem over the years that may have caused him to cross the line."

"Excuses, excuses." Rosamund wrinkled her nose unsympathetically toward her former boss. "For Johnnie, Leah, and Holly, I hope he rots in jail."

"He will," Russell asserted, knowing there was no way out of this for Paxton. He realized that, for Rosamund, seeing the man she once looked up to pay the price for his criminality would be one big source of satisfaction. With another being the dismantling of Simon Griswold's human trafficking business and with that, less victimization of innocent children, women, and men as a result. "Let's go home," Russell told her, feeling that this really would be home for him, or wherever Rosamund wanted to be, now that his time in Weconta Falls had come to an end.

"So, I quit my job," Russell said to Rosamund that evening, as if it was a routine thing, as he sat beside her on the sectional in her loft, a bottle of beer in hand. She had been debriefed by the various powers that be as was standard procedure in a federal investigation of this magnitude. The replacement deputy U.S. marshal Joel Elizondo, a tall and thickset forty-year-old with walnut-colored eyes and dark hair in a Caesar cut, stood guard outside the door, just in case there was more trouble. Holly Kendall had gone into surgery immediately and everything had gone well according to doctors, with the belief among them that Holly would miraculously make a full recovery. Virginia was home, but just a phone call away, if needed.

"Seriously?" Rosamund's eyes widened with surprise. They had talked about one or the other shifting careers to be together, but nothing definitive.

"Yeah, I'm officially no longer Detective Lynley, Weconta Falls Police Department." He grinned and sipped the beer. "Getting out of Dodge," he joked. "Put the house on the market and, hopefully, it will sell soon."

"Are you sure about this?" she had to ask, knowing it was probably too late to have a redo. She sipped her own beer.

"How can I not be?" he responded coolly. "It wouldn't have been fair to ask you to give up what you do, given your dedication to the job. In fact, once the trial is over, I wouldn't be surprised if you got a promotion to move up the ladder with the DHS or Homeland Security Investigations."

"I wish." Rosamund tsked, not wanting to get ahead of herself in merely doing her duties, hazardous and all. "But anyway, this is about you," she told him, feeling a little guilty that he was suddenly unemployed. "What will you do now?" With his law enforcement résumé, she was sure he would find gainful employment soon.

"Actually, I'm about to rejoin the Bureau," Russell uttered proudly.

"Really?" She gazed at him with excitement. "That was quick."

"I've been thinking about it for a while," he admitted.

"Even before you came into my life, truthfully, I was starting to feel a little restless, wondering if I could ever settle for small-town detective work when there were so many interesting assignments potentially awaiting me with the FBI. I'm ready to get back in the saddle, if you will. Scott seems to think that it's more or less a done deal. I'll take him at his word for that. Unless I find out otherwise, I should be reemployed with the Bureau in no time flat. In the meantime, I'm here to support you every step of the way as you put the screws to Simon Griswold and his new jail pal, Harold Paxton."

"Thank you," Rosamund gushed, eager to put this case and those bad actors in the rearview mirror, so her focus could instead be more on the evolving relationship between her and Russell. "Just know that the support works both ways," she stressed.

"I do know that." He grinned and kissed her. "I also know that I love doing that."

She blushed, touching her tingling mouth. "And I love you doing it," she said. "Along with kissing you back."

"Anytime you like," he challenged her.

Rosamund didn't disappoint. "How about now and forever," she teased him.

He grinned. "Works for me."

As it did for her. She kissed him and let it linger for a while, welcoming the respite from escaping death more than once and readying herself for the big day in court.

ON THE FIRST day of the trial, Rosamund entered the Earle Cabell Federal Building, accompanied by Russell, Virginia, Deputy U.S. Marshal Joel Elizondo, and Rosamund's sister, Gabby Ulrich, who flew in the night before to show her support. Gabby was basically a slightly younger version of herself, Rosamund felt, only an inch shorter with long, straight dark hair with cappuccino highlights.

"I know you'll do great," Gabby encouraged her, after they were brought to a waiting room till it was time for Rosamund to testify.

"Absolutely," Russell agreed. "You're well prepared to take whatever Griswold's attorney throws at you."

"Thanks." Rosamund welcomed the confidence they showed in her and was happy to see that two of the most important people in her life seemed to have hit it off. She looked forward to meeting Russell's siblings in person. "I'll do my best," she promised, knowing her testimony could make or break the federal case against Simon Griswold. She fully expected that she would also be called upon to testify against Harold Paxton, once he went to trial for murder, attempted murder, money laundering, and other serious charges.

"And I'll be there with you every step of the way," Virginia pitched in, as someone also slated to testify later regarding her investigation into Griswold's human trafficking operation while Rosamund was under the federal program.

"I know," she said, smiling at her partner. Before she could contemplate further, Rosamund received word that it was time, as she was being called as the first witness.

She received a warm hug from Russell, who whispered in her ear, "Good luck."

Her eyes crinkled as she whispered back, "That's already come in meeting you."

"I feel the same," he promised with a grin, while looking dapper in a gray suit and black loafers.

She took that to heart and left the room, where Rosamund was led to the courtroom by Deputy Marshal Joel Elizondo. He'd been shaken up by the near-death experience of his colleague Holly Kendall, and was determined to do his part to look after Holly's two children till she recovered.

Rosamund wore a navy blue houndstooth-print skirt suit and black pumps as she made her way toward the witness box. Her hair, which had started to grow out, was in a twisted updo. She looked at Laura Gibson-Norcross, who would be questioning her. Laura flashed her a soft smile. Next to Laura at the prosecutors table was fellow assistant U.S. Attorney Neil Rivera, who was thirtysomething, very tall, lean, and bald-headed. He also acknowledged Rosamund.

She turned to the defendant, Simon Griswold. He wore a charcoal gray suit, and she noted his pompadour fade hairstyle was now grayer. Next to him was his attractive attorney, Alicia Aotaki, whose long brunette hair was in a bubble ponytail. Griswold favored Rosamund with a menacing stare before she looked away, determined not to let him get to her. On the contrary, she was more than ready to do her part to put Griswold away for life, in memory of her late partner, Johnnie Langford, and for the many victims of Griswold's human trafficking.

Rosamund took the stand, steeling herself for what was to come. Laura Gibson-Norcross left her table and approached confidently, as she offered Rosamund another supportive smile, then said respectfully, "Agent Santiago, why don't we start with you telling us who you work for?"

"I work for the United States Department of Homeland Security," Rosamund told her.

"And what is it that you do for the DHS?" she asked.

"I'm a Homeland Security Investigations special agent in its Center for Countering Human Trafficking."

Laura waited a beat and continued, "Tell us a bit about what your duties entail?"

Rosamund adjusted in the seat and went through the CCHT's mission of countering the crimes involving human trafficking, protecting and rescuing victims, and increasing deterrence efforts, using the DHS's strengths and resources, often in cooperation with its partners in law enforcement across the country. "Our entire goal is to stop the trafficking of humans through all the legal means at our disposal, saving lives in the process," she concluded.

Again, the assistant U.S. attorney allowed that to sink in before saying evenly, "Let's turn to your purpose for being a witness for the prosecution today, Agent Santiago." Laura glared at the defendant and turned back to Rosamund. "Why don't you tell us about your mission as an undercover agent that led to this very moment in time."

Rosamund sucked in a deep breath and met the cold stare of Simon Griswold, who had tried to kill her twice, one of which was by his own hand. She had cheated death both times and now had the opportunity for justice to be served. She was more than up to the task. She was determined to make sure he paid for his terrible crimes and for snubbing his nose at the laws of the country he lived in for profit and total disregard for anyone but himself. Similar to his partner in crime, Harold Paxton.

RUSSELL QUIETLY SLIPPED into a seat in the spectator section and listened in as Rosamund took it to Simon Griswold, detailing his sordid human trafficking operation and various means of coercing, recruiting, capturing, and separating victims for forced labor, sexual exploitation, and sex slavery. She withstood a withering cross-examination by the defense lawyer, as Rosamund more than held her ground in making the case against Griswold.

During the afternoon session, it was much of the same as Rosamund testified with grit and determination. When it was time to point the finger at Griswold for the murder of Johnnie Langford, she didn't hold back.

"The defendant, Simon Griswold, showed no hesitation or mercy when he pulled the trigger of his gun and shot to death my partner, Homeland Security Investigations Special Agent Johnnie Langford, at point-blank range," Rosamund recounted, grimacing at the painful memory. "Were it not for the defendant's firearm jamming, I wouldn't be here in this courtroom today." She sighed. "But I am here and doing the right thing by exposing the defendant for the monster he truly is."

Russell could see that the jury was moved by her testimony, which was met with approval by the prosecutors. It made him love Rosamund all the more, knowing what kind of a woman he was getting as a romantic partner and, hopefully, future wife and mother of his children. When her testimony was finished, Rosamund left the witness stand with her head held high, after giving everything she had toward securing a conviction for Griswold. Russell was proud of her and more than ready to begin the next chapter of their lives together.

TWO WEEKS LATER, the jury returned a guilty verdict against Simon Griswold, who would be spending the rest of his life behind bars. And with this, her round-the-clock security was no longer needed. Rosamund celebrated the verdict with Russell over dinner at one of her favorite restaurants, Eve's Steak Castle, on Main Street in Downtown Dallas.

"We did it!" she declared, raising her goblet of red wine triumphantly, while feeling good knowing that Griswold would never again be able to practice the trading of humans for commercial sexual exploitation, forced labor, and other illicit purposes.

"Never doubted you would," Russell said coolly, cutting into his filet mignon. "Between your testimony and the strong evidence the feds had going for them, it was evident that Griswold was going down. It was just a matter of time, which for him has now run out."

Rosamund smiled. "Thank goodness for that." She forked a slice of her Wagyu strip steak. "Next up is Harold Paxton," she stated. "I hear they're throwing the book at him, and deservedly so."

"I'll say." Russell took a sip of his wine. "He's the worst of the worst in using his position of authority to profit off victims of trafficking, even to the point of being willing to kill to continue lining his pockets."

She twisted her lips at the thought of the former special agent in charge attempting to murder her, and very nearly succeeding. But she wasn't about to let that spoil the evening and spending quality time with the man she loved. When Rosamund looked at him, she realized that Russell was staring at her across the booth. "What?" she asked, wondering if she had stained her floral appliqué midi dress with food or something.

"Well, I have news," he began mysteriously.

She eyed him musingly. "What news might that be?"

Russell sat back. "Thought you might like to know that I'm officially back with the Bureau," he said. "We still need to iron out a few minor details but, as of now, I'm a full-fledged FBI special agent again."

Rosamund smiled. "That's terrific!" She knew he had been working toward this and even considered other options, had it fallen through. But now that it was a done deal, she couldn't be happier for him. And them, with her own job as a DHS special agent still intact.

"I thought so." He sipped more wine and then gave her a big smile. "There's more…"

"More…?" She listened intently.

"It just so happens that I am very much in love with you," Russell said earnestly. "But the only way that love can be complete for me is if it's in the context of husband and wife. So, with that being said…" He paused long enough to remove a small velvet box from the inside pocket of his solid weave blazer. Opening it to reveal a ring, he continued, "I wonder if you would do me the great honor, Rosamund Santiago, and make me the happiest man in the world, by marrying me and, if you like, raising a family together?"

Russell took the ring out and Rosamund put a hand to her mouth with sheer exhilaration. Before he could change his mind, she grabbed the fourteen-karat, two-tone gold, pear-shaped halo frame diamond engagement ring and slid it onto her finger. It was a perfect fit.

"Can I take that as a yes?" he asked lightheartedly.

"Yes, yes, and yes!" she declared enthusiastically, marveling at the ring before meeting his eyes. "I will gladly marry you, Russell Lynley. Nothing would make me happier than to become your wife. And also, the mother of our children." Whether two, three, or even four kids, they could decide that in time.

"Those words are music to my ears." Russell beamed, and scooted over in the booth to give her a hearty kiss. "Thank you."

"The pleasure is all mine." Rosamund giggled. She kissed him again, feeling giddy, and admired the ring. "We should probably have a big wedding, so we can invite all of your family, my family, and even some of our friends and coworkers we left behind in Weconta Falls." She especially wanted to invite Tracy Sheridan, whom she had stayed in contact with, and Shailene McEnany, who had provided Rosamund with a job to keep busy while living a life as Tisha González.

"I wouldn't have it any other way," Russell said in complete agreement.

Rosamund laughed. "Somehow, I didn't think you would."

"Shall we seal the deal again with another kiss?"

"Do you even need to ask?" she said, before doing the honors.

Epilogue

Homeland Security Investigations Special Agent Rosamund Santiago was in on a major crackdown on human trafficking in Texas. Following the convictions and life sentences of Simon Griswold and Harold Paxton, she had been reassigned to the HSI Houston Field Office six months ago. There, Rosamund cherished her role in taking down those individuals who would seek to sexually exploit women and children or coerce those trafficked into domestic servitude with no moral compass. Working as part of the Human Trafficking Rescue Alliance of the U.S. Southern District of Texas that brought together law enforcement agencies on the federal, state, and local levels, the Department of Homeland Security was more than happy to play its part in successful operations. Such as the latest case involving the rescue of more than two dozen undocumented minors who were being sex trafficked across Houston and otherwise kept as prisoners at a house on the northwest side of the city. The six adult traffickers were placed under arrest and would be fully prosecuted.

Beyond work and a new location to call home, Rosa-

mund could barely believe how much her life had changed
for the better, now that Russell Lynley had entered it.
With a huge wedding planned for midyear, he had proven
to be everything she could have ever asked for in a fi-
ancé and future husband. That included actually working in the same city and occasionally even together in
crossover investigations. On the personal front, they both
wanted children and had even taken to picking out potential names for them, depending on whether male or
female. And they had pooled their resources and purchased a big two-story house on Moody Street with all
the trimmings and a large backyard, in anticipation of
starting a family and giving them something to grow into.
Not to mention, a place spacious enough to accommo-
date the numerous visits from their families and friends
that were expected.

Having completed her work shift, Rosamund headed
home just long enough to change into running attire for
a date with Russell at their favorite spot for jogging and
enjoying quality time together. As he never seemed to be
late, she stepped up the pace, before hopping in her crim-
son red Subaru Forester Sport and heading off to the park.

RUSSELL CONSIDERED IT a stroke of luck and more that
he was able to secure a spot with the Bureau, based at
its FBI Houston Field Office. As an experienced special
agent, he was given choice assignments, along with the
full confidence of the special agent in charge, Jacquelyn
Hernandez. But more importantly, he got to do his thing
in Houston, where his gorgeous fiancée, Rosamund Santiago, was employed as an HSI special agent. After her

ordeal in Dallas, including losing her partner, Johnnie Langford, and being forced into the WITSEC, Russell had expected that she might put in for a transfer to some-place where she could start fresh. It was something he had needed as well, having tried to escape his troubles in St. Louis after the tragic death of his wife and daughter by fleeing to Northern California. As it turned out, he discovered that he didn't belong in Weconta Falls after all, at least not for the long run.

But that move had allowed him to meet the waitress Tisha González, who had more layers beneath the attractive surface than he was able to peel back. He and Rosa-mund clicked and fell in love, giving Russell every reason in the world to want to face his own demons and jump-start his career with the Bureau. So far, it had proven to be a perfect fit. He had just wrapped up a domestic ter-rorism case in southeast Texas and, as part of an FBI Vi-olent Crime Task Force, moved on to an investigation of an armed bank robbery on the northeast side of Houston.

After work, Russell changed into his jogging clothes and climbed in his Jeep Grand Wagoneer for a workout date with Rosamund at Hackberry Park on South Dairy Ashford Road. He was running late, but suspected he would still beat her there. Both passionate about stay-ing in shape and jogging, in particular, it was a great bonding experience, now that they were more settled in their careers and location. He loved their new house and was happy they were both able to sell their separate resi-dences. The new house was in a great neighborhood and was a perfect place to raise a family. He couldn't wait till they were married and could get started in that respect, as he felt they were certain to be wonderful parents. Just as Russell felt his own parents were and Rosamund's continued to be from what he could see. He looked forward to their families bonding over time and having visits back and forth. Rosamund had even talked about getting a dog when time permitted, and had told him about the Jack Russell terrier she had as a little girl.

When he arrived at the park, Russell was still hopeful he could get in a quick warm-up before Rosamund arrived. Only she had beaten him there and was already in her element as a runner, waiting for him on the jogging trail. "Finally decided to show up, huh?" she teased him.

"Sorry I'm late," he said. "Traffic and all that."

"Yeah, right. Any excuse to try to justify your tardiness, Special Agent Lynley."

Russell grinned, knowing when he had come up short. "Guilty as charged," he relented. "Come on, let's run."

Rosamund smiled. "I'll try my best not to leave you behind."

He laughed. "Sounds like a challenge to me."

"Maybe it is."

"You're on," he accepted.

She took off down the scenic trail, leaving him in the dust, before Russell caught up and ran parallel with her. "So, how was your day?" he asked. Rosamund brought him up-to-date and asked the same. He beamed. "Honestly, it got a whole lot better the moment I laid eyes on my stunning fiancée."

She blushed. "Oh, that's what every woman wants to hear, whether true or not."

"It's true," Russell promised, taking her hand and

slowing them down. "I love you, Rosamund, and you'll always be the very best part of my day."

"You know what," she uttered, "I feel exactly the same way, Russell. Maybe it's something in the water here."

He laughed. "More likely, it's something in the heart and soul."

Rosamund's face lit up. "I like that answer much better." She wrapped her arms around his neck and kissed him on the lips. "So much better."

Russell felt his heart skip a beat, before he stopped the kiss long enough to say, "Me too."

* * * * *

PROTECTING COLTON'S SECRET DAUGHTERS

LISA CHILDS

With great appreciation for Patience Bloom, for including me in this continuity and for letting me continue my Bachelor Bodyguards and Hotshot Heroes series. Thank you so much for supporting the series and the characters I love to write!

Chapter One

Since the killings had begun, FBI special agent Cash Colton had spent more time at the Manhattan field office than he had anywhere else, so it felt strange to be outside now. Well, inside an SUV driving toward Coney Island, but it wasn't the office or a crime scene, which was the only other place he'd been besides his office.

At least Coney Island wasn't a crime scene yet. But after the text he'd received, the text that haunted him, Cash couldn't help fearing that he might be heading to the site of another murder soon and not just because of the way the killer kept killing. That fear, because of that damned text, compelled him to make the trip to Coney Island to make sure *she* was okay.

Even before receiving that text, he'd been as determined as the rest of his special unit to catch the Landmark serial killer. The first victim, Mark Wheden, had been shot in Central Park, and found with a typed note stuffed in his pocket: *Until the brilliant and beautiful Maeve O'Leary is freed, I will kill in her honor and name. M down, A up next.*

Like this lunatic actually expected them to free a serial killer because of his threats? Then there would be two serial killers terrorizing New York—although Maeve hadn't limited her killing to just the Empire State. She'd killed wherever and whomever she'd married. She'd also tried to kill a lover's wife in order to inherit that woman's fortune. Anything for money...

Insatiable greed was Maeve's motive for murder.

Why was the Landmark Killer killing? What was his motive? Had Maeve somehow brainwashed him the way she had that poor psychiatrist? Like she had all her husbands?

But even she had to see that there was no way she was getting released; she was being held in custody without bail because of all the murders she'd committed and the likelihood she would flee.

That hadn't stopped her admirer, though. The Landmark Killer's second victim, Andrew Capowski, had been found on the Empire State Building observation deck with a typed note in his pocket that had read nearly the same as the first but the second line said: *MA down, E up.*

Not long after that, a man named Edward Pendleton was murdered after leaving the Metropolitan Museum of Art. The next attempt had been on Broadway, but that victim had fortunately survived. Unfortunately, since his assailant had worn a mask and a hoodie, he hadn't been able to provide much more than a vague description. Male, maybe on the younger side...

The fact that the killer had been sending the Coltons personal texts told Cash and his team one thing: the killer was probably closer than they'd realized. Closer to them than they were to finding him.

He had to be stopped before anyone else died, and before anyone else was threatened. The way Valentina had been threatened…

Maybe she hadn't been named specifically, but the threat had been implied in the text Cash had received; he was the latest one singled out on the FBI serial killer team. His twin had been the first to be taunted.

Who the hell was it? Was it someone close to them as they had come to suspect? Someone within the FBI or within the Ninety-Eighth Precinct that had worked to hunt down the Black Widow serial killer, Maeve O'Leary? Someone who'd come to admire her for some sick reason?

The note about Valentina had been a text sent to Cash's phone after the first victim was shot on Broadway. No worries. Lots where that dippy actor came from. Tsk-tsk, Cash—murdered daddy and a sad ex-wife.

Instead of trying for another actor, the killer had claimed the life of an assistant theater director after that text. And what about Valentina?

Was she in danger? Had that text been meant as an actual threat or was it just a ploy to distract Cash from the case? While it likely was a ploy, Cash wasn't immune to the text. It had worked. He *was* distracted. He couldn't stop worrying about Valentina even though he'd told a friend at the local police precinct about the note and had asked Sergeant Dave Percell to watch out for her, to make sure that nobody was lurking around her, trying to hurt her.

Was she really sad?

Why?

She couldn't still be unhappy about their divorce. More

than three years had passed since Cash had set her free to have what she'd really wanted: a husband who wasn't consumed with his work and most especially one who wanted children. More than anything else, more than him, Valentina had wanted a family.

Because Cash hadn't been able to see how he could handle his career, marriage and fatherhood, he'd done what he'd thought would make Valentina the happiest. After she'd moved out to get some space from him, he'd filed for divorce. He'd wanted her to have the happiness she deserved. So why wasn't she happy? Or was the texter lying about that?

He hadn't lied about Cash's murdered daddy. That had happened; a serial killer was responsible for Cash's cop father losing his life.

And inadvertently responsible for Cash and all his siblings going into law enforcement.

So since he'd told the truth about that, he might have been right about Valentina as well. But how would the Landmark Killer know if Cash's ex-wife was happy or sad unless he'd gotten close to her? Did he know her? Or had he been stalking her like he had the victims whose lives he'd taken?

Those worries kept Cash awake at night, kept him on edge. Even though his buddy Dave at the local precinct had promised to keep an eye on her, Cash had also called Valentina to let her know about that text. To make sure she was aware of the potential threat. She'd been short with him, as if he'd caught her at a bad time. And maybe he had...

And ever since he'd heard her voice, he hadn't been

able to get it out of his mind. Just as he'd never gotten Valentina Acosta completely out of his heart. Cash suspected that the Landmark Killer had known that when he'd sent Cash that text. He'd known how badly it would bother him, so somehow he knew Cash.

Maybe better than Cash knew himself, because in the past three years he hadn't let himself admit how he felt about Valentina. He rarely let himself think about her at all. If not for that damn text...

And then that call he'd made to her, to the same cell number she'd always had. Brennan had offered to make the call for him, as if it was somehow his fault that Cash had received the text even though their entire unit was hunting this sick serial killer. But he'd sent Brennan the first text: Shouldn't you be out looking for me skulking around Broadway theaters instead of shacking up with a murder suspect? I thought you Coltons didn't like killers because of what happened to poor Daddy.

Brennan had been reluctant to share the text with them. Probably because of the shacking up part. Cash smiled and caught a glimpse of his own reflection in the rearview mirror. Despite being twins, he and Brennan looked nothing alike because they were fraternal, not identical. Brennan had pale blond hair and pale blue eyes and a baby face while Cash had brown hair and green eyes and always looked like he needed a shave even if he'd just shaved. But given how busy he was, he'd given up and wore a beard now.

Valentina had always told him that she thought his scruff was sexy. But that was when he'd kept his beard neatly trimmed. He didn't look neat now. He probably should have stopped home and showered after leaving the office, but for some reason he'd had this compulsion to drive to Brooklyn and Coney Island. To see for himself that Valentina was really all right, that she was safe and not sad.

"VALENTINA? ARE YOU all right?"

The voice startled her, drawing her attention back to the present, and not the past where it had been constantly slipping since that call a week ago. From Cash…

She had not heard the sound of his deep voice in three years, but she'd immediately recognized the rumble of it in her ear, raising goose bumps on her skin like they were rising now despite the warmth of the library.

"Valentina…" he'd murmured.

"Valentina!" the older woman repeated. "Are you all right?"

She shook her head and blinked and squinted against the late-afternoon sun pouring through the tall windows. Then she tried to focus on the woman standing in front of her, blocking her path as Valentina tried to push the double-wide stroller between the rows of children's books.

"You're not all right," Mrs. Miller remarked, and she reached over the top of the stroller to pat Valentina's hand. "What's troubling you, honey?" The back of the woman's hand had thick veins crisscrossing it, and on every finger, below the swollen knuckle, she wore a ring with big stones that sparkled and reflected the sunlight. The sun also glinted off the jewels hanging from the chains around her neck.

Four pudgy little hands stretched out from the stroller,

reaching toward those shiny pendants. The girls loved shiny things.

She smiled. "Nothing, Mrs. Miller, I'm fine. Really."

The woman stepped back then and leaned down to smile at the toddlers in the stroller. "How could you not be happy all the time with these two gorgeous girls?"

Mother's pride suffused Valentina. "I just picked them up from day care." If they didn't love going to school, as they called it, she might have regretted having to work full-time. But as a single mother, she didn't have a choice. At least she had a job that she enjoyed.

"And you came right back to work?" Mrs. Miller asked with surprise.

"We're picking out a book for bedtime. Well, two books. They each get to choose one."

"You're passing your librarian's love for books on to your little girls, that's wonderful," Mrs. Miller enthused. "And speaking of books…"

"I tracked down that memoir you've been looking for," Valentina assured her.

"That's wonderful!" the woman exclaimed, her pale blue eyes sparkling like her rings with excitement.

"I ordered it to be sent here from the branch where I found it. If it arrives while I'm off this weekend, I asked Randall to call you and let you know," Valentina said.

"I can wait until you're back on Monday, honey," the woman said. "Then you and I can discuss it."

That was one of the parts of Valentina's job that she enjoyed most. Discussing books with other avid readers.

The older woman loved reading the memoirs of famous theater actors and actresses and socialites and artists from years past, probably looking for a mention of herself. She'd once been an actress before marrying well and becoming a socialite; there was even a rumor that she had also been a famous artist's model and muse.

"When are you going to write your memoir?" Valentina asked. "Yours is the book I would love to read."

The older woman blushed and giggled and waved a hand in front of her face, and the sunlight glinted off the bright stones on her rings. She had the air about her, with the furs she wore and her perfect makeup and clothes and jewelry, of old Hollywood glamour. "I might be scribbling down a few notes here and there," she admitted with a sly smile. "But I find myself focusing on other far more interesting people and events than myself. I'm definitely not the type to kiss and tell. But I certainly enjoy reading the stories from the people who do."

Valentina laughed now, and the girls echoed it, despite having no idea what she was laughing about.

Mrs. Miller giggled again, and she looked much younger than her probably eighty or ninety years. "You enjoy your bedtime stories," she told them, and she patted Valentina's hand again as she walked past them.

The little girls leaned out either side of the stroller and stared after the older woman.

"Sparky..." Luciana murmured.

"Sparky," Ana repeated.

They must have been talking about the older woman's jewelry. Valentina smiled as her heart filled with love. They were so adorable with brown curls framing their little faces. Ana had dark eyes, like Valentina, while Luci's were green, like...

No. She wasn't going to think about him anymore. And for the next while, she managed that while helping the girls pick out books. But they knew the routine, so they chose quickly once they ruled out the ones they'd already read. Then they checked out and were back in the stroller, heading toward home, shortly after Mrs. Miller left.

The distance between the library and the high-rise condo complex where they lived was far enough that it was easier and safer to push the girls in their double stroller than for them to walk. The only problem was that with the street noise from traffic echoing off the commercial buildings, Valentina couldn't hear all of their chatter. Not that she understood much of it; they had their own little twin language. While they always understood each other, it wasn't as easy for Valentina all the time.

She still wasn't certain she understood Cash's call, either. He'd received a text about her from a serial killer? Or so he and the rest of his unit suspected, but nobody at the FBI had been able to trace it. With all their technology, how was that possible?

And why send Cash a text about her?

She had not had any contact with her ex-husband since that day she'd moved out to take some time to think, to figure out if she could accept what he was willing to give her. Whatever time that was left over from the job that consumed him. But she'd wanted more than that; she'd wanted a family. And that was the one thing he'd told her he would not give her. But he actually had…

Neither of them had known it when she'd moved out, though. She hadn't even known it yet when the divorce papers had come. Thinking he didn't care enough to figure out a compromise with her, Valentina had just signed them and ended it without an argument, without a fight. And she'd thought it was done, that she would never see or hear from him again. And she hadn't for three years...

Until that night a week ago.

"Valentina..."

And just the sound of his deep, rumbly voice had all the feelings rushing back, overwhelmingly intense. The pain, the loss, the guilt...

She should have told him all those years ago when she'd first found out herself that she was pregnant. But she'd figured that it was too late then, because she had already signed the divorce papers. And in sending them, Cash had clearly also been sending her the message that there was no hope for them as a couple. They were over. Done. He hadn't wanted the same things she had. He certainly hadn't wanted—

A loud pop rang out, startling her and making her jump. It wasn't so much the noise, which must have been a backfiring car that had passed or started up along the curb or in one of the alleys they'd passed. It was that she'd been so distracted again that she hadn't even realized where she was. That she had almost walked past the street she needed to turn on and cross to head home. She had to put that phone call out of her mind.

Cash hadn't called again. And he probably wouldn't. She knew he was busy chasing another killer, like he always was. The Landmark Killer. She'd watched the news and had read the article the *New York Wire* had recently run about the investigation.

That article had been more about the investigators than

anything else. It had been about the Coltons, who worked in the elite serial killer unit of the FBI. And it had revealed the reason why they were all on that unit and so dedicated to hunting down killers: because a serial killer had murdered their police officer father, to some of the investigators like Cash and uncle to a couple others, so many years ago.

But were they hunting the Landmark Killer or was he hunting them with the notes he left in his victims' pockets and with the text he'd sent Cash?

She didn't know exactly what the text had said, just that it had mentioned her. Since she and Cash had had no contact since their divorce, how had this serial killer known about her at all?

So was she in danger? And the girls?

Or were Cash and his siblings really the ones who were in danger, and the serial killer was just texting to taunt them as he had with those notes he left on his victims?

HE HAD KILLED AGAIN.

Like he had so many times before. That didn't even bother him anymore.

Taking a life.

It wasn't a big deal. It was just what he did like other guys played video games. But this wasn't a game to him. It was a vocation.

One he had to protect at all costs.

This time he couldn't be certain that he wouldn't get caught. He couldn't be certain unless he *made* certain. He had to eliminate any possibility of being identified as the killer.

So he settled into the driver's seat and pulled the mask over his face and drew up his hood, pulling it tight around that mask so that nothing of his face reflected back at him from the rearview mirror. Nothing but his eyes: his cold, dark eyes.

Chapter Two

Cash knew Valentina's address. She'd given it to him to forward her mail after she'd moved out of the apartment they'd shared in Manhattan. She'd moved to Coney Island, into the condo where her grandparents used to live. Her grandparents, knowing how much their only granddaughter had loved visiting them there, left the condo to her in their will when they'd passed away shortly before Cash and Valentina's divorce. Valentina had wanted to move out there then while Cash had wanted to stay close to the Manhattan office.

Maybe losing so much of her family had made Valentina even more desperate to start one of her own. That was when she'd really started pressuring Cash into having kids, and she'd wanted to raise her children in a place she remembered so fondly from her own childhood. Cash didn't have that many fond memories of his childhood; his father's brutal murder had overshadowed all the happy ones.

It overshadowed his adulthood, leading him to a life in law enforcement. With his job consuming so much of his time and attention, he shouldn't have become a husband, let alone a father.

Valentina had often told him, during the three years that they'd been married, that she'd felt like a mistress, and his career was really his wife. She only got stolen moments of his time, and he'd almost seemed guilty about the time he'd spent with her, the time away from his job. It hadn't been fair to Valentina. She shouldn't have been alone so much while he'd been working nights and weekends in addition to all week long. She'd deserved so much more from their marriage, from him. She'd deserved everything she'd wanted.

She was so sweet and loving and smart and beautiful. So very beautiful...

He could see her now in his mind, and maybe he even conjured up her image through the side window. Her thick dark hair flowing nearly to her waist, her hips swaying as she walked along the sidewalk. But she was pushing something in front of her. A stroller?

Was she babysitting for a friend?

Or had she started that family, the one she'd wanted with him, with someone else? That was what he'd hoped for her when he'd divorced her, but knowing that she had actually moved on with someone else...

And he hadn't. He was still stuck in their past, dreaming of her smile, of her laugh, of her wicked sense of humor flashing in her dark eyes, and the love...

A car horn tooted behind him and he realized the light had changed to green and the traffic in front of him had moved. But he was still stuck...

He pressed on the accelerator and surged forward

through the intersection. The light green at the next one, he drove through that as well because he spied an open parking space ahead on the curb. He was nearly to her condo building. That had to be where she was heading. So he pulled into that spot and hopped out of his SUV. She would be coming this way if she was going home.

But maybe she'd been babysitting for someone and was taking the child back to their parents. Or was she the parent? Had she had the child she wanted? The family?

He wanted to be happy for her. But a part of him had never stopped wanting her. And if that was her he'd seen on the sidewalk, she was every bit as beautiful as she'd always been. As sexy…

His heart pounded hard as he skirted his SUV and stepped onto the sidewalk. He'd gotten only a couple of blocks ahead of her. She should appear soon, but the sidewalk was packed with people heading toward him, probably intent on enjoying the sunny day at the amusement park or the beach. And her complex was so close to both.

Instead of waiting for her to pass by him, Cash started through the crowd, moving against the throng of people. It had been three years since he'd seen Valentina; maybe that hadn't even been her he'd glimpsed on the sidewalk. Maybe that woman just looked like Valentina with the same curves and the same walk.

But if that woman wasn't his ex-wife, he doubted his heart would be pounding as fast and hard as it was. It wasn't just attraction or anticipation coursing through him, though; it was fear. Something had compelled him to drive out to Coney Island today to make sure she was safe. He'd been worried since he'd received that text, but that worry had intensified, twisting his guts, because he had a sick feeling, almost a premonition, that she was in danger.

He moved faster through the crowd, drawing grunts and curses as he accidentally banged into people. Maybe if they hadn't been on their phones and distracted, they would have seen him coming, but he grunted back apologies. Until he neared the next intersection and he saw *her* standing on the other side; then he was the one distracted.

The woman was definitely Valentina. She stood at the curb, in front of that stroller although she was half-turned toward it, her hand on the top of it as if she was protecting it from the traffic on the street in front of her. The breeze coming in off the ocean played with her hair, swirling the long chocolate-brown tresses around her, while it plastered her light blue cotton dress against her curves. He knew that body so well that his tightened with the desire coursing through him. He'd never wanted anyone the way he'd wanted her.

The way he still wanted her...

She didn't see him. Her focus was split between that stroller and the crosswalk light. Once it turned green, she held back a moment, letting other people pass by her. Then, finally, she started across, and just as she did, Cash heard an engine rev, brakes squeal and metal scrape as a car sideswiped the one stopped in front of it to pass it and roar toward the intersection, toward Valentina and that stroller with not one but two children in it.

His heart slammed against his ribs as fear shot through

him. He'd been right to worry about her; she was definitely in danger.

Mortal danger...

THE ASPHALT WAS hard and hot beneath her back. The
impact with which Valentina had struck the ground had
knocked the breath from her lungs, and she couldn't get
it back, not with the heavy weight lying on top of her,
pressing her into the ground. Panic gripped her, and now
her lungs burned with a scream as well as lack of breath.

The kids!

The stroller. Had it been knocked over as well? Or had
the car done that?

It wasn't the car lying atop Valentina; it was a long,
hard body. A familiar body even now, after three years;
she recognized the feel of it pressed against hers. Instead
of savoring the sensation, Valentina shoved at his shoulders, pushing him off. She had to find her babies.

Their babies...

The stroller was still upright, but the girls were crying and reaching out toward her. Fortunately they were
strapped in yet, and while they were scared, they didn't
appear harmed. Tears streaked out of Valentina's eyes.

Cash, who'd rolled off her, vaulted to his feet and
helped her up. "Are you all right?"

She didn't care about herself; she ran toward her children, checking on them. Making sure they were okay. No
scratches. No bumps or bruises. So, thank God, the car
hadn't struck the stroller at all. Cash must have shoved
it out of the way when he'd knocked her down.

"It's okay, it's okay," she murmured to them. Then she turned back toward Cash and asked, "What happened?"

"A black Ford Taurus nearly ran us down," Cash said, but he was speaking into his cell phone, reciting a plate number that he must have somehow been able to read. He wasn't even looking at her. Or the kids.

She didn't want him to; she didn't want him to see her and definitely didn't want him to get a good look at the girls. Most of all, she didn't want to have to explain what she'd done and why she'd kept the secret for so long.

Right now she just wanted to get herself and her daughters safely away from there, far from that car and even farther from Cash.

But as she reached for the handle of the stroller, she heard the deep rev of an engine again and the squeal of tires. And she turned and saw that the black car had started back toward them...

Damn it!

How the hell had he missed?

He'd been so close. Too close to give up so soon. No matter how many people had called 9-1-1, the police wouldn't get there for a few minutes. So he turned around at the next intersection, scraping cars that were parked along the curb as he made that sharp U-turn so that once again he was facing that intersection.

The woman was standing again, right in the middle of the street, next to that big stroller.

Totally focused on his target, he pressed hard on the accelerator and headed straight toward them.

This time he would not miss.

Chapter Three

Cash dived for Valentina and the stroller again, shoving them out of the way even as he drew his weapon and aimed at the vehicle, at the person in the driver's seat, his hands gripping the steering wheel. The person wore a mask, and his hood was pulled tight around his face.

It had to be…

The Landmark Killer.

Cash stared down the barrel of his gun at the masked driver, but then he aimed for the tires and squeezed the trigger. One tire blew and another, but the car continued on, turning sharply with a squeal of rubber slapping against asphalt and another screech of metal as it scraped another car.

Then it sped away, sparks flying from the rims hitting the road.

Even though he'd shot out two of the tires, he couldn't be certain that it wouldn't come back, that it wouldn't try for them again. And the driver was probably armed, too.

Some of the Landmark Killer's victims had been shot.

None of them had been run down.

And none had been women or children. But the killer

wasn't really after them; he was probably only trying to send Cash a message.

People were in danger because of him, because of their special unit's determination to catch and stop the serial killer. And if they stayed on this busy street, more innocent people might get hurt because of him.

"We have to get out of here," he told Valentina. Checking to make sure the black car was gone, he holstered his weapon and reached for the stroller. Instead of pushing it, he picked it up and rushed down the sidewalk toward her building.

Valentina kept pace with him, running either from danger or to stop him from rushing off with the kids, who cried as he carried them.

They had to be terrified, like Valentina obviously was. Her dark eyes were wide with fear and shock. "This way," she said, her voice shaking as she started across the street.

But Cash caught her arm, holding her back, making sure that neither the black Ford nor any other vehicle was careening toward her. When he saw a break in the traffic, he hurried across with her and that stroller.

Once across the street, she ran for a gate, punching in the code so that it opened to a parking lot and the high-rise building beyond it. Then she released a shaky breath as if they were safe. Cash wasn't as convinced. Since the Landmark Killer could send an untraceable text and know so much about him and his siblings, the smart psychopath could probably figure out the code to that gate as well.

They weren't safe just because the gate closed behind them. It could open again. It could let the killer back inside. So Cash didn't slow down and didn't let her slow down, either, until they were inside, up the elevator, down the hall and locked inside her condo.

Then finally he released a ragged breath of relief and his tight grip on the stroller, settling it onto the floor in the narrow foyer.

"It's okay, it's okay," Valentina said, repeating what she'd been telling the kids since the car had nearly run them down. She knelt in front of the stroller and unclipped the belts securing them into their seats. Then she pulled them into her arms, hugging their small, trembling bodies close against her. They were the same height so probably the same age. They were somewhere in that toddler range. Twins? "You're safe now, my babies. We're home."

"Home?" His voice cracked on the word.

They were home? They lived here…with her? But as he noticed the finger-painted and crayon artwork framed and hanging on the foyer walls as well as pictures of them at all different stages of their lives, he realized that they did live here.

With Valentina…

They were hers.

Their hair was a little lighter brown, though, and curly, like his if he didn't get it cut often enough. Then one of the little girls raised her head from Valentina's shoulder and stared up at him with green eyes the exact same shade as his. And his heart contracted as it had when he'd seen that car heading toward Valentina and that stroller.

Were they his, too?

DESPITE BEING HOME, in the place where she'd always felt the safest and happiest, Valentina was scared and on edge. The door was locked. And with their being on the eleventh floor, there was no way a car could come up here and ram into it, like it had tried ramming into them on the street. Not once but twice...

She trembled as she thought of it, of the close call she and the girls had had, but she forced a smile for her daughters. The car was no longer a threat, but Cash was.

He was still here. And she was tense, on edge, because she knew what was to come. Cash had only had a chance to ask Valentina one question, if his just repeating the word *home* in that strangled-sounding voice had actually been a question, before his cell had rung and vibrated loudly in his pocket. With its persistent ringing, he'd had to pick it up. He'd been on his phone ever since, explaining why he'd chosen to leave the scene instead of waiting for the local police to arrive.

To protect them and to protect the other people on the street. With the way the car had kept coming at them, the driver had been so determined that he might have tried again even after Cash had taken those shots at the tires.

Who was the driver? The person who'd sent Cash that text about her?

Her ex-husband hadn't even told her what it had said specifically, just that it had mentioned her and that made him uneasy. He'd warned her that the killer was very dangerous, and she needed to be alert and aware of the potential threat.

But she hadn't been alert and aware since that call,

or at least not enough. She'd been distracted, and if he hadn't showed up when he had today...

She shuddered again, thinking of what could have happened to her daughters. To their daughters.

She struggled to comfort them now. They were clinging to her yet, trembling within her embrace. Or maybe she was the one shaking with fear in reaction to what had happened and over what could still happen when Cash realized what she'd done.

The secret she'd kept.

The secrets...

Luci and Ana.

"Mommy..." Ana whispered, her usually soft voice a little raspy from all the crying she'd done. "Who that man?" she asked, pointing one small hand toward Cash, where he paced in front of the windows, his cell phone pressed to his ear instead of on speaker.

He probably didn't want them to overhear the other side of his conversation. Was he getting yelled at for leaving the scene?

She was grateful that he'd picked up the stroller, that he'd whisked the twins away from the chaos and danger. They'd been scared when he'd picked up the stroller and run with it, but they probably hadn't realized he'd been protecting them. Were they even aware of what had happened? How much danger they'd been in?

Not yet three years old, they were so young, but they were smart and observant, too. And they'd known enough to be afraid when that car had nearly run them down, or as empathetic as they were, maybe they'd just felt her fear.

That fear hadn't left her yet. She'd never been so scared

in that moment when she'd been knocked to the ground and she hadn't known what had happened to the stroller, to the girls.

Her heart ached with that fear, and her arms were starting to ache, too, from holding them so close.

Luci wriggled away from her now and turned around to face her. "Who that man?" she repeated her twin's question, as if Valentina hadn't understood Ana and she'd needed to translate for her sister as she often did.

Valentina understood. She just wasn't certain how to answer it. With the truth...

Or...

"He's an FBI agent," she answered with the most information that she cared to reveal right now and in order to soothe their concerns about him. His having the gun and firing it at the car had probably scared them into thinking he was a bad man, and then he'd picked up the stroller, probably scaring them even more and making them worry that he might hurt them.

She was more worried about his hurting her for keeping them secret from him. He wouldn't physically hurt her; Cash was too gentle a man for that. But he had every right to be furious with her.

"What?" Ana asked.

"What fib?" Luci added her question.

Their little brows creased beneath the fall of their curls. Clearly they didn't understand what an FBI agent was.

"An FBI agent is like a policeman," she explained. "He's a good guy." And he really was. He deserved to have known the truth, that he'd become a father.

But that was a responsibility he'd never wanted to have,

not when he already shouldered more than he could physically handle with his job on that serial killer task force. So when she'd finally figured out she was pregnant, after the divorce papers had already been signed and filed, she hadn't wanted to saddle him with more responsibility, especially one he hadn't wanted.

But she was honest enough with herself to admit she'd acted selfishly, too. She'd known the only way she would ever get over losing him was to have no further contact with him. But as she stared at him now, looking so handsome and serious, his brow creased like his daughters' as he listened to his caller, she knew it hadn't worked. Her heart reacted the way it always had to him, beating faster, fluttering in her chest.

His hair was getting long enough that it was starting to curl, and his beard was longer than he usually had it. But she'd never minded if he hadn't trimmed it. It was soft, and she'd loved it brushing across her face when they'd kissed as well as the other parts of her body that he'd kissed. He'd always been such a thorough lover. She'd never even tried to be with anyone else since the divorce.

She'd told herself that it was because of the girls, because they needed all her time and attention. But it was really because she'd known no other man would compare to Cash Colton.

Despite not seeing him for three years, she wasn't really over him.

She wondered if she would ever be…

ASHLYNN COLTON HAD been so afraid when she'd gotten that call from her brother Cash. As an FBI special agent, he was often in danger; she knew that. But one of her other brothers, Cash's twin Brennan, had recently had some close calls, too. And knowing she could have lost him, like they'd lost their dad, had had them all on edge.

Then Cash had received the next text after Brennan received his. Their cousin Sinead, the FBI profiler, had gotten the first one. But no matter how hard Ashlynn had tried, she'd been unable to trace any of them. They were sent from burner phones and rerouted through ISPs so they bounced off so many towers that she couldn't even pinpoint a location.

New York.

She knew that. It had to be. But she hadn't been able to figure out any more. Frustration gnawed at her over that; she was an FBI tech expert. She should have been able to find out more about the phones, about who'd purchased them.

Should have been able to track down the sender of those damned texts. And maybe if she had, Cash wouldn't have been in the danger he'd been in just a short time ago.

He'd called her from the scene, firing off that plate number to her, but then she'd heard an engine revving and the squeal of tires on asphalt, and she knew the vehicle had returned, the driver coming back after Cash.

Her brother had cursed and disconnected the call. And she'd spent a long while wondering what had happened even as she'd called 9-1-1 for him. Even as she'd run the plate number he'd given her...

"That car was just reported stolen twenty minutes ago," she said now.

The owner had been shopping on Coney Island and

had worried that they'd forgotten where they'd parked. But they hadn't been able to find it anywhere until they'd witnessed it careening down the street toward a young family. That was what they'd said in the 9-1-1 call Ashlynn had "borrowed" from the Coney Island emergency services department.

"Cash?" she asked. "What the hell happened?"

"I told you," he said. "That vehicle tried running us down."

"Who's us, Cash?" she asked, but she had a feeling she knew at least part of it. But family...what did that mean?

Predictably he replied, "Valentina..."

But a man and a woman would have been called a couple, not a family. "And?" she prodded. She could tell there was more, and not just because of that 9-1-1 tape she'd heard and the police report she'd read about the stolen vehicle, but because she knew her brother.

He sounded distracted and upset, and Cash wasn't easily rattled. That text had rattled him, though. He'd never gotten over his ex-wife. None of them really had; Valentina Acosta was so fun and sweet and so good for Cash, who'd tended to work too much and take on way too much responsibility.

Ashlynn wasn't certain why Valentina and Cash had gotten divorced. They'd seemed crazy about each other; they'd had the kind of relationship other people envied. The way they'd looked at each other, the love that had radiated out of their eyes. She'd envied their relationship, but she could also understand why it might not have lasted.

She and all her siblings had a tendency to let the job

consume them. Because of how they'd lost their dad, they understood all too well how hard it was to lose someone you loved to a serial killer in a senseless act of violence that had nothing to do with the victim.

Except wrong place, wrong time...

Was that the case with Cash, though? Or was the Landmark Killer stalking him now even though Cash certainly didn't match the profile of the other victims?

While the Landmark Killer had sent Brennan and Sinead texts, he hadn't made attempts on their lives. Why Cash and Valentina?

"Cash?" She prodded him again when she realized he hadn't answered her yet. "Who else was there besides you and Valentina?"

"Her daughters," he mumbled into the phone.

"Her daughters?" Ashlynn repeated. "Valentina has a couple of kids?"

"Twins," he murmured faintly.

Like him and Brennan. She wanted to ask more, but before she could fire her questions at him, he said, "I have another call coming in, Ashlynn. I need to go."

She hadn't heard anything on the line to indicate that he was telling the truth. She suspected he had another reason for ending the call. He didn't want to give her a chance to ask any more questions about Valentina and her twin daughters.

Why?

Because the answers were too painful for him or because he didn't know them?

"Cash, please be careful," she said. But she was too late. Her brother had already hung up.

He hadn't heard her warning, but she didn't know if he would have heeded it even if he had. Cash had already been intent, as they all were, on catching the Landmark Killer, long before he'd sent that text about Valentina.

Now...

If it had been the Landmark Killer driving the stolen car, then Cash was undoubtedly even more determined. But at what risk and what cost?

The same one their father had paid?

With his life?

Chapter Four

Cash hadn't had another call. But he'd known where the conversation with his sister was heading, to questions he couldn't answer until he'd asked them himself.

But even though another call hadn't been coming in, a knock had come at the door. And, just like Ashlynn, he hadn't had the chance to ask the questions he needed the answers for, of the only person who could really answer them: Valentina.

He wound up answering questions, though, when he opened the door to an officer from the local precinct, the one he'd asked to periodically check on Valentina. This wasn't the officer he'd asked, though; this guy was older than Dave. Probably closer to retirement, whereas Dave Percell was just a couple years older than Cash. Why hadn't Sergeant Dave Percell warned him about the twins? If he'd been watching out for her like Cash asked him to, then Dave had to realize that they were with her all the time so they were hers. That she wasn't the only one in danger because of him.

But he saved those questions while he answered this older officer's questions about what had happened in the street, with the stolen car. He wished Dave had come instead to take the report, but he was off for the day, which was why Cash had felt compelled to check on Valentina himself.

That and he'd just wanted to see her for himself, to make sure she was really okay since he'd had that nagging feeling in his gut that she wasn't. And he'd been right.

He didn't explain all that to this officer, though. Just kept everything quick and impersonal. Or as quick as he could, given that the officer asked Valentina all the same questions he had Cash and then he crouched down to fire those same questions at the kids.

Dave might have done a better job getting the kids to talk since he had five of his own. Cash had known the man a long time; they'd both been up for the same job with the FBI. But Cash had beat him out for it, which Dave had repeatedly assured him was a blessing because he wouldn't have had time for his family if he'd had Cash's job. A family obligation was why he was off today, leaving this loud, awkward officer to take the report.

But the girls were shy. They ducked behind their mother and refused to answer any of the officer's questions. Cash had heard them talking to Valentina while he'd been on the phone with his sister. They'd asked about him. They didn't know who or what he was. And at the moment neither did Cash for certain; he just had his suspicion.

The older officer focused on Cash again. Obviously he knew what case he was working on, maybe because of that damn article in the *New York Wire* or maybe Dave Percell had let him know. The guy asked, "So you think it could be the Landmark..." He trailed off with a glance at the girls and Valentina.

"I'll take them into their room now," she said, probably anxious to get them away from that conversation. Or away from Cash?

But before he could let them go, Cash had to ask, "You're sure they weren't harmed?"

She nodded. "The stroller never tipped over. They're fine. Just scared." Like she clearly still was.

Like Cash was...

"And you?" Cash asked.

He should have asked her that earlier, after he'd pushed her out of the way of the vehicle and they'd hit the asphalt. But she'd gotten right up; she'd run to the stroller. She'd run to her building, keeping up with him as he carried the stroller. So he'd assumed she was fine, and he really hadn't had a chance to ask her before now.

But he could see how mussed her long hair was, and the torn material of one dress sleeve revealed a scrape on her skin. He must have done that when he'd knocked her to the ground.

"Did you get hurt when I pushed you down?" he asked her, his voice gruff with concern and guilt. He hadn't just pushed her; he'd pretty much tackled her.

She shook her head. "No. I'm fine. Really." But her voice had cracked as she made the claim.

And he knew she wasn't fine at all. But before he could challenge her assertion, she turned away from him and the officer and, holding one of the hands of each of the twins, she steered the children through the living room to the short hallway off it.

She'd changed the condo a lot since he'd visited her grandparents with her more than three years ago. Their cold red leather couch had been replaced with a soft, brushed-looking suede sectional, and the glass coffee table was gone, replaced by a brightly patterned cloth ottoman.

Everything about the place looked brighter and warmer and softer...even Valentina, except when she looked at him. If she looked at him...

She didn't even spare him a backward glance as she disappeared through the doorway off the living room.

"So you think it's the Landmark Killer?" Officer Hooper finished the question he'd been asking before Valentina had whisked away the twins.

Cash tensed with fear and dread about the danger his ex-wife and her daughters were in because of him. Because of his job. And were Valentina's daughters his? They looked to be around two or three, not that he was an expert on kids, but that was the age they would be if she'd been pregnant when she left him.

He had to ask her. Had to know...

But right now he needed to focus on how much danger they were in.

"I don't know if it's him," he answered the officer. "We only have a vague description of the Landmark Killer, and with the driver wearing a mask and a hoodie—" which was part of that vague but also very common description of the serial killer "—I can't tell you much about his appearance."

And now that he knew the car had been stolen, it was just another dead end leading to nowhere.

The best lead the FBI special unit had to the killer was the texts he'd sent to taunt them. Because of everything he knew about them personally, they all had realized that he had to be close to them somehow and maybe he was also in law enforcement.

Cash could really only trust his family and a few other select individuals who were either becoming part of the family or had been friends for many years. Like Dave Percell. But maybe it was good that Dave had been off today and out of the area, or Cash might not have been so compelled to check on Valentina himself. He might have sent his friend instead, to make sure she was safe.

She wasn't, and neither were her daughters. He really had to know if they were his, too. And if they were, why she hadn't told him…

"A few other officers stayed behind at the scene to interview pedestrians and shop owners and street vendors who might have seen something, too," Officer Hooper said. "Hopefully they'll come up with something more to go on than…"

A stolen car and a description that could have been anyone wearing that disguise. A man or a woman, young or old. It wasn't enough to prove to the local authorities or to Cash that it had been the Landmark Killer behind the steering wheel. But whoever it was, the person had been so intent on killing that they'd turned around and tried again.

And would they keep trying?

"Will you be staying here?" the officer asked. He'd probably noted that for the report Cash had given a different address for his home than this condo. Though his last name and Valentina's were still the same. Even after the divorce, she'd kept Colton. Was that the girls' last name, too?

He had to talk to her, his gut as tight with dread as it had been when he'd sensed that she was in danger. "I'll let you know," he told the officer as he walked him out the door. As he closed it behind him, his cell vibrated with another call. The sergeant from the local precinct that Cash fully trusted.

"Hey, Dave," he answered.

"I heard about what happened," Dave Percell said. "Sorry I wasn't in the area today."

"How many people knew that?" Cash wondered.

"That I had an appointment in the city?" Dave asked. "A lot of people in my precinct."

So there could be someone even here who could be working with the killer or could be the killer. Maybe that was how he'd known Valentina was sad.

But was she?

She'd been scared, rightfully so, over that car trying to run down her and her daughters. But sad…

"I'm back in Coney Island now," the guy continued. "I can come by…"

"The condo," Cash said. "As soon as you can." Cash had some things he needed to do, but he didn't want to leave Valentina and the girls alone again.

The first thing he needed to do, though, before anything else, was to figure out the truth. Once Dave assured him that he was on his way, Cash disconnected the call and went to find Valentina.

She sat on the floor in a narrow space between two

twin beds. Each bed had a curly-haired twin tucked under a bright pink fleece blanket. The walls were a pale pink, almost blush color, while the curtains were bright pink like the blankets. One girl had a purple teddy bear clasped in her arms, the other a stuffed white bunny.

As Valentina read from a book she held up between them, their eyelids began to droop, falling down over first the set of dark eyes that looked so much like her mother's, and then the others over the green eyes that looked so much like Cash's.

Their little bodies slumped and relaxed, and soft snoring emanated from first one and then the other. And some of the tension eased from his body that they felt safe now.

"They're asleep," he whispered to Valentina who'd continued to read.

She'd probably realized they were out but hadn't wanted to stop reading because she suspected what he was going to ask her. What he had to know…

He waited until she got up from the floor and joined him in the hall, closing the bedroom door behind her, before he asked, "Are they mine?"

She sucked in a breath and stepped around him, walking into the living room. Maybe she hadn't wanted their conversation to wake the twins. Or maybe she was worried about how he was going to react. Or maybe she just had no intention of answering him and that was why she'd walked away from him.

He followed her to where she stood before the windows that looked out onto Coney Island. The myriad lights of the rides at Luna Park sparkled down below. The condo building was close to the amusement park and to the water that glistened beyond the rides, its surface reflecting the last pinkish glow of the sun that must have just set. Days were already starting to get shorter now that summer was slipping away in September.

"Valentina?" he prodded her.

She stood in front of those tall windows, her arms wrapped around herself as if she was cold or, more likely, scared. Of what had happened? Or of his reaction to what she'd clearly kept from him?

His children.

"Are they mine?" he asked again.

As if preparing herself for a fight, she drew in another breath and straightened her shoulders before she turned around to face him. Then she quietly replied, "Yes."

And Cash wished he'd prepared himself for her response, because he felt like he had when that car had come at them. Stunned. Scared. But this time, instead of getting out of the way, he'd let it run him down. The wind was knocked out of him and his heart pounded furiously and for a moment he couldn't breathe, couldn't even think, as if he was in shock.

And, despite the suspicion he'd had when he'd seen the one little girl's eyes, he *was* shocked. He was shocked that he was a father. And he was even more shocked that Valentina had never told him he was.

HER HEART HAMMERING in her chest, Valentina waited for him to yell at her. She'd braced herself for him to react that way with the breath she'd drawn in, the one that burned now in her lungs. She released it in a ragged sigh as she continued to wait for him to do something. Anything...

But he just stood there, the exact same way she'd stood in the street as that car had barreled toward her and the stroller. She hadn't done anything then; she'd been too frozen with fear and shock to react.

Was that Cash's issue?

Realizing that she hadn't expressed her gratitude yet for his saving her and their daughters, she murmured, "Thank you."

He tensed then and stared at her, his green eyes wide with that shock he was obviously reeling from. "Are you thanking me for them?"

"I'm thanking you for saving them," she explained. "And me from that car. That was...that could have..." She could have lost their daughters and her own life if he hadn't been there, if he hadn't reacted as quickly as he had then. Maybe that was why she found it so unnerving that he hadn't reacted now, to her admission that the girls were his, too.

"It's probably my fault that you're in danger," he said. "That text..."

"Did it specifically threaten me? Us?" she asked.

When he'd called her a week ago to tell her about it, she hadn't asked any questions because she'd been anxious to get him off the phone before he overheard the girls chattering in the background. She hadn't wanted him to ask about them like he just had.

He shook his head. "It didn't mention *them* at all. Just my ex-wife..."

She narrowed her eyes, suspecting there was more.

Something he'd left out. "What about me?" She should have asked that a week ago; she probably should have asked to see the text since it had mentioned her. Then she might not have been so shocked today. "Tell me what it said."

He hesitated.

"I have a right to know," she pointed out. "Since it mentions me."

"I had a right to know about them," he replied, his voice gruff with anger.

And she flinched, but she couldn't argue with him. He had had a right to know, and she had struggled with guilt all these years over keeping them secret. "Yes, you did," she conceded.

"Why didn't you tell me?" he asked.

She flinched again and reminded him, "Because you didn't want them."

"I didn't know—"

"You didn't want to be a father," she said. "You made that very clear to me." He hadn't done that until she'd told him she wanted to start their family. With as much as they'd worked, and all the passion between them when he was home, the conversation that they should have had before they got married hadn't happened until it was too late.

He didn't argue with her now, just sucked in a breath as if she'd struck him.

"And when you had your lawyer serve me with divorce papers, you made it very clear that you didn't want to be a husband, either." She wondered then as she had over the course of their three-year marriage and the three years since they'd divorced why he'd proposed, why he'd married her at all, if he'd never wanted the same things she had.

If he'd never really wanted her...

The minute she'd moved out to clear her head, to think about what compromise could work for both of them, he'd served her...as if he'd wanted to make sure that she wouldn't try to come home again.

But she'd been home the minute she'd moved into the condo on Coney Island that she'd loved so much. But not as much as she'd once loved him.

"All you wanted was your job," she pointed out.

Finally he moved then, stepping closer to her, so close that she could feel the heat and tension in his long, lean body. His body was so hard, so muscular that he'd always made her feel so soft and feminine, so sexy, especially when he looked at her like was looking at her now, with all that heat and desire in his green eyes.

"That's not true," he said. "I did want you, all the time."

She closed her eyes as memories rolled through her mind, of his kisses, his caresses, of the passion that had burned so hotly between them. But maybe it had been too hot, and that was why it had burned out so quickly.

Or had it?

She felt the attraction to him that she always had, the tingling in her skin, the rapid beat of her pulse, but maybe that was just fear over what had happened and over what he would do now that he knew the truth.

About their girls...

"I'm staying," he said.

She opened her eyes and stared up at him in surprise. "What?"

"I need to get some things from my place first, but I have a friend from the local precinct coming by to stand guard in the hall until I get back. Dave Percell. Do you remember him?"

She shook her head. She hadn't met many of his work friends. When he hadn't been working, they spent all their time together or with their families.

"But I am coming back, Valentina," he told her.

"You…" She shook her head. "You can't." She wouldn't feel safe with him staying here with her and the girls. She wouldn't feel safe not because she was afraid of what he might do or expect but because of what *she* might do or expect. Like for him to stay…

And it would be even worse if the girls expected that, too, because they would get as disappointed and heartbroken as she'd been.

"You and…" His voice trailed off as his throat moved as if he was choking on something, then he continued. "Our daughters might be in danger because of me. I'm going to stay here to protect you all until this sociopath is caught."

She shook her head. "That's not necessary. We'll be fine without…"

"Without me?" he finished for her. "I guess you were fine the past three years."

But she hadn't been fine without him. Not really. And especially not today. In fact without him, she and the girls might have been killed.

"I see that you've managed just fine," he said. "But this

is different. This is real danger. Surely you had to realize how close a call you had today, that you all had today?"

She shivered and nodded. "Too close."

If he hadn't been there...

She couldn't think of what might have happened to their daughters. To her...

"I just don't understand why this killer would come after me," she said. It wasn't as if Cash was still in love with her, if he'd ever been in love with her. Because if he had, wouldn't they have been able to find a compromise, a way to stay together that would have made them both happy?

He pulled out his cell phone then and pulled up a text that he showed her.

The text...

She skimmed over the line about the actor and read the last part. Tsk-tsk, Cash—murdered daddy and a sad ex-wife.

She bristled with indignation and wanted to deny this sick killer's claim. She wasn't sad. She had her daughters who made every day, every moment, special. A job she enjoyed. A home she loved. And friends...

But she didn't have Cash.

She never really had, though. Because even though they'd shared a bed for three years, he'd never really shared his life with her.

Another text came into his phone. I'm here.

And she let out a little gasp, wondering if that was from the killer as well.

But Cash headed toward the door. "Dave's here. I'll

have him stand guard outside the door. He'll protect you and the girls until I get back."

Who would protect her then, once he returned? Who would protect her from falling for him all over again?

BEFORE BULLETS HAD taken out two of the car tires, the gun had been aimed right at him, and if it had fired then, it could have struck him right in the face. In the mask…

He was so damn glad he'd put the mask on after he'd stolen that car. If only he'd been wearing it earlier, when he'd killed…

But it was too late to undo what had already been done. All he could do was try to fix it now. Like he'd tried to fix it by running them all down.

But that hadn't worked. He stared at the car, that sat lopsided with the two flat tires, in an empty parking lot. He was lucky that he'd managed to keep driving, to get away. He'd had a close escape.

Too close.

He had to be more careful next time. Had to make damn sure that he didn't miss, with the car, or with whatever weapon he chose next.

He had to get rid of this weapon: the car, which had proven ineffective. He had to make sure that there was nothing left inside it that could be traced back to him.

So he dragged in a deep breath of gasoline fumes from the liquid he'd poured all over the seats. The acrid scent burned his nose and throat, making him cough and sputter. He glanced around to make sure nobody lurked in the shadows, in the dark.

Then he lit a match, striking it to a wad of cloth, and

tossed it inside that car, onto the seat. And with a whoosh of air, flames sprang up, burning the upholstery, burning his DNA...

Taking away every trace of him inside that vehicle. But he wasn't done yet. He couldn't leave until he'd accomplished everything he'd promised to do.

Chapter Five

Cash pushed open the door to his apartment to a rush of stale air. He didn't even remember the last time he'd been here. He'd been staying mostly at the office, using the locker room to shower and wearing the clothes he'd stashed in his locker. He'd run out of clean ones, though.

That was why he'd left the office today. To clean up and grab some fresh clothes. But he'd figured, with Dave not working today, that he should drive out to Coney Island first and make sure that Valentina was okay. Especially with that gut feeling nagging at him.

He'd also wanted to find out if she really was sad. He thought of how she'd looked standing at that curb, waiting for the light to change. She hadn't looked sad to him. Beautiful. So damn beautiful…

And distracted maybe…like he was whenever he thought of her.

With being a single working mother, she had every reason to be distracted and stressed and tired.

She was single, wasn't she?

He'd never asked. He'd just assumed, and when he'd told her that he was staying at her place, she hadn't told him that he couldn't because she had a partner. Not that he was staying with her in that capacity.

Clearly he'd never really been a partner to her, and all he could offer her right now was protection. Because she wasn't wrong. He hadn't really wanted to be a husband or a father. And if he hadn't fallen so damn fast and so damn hard for her, he wouldn't have even tried to change his mind, to change the plan he'd always had for his future. To catch and stop as many serial killers as he and his team could.

But once he'd met her, at a library in the city, he hadn't been able to imagine his future without her in it. But she'd wanted a future he hadn't been willing to give her.

She had it now. She had the children she'd wanted. She lived where she'd wanted them to move, into the condo where she'd made a warm and comfortable home for her and the girls.

So he should be happy for her. He shouldn't be sad, and he shouldn't be angry and resentful, which was how he felt now, which was what churned inside his empty stomach. He wasn't going to take the time to eat now; maybe he would pick up something on the way back to Valentina's. The pizza she'd always loved from the place down the street.

Unless they'd eaten before he'd seen them walking back to the condo, she had probably not eaten, either. The girls hadn't.

But they must have been so exhausted over their ordeal that they'd fallen asleep without thinking about it. Hopefully they wouldn't think about what happened; they wouldn't have nightmares about it.

He suspected he would, that he would keep seeing that car aiming for them, the driver hell-bent on hurting them or worse. Killing them...

Why?

They certainly were not at all remotely similar to the Landmark Killer's other victims, who'd all been male, as the victims of Maeve O'Leary, the Black Widow, had been. She'd tried to kill a woman, too, though. And since the Landmark Killer obviously idolized her, was that why he'd made this attempt on Valentina's life?

Or hadn't it been him at all?

Cash really didn't know anything about Valentina anymore, if he ever had. He'd always thought she was so straightforward and honest, but she'd kept a life-changing secret from him for three years.

She'd kept his children from him for three years. That anger surged through him again, and he hurriedly packed up some clothes and toiletries into a duffel bag. With its handle clutched tightly in his hand, he stepped out his door, locked it behind him and headed down the stairwell at the end of the hall to the parking garage in the basement.

As he started toward where he'd parked the SUV, he heard a door open and close behind him. Had someone else been in the stairwell?

It hadn't been a car door he'd heard; it had been heavier, like the steel door to the stairs. It could have just been another resident leaving when he was, but when he turned back, he noticed no one walking behind him. Nothing but shadows in the dimly lit concrete structure.

He turned back and continued walking to where he'd

parked the FBI SUV, but then he heard the scrape of shoe soles against the concrete. And he knew for certain that he was not alone.

Someone else was inside the parking garage. Someone who clearly didn't want to be seen.

Cash carefully reached inside his jacket for his holster, pulling out the weapon he'd fired already once that day, and he was prepared to fire again.

To do whatever necessary to get back to his family...

Family.

For so long after his dad's death, that had been just his mom and siblings. That was the only family he'd ever intended to have, so that he didn't leave anyone behind mourning him like they'd all mourned his dad.

The footsteps hastened behind him and he whirled around with his weapon. He wasn't going down without one hell of a fight.

THE GIRLS HAD been fighting so hard to stay awake earlier, but once Valentina had started reading to them, it had been clear how exhausted they'd been from their long day and from that scare with the car and with Cash.

He had frightened them when he'd picked up their stroller and run with it like he'd had earlier. But he'd only been trying to keep them safe. To protect them.

And he intended to move in to do that, to keep them safe. She believed that was his only intention, or she would have definitely refused. But after what had happened, how the car had turned around and come back, she couldn't deny that they were in danger.

From whom?

A serial killer?

Was that who had really been driving that car?

But why come after her and the kids?

Cash's sad ex-wife…

She shivered as she realized this person must have been watching her. Following her…

Why not mention the children to Cash? Because there was no doubt he'd been shocked to learn about them. Maybe that was what the texter had intended, though. For Cash to seek her out and find out the secret she'd been keeping from him.

Was this all some sick joke this person was pulling? Manipulating Cash into contacting her again, into finding out the truth? To hurt him? To rattle him? To distract him from his quest for justice?

She hated that she and her children had become pawns in this game a killer was playing with Cash and his team. That article in the *New York Wire* had mentioned every member of the FBI's special serial killer unit as well as dredging up what had happened to Cash's father.

Murdered daddy…

Sympathy flooded her heart for Cash and his siblings and for her daughters as well. They'd lost their grandfather without ever getting the chance to know him because of a killer. She was the one who'd denied the rest of them knowing the girls.

She felt almost guiltier about that than she did about keeping them from Cash. His mother would have loved spoiling her granddaughters, might even have moved home from Florida where she'd relocated after retiring. And Brennan and Patrick would have struggled to relate to the girls, probably like their father would have, but they would have made the effort because family mattered to them.

And Ashlynn...

Valentina smiled as she thought of the brilliant young woman she'd been fortunate to call her sister for three years. She'd missed Ashlynn the most of her in-laws because she'd always wanted a sister.

But Valentina had known that in order to get over Cash, she'd had to make a clean break from all the Coltons. She hadn't known then that she was already pregnant with two more of them.

And now a killer was after all the Coltons on that special serial killer unit and maybe Valentina as well. And even her daughters?

A cry broke the silence in the condo, startling Valentina into releasing one of her own. She ran to the bedroom, desperate to make sure the girls were okay. When she opened the door, she found Luci wrapping her arms around Ana, as if trying to comfort her as Ana cried, tears streaking down her face.

"What's wrong?" Valentina asked with concern. They'd been through too much today.

Ana pulled away from her sister to raise her hand and point. "Bad...bad..."

"Just a bad dream?" Valentina asked.

Ana shook her head. "No. Bad man..."

Valentina glanced around the room, but there was no monster hiding in the shadows. Just their dollhouse and toys.

But she shouldn't have expected to see anything else.

The only way in or out of the condo was through the door that one of Cash's friends and colleagues guarded.

They had to be safe.

Now.

For the moment.

She crossed the room to join the two of them in Ana's bed, hugging them both close to her. "There's no bad man here," she said. "You're both safe now. Nothing's going to happen to you."

And not just because of Cash protecting them, but because she would do her best as well to keep them safe. From danger and from the heartbreak their own father might cause them.

The heartbreak Valentina had suffered when they'd separated, and then without trying to patch things up, he'd had her served with divorce papers.

She wouldn't let him hurt and disappoint their daughters the way that he had her. While Cash protected them from danger, she would have to figure out how to protect Luci and Ana from the potential heartbreak of getting too attached to him.

Like Valentina had...

So much so that that text hadn't been wrong. She was sad whenever she thought of him, which over the past three years had been all too often. Maybe that was because she saw him every time she looked at their daughters. She saw him in Luci's vivid green eyes and in the curve of Ana's lips when she smiled and with the intensity they both showed when they listened to a story Valentina read or when she told them about something that had happened at the library.

They were such good little girls. So sweet.

They had to be safe.

Ana clutched at her, her chubby fingers grasping the torn sleeve of Valentina's dress and the scraped skin beneath it. Valentina bit her lip to hold back a cry of pain.

"Bad man," the little girl murmured again.

Was she talking about the one who'd been driving the car? Or Cash? Had he scared her too badly when he'd picked up the stroller?

"The man who picked up you two and carried you back here in the stroller, he is a good man," she assured them.

He's your father...

But she couldn't tell them that until she'd talked to Cash, until he'd told her what he planned to do about them. Did he just intend to protect them from this serial killer? Or did he want to be part of their lives?

"Fib," Luci said. "He a fib..."

A lie? Valentina was the one who'd lied, at least by omission. She hadn't told Cash about them, and she hadn't told them about Cash. While they'd been curious when they'd seen other kids with their dads at the day care or on the playground, they'd never asked about theirs. Maybe because he'd never been around...

"Where the fib?" Luci asked.

Then Valentina remembered when she'd told them when they'd been so shy with him when they'd first gotten back to the condo. "FBI agent," she said. "Yes, he's a good man."

"Like a poly man," Ana added.

Realizing the toddler was trying to say policeman, Valentina smiled and nodded. While the twins were very smart for their ages, they also had slight speech impediments that made them a little harder to understand. "Yes."

"Where is he?" Luci asked, and she glanced around the room now like Valentina had.

"He left for a little while," she said, "but he will be coming back soon." She wasn't sure if that was a good thing or a bad thing. But then she heard the sound of male voices, loud male voices, coming from her front door, and she wished he was here now. Inside with them, to protect them like he'd promised her he would because neither of those voices she could hear was Cash's.

Was someone trying to get past the police officer, trying to get inside, to get to her and the girls?

Cash had made her turn the dead bolt behind him when he'd left. But that didn't mean the lock would keep out whoever was out there arguing with the officer. Locks and doors could be broken.

Just like hearts...

Valentina wasn't going to take a chance, not with her daughters. "Let's play hide-and-seek," she told them, infusing fake excitement into her voice; maybe it would disguise the fear she was really feeling. "Let's hide so well that nobody can find us..."

The condo wasn't that big, though; they wouldn't be able to hide for long before they were found.

Chapter Six

Cash's shadow in the dark had never materialized. While he'd heard the person, he hadn't seen him. So he'd taken his time driving back to Valentina's place, making sure he wasn't followed. Not that the person who'd tried running them down didn't know where Valentina lived, or he probably wouldn't have known what street they'd be crossing and when...

He had to have been tracking her. How else would the text writer have known how sad she was?

Unless that had been a bluff. Unless the texter and the driver of the car weren't the same? While Cash couldn't imagine who else it could be, he hadn't wanted to take any chances, so he'd made certain nobody followed him.

And so he'd been gone longer than he'd wanted to be, longer than he should have been, because when the elevator doors opened onto her floor, he could hear the yelling. Two men, voices raised, argued hotly.

"You need to turn around and leave," Dave advised, his voice shaking with fury.

"I need to see Valentina!" the other man shouted. "I need to know what's going on!"

"It's late," Dave replied. "You need to leave."

"I need to know what the hell you're doing here!" the guy hurled back at him.

"Why?" Cash asked the question as he reached beneath his jacket, his fingers close to the gun handle sticking out of the holster. He'd already drawn his weapon too many times today. The first had been as a desperate measure to save Valentina and the girls.

The second had been out of paranoia, probably, since he hadn't actually seen anyone else in the parking garage earlier. Maybe some dumb kid had been about to try to mug him and had quickly changed his mind and career choice when he'd seen the gun. Either way, Cash didn't want to overreact now, especially if this guy had a reason for so desperately wanting to see Valentina. Was he dating Cash's ex-wife?

Cash studied the guy, whose face was flushed as if he'd been drinking or maybe just because he was angry. He wasn't quite as tall as Cash and probably a little older with dark eyes and a mouth drawn into a tight grimace of annoyance.

"Why what?" he asked Cash.

"Why are you so desperate to see Valentina at…" He glanced at his watch. He'd thought it was later than nine; it felt later to him and it had already been dark when he'd driven back over here, dark in the parking garage, too, as if some of the lights had burned out. But nine o'clock on a Friday night wasn't really late, especially not if this man had had plans with Valentina.

A date?

She hadn't mentioned anything earlier, but they'd had

so much else to talk about that it could have easily slipped her mind. Cash felt a small jolt of satisfaction if she'd forgotten her date. And a small stab of jealousy that she might have had one.

But that was crazy. Of course she'd dated over the past three years. She was too beautiful and smart and funny not to have men chasing after her.

Men like this guy?

"Who are you?" Cash asked him. But he wanted more than his name; he wanted to know the man's relationship to Cash's wife. Ex-wife...

The guy looked from Dave to him and back. "The question is what's going on? Why are you two lurking outside Valentina's door?"

Valentina. So they were on a first-name basis.

"How do you know her?" Cash asked, and he wasn't sure he was asking as an investigator or as the man who'd once loved Valentina, who'd been married to her. But they'd been divorced as long as they'd been married, so he really had no right, except that she was in danger and he wanted to protect her. At least that was the excuse he gave himself and he would give her if she asked why he was interrogating her date.

The guy narrowed his eyes. "What's going on?"

"Why won't you answer any questions?" Cash asked. He nodded at Dave, who pulled out his shield and showed the guy.

"The police!" the guy exclaimed. "Oh, my God, why didn't you tell me who you are and what you're doing here?" He asked Dave that question before he turned back to Cash. "And if he's the police, who the hell are you?"

Dave, who'd clearly lost his patience with the guy, snorted. "You have the potential to get in a lot more trouble with him than you have with me if you don't do what I told you to and back off right now."

But the man was bristling with belligerence and stepped closer to them both, closer to the door, as if he was going to shove his way inside. "What's going on?" he persisted, almost desperately. "Is Valentina all right? And the girls? Those little girls of hers?" His face was more flushed now, his eyes looking a bit glassy with unshed tears or maybe inebriation.

Cash didn't know what to think of the guy. "Who are you?" he repeated his question. "And you better damn well answer me or Sergeant Percell here will be booking you—"

"Blake Highland," the guy finally replied, blurting out his name.

"And how do you know Valentina?" Cash asked, and he held his breath now as he waited for the answer, as he had earlier when he'd asked Valentina if he was the father of her twins.

The guy pointed toward a door down the hall. "I live on the same floor. I keep an eye out for her, single mom living alone with those little girls."

They were vulnerable and an easy target for a serial killer and for men like this neighbor of hers. Pushy guys who got pushier when they'd been drinking like this guy must have been. Cash was close enough that he could smell the scent of liquor wafting from his mouth.

Highland shook his head. "Poor Valentina. The dad of those girls is a deadbeat..."

Deadbeat. The word was like a blow to Cash's gut, making him feel physically ill. Deadbeat. This guy probably wasn't the only one who thought so, who wondered why she had no help with the kids, financial or otherwise.

"He's never around. She handles everything on her own," Blake Highland continued. "It's a damn shame. She deserves better. She's a really sweet, hardworking lady and a great mother." His lips curved into a faint smile. "And she's pretty damn hot, too."

Pride stinging from that deadbeat comment, Cash asked, "So is that why you're hanging around outside her door? Why you're harassing her?"

The guy sucked in a breath now like he'd been punched. "No. I saw this guy hanging around her—"

"This guy is a police officer," Cash reminded him.

"So what's happened? What's going on?" Highland demanded to know. "Are they okay?"

Cash glanced toward the door. Were they?

Since he'd heard the arguing the minute the elevator doors had opened, Valentina must have heard them, too, since they were right outside her door.

He reached around Dave and knocked. "Valentina?"

He didn't want to wake the girls, but he couldn't imagine they'd slept through the arguing, either. And he doubted Valentina had gone to bed yet. So why wasn't she unlocking the dead bolt he'd made her turn as he'd been leaving earlier?

There was only one way in and one way out, right? He hadn't checked out the place as thoroughly as he should have before he'd left, but that was what he'd remembered from when Valentina had shown him the condo when she'd first inherited it. She'd been so excited about it, had wanted to live there so badly, but he'd shut her down with the excuse that it was too far from his office and her job at the time. Just as he'd shut her down about starting a family.

She had it anyway.

He knocked harder. "Valentina. It's safe for you to open the door now."

Maybe it was him she didn't want to let back in; she hadn't been thrilled that he'd wanted to stay at the condo to protect them. But she hadn't been able to argue that it wasn't necessary, either, not after that car had nearly run down her and the girls.

He hadn't been there for them the first few years of their lives, but now that he knew about them, and knew that they needed him, he intended to be there now.

If Valentina would let him in…

SHE DIDN'T WANT to let him in again. Not into the condo and definitely not into her life and the lives of her daughters. Their daughters. While they were hiding yet, she could hear them giggling together because, of course, they had stuck together. They never hid separately from each other even when playing hide-and-seek with just her. Even though they didn't know it, they were playing hide-and-seek now with someone else, with whoever she had heard arguing out the door.

Probably Cash's friend and…

She hadn't recognized the other voice. But she identified Cash's the minute he'd joined them. She recognized it now as he called her name and told her it was safe for her to let him in. But it wasn't safe. Even though he claimed he wanted to protect them, she knew that he would eventually wind up hurting them himself. When he left…

Because he would. He wouldn't stay with them here on Coney Island and play happy family; he'd made that clear to her three years ago. So that was why she didn't open the door when he called out to her. She stood in front of it, her fingers on the dead bolt.

"Valentina, are you all right?" he asked, his voice lower as if he knew she was standing there, as if he felt her presence like she felt his.

She'd always been so damn aware of him, so attuned to him and attracted. And because she knew him and his overdeveloped sense of responsibility and protectiveness, she knew he would break down the door if she didn't open it. So she turned the dead bolt and let him in. Again.

He didn't step fully inside, though, just stood on the threshold as if trying to keep her in the condo and the other two men out in the hall. One must have been his friend and the other was one of Valentina's neighbors.

Blake…something; she couldn't remember his last name. She usually tried to avoid him because he made her uncomfortable with the way he looked at her, as he was looking at her now, with that glazed-eye gleam in his eyes. She'd learned over the past three years that some men preyed on single mothers, thinking they would be grateful for whatever attention a man chose to give them. Valentina preferred for men like that to show her no attention at all.

She especially hated how Blake timed his drop-in visits for after the girls were in bed and after he'd been drinking. "I asked you to stop coming over," she reminded him now.

The guy's face flushed. "I saw this person loitering in the hall outside your door, and I was worried about you," he said as if he deserved a medal.

He was one of those guys who wanted everyone else to think he was a good guy, a hero, when he was really just a shallow opportunist.

He was the opposite of Cash, who'd always been reluctant to tell others what he did for a living. He was a true hero who didn't want anyone to know that he was.

Maybe for reasons like this...

So his *sad ex-wife* didn't get threatened.

"I'm fine," she insisted.

"But something must have happened for the police to be here. Are the girls okay?"

As if he really cared. He never paid them any attention when they saw him in the hall or elevator.

"They're fine," she insisted. But she wondered how long they would stay hiding before they came out to see who was at the door. "You have no reason to worry about me."

The guy looked from the police officer to Cash again. Then he remarked, "You never told me who you were. Another cop?"

The other man, who must have been Cash's police friend Dave even though he wasn't in a uniform, snorted. "He's FBI, man."

Valentina swallowed a groan, fearing her neighbor's reaction to that news.

His eyes widened. "FBI? What the hell's going on,

Valentina? You gotta let the co-op know if you're putting all of us in danger."

She did not need to get in trouble with the co-op board. Several of her neighbors had already been upset that a young single mother with active toddlers had replaced the prior owners, the quiet, sweet old couple that were her grandparents. They'd died during the pandemic, as they'd done everything, together, holding hands between their hospital beds.

She'd wanted a relationship like that for herself. Like her grandparents and like her parents who were traveling in their retirement, determined to enjoy every minute of life they had left together.

"Nobody is in danger," she assured Blake. At least not physical danger at the moment.

Blake shook his head, refusing to accept her claim. "The police and the FBI don't get involved unless it's big—"

"I'm her husband," Cash said. Before Valentina could correct him to add the ex, he continued, "You know. The deadbeat dad."

That was what Blake must have called him. But it wasn't Cash's fault that he hadn't been around; it was hers. Would he have come around even if he'd known about them?

Just before she'd left, he'd made it absolutely clear to her that he never wanted to become a father; he never wanted to have a family. She suspected he hadn't wanted a wife, either.

She wasn't sure even now why he'd married her. But they'd had so much passion, and she believed they'd been so in love. At least she had been. And because of that passion and love, she hadn't asked him the questions she should have before they got married. And even when he'd first told her he didn't want kids, she'd figured he would eventually change his mind. That he would want to share their love with children.

"Come out! Come out wherever you are!" a little voice called from the direction of their bedrooms.

A smile tugged at Valentina's lips. She was the one who was supposed to say that when they were hiding. Not the other way around, but sometimes they forgot the rules. Today, of all days, with the car nearly running them down, with Cash saving them, with taking a nap before dinner, they were going to be distracted and confused.

Like she was…

So she didn't protest when Cash slid his arm around her waist and drew her close to his side. "You and your neighbors have nothing to worry about," he told Blake Highland. "There is no threat to anyone in the building." But the way he narrowed his eyes and the hard stare he sent the other man suggested otherwise, especially when he added, "Just remember and respect what Valentina told you, you need to *stop* dropping by."

Blake raised his chin and returned Cash's stare with a hard, resentful one of his own. "Yeah, well, I was only looking out for her like a lot of the other neighbors do."

Valentina acknowledged that some of them did. The ones who'd known and loved her grandparents like she had. They didn't judge or resent her or want to take advantage of her. They even offered to babysit sometimes for the girls when she had to run out quickly for something.

This man she wouldn't have trusted alone with her girls and especially not alone with herself. So she was glad she hadn't pointed out that Cash was her ex, especially when the guy finally turned around and walked away, slightly unsteady on his feet.

Cash turned then to his friend who gave him a sharp nod. "I'll check him out."

"Thanks," Cash said. "And thanks for standing guard until I got back."

"I can stay," Dave offered.

"I appreciate the offer," Cash said, but he shook his head. "But go home. You weren't even on duty today. Enjoy the rest of your evening."

"Thank you," Valentina added, and forced a smile when really she wanted to call him back, wanted him to stay and for Cash to leave.

But Cash had dropped a duffel bag on the floor when he'd stepped inside, and his arm was still looped around her waist, familiarly, possessively. Clearly he was determined to stay even if his friend did.

Of course she could have refused to let Cash back in the condo at all. She could have insisted that they were perfectly safe inside with the door deadbolted. But she didn't feel safe, not after what had happened today, what could have happened to her and the girls. She didn't feel safe with Cash here, either, though.

A soft voice called again, "Come out! Come out wherever you are…"

And she knew it wasn't fair to them or to Cash to keep them apart any longer than she already had. She felt guilty about that, because she'd done so mostly to protect herself. To protect her heart.

But she had believed she'd been protecting the girls, too, from Cash rejecting them or disappointing them. But if Cash hadn't shown up when he had today, she might have lost them forever. She might have lost her own life as well. So instead of pulling away and pushing him out the door with his friend, she leaned against him, grateful for the support of his arm around her, of his strong body against hers.

And she wondered which was the bigger mistake that she'd made.

Never telling him about the girls.

Or letting him stay...

Chapter Seven

Cash could have lost his daughters today without ever knowing they existed. He could have lost them without ever seeing their sweet faces and hearing their soft, giggly little voices.

That knowledge wrapped around Cash's heart, squeezing it so tightly that he sucked in a breath over the sharp pain. He *looked* for them now, opening closet doors, peering behind curtains.

But from the giggling, he knew where they were. Under Valentina's bed…

"Come out, come out wherever you are." He said it now like they had called out just moments ago.

Valentina had tried to pull away from him to find them, but he'd held on to her a moment longer because her body had felt so damn good against him. Her warmth, her softness and the sweet scent of her honeysuckle perfume had overwhelmed him, and he hadn't wanted to let her go.

Again…

But he was the one who released her, just as he had three years ago. "Wait," he'd said, before she could rush off toward the sounds of giggling. "Let me find them."

"You might scare them," she'd warned him. "They're really very shy."

"You told them that I'm a good guy," he'd replied. "Remember?"

And her face flushed as if she was embarrassed or maybe frustrated. Did she consider him a good guy? Or did she hate him for refusing to compromise in their marriage and for divorcing her when she'd left?

She must hate him, or she would have told him about her pregnancy. She would have let him be a father to the child, children, she was carrying. Unless she'd really believed that he would reject them, that he wouldn't want to be a part of their lives.

He had missed so much of that already. And he should hate her for that, but he couldn't. He understood her reasons, which were the very reasons he had given her for ending their marriage.

Because he hadn't wanted to be a father...

When she'd first brought up starting a family, he'd used the explanation he'd heard other childless people use: *I don't want to bring a child into such a dangerous and evil world.*

As an FBI special agent in the serial killer unit, he knew better than most just how evil and dangerous the world was. And after today, after she and the girls had nearly been killed, Valentina had to realize that he was right.

But the girls were here now. So all he could do was his very best to keep them safe. Tears had stung his eyes, and he'd implored her, "Let me find them."

Her dark eyes had glistened as she'd nodded. "Okay."

And so he'd followed the sounds of giggling through the living room to the short hall. He passed the open door to their very pink bedroom and pushed open the one that had been left ajar to Valentina's room.

It smelled like her, like honeysuckle and sunshine, but the walls and bedding and furniture were all white. The color was in the pillows and the decorations, which were all bright pops of orange and deep green like the shag rug on the dark wood floor. He dropped down onto it and peered under the bed.

Two sets of eyes stared back at him. The dark ones that were so like Valentina's and the green eyes that were so like his. He opened his mouth to talk to them but realized that he didn't even know their names.

And they didn't know his. They didn't know that he was their daddy.

"You da fib," one little girl murmured as she worm-crawled toward him.

"Da fib?"

"FBI," Valentina said from where she stood in the doorway, as if she hadn't trusted him alone with their daughters. "Remember, we told them who you are."

"I want to tell them what else I am," he said, his heart pounding so hard and fast that it was as if it was going to burst if he didn't then reveal that he was also their father.

"You and I need to talk about that first," she said.

Did she not want them to know?

Why?

But then he realized she was worried that he wasn't going to stick around, that he would disappoint and let them down like he had her during their marriage. And that worry settled heavily in the pit of his stomach; he didn't want to hurt them, either.

"Do you wanna hide now?" the little girl asked as she rolled out from beneath the bed.

It was the one with the green eyes that matched his. Her twin crawled closer but stayed under the bed yet and a little behind her sister, as if she was shy or scared.

He didn't want them to be scared of him or of that bad man, but he didn't want to lie to them, either. "Not yet," he said. "But I will take a turn another time." He was going to be there a while, which would give him time to get to know his daughters. But he wanted even more to catch the Landmark Killer than he already had.

He had more of a reason to catch him now that the psychopath had threatened Cash's family. But had it really been the Landmark Killer who had come after them?

Why would he have gone after two little girls and their mother? Unless their names somehow would help him spell out his idol's.

"What are your names?" he asked them.

"Luci," the green-eyed one replied.

"Luciana," Valentina added. "And Ana."

There were an *L* and two *A*s in Maeve O'Leary's name, but the girls definitely didn't fit the description of the other victims: blond, blue-eyed men in their thirties. Maybe nearly running them down had just been a warning to Cash, intending to make him back off from the investigation, which was probably what he'd intended with that text: to distract him. But trying to run down the girls and Valentina had taken it much further. Unless the driver behind the wheel of that stolen car hadn't been the serial killer and maybe had had nothing to do with the Landmark Killer at all.

Whatever the driver's motivation was, the girls were definitely in danger.

"Luciana and Ana," he repeated, and turned back toward Valentina. "Your grandmother and mom's names."

"Ana's middle name is Michaela for your dad," she said.

A pang of loss struck his heart. Over her honoring his dad, Michael, in that way, and because he'd had no part in naming them. He cleared his throat and asked, "And their last name?"

While she'd honored his father, had she made it clear that Cash was their father? Or had she intended to keep him entirely out of their children's lives?

"Acosta—"

He sucked in a breath.

"Acosta Colton," she finished.

"Casa Colton," Ana murmured, and her eyelids were beginning to droop, her little chin dropping back onto the carpet. She'd scooted half out from under the bed but was still partially beneath it. Maybe she felt safer there after what had happened today.

The car. The loud voices in the hallway.

Luci was sitting on the floor next to him, and she reached out and touched his hand. "Did you get 'im?"

"Get who?" Cash asked, and he reached out to tickle her tummy. "You? I got you…"

She giggled and wriggled away from him. "Not me. I not bad. Did you get the bad man?"

Cash tensed. "Bad man?" Had the little girls witnessed

But how could she not? Didn't the world need more good in it to combat that evil, to fight it like he was fighting it?

And her children were so good, so sweet. And while it wasn't their reason for crying, they were tired and hungry right now, too. She could hear one of their bellies rumbling, and an echo of it coming from the other one.

"Okay, you two, go wash up, and I will make us something to eat."

"'roni and cheese," Ana requested.

"Pancakes," Luci said.

"Pancakes for beckfast?" Ana queried with a giggle snort.

"Dinner, too," Luci said.

Sometimes they did have breakfast for dinner, but Valentina was already worried about Cash judging her parenting so she wanted to fix something healthier, especially as they were going to bed soon.

Fortunately she had some leftover turkey tetrazzini that would heat up fast and that the girls actually loved. While they headed into her bathroom to clean up, she stepped into the hall where Cash was leaning against the wall.

She pressed a hand to her heart, which pounded fast with surprise. "I didn't know you were standing there. I thought you had a call…" She'd suspected then he'd used it as an excuse to escape from his crying daughters.

His face flushed a bit. "It was Ashlynn. I need to call her back."

But clearly he'd been waiting to do that.

"Are you going to tell her…about them?" she wondered. She'd loved Cash's family and would have loved to maintain relationships with them after the divorce, but it had been easier for her to cut ties with all the Coltons completely. She'd figured it was the only way she would get over Cash.

She wasn't sure that it had worked, though, because her heart hadn't slowed from its frantic beating. Maybe that wasn't because of him but because of the situation. The entire dangerous out-of-control situation.

"Before I tell any of my family about them, I want to tell the girls first," he said. "I want them to know that I'm their father."

Valentina's heart rate quickened even more, and panic overwhelmed her, making it hard to breathe. "I—I…" She couldn't deal with this right now. "Not tonight," she implored him. "It's getting late. They haven't eaten yet, and they need to go back to bed and sleep."

And hopefully not wake up with another nightmare like the one Ana had had earlier during her brief nap.

He levered himself away from the wall then and stepped closer to her, so close that she could feel the heat and strength of his body. A body she'd once loved so much…

She'd loved his strong arms wrapped around her, holding her close. His chest where she would lay her head to sleep at night, on the nights he hadn't spent in the office, working on some case, on finding some killer.

That was all he was doing here: working. Protecting them from one of the serial killers he'd devoted his life to hunt.

"This feels like you're stalling, Valentina," he said.

"Don't you think three years was long enough to do that? Or did you never intend to tell me at all?"

She really wasn't sure. Maybe when the girls asked, she would have told them then. And if she'd told them, she would have had to let him know as well in case they'd wanted to meet him.

Or maybe not...

She shrugged.

"Do you hate me that much?" Cash asked. "That you would purposely keep them from me?"

No. That was the problem. She'd loved him too much. Too much to ever get over him if she'd had to see him regularly over the years.

But even as much as she'd loved him, she loved her daughters more.

"I was just trying to do the same thing you're trying now," she said.

His brow furrowed. "What?"

"To protect them."

He flinched. "I would never—"

"Not purposely," she agreed. "But you would..." Just like he had hurt her.

"Valentina..." He stepped even closer then until their bodies touched, and his tensed.

Hers softened with desire. A desire she hadn't felt in so many years. Since Cash.

She stared up at him as he stared down her, and the way he looked at her was how he used to, with so much desire, with so much...

No. She couldn't think it was love, not now, or he

wouldn't have divorced her as quickly as he had. He would have tried to work things out.

Maybe it was just lust, and maybe that was all she was feeling, too. That had her pulse racing, was making it hard to breathe and had heat rushing through her.

He was so damn handsome, and she wanted to reach out, wanted to skim her fingertips over the softness of his beard. She wanted to feel that against her face, his lips pressed to hers...

He might have wanted it, too. His chest was moving as if he was having trouble breathing. He started to lean down, lowering his head toward hers.

But then little giggles rang out from the bathroom with the sound of splashing. And his cell phone vibrated again.

"You better take that," she said. "And I better save my bathroom..." She stepped around him to head back into her bedroom. But she stopped just inside the door, her legs, and she needed a moment to collect herself and to remind her that he was only here because of a killer.

ASHLYNN'S HAND WAS shaking as she held her ringing cell. If it went to voice mail this time, she was going to go to Valentina's condo. That had to be where Cash was since his cell phone was pinging off a tower on Coney Island. She was close, had ridden with their brother Patrick out to this scene, this abandoned parking lot.

She was scared, but not for herself. She was scared for Cash and Valentina and the girls.

Were they okay?

Had something happened?

"Hey."

Cash's voice suddenly emanating from the speaker startled her, and Ashlynn nearly dropped her phone. "Thank God," she murmured. "I thought something had happened..."

"Not here," he said, then cleared his throat as if it was a lie he was having trouble swallowing.

"Fib..." A child's voice emanated from Ashlynn's cell now, as if a kid was calling out Cash on his lie.

One of her daughters. Had they already bonded with Cash enough to call him a liar? "You're at Valentina's?" she asked, just to confirm.

"Yeah, I'm going to be staying here for a bit to make sure nothing happens to her or the twins."

The twins? Not *his* twins. Did he know? She did; after talking to him earlier, she'd pulled their birth certificates. Maybe he did know; maybe that was why he was staying there to protect them.

"That's good," she said. Because they needed protection. She drew in a sharp breath, then coughed and sputtered as the smoke burned her throat.

"Where are you?" he asked her. "And why are you calling?"

She glanced around the parking lot of the abandoned warehouse. It didn't look all that abandoned now with firefighters and police officers and crime scene techs hovering around the smoldering metal of a burned car.

"I think we found the car that was used to nearly run you down," she said.

Cash's ragged sigh of relief rattled the cell speaker. "That's great. Thank God. What did you learn? Any prints? DNA?"

She sighed now. "No. And whoever it was made sure that there wouldn't be anything left behind to trace back to him. He torched it."

"Sometimes there is still a print or something…"

"Sometimes," she agreed. "But according to Patrick, this was a hot fire with a lot of accelerants." As cohead of the FBI's CSI, he was the expert. He could have trusted someone else to come out, but he'd wanted to check this out himself because it involved Cash. He was suited up, checking out the burned shell of that car. "I don't think we'll find anything. Whoever this is, they know what they're doing, Cash. They're professional."

"A hit man?" he asked. "Is that what you're saying?"

"Just someone who's done this before," she said. Like a serial killer determined not to get caught or someone in law enforcement who knew the ins and outs of investigations. "Or has been on the other side of this."

"One of us," Cash murmured.

"Law enforcement maybe," Ashlynn admitted, although she didn't want to believe someone within the FBI or a local precinct could be responsible for murders. "You need to be careful," she told him.

"You, too."

She hadn't gotten one of those texts that her twin brothers and her cousin Sinead had received. But none of them had fit the description of the killer's victims. He was fixated on blond men. Those were the victims whose lives he'd taken.

So why go after Valentina?

Just to mess with Cash? Or was there someone else after her for another reason?

"Have you talked to Valentina over the past three years?" she asked. If he'd known those kids were his, he would have. Wouldn't he? "Do you know what she's been doing?"

While Brennan had received a weird text like Cash had, it hadn't been the Landmark Killer who'd gone after the woman Brennan had been falling for but someone else who'd wanted to kill her and very nearly had.

"Could there be someone else after Valentina?" she asked. "Someone who might want to hurt her?"

"Valentina?" he asked, as if the thought of anyone wanting to hurt her was inexplicable.

It was to Ashlynn, too. "You know the world we live in," she reminded him. "Dangerous people go after innocent people all the time. They actually seem to prey on them."

He made a strange, strangled sounding noise...either a grunt of agreement or a gasp.

"Gobble, gobble," a little voice murmured out of the speaker. "Turkey for beckfast."

Cash chuckled then.

That was a sound Ashlynn hadn't heard him make in way too long. She smiled. The kids sounded adorable, and knowing how beautiful Valentina was, they were probably cute. And they were Coltons, too. For some reason Coltons seemed to attract danger.

Her heart rate quickened. "Cash—"

"I have to go now," he cut her off. "Let me know if you find anything more out about the car."

Then he disconnected the call, leaving Ashlynn as scared as she'd been when he first hadn't picked up. Even now that she knew where he was, she wasn't convinced that he was safe...that he, Valentina or her nieces would ever be safe until this killer was caught.

Chapter Eight

Cash dreamed of danger, and not from careening vehicles or gunshots but from giggling little girls. And their mother.

Beautiful, patient, so very good with them during dinner and throughout their baths and then tucking them into bed with those stories again.

He dreamed of every moment, savoring it, as he considered all the moments he'd missed. And that hurt so damn bad.

That was the danger. Wanting this forever...

Wanting them forever.

But if Valentina still wanted him, she wouldn't have signed those divorce papers and kept his children from him. While she'd let him spend the night, on the couch, he knew it was just because she wanted to keep the girls safe as badly as he did.

She wouldn't take any chances with their well-being, which was why she didn't want to tell them who he was. Their father...

She didn't trust him.

He could understand that; he trusted few people himself. Even now he wasn't sleeping deeply. He stayed aware enough to notice the shift in the air around him, the faint vibration of footfalls on the floor beneath the couch on which he lay. And he felt the intense gaze of someone watching him.

He reached beneath the blanket that Valentina had given him, touching the handle of the gun in the holster he wore. He hadn't taken off his clothes or his weapon, worried that he might need to act quickly if something happened. If that person came for them again...

A pro.

Ashlynn had warned him that was what she and Patrick thought the person was: a professional criminal. Killer. Or someone with inside knowledge of investigations. His unit had already determined that about the Landmark Killer, that he had to be close to them.

Too close...

Like whoever was watching Cash sleep.

Then he heard a little giggle, and a smile tugged at his lips as he opened his eyes. The twins were standing at the end of the couch, peering over the arm at him. And behind them stood Valentina, her beautiful hair mussed, her face flushed from sleep and maybe because she'd been staring, too. Like she'd stared at him last night when they'd been alone in the hall and he'd been so tempted to kiss her...and he might have if the girls hadn't started giggling.

"Mornin', seepy head," Luci greeted him.

And he chuckled. They were so cute.

"You seeped over," Ana added.

He wanted to scoop them up and hold them close like

Valentina had last night as she'd comforted them. He didn't know how to do that, how to interact with them naturally. While he wanted to blame Valentina for that, for denying him a presence in their lives, he knew that was on him. He'd never been good with kids.

"You probably didn't get much sleep on the couch," Valentina remarked.

He shoved his fingers through his hair, which felt like it was standing on end. "It wasn't the couch." He'd not slept well for so many other reasons, the biggest one being so close to her again.

Seeing her...

Smelling her...

Wanting her as passionately as he always had.

But she was in danger even as his ex. If they were to-gether...

She would be in more danger, and so would Cash. He would be in danger of disappointing the girls just as he had her so many times. Late for dinner. Canceling an-niversary trips.

Not making her feel as special as she deserved to feel. She was so beautiful, even with the dark circles beneath her eyes that hinted at her not getting any more sleep than he had.

She touched her face, as if self-conscious of his staring. Then she turned away and headed toward the kitchen. The girls stayed behind, still studying him over the arm of the couch. And his heart yearned to tell them the truth.

He wanted them to know who he was, what his rela-tionship to them was. "We never had that conversation I wanted to have," he said to Valentina as he got up from the couch and folded the blanket he'd used.

He heard her suck in a breath and she peered at him over the kitchen island, her dark eyes imploring him. "Let me get some coffee first."

The kitchen was in a corner of the open space that encompassed the living room and dining room, too. The cabinets were white and so were the counters, but like her bedroom, there were pops of color in the reclaimed glass backsplash and in the teal pots and pans that dangled from a copper pot rack over that counter. There was also a teal coffeepot, which was currently brewing, and other small teal appliances.

He smiled. "You're still not a morning person?"

She glared at him. "No. But these two are, like you always were."

Were they like him? If so, it had to be from genetics, since he hadn't been part of their lives. He hadn't been able to nurture them.

But it was clear that Valentina had.

They joined her in the kitchen. "Helping" her with "beckfast," which was pulling boxes of cereal from a cupboard and a bag of bread from the counter. A small step stool was pushed against the cupboard, and they both tried to climb onto it to put bread in the toaster.

Valentina moved around them, moderated their argument and made the breakfast as if performing a waltz. With grace and patience and affection...

She was a great mother. The mother he'd always suspected she would be. That was why he'd filed those divorce papers, so that she could have this family she'd always wanted. The family he hadn't wanted to give her.

But yet he had. And he wasn't sure what to do about it, what to do about this feeling of being on the outside looking in...like he was Scrooge and a ghost was showing him what his future could have been had he made better choices.

At the time, he'd thought he'd done the right thing. But now, he had no idea what to think and worried that if he didn't protect them from the danger they were facing, he was going to see the consequences of bad decisions and of bad things happening to Valentina and the girls.

Because of him.

WHILE VALENTINA HAD made breakfast, Cash insisted on cleaning up with the girls. She could hear the deep rumble of his voice and their giggles as well as the rushing water of the faucet.

Her heart had yearned for this for so long, to have this family with him, share these moments with him and their children. But when she'd told him she wanted to have children, he'd used his job, hunting serial killers, as an excuse not to have a family, not to give her what she'd wanted. So it was kind of ironic that he was only here now because of the serial killer's implied threat, not because Cash wanted to be here.

Not because he wanted to be with her and their daughters.

She wasn't sure what he wanted. The way he looked at her, with all that heat in his green eyes, reminded her of the past, of the passion that had burned so hot between them. So hot that it had probably been inevitable they would get burned alive from it.

Her knees trembled a bit, and she leaned back against the wall of her bedroom, next to the open door through which she eavesdropped. She didn't entirely trust him not to tell the girls that he was their father.

And she couldn't really blame him if he did. She had denied him his rights for too long already. To continue to put off the moment of truth was probably unfair to him and to their children. She just didn't know how to tell them, how to explain what she couldn't even really explain herself.

But maybe it was better to do it now, before the girls were old enough to understand what she'd done and hated her for it. Like Cash probably hated her...

She heard more giggling, louder, closer, and footsteps running. She forced a smile, expecting the girls to burst into her room as they always did, but the running stopped at their bedroom and the door slammed shut. She stepped away from her wall to go out and see what had had them running like that, but a big, hard body blocked her doorway.

"Oh…" She nearly slammed into Cash's chest. The T-shirt he wore beneath an open-collared shirt was molded to every muscle of it right now, the cotton soaked. His hair was wet, too. "I thought you were washing the dishes." She tried to fight the smile tugging at her mouth.

"Apparently I looked like a dirty mug," he remarked with a grin. He touched his beard, which looked as damp as his hair and shirt.

She found herself giving in to the temptation she'd

fought last night, and she reached out, running her fingers over the damp, soft hair of his beard and over the rigid jaw beneath it. "Your mug looks pretty clean now," she murmured. And just pretty...

She'd always thought he was one of the most attractive men she'd ever seen, since that first day he had walked into the library where she'd worked in Manhattan. He'd been looking for something, some obscure book written by a suspected serial killer.

She'd found it for him. Even after he'd caught and put away that serial killer, he'd kept coming back to see her, and they'd started dating. They'd only been going out for a little while before he'd proposed, and they'd had their whirlwind wedding on Coney Island.

She blinked against the sudden sting of tears in her eyes as she remembered the beauty and promise of that day. How naive she'd been to think they would live happily ever after...

"What's wrong?" he asked, and his hand covered hers on his face, holding it there against his beard.

"What's right?" she asked. "I feel like that car hit me yesterday." And had knocked the sense completely out of her so that she wanted to kiss her ex-husband, wanted to be with him like they'd once been.

Happy.

Passionate.

In love...

No. *She'd* been in love. If he'd loved her as much as she had him, he would have tried to make it work, tried to find a way that they could stay together. That was why she'd left, so she could take some time to clear her head and try to figure out what she could give up so she wouldn't have to give him up.

He moved his hands to her arms then, gently running his palms from her biceps down to her wrists. "Your sleeve was ripped. Do you have bruises? Anything feel like it's broken? I should have taken you to the ER to get checked—"

She pressed her fingers over his lips to stop him. "I feel fine. Physically..." That wasn't entirely true, though; she did have bruises and she was sore. "It's just that this feels so unreal, what happened, you being here, it's like a dream..."

"Or a nightmare?" he asked, arching one dark eyebrow.

She'd had both about him. Nightmares where he found out about the twins and was so furious that he threatened to take them away from her because of her being so cruel to keep them apart for so many years. And dreams that he'd been with them the entire time...

"We need to talk about the girls," she said.

"About telling them that I'm their father?"

She nodded. "I don't want to tell them if you don't want anything to do with them. I don't want them to get hurt..." Her voice cracked on that last word with the pain she'd felt when their marriage had ended.

He flinched and closed his eyes as if he was feeling that pain, too. "I don't want that either," he said.

"What do you want?" she asked. "Do you want to be part of their lives? And how would that look? How much time can you give them? More than you gave to us?"

He sucked in a breath as if she'd punched him. And as he stepped back, a door opened and a little girl shrieked.

Ana ran into the hallway, screaming while Luci chased after her, yelling, "Bang. Bang." And she pointed her index finger while pulling back her thumb as if she was pulling a trigger, as if she was shooting her sister.

BRENNAN HAD CALLED an informal meeting instead of an official one since the FBI director, Roberta Chang, was out of town at a conference. She'd considered canceling her appearance at the conference because of the Landmark Killer, but Brennan and the rest of the team had insisted they had it under control.

But they didn't.

Bodies kept turning up. And the notes...

Not just the ones in the pockets of the victims, but the ones texted to him and to Cash. Where was Cash?

Brennan looked around the conference room he'd commandeered for the meeting. But only his sister Ashlynn, brother Patrick and the director's assistant, Xander Washer, were in the room. Ashlynn and Patrick were standing near the entrance, like they were half out the door, while Xander sat in a chair, a pen in his hand as if he was going to take notes for them.

Or more likely taking notes for his boss, who undoubtedly had told the young man to keep her apprised of the investigation. Hell, at the moment, Xander probably knew more about what was going on than he did.

"Where's Cash?" Brennan asked uneasily. Fraternal twins, they didn't quite have that twin-tuition thing where they knew when each other was in danger or anything. But with a serial killer taunting them, it wasn't much of a stretch to think that something might have happened to Cash.

"You didn't hear?" Ashlynn asked.

"About what?"

"Someone nearly ran down Valentina yesterday."

Brennan cursed. He didn't need twin tuition to know how much Cash loved his ex-wife, even now, years after their divorce. "Is she all right?"

Ashlynn nodded. "Yes, Cash was there and saved her. And the car that was used was tracked down last night. It had been stolen right before the attempt."

"And afterward, it was burned," Patrick added. He was the co-head of the FBI crime scene investigation division. "We went over it. No DNA, no prints. No evidence to figure out who stole it."

"Nothing?" Brennan asked, his stomach sinking at the thought of someone else being out there, trying to take out another Colton.

Patrick shook his head. "No evidence, but from the distance between the seat and steering wheel, we can conclude that the last person who drove it was probably close to six feet tall."

Xander's pen moved across the page.

"You probably don't need to take notes about this," Brennan said. "I doubt it has anything to do with the Landmark Killer."

"Why not?" Xander asked. "Didn't Cash get a note about his ex?"

"A text," Ashlynn corrected him. "But this isn't the Landmark Killer's MO. He doesn't use vehicles or go after women and kids."

"Kids?" Brennan asked.

Ashlynn nodded. "Yes, Valentina has twin girls."

"How old?"

"Old enough that I heard them talking while he was on the phone with me," Ashlynn said. "But I don't know anything about kids."

Something about her tone, and the way that she looked away as if unwilling to meet his gaze, had Brennan wondering if she knew more.

"If they were talking," Xander said, "they must be at least a couple years old."

Either Valentina had moved on quickly, while Cash hadn't moved on at all, or...

Those kids were his.

No wonder Cash hadn't shown up at the office today. He'd put work before his marriage and lost his wife three years ago. If those kids were his, he'd probably do whatever he could to make sure he didn't lose them, too.

To a killer, like they'd lost their dad.

But Brennan wondered if it had really been the Landmark Killer going after Valentina. Or someone else, like the person who'd gone after Stella recently.

Did Valentina have an enemy? A stalker? Someone obsessed with her besides Cash?

Chapter Nine

"No bang, no bang!" Ana cried, tears streaking down her face.

Cash bent over to pick her up, but before he could reach for her, Valentina pushed him aside and picked up the toddler herself. Didn't she think he was capable of comforting a crying child?

"Your holster," she whispered at him. "They must have seen your weapon."

He'd made a point of keeping his shirt over it, but maybe when they'd been washing dishes, they'd caught a glimpse of it, especially when they were spraying water at him. He didn't know if they'd noticed it, but with as bright and observant as they were, they probably had. Or maybe they remembered him drawing it in the street and shooting at that car if they'd been able to see that from their stroller.

Since he couldn't comfort Ana, he reached for Luci instead, catching her shoulders and stopping her from mock-shooting her sister, who was clearly terrified. "Hey, no bang bang here," he said.

He and his siblings hadn't even played cops and robbers growing up like other kids had because, as the kids of an officer, they'd known how serious crime and how dangerous guns really were. Knowing that, they'd all wanted to be in law enforcement, like their dad, even then. And after his death, they'd been even more determined, which had probably broken their mother's heart.

Celeste Colton never said that, though, had never discouraged them from their careers. But maybe that was why she'd moved to Florida some years ago, to remove herself from the front-row seat to their dangerous professions. News of the Landmark Killer had probably made it to West Palm Beach, though, and if not through the media, then through one of his siblings' weekly calls to her.

He would have a lot to tell her on his next call. That is, if he could convince Valentina to let him tell the girls first that he was their father. But now she blamed him for their violent playing.

"Pretending to shoot someone is not a good game to play," he told Luci.

But the little girl stared up at him with a blank expression in her green eyes. She clearly had no idea what he was talking about. And she was too young for him to try to explain.

"You scared your sister," he pointed out, hoping that would get through to her.

"Bang bang," she said. "The bad man go bang bang."

The bad man hadn't shot at them, though. He'd driven a car at them. "Did you see that on TV?" he asked. "Is that what you're talking about?"

She shook her head, tumbling curls around her face.

"I don't let them watch shows like that," Valentina said, her voice sharp as if she was offended that he would think she had.

"Even cartoons are violent nowadays," he said, which was one of the many reasons he'd given her for why he hadn't wanted to bring children into the world. It was too full of violence.

But she'd countered that was why good was necessary, to counteract the bad. If only that was how it worked...

"They must have seen your weapon," she insisted. "When you shot at the car."

That had all happened so quickly that Cash couldn't recall where everyone had been and what they might have seen. His focus had been on stopping that vehicle from hitting them.

"Am I the bad man then?" he asked. He certainly had been in their marriage, the one who'd denied her what she'd wanted. His time and a family.

Luci reached up and touched his face. "The fib..."

He was so much more, but now he worried that Valentina might never let him tell them. Of course that didn't mean he couldn't tell them himself. But he didn't want to upset her either, especially when she had valid concerns that he might disappoint and hurt them. He was concerned about that, too, with that sick feeling in his gut again.

"You two are soaked," Valentina remarked.

Three, if she'd included him.

"You were supposed to wash the dishes, not yourselves," she said. "Go back to your rooms and change into dry clothes. Then bring me your wet pajamas and

I'll put them in the dryer." She set Ana on her feet and she and Luci ran back into their room, their earlier scuffle forgotten.

By them...

It was clear from the tension gripping Valentina and the line between her eyebrows that she was worried.

"I didn't show them the gun," he said quietly. But he couldn't swear that they hadn't seen it, and she knew that as well.

"I don't want them getting hurt," she said, and she stepped into her bedroom and gestured for him to follow her. She probably didn't want the girls to overhear this conversation.

Because she didn't want them to hear any more about the gun? Or about his being their father?

"By whoever tried running them and you over or by me?" he asked.

"Both," she said.

"I don't either," he said. "But I feel like they should know who I am to them. Something I should have known before this, too."

Her face flushed, and she dropped her gaze down to her hands, which she twisted together now that she wasn't holding their daughter. "I know."

He hadn't expected her to admit that.

"But you told me you didn't want kids," she reminded him. "So I didn't think you would want to know, that you would want to be responsible for something you never wanted..."

A pang struck his heart; it hurt him that she'd thought he would reject his kids. That he wouldn't want them.

Because even though he didn't know them, he was falling for them as hard and quickly as he'd fallen for their mother when he'd met her. He'd loved her so much that he'd ignored the decisions he'd made so long ago about never getting married and focusing only on his career. But when she'd been unhappy with him being gone so much and missing holidays and anniversaries and canceling planned vacations, he'd known he'd made a mistake.

That he'd been selfish then. Was it selfish now to want the girls to know he was their father if he couldn't figure out how to give more of himself to them than he had their mother?

VALENTINA HELD HER breath as she waited for Cash to say something, anything to indicate that he wanted to be a father to their daughters. That he didn't regret her having them. That he could love them like she loved them.

Like she'd once loved him. Because she'd loved him, she hadn't wanted to hurt him just as she didn't want him hurting the girls. But she had, by keeping the girls from him and how she'd just reacted.

"I'm sorry," she said. "I should have told you the minute I learned I was pregnant." She had a lot of excuses why she hadn't; excuses she'd already given him to justify what she'd done. She'd been giving herself those same excuses the past three years, but she knew she'd acted selfishly.

He didn't say anything, didn't acknowledge her apology at all.

She knew it wasn't enough to make up for the years of their daughters' lives that he'd missed. She would never be able to compensate for that, and guilt swirled around her stomach with all the coffee she'd drunk to wake up after she'd spent the night before reeling from everything that had happened.

"And I shouldn't have blamed you for the bang-bang thing," she added. "They could have picked up something at day care. Anywhere, really..."

He continued to just stare at her, as if not following what she was saying. And that unnerved her. That stare. And how his wet shirt molded to his chest.

Nerves and attraction getting to her, she continued to ramble out more apologies. "And I'm sorry that I haven't let you change and put your shirt in the dryer—"

As she had earlier, he pressed a finger to her lips. "Shh, it's okay."

She had a feeling that he wasn't talking about everything she'd done and had just apologized for doing. Probably just the shirt...

Especially when he stepped back and shrugged off the one he wore over the wet T-shirt. Then with a glance at the door, he quickly took off his holster and reached above her armoire, setting it atop there and well out of the reach of the little girls. Then he lifted his T-shirt over his washboard abs and then over his chest.

Valentina's pulse raced as her skin heated. She'd never wanted anyone the way she'd wanted him. He was so sexy, with lean muscles lightly dusted with dark hair. Soft hair...

Hair that had tickled her skin when she'd lain in his arms, her body against his body. Touching everywhere...

She wanted to touch him again like that, wanted to be close to him, wanted to kiss him.

And maybe he saw that desire on her face, because he stepped close to her again. Almost involuntarily, she reached for him, sliding her hands over his chest like she had so many times before. She loved how the soft hair tickled her skin.

He leaned down, his head close to hers, and she rose up on tiptoe just enough that her mouth brushed across his. He wrapped his arms around her, pulling her closer as he kissed her back, deeply, passionately.

He tasted sweet, like the syrup from the pancakes, but he acted like he was hungry yet, like he couldn't get enough of her mouth, of her kisses.

And she kept kissing him as she ran her hands over his chest. His heart beat hard and fast beneath her palm. And he panted for breath, like she panted.

"Mommy!"

Startled, she jerked away as Cash stepped back. And they both whirled toward the doorway where two little girls stood, staring at them in shock. They'd never seen her kissing anyone before.

She hadn't dated since the divorce; hadn't found anyone that sparked her interest enough.

Because no one could ever be their father.

HE STARED DOWN at the gun that he held in his gloved hand, the gun that had taken so many lives. He needed another gun. One that couldn't be traced to other crimes.

So many other crimes…

He'd gotten sloppy.

Complacent.

That was what had gone wrong yesterday.

It had gotten too easy for him to kill. And he'd begun to take it for granted that he would never be caught. That there was no way anyone could identify him. But that had been before yesterday.

Before…

He couldn't miss again. And with a gun, he had a far better track record than he had with a car. That had been so damn sloppy yesterday; he was lucky he hadn't gotten caught or shot then.

With the gun, he wouldn't miss the next time. He just had to wait for another chance to present itself. And he wasn't sure when that would be…

When they would be as vulnerable as they'd been yesterday.

But eventually, if he watched and waited, the moment would come, and he would be ready. He would make certain that he ended it this time. And that there would be no way to trace any of his crimes back to him.

And nobody around to identify him.

Chapter Ten

Cash's body went from hot to cold. One minute he was burning up with desire for Valentina, his skin on fire wherever she touched him, and the next...

"Mommy!"

The word hit him like a bucket of ice. And it must have hit her just as hard because she jumped back, away from him, as if he was the one who'd thrown the cold water on her.

The girls looked just as stunned as they stared at him from the doorway, their eyes wide. He grabbed his button-down shirt and thrust his arms in the sleeves. Clearly they weren't used to seeing their mother kissing shirtless men. That tension inside him eased some, but then he felt a pang of guilt as well.

He'd divorced her so she could move on and be happy. So she would find the happiness she deserved. The family she'd wanted...

He hadn't figured on her being a single mother; he knew how hard that had been on his mom after his dad's murder. And he hadn't wanted that for Valentina. Even if he'd agreed to try for the children she'd wanted, he'd known that with the time his job took that she would have essentially been raising them on her own.

Like she'd wound up doing anyway.

He should have hoped for her to have someone in her life to take care of her for once instead of her taking care of everyone else. But selfishly, he wanted her, and if the little girls hadn't come to find their mommy, he wasn't sure what would have happened between them.

"Mommy? Why you kiss fib?" Luci asked the question.

And Cash nearly groaned at the name his children called him. He knew they meant FBI agent, but to him, it just sounded like fib, like a lie, for so many reasons. For one, he didn't even feel like much of an FBI agent since he had no idea who the Landmark Killer was, and for another, because of his hunt for the serial killer, he had put Valentina and the girls in danger. And for another, he hadn't even noticed them sneaking up on him because he'd been so distracted kissing their mother.

What if the killer had gotten into the condo?

What if it had been him instead of them?

He had to be more careful. He had to ignore the attraction he'd always had for Valentina. No. It was more than attraction. So much more…

Valentina drew in a deep breath before smiling, albeit a little too brightly, at their daughters. She stepped back and settled onto the edge of her bed, then she patted the places on both sides of her and said, "Come here. I need to tell you who this really is."

And Cash's heart kicked back into the high gear it had been in during their kiss. But this was different. That had been passion; this was panic. He'd been bugging her to tell them, but now…

The little girls climbed onto the bed next to their mother, and she scooted them around until they all sat against the profusion of colorful pillows she'd always liked to have on the bed.

"What, Mommy?" Luci asked with curiosity. "He not the fib?" She pointed a small hand at him, and her green eyes, so like his, narrowed with a trace of suspicion.

"He is an FBI agent," Valentina said. "He catches bad people and puts them in jail."

"Bang bang bad guys?" Ana asked, her voice a bit squeaky and shaky.

"I don't shoot them," Cash assured her with a glance up at where he'd concealed his weapon from them. He couldn't understand their fascination with guns. He was more uncomfortable with that than the lie he'd just told them; he had had to use his weapon in the past. But he didn't want them to think he killed people. "I don't want anyone to get hurt," he said. "Especially good people."

"Sparky," Ana murmured. "Sparky…"

Cash looked at Valentina, trying to understand what the little girl meant, but she raised her shoulders in a shrug, then pointed at the window. "The sun's a little bright. Maybe that's it…"

Cash stepped in front of the window, blocking some of that light, casting a shadow over the bed where the people he wanted most to protect were cuddled together. And it was as if that beam of sunshine pierced through his heart now, warming it.

Valentina looked cold, though, as if she pulled the

little girls closer for warmth or comfort. "I should have talked to you two about this a while ago. I should have talked to…" She glanced up then and met his gaze, and tears glistened in her dark eyes. "But I didn't know how to tell you…"

Luci reached up then and touched her mother's cheek. "What, Mommy?"

"You know how some kids at day care have daddies that come pick them up?" she asked.

Ana nodded.

"We don't have a daddy," Luci said.

Now pain pierced Cash's heart.

"You do have a daddy," Valentina said. "This is your daddy." And like Luci had, she pointed at him, and her hand was shaking.

The girls followed the direction of her index finger to him. And their eyes widened.

"The fib?" Luci asked.

"Daddy," Ana murmured, and tears glistened in her eyes as if she was moved that she could use that name.

And tears stung Cash's eyes that she'd used it for him. That he was a daddy…

"Daddy!" Luci said it, too, with conviction, and then she jumped up and ran across the bed toward him, vaulting into his arms.

He caught her and held her close. And then Ana was there, too, tentatively, shyly, following her twin across the bed. She stood behind Luci, waiting.

He reached for her, too, with his other arm, folding her against him, holding them both. He'd had no intention of ever becoming a father, but now that he was, he couldn't imagine these little girls not being in the world. He had to do his best to protect them. To keep them safe. But he knew that he didn't have to protect them just from bad men; he had to protect them from himself.

VALENTINA COULDN'T GET over the sense of panic that had been pressing down on her chest since that morning when she'd told the girls that Cash was their father. No. She'd been panicking even before that, when she'd kissed Cash. When she'd wanted him so badly that they would probably have made love if the girls hadn't interrupted them when they had.

Well, for her it would have been making love. She wasn't sure what it would have been for him. She struggled to believe that he loved her, that he'd ever loved her, or he wouldn't have served her with divorce papers so quickly. He would have tried to find a way to meet her halfway.

But then she wasn't sure what that would have been. What was the compromise between having a family and not having one? She couldn't imagine not having the girls in her life.

Even now she could hear them giggling as they played in their room. And the deep rumble of Cash's voice as he played with them.

And that panic pressed harder, squeezing her heart. She couldn't fall for him again. She couldn't.

Because nothing had changed. He was still all about his job. And she knew why...

She'd always known. She pulled the *New York Wire* from the drawer of her bedside table. The article told everyone else the story of how a serial killer had murdered his father, leading to Cash and his siblings dedicating their lives to catching and stopping other serial killers.

His crusade was admirable, one of the many reasons she'd fallen in love with him. She hadn't wanted him to stop, just to give her some of his time and energy as well. And to give her the family she'd wanted…

She had that now. At least she had her girls. She doubted she would ever have Cash, but now that he knew he was a father, she hoped he would make an effort with them. That was why she'd decided to tell them, and so that they would stop calling him the fib.

She'd kept the truth too long from everyone. Even herself.

She'd known she needed to do this, to tell them. Her parents had urged her to do it, had even threatened to tell Cash for her. But she'd insisted that she was doing the right thing for all of them. And she'd thought she was right.

Until the girls had called him Daddy…

Tears stung her eyes, and she blinked furiously.

"Are you okay?" a deep voice asked.

And she turned to find Cash leaning against the doorjamb, staring at her. Usually she would have sensed his presence. She would have reacted as she did now, with an increased pulse and tingling skin. She'd wanted him so badly earlier when his mouth had moved over hers, when her hands had moved over his naked chest.

She still wanted him that badly, so badly that her hands shook on the newspaper when she tried to put it back into the open drawer.

He stepped forward and took it from her, his handsome face twisting into a grimace of disgust and frustration.

"Stella Maxwell knows you well," she remarked, trying to ignore the little sting of jealousy she felt.

Cash grinned. "Not me. Brennan. They're together now."

"I'm glad he has someone," she said. She had always liked Cash's twin, so much so that she didn't like how that reporter had betrayed Brennan's trust for a story. "But that article…"

"Stella didn't write it," Cash said. "Well, maybe she did write some of it, but she didn't submit it to her editor to print. She wouldn't have done that to Brennan. Somebody hacked her computer and added to the article, then submitted it to her editor."

"Somebody?"

"Either a mole in Stella's office or the Landmark Killer," he said with a glance over his shoulder as if checking to make sure the twins hadn't sneaked up on them again.

"You think he could have been behind that, too?"

He nodded. "He's been messing with Brennan and me, and he sent a text to our cousin Sinead, too."

"The FBI profiler?"

He nodded. "Whoever it is, he knows everybody working the case. He knows how to get a hold of us without the texts getting traced back to him."

She shivered.

"I'm sorry," he said. "I never wanted this part of my life to touch you, to affect you, and I definitely never wanted to put you in danger." He glanced toward the doorway again. "Or them…"

"Did they fall asleep?" she asked. She hadn't heard any giggling or movement since she'd noticed him in the doorway.

He nodded, a small smile curving his mouth. "They were playing so hard, and then they just crashed into their beds. At first I thought they were pretending they'd fallen asleep, but they're out."

She smiled. "They usually take a nap about this time of the afternoon."

His smile slipped down into a frown. "I don't know anything about them. Their schedules. When they took their first steps, their first word…"

Mama. But she wasn't about to share that with him. "I'm sorry," she said. "I really thought I was doing the right thing, that you didn't want…"

He nodded.

But then she let out a soft curse, at herself. "But I was really just doing what was easiest for me."

"Raising twins all by yourself?" he asked. "That was easiest?"

"Easier than seeing you again," she admitted.

And he flinched. "I didn't realize you hated me that much."

It was just the opposite, but she couldn't admit it without revealing that she still had feelings for him. Feelings that she knew would only lead her back to the same heartbreak she'd felt before.

But she couldn't let him think she hated him, so she shook her head. "It wasn't that," she assured him. "It was just easier to have a clean break. You must have thought the same, because you had those divorce papers served to me so quickly after I moved out. I got them before I even realized I was pregnant."

She'd thought it was just stress over the separation that had made her so sick after she'd moved into her grandparents' condo. She'd been using an IUD as birth control, so she hadn't considered that she could actually be pregnant.

"I thought it would be easier that way," he said. "I was so focused on the case at the time, and I kept disappointing you..." He glanced toward that open doorway, and she knew he was worried about the same thing she was, that he would disappoint them as well.

"The longer you stay here, the more attached they will get to you," she warned him. But she was worried that they weren't the only ones who would get used to him being here.

"I have to stay," he said. "I have to make sure nothing happens to any of you."

She knew they'd had a very close call the day before, and without Cash there to save them, they might not have survived it. But she'd had a close call just a short while ago...with him.

With kissing him, with wanting him...

His staying here was bad enough, but if she let him back into her bed as well as her life, she wasn't sure she would be able to let him go again. She wasn't sure that she would want to.

So she drew in a deep breath and braced herself to resist the temptation he'd always posed for her. She could not touch him again. Or kiss him.

Or even look at him too long like she was looking at him now standing in the doorway. So tall. So intense. His gaze was focused on her with that look in his green eyes again, that heat.

She jumped up from the bed, knowing that she had to get out of it before she did something stupid, like pull him into it with her.

"I have baby books for them," she said. "They're on the shelves by the TV. There are DVDs, too, of them. They love getting their pictures taken and having me record them." But as much of their lives as she could show him, he hadn't been there in the moment. He hadn't shared the experience with them. But would he have, even if he'd known about them? Or would work have consumed him then as it always had?

And probably still did...

His phone vibrated with an incoming text. His hand shook a bit as he pulled it from his pocket; maybe he was worried that it was another one from the Landmark Killer. Another taunt...

Whatever it was, it drew his attention away from her. And she was happy for that this time. Because if he'd kept looking at her the way he'd been, she wasn't sure how long she would have been able to resist temptation.

Chapter Eleven

A week had passed since Cash moved into the condo. A week he'd taken off work, which was unprecedented for him. A week he'd asked Valentina to take off from the library as well, and to keep the girls home from day care.

He could keep them safe here.

He was the only one in danger in the condo.

Danger of getting used to this, to living in the sun-filled home with the view he was appreciating at the moment, as he stood in front of the windows staring at the Cyclone roller coaster and the Ferris wheel at Luna Park. Beyond the rides, the water glistened in the morning sunshine.

Even more than the place, he was getting used to the people who lived here. His family. While Valentina was his ex-wife, she would always be the mother of his children. Always be part of his life now...

And she would always hold a part of his heart, if not the whole thing. No. The little girls had taken the rest of it. Every minute with them, every smile and giggle and hug, had love overwhelming him. The love he felt for them...

And the love he thought they were beginning to feel for him. They were getting attached to him, just as Valentina must have been worrying about. They were getting used to him being part of their everyday lives.

They'd watched all the DVDs with him that Valentina had taken to document every one of their milestones. Part of him hoped she'd been documenting them for him as much as for herself. That she had intended to show them to him one day. The girls showed him their baby books and photo albums themselves. And they'd taught him how to play Chutes and Ladders and Hungry Hungry Hippos and all the other board games they'd been playing over the last week. They'd also watched a ton of movies and cartoons, with their mother letting them stay up past their bedtime more often than not.

He wondered about that. Had she done it because they were excited about him being there and she hadn't wanted to limit their time with him? Or had she done it because she'd wanted to limit her time alone with him?

Once the kids went to bed at night, she slipped off to her room shortly after, closing the door in his face, closing him out. But despite that, they'd talked about their lives over the past three years.

About his job and his family. And about her job and her family.

They'd even talked about how crazy the world had gotten with polarizing politics and inflation and all the things that ordinary married couples probably discussed. They'd never talked that much when they'd been married, though.

The nights he'd been home from his job, they had spent

in bed together, and they'd done very little talking at all then, making up for the time they'd been apart. His body ached to make up with her that way, for all the lost years. He wanted her so damn badly. Wanted to kiss her again and hold her and join their bodies together the way they used to, where he'd felt like he was coming home.

Like she was his home. Not an apartment or a condo, but her. He'd never felt as though he'd belonged anywhere as much as he'd belonged in her arms.

"They fell asleep," Valentina remarked as she joined him in the living room. She seemed nervous, on edge.

He was, too, had been since that kiss. Sleeping on the couch, so close but yet so far from Valentina, was killing him. He wanted—no, he needed—to be back in her bed, back in her arms and she in his. He ached for her.

"Is that bad that they fell asleep?" he asked.

Maybe she was worried what would happen if they were alone together too long, if she would kiss him again, like she had that day, like he'd wanted her to kiss him and touch him again ever since.

"It's morning," she said. "They never take a nap this early in the day."

"They get up at the crack of dawn," he said with a smile.

"Like you," she murmured.

They were like him in some ways, ways he wouldn't have expected since he hadn't lived with them until this week, until now. The early rising, the things they liked to eat, the shows they liked were even some of the old cartoons he'd watched as a kid, the Disney movies he'd loved when life had still been innocent and simple for him.

When his dad had been alive…

But when his dad had died, Cash's innocence and optimism had died with him. He'd known then how much evil there was in the world, how innocent people could be killed for no reason.

Like whoever had tried to kill Valentina and the girls when he'd aimed that car at them, not once but twice. That hadn't been an accident, especially not when the stolen car had been set on fire just a short while later. Ashlynn and Patrick thinking it was the work of a professional made him even more determined to stay here, to keep them safe.

But what motive would anyone have to want to hurt those sweet girls and their mother? Besides the Landmark Killer messing with Cash?

"I need to go back to work," she said. "And they need to go back to day care, back to their usual schedule." The desperation was in her voice and in the dark circles beneath her eyes. She didn't appear to be sleeping any better in her bed than he was on the couch.

If only…

He started toward her then, wanting to kiss her again as they'd kissed that day. Wanting to be with her.

But he'd only taken a couple of steps before his cell rang and vibrated in his pocket. So it wouldn't wake up the twins, he grabbed it quickly, and instead of rejecting the call as he'd intended, he accidentally accepted it. Maybe because his hand was shaking from the desire for Valentina that was coursing through him.

"Cash?" Brennan's voice emanated from the cell speaker.

"I'll give you privacy," Valentina said, and she darted

back into the hall as if she'd been looking for an excuse to escape from him, as if she'd known what he'd been about to do. To kiss her...

"Cash?" Brennan called out again.

"I'm here," he said, and he took the phone off speaker so that the sound of their uncle's voice wouldn't wake up the girls.

It was early for them to fall asleep, though they'd all stayed up a little late last night, eating popcorn and watching *Aladdin*. Then they'd wanted to have a slumber party in the living room with him, but Valentina had insisted that the couch was too small for all of them.

He could have suggested that they move the slumber party to her bedroom, to her big king-size bed. But he hadn't wanted to put her on the spot like that, and he wasn't certain he could share a bed with her and not want more.

It was probably good that Brennan had called when he had, so that Cash hadn't kissed her again. He wouldn't have been able to stop at just a kiss.

But he released a ragged sigh, of disappointment, before asking, "What's up?"

"You tell me," Brennan said. "I haven't seen you all week."

"You know why," he reminded him. He'd let Brennan know that he had to work remotely for the time being instead of going into the office. Not that he'd really been doing much working on anything but catching up on his daughters' lives and all of it he'd missed. "I can't let anything happen to Valentina or the girls..."

"You can have Dave Percell keep an eye on them for you like he did the week after you received that text."

"That was just a text," Cash said. "That wasn't a car trying to run them down."

"You don't know that that had anything to do with the Landmark Killer," Brennan pointed out. "In fact I'm pretty damn sure that it didn't. His victims have all been blond, blue-eyed men in their thirties."

"He's going after us, too," Cash reminded him. "With those taunting texts, with that article in the *New York Wire*. He's messing with us, and if it wasn't him that was driving that car, it might have been someone he hired."

Brennan sucked in a breath. "I hadn't considered that. From Sinead's profile of him, it seems like he would be someone who'd work alone."

"He works with us," Cash said.

Brennan cursed. "We need to figure out who. We've got to stop him. So I called a meeting for this afternoon, and you need to be there, too, Cash. We can't meet here because that damn Landmark Killer would know about it, would know that we're onto him, so I called it outside the office. Because you need to be there, I booked a hotel room not that far from where you're staying."

"Ah..." He appreciated that Brennan had considered him when he'd chosen the location. But he was torn. Getting out of the condo for a moment, getting some distance between him and Valentina, might clear his head and protect his heart.

But...

"I called Dave Percell, too," Brennan said. "He's on his way over to watch the door for you."

"That didn't go that well last time," he said. "Her neighbor got all uptight about it and was saying that the condo board wouldn't approve of her being here if it put other residents in danger." Of course he'd probably been saying all that out of spite, because he'd been hitting on Valentina. Blake Highland wouldn't do that anymore if he knew what was good for him.

"You need to be here, Cash. We need to stop this guy before he claims another victim. And if he hired someone to go after Valentina and the girls, that would stop that, too," Brennan said. "That would make them safer than your playing house is making them."

Cash flinched. Playing house. Was that all he was doing?

"And if he's not behind that attempt on their lives, you need to figure out who is."

"What are you saying?"

"You could have other enemies. With our job, we've all made enemies," Brennan pointed out. "Hell, anybody can make an enemy, some without even realizing it. Like Stella. That attempt on the lives of Valentina and the girls might have to do with something else. Even with Valentina…"

Cash snorted at the thought of her making an enemy. "Stella is a reporter. Valentina is a librarian. She doesn't make enemies."

"Maybe someone really doesn't like being shushed," Brennan joked.

But Cash couldn't laugh about someone going after his family. His brother was right, though. The best way to keep them safe was to figure out who was behind the threat and the attempt on their lives and stop them.

"Okay, I'll be there," he said. He could trust Dave to protect them like he had that first night, making sure that the predatory neighbor hadn't been able to even speak to Valentina until Cash had had her open the door.

Just how predatory was the guy? And how angry that Valentina kept rebuffing his advances? Angry enough to try to kill her?

Cash shook his head at the ridiculous thought, at the idea that Brennan had planted in his mind that the person who was after Valentina and the girls was someone in her life, someone she knew, who wanted to hurt her.

SHORTLY AFTER HE'D taken that call, Cash was gone. Valentina should have been relieved to get a break from him and the feelings that kept overwhelming her in his presence. Guilt and regret that she hadn't told him about their daughters sooner, that intensified every time she watched him with them. With every hug they gave him, she thought of all the other hugs she'd denied him.

But she couldn't know how many he would have had, how much he would have been around them if he'd known about them when she was pregnant. He might not have been there for her or them then. He was only here now because of that text and his saving them from someone trying to run them down.

But guilt and regret weren't even the most overwhelming feelings she had. Desire was. She wanted him so badly. Maybe it was just because she'd denied that part of her life for so long, that she'd pushed aside her needs as a woman and had totally focused on being a mother.

She didn't feel much like a mom at the moment, though, because she wasn't protecting her kids from the heartbreak that was sure to come. The heartbreak that Cash would inevitably cause them, just like he'd caused her, when he'd been unable to give her the time and attention she'd needed from him. Which hadn't been much...

Little kids needed more.

And now the guilt surged back because Valentina realized she hadn't checked on them lately. They'd been napping for a while and at a time when they usually wouldn't have napped at all. Concerned, she hurried from her bedroom to theirs.

Ana sat up in her bed, flipping through the pages of one of her picture books, while Luci was huddled under the covers in hers. "Shh, Mommy," Ana said. "Luci seepy."

Valentina dropped to her knees between their beds. "She's been sleeping for a long time."

"Long time," Ana agreed.

"It was sweet of you to let her sleep," she praised her daughter. But it had been neglectful on Valentina's part; she should have checked on the girls earlier. She reached out now to do so, pulling back the blanket to touch Luci's forehead. It was damp and hot, like the hair plastered to her head. She was burning up.

Luci shivered, her bottom lip quivering. "Sooo cold..." she murmured, and she grabbed at the blanket to pull it over her head again.

"Oh, baby." Panic gripped Valentina, but she forced

herself to appear calm as she hurried to the medicine cabinet in her bathroom and grabbed a thermometer and the bottle of children's pain and fever relief.

She had to pull back the blanket again to get a reading with the forehead thermometer. And she swallowed her gasp of alarm over how high it was.

"Come on, Luci," she said. "You need to take some medicine." She poured the recommended dosage into the liquid medicine dispenser and pressed it to the little girl's lips, which were already starting to crack. Once she got Luci awake enough to swallow the medicine, she hurried to put that bottle away before getting some Pedialyte from the refrigerator. The poor little girl was already getting dehydrated. Valentina got her to drink some of that before Luci fell asleep again.

Then, shaky with fear for her sick child, Valentina ducked back into her own bedroom to call the girls' pediatrician's office.

"If her fever doesn't come down, you need to bring her into the office," the nurse advised.

Cash had been insistent that they didn't leave the condo. He'd even told his friend as much when Sergeant Percell had shown up to guard the door.

But if Luci's fever didn't go down, it was going to be more dangerous for the little girl inside the condo than it would be to make the short trip to the doctor's office, especially since there had been no more threats or attempts on their lives.

Maybe the whole thing with the car had just been a warning for Cash to back off. And since he'd stayed with them the past week, he had. So maybe there was no more threat to them but the fever that was currently ravaging poor Luci.

If her fever didn't go down soon, there was no way that officer or Cash or anyone else, even a serial killer, was going to prevent Valentina from getting her daughter the medical help she needed.

Chapter Twelve

Ever since he'd left the condo, Cash had been on edge. Hell, he'd been on edge even before he'd left. He'd been on edge since he'd received that anonymous text about his murdered daddy and his sad ex-wife.

Staying with Valentina and the girls the past week had nearly pushed him over that edge. He'd wanted to do more than protect her; he'd wanted to be with her, with all the passion that had always burned so hot between them. But that would have been dangerous for both of them. He couldn't afford any distractions right now, and neither could she and the girls. He had to keep them safe.

Dave had promised he'd make sure they didn't leave the condo and that nobody got inside, but he was just one man. What if more than one person came after them or...

"You're here, but you're not here," Brennan commented from where he sat at the desk in the hotel suite he'd booked for the meeting.

Cash knew who his twin was talking about and released a ragged sigh, and suddenly he was so weary, he considered lying back on the bed where he was sitting to close his eyes. "I'm sorry. I know I haven't been doing my part in catching this psychopath."

"You've been busy," Ashlynn said sympathetically, "with Valentina and the girls..."

She trailed off, and he knew what she was asking, what, knowing his sister, she'd probably already investigated to find out.

To confirm what everyone else either knew or at least suspected, Cash said, "Valentina's daughters, Ana and Luciana, are mine."

Predictably, nobody looked surprised. They were concerned and maybe confused, though, as they stared at him with sympathetic expressions on their faces.

"I can't believe Valentina didn't tell you about them," Ashlynn said.

"She didn't think I wanted to be a father," Cash said in her defense.

"You didn't," Brennan reminded him. "So how do you feel about being one now?"

"I guess it's possible to change your mind, right?" Cash asked him. Brennan had vowed to stay single, probably partly because of seeing how hard Cash's divorce had been on him.

Hell, he'd never really recovered from it. He'd never gotten over losing Valentina.

"Is it?" Patrick asked the question now, arching one of his light brown eyebrows over one of his hazel eyes. He sat on the edge of the bed across from Cash.

"It's really hard for us Coltons," Brennan said. "But it is possible."

Ashlynn snorted. "Not for all of us Coltons. I'm over

dating. So over it…" Her forehead creased beneath the lock of dark hair that had escaped from her ponytail and fallen across it.

"You didn't call this meeting for us all to discuss our personal lives," Cash reminded them, embarrassed that his had taken over the conversation. He was also embarrassed over how badly he'd screwed up his personal life.

If only he could have figured out a way to balance work and his wife…to give them both his attention…

Maybe he wouldn't have lost her. But that had only been part of their problem. The other had been his refusal to start a family with her. Hell, they'd just wanted different things out of life.

"No, I called this meeting to talk about the Landmark Killer without the risk of him overhearing us," Brennan said. "We've been going through these lists of employees from our office and from the 130th Precinct. Using Sinead's profile of a male in his twenties, we've narrowed it down to six. Two rookie cops at the 130th as well as a PI who works out of the precinct a lot."

"And the other three?" Cash asked.

"Are the reason I booked this room for the meeting. They work out of our office," Brennan said.

They'd already suspected that someone close to them was the killer, someone who knew about their personal lives. "Yeah, but who?" Cash asked.

"A researcher, an IT employee and—" he lowered his voice as if he was worried the guy might be lurking outside the hotel room door "—the director's assistant, Xander Washer."

Cash whistled between his teeth. "Good thing the director's out of town. She's not going to appreciate her right hand being a suspect."

Patrick grunted. "Sucks when you can't trust the people you work with…"

They all nodded in agreement. "But it has to be someone close to us," Cash repeated what they'd already suspected. "Someone who knew about our dad and Valentina…"

"Or it could just be someone who did his research on us. Why don't you take Perkins, the researcher?" Brennan asked Cash.

"Jonathan Perkins?" Ashlynn asked.

Brennan nodded. "Yeah."

"He asked me out a few months ago," she admitted. "But I shot him down." She groaned. "So over dating…"

"Probably a good thing you shot him down," Cash said. "He might be a crazed psychopath."

Ashlynn snorted. "Sure, under his sweater vests."

"Maybe your rejection set him off," Brennan teased. Their family often handled difficult situations by using humor to diffuse them.

"I'll check his alibis for the murders," Cash said.

Brennan divvied up the rest of the suspects, giving Xander Washer to Ashlynn. There was also an IT employee at the FBI, two rookie cops at the 130th and a PI who worked out of there a lot as well. Then he tossed computers at each of them, and they proceeded to deep-dive into the suspects' phone records and credit card invoices, checking specifically the dates and times of the murders.

But Cash was distracted, thinking of Valentina and the kids. His family...

He was worried about them, worried about their safety and worried that the little girls weren't the only ones getting used to him being part of their lives. He was getting used to them as well, to being Daddy to Valentina's Mommy, to being the family he'd sworn he never wanted.

Panic pressed on his chest at the thought, making it hard for him to breathe. So hard that he could only take short, shallow breaths like he was hyperventilating.

"Are you okay?" Patrick asked.

He nodded. "Yeah, yeah, just..."

"Distracted," Brennan finished for him. "You don't have to worry about Valentina and your daughters. Sergeant Percell is at the door. He's protecting the—"

Cash's cell ringing interrupted his twin's assurances. And when Cash saw that it was Dave calling him, he was worried that his brother was wrong. That Dave hadn't protected them at all, and Cash shouldn't have left them.

LUCI'S FEVER WAS not dropping. And she was more listless and dehydrated. She needed to get to the doctor's office fast. Even though she didn't use it often, Valentina had a car parked in the garage beneath the condo building; she could drive the twins herself. She shouldn't have waited for Cash to come back. She should have just shoved his friend aside and carried her kids out.

But when Sergeant Percell had handed his cell phone to her, Cash had been on it, vowing that he was close and that he would be there right away.

Even if he was on his way and it wouldn't take him

long, those precious moments with a sick child felt interminably long to Valentina as she paced the living room as she waited for him.

The medicine and Pedialyte hadn't worked. Even a cool bath hadn't lowered Luci's fever. The poor kid was so sick that Valentina's heart ached for her. Luci was always so energetic and upbeat and usually very healthy. She didn't get sick, not like this. Sniffles had been the most serious illness the little girl had ever had.

Valentina was scared, especially after how she'd lost her grandparents. She couldn't lose a child, too. When the knock finally came at the door, she was ready, the children already in their double stroller. She jerked open the door.

"You're supposed to wait to confirm who is knocking," Cash admonished her.

And her fury bubbled over. "I've been waiting long enough. No, Luci has. She needs medical attention right away."

Cash bent over the stroller. While Ana was awake, she was quiet as if she felt Valentina's fear. Or maybe she was so attuned to her twin that she knew how sick she was, that this was serious. Luci slept, slumped in her seat in the stroller. "She's so flushed," Cash remarked, his deep voice gruff with emotion. "Let's get her to the ER."

"My doctor's office is in the urgent care center not far from here," she said. "They're like a small emergency room and are ready to set up an IV to treat her."

"I'm sorry," Cash said as he stepped back and helped her get the stroller through the doorway. Then he guided it down the hall toward the elevator that Sergeant Percell was holding open for them. "I didn't know. I wouldn't have left if I knew she was sick."

Valentina felt a twinge of regret for being short with him. She hadn't known, either; she should have checked on the twins sooner, should have found out why the kids had been so tired as to fall asleep in the morning. She wanted to comfort Cash, but she needed comfort, too.

No. She needed to focus on her children; she'd let Cash and her desire for him distract her from that, from what mattered most.

She pushed the stroller into the elevator and barely waited for Sergeant Percell and Cash to step inside before she closed the doors and pressed the button for the basement. Once the elevator started its descent, she crouched down in front of the stroller. "You'll be feeling better soon," she assured Luci.

But the child didn't open her eyes, as if the lids were too heavy to lift; they just fluttered a bit. A quiet murmur slipped through her lips though as if she was trying to tell Valentina something.

"She said Daddy," Ana translated for her.

And Cash sucked in a breath before he crouched down in front of the stroller next to Valentina. "You're going to be okay, sweetheart," he told the little girl, and he brushed his fingers across her flushed cheek.

Luci's lips curved slightly as if she'd heard him and believed him.

Valentina wished she had the same faith. But the little girl's fever hadn't come down; her body was working too hard trying to fight whatever virus she'd picked up. Probably at day care…

Though it had taken a week for it to get her this sick, Valentina should have seen the earlier signs. Luci was the one who loved going to the amusement park, who loved being outside, but she hadn't pushed once to leave the condo.

Valentina had thought it was because of the novelty of Cash staying with them that the girls had been happy to stay inside with their new daddy. But now she wondered...

She reached out and checked Ana's forehead, too, but it was still cool, like it had been. She wasn't sick yet, but she usually got what Luci had. Actually, she usually had it first and the worst.

"Let me know if you start feeling bad, too," she told her.

"I 'kay, Mommy," she replied. "Luci sick."

"Yes, but we're getting her to the doctor now." And Valentina would have the pediatrician check out Ana, too.

The elevator dinged as it finally stopped in the garage. The trip had seemed to take forever, just as it had for Cash to get here. Tears of frustration stung Valentina's eyes. She just wanted to scoop them up and run with them to the doctor, to get them help.

But Cash held the stroller back and her as the sergeant started out first. Dave walked a short distance away from the elevator, turned around and nodded, probably indicating it was all clear.

At least that was what Cash seemed to think because he started out with the stroller. But he pushed it with one hand while he reached for his holster with the other, as if he wasn't entirely sure that there was no danger lurking in the dark shadows of the garage.

Valentina was more worried about Luci's fever. That was the real threat to her child. Not some car careening out of nowhere at them again like had happened a week ago.

She shouldn't have let Cash hold them hostage in the condo the last week like he pretty much had. She should have made sure that the girls got out, got fresh air, and maybe Luci wouldn't have gotten so sick.

Tears of frustration stung her eyes, and she wanted to hurl accusations at him, to blame this illness on him. But before she could open her mouth, someone stepped from the shadows. Wearing dark clothes with a hoodie pulled tight around his face, he looked like a shadow but for the glint of his eyes in the darkness and the glint of the gun he held.

Ana screamed. "Bad man!"

And Cash drew his weapon just as the man pointed his gun toward them.

She wasn't sure who fired first, just that the gunshots echoed throughout the parking garage. Ana covered her ears and closed her eyes as she screamed. And Valentina's scream echoed her daughter's. She stepped between them, crouching over them, trying to protect them as the elevator doors closed behind them, cutting off their chance of escape.

Cash was between them and the shooter. And she heard his grunt of pain and felt his body jerking as he took a bullet. And she screamed again.

Chapter Thirteen

Cash got hit. But the bullet just grazed his arm, burning more than it hurt. He was worried that after grazing him, the bullet had hit the stroller, though, or Valentina. He had to get them to safety. The elevator doors had closed.

"Dave!" he called out, worried for his friend.

Dave waved to him from behind a pillar he used as a shield. But the shooter wasn't firing in the sergeant's direction. He'd fired at Cash or at Cash's family.

Cash had returned fire, but he wasn't sure if he'd hit the guy, or if he was just hiding. He moved quickly, glad that he'd parked near the elevator. He clicked the locks and got the kids and Valentina into the FBI SUV with its bulletproof glass. They would be safe.

Which was proved when bullets pinged off the vehicle, striking the metal and the windows. He turned toward the direction of the shots, ready to go hunt down the man. But Valentina, who was in the back, yelled, "No. We have to get out of here!"

She was right. For Luci's sake, he needed to get them to the urgent care.

He shut the driver's door and started the ignition, but as

he did, the shooter continued to fire at them from somewhere in the shadows. Pressing hard on the accelerator, he sped away, careening around the corners toward the exit to the street. He could only hope that Dave would be okay and that the sergeant would get some shots off that did hit the man. At the moment, protecting his family was Cash's main responsibility, but he called 9-1-1 as well, identified himself and requested backup for Dave. A unit was close, the sirens blaring loudly as he exited the garage.

"You're bleeding," Valentina whispered, her voice raspy from her screaming or from her fear.

That fear gripped him that she was talking to one of the kids. But she reached between the seats, from where she sat in the back with the girls, and touched his arm.

"I'm fine," he insisted, even though the wound was still stinging and burning like the guy had shot a bee through his arm instead of a bullet. His arm was bleeding, though, he could feel the blood trickling over his skin.

"Daddy..." Ana whispered, her voice cracking with the tears that slid down her face. "The bad man got you, too."

"Too?" he asked, and he chanced another glance into the back seat. "Are you hurt? Is anyone hurt?"

"Sparky..." Ana murmured.

"She must be getting a fever, too," Valentina said as she pushed back the girl's damp curls and touched her forehead.

Cash swallowed a curse. They had enough going on right now with being sick, and he'd brought that damn shooter into their lives. He must have followed Cash from the hotel, somehow gotten into the garage...

Unless he'd been here. Unless he lived here, too.

"What do you know about Blake Highland?" he asked Valentina.

She sucked in a breath. "Why are you asking? He just lives down the hall and drinks too much. That's all I know."

Fortunately the urgent care was close, and he got the girls and Valentina safely inside. As they checked in, he was able to follow up on what had happened in Valentina's garage. Dave was okay. He'd lost the shooter, but he hadn't been hit. Unfortunately, ducking bullets hadn't given him a chance to get a description of the man or the vehicle he'd been driving, if he'd been driving one at all.

One minute he was there, and the next he was gone, the second Cash had driven off. Cash and his family had definitely been the intended target.

"Find out where that Highland guy was. Check his alibi," Cash advised. Just as he and his unit had alibis they needed to check. He called Brennan next, bringing him up to date on what had just happened.

Brennan cursed. "We're on our way."

Because the hotel was close, it didn't take long before his family stormed into the urgent care waiting room. He could hear their voices from where he was in the back, sitting next to the bed where his little girl was hooked to an IV.

He got up from his chair to head off his family. But Valentina grabbed his uninjured arm and insisted, as she had been insisting since they'd arrived, "You need stitches."

He shrugged off her concern, but he couldn't shrug

off his guilt. Somehow this was his fault; he just knew it. Maybe not Luci getting sick, but the shooting and the nearly getting run down had to be. He'd put his family in extreme danger because of his job, because of what he did, hunting serial killers.

That probably meant that the rest of his family was in danger, too. He stepped through the door to the waiting room, and they turned toward him.

"Are you all right?" Ashlynn asked as she rushed toward him. She reached out as if she intended to hug him but jerked back before she touched his arm. "You're bleeding!"

"So I've been told."

"You got shot," Patrick said, his face getting pale.

The co-head of FBI CSI was definitely not squeamish. He was just concerned. They'd already lost their dad; they didn't want to lose anyone else in their family.

"I'm fine," he assured them all. "Just got grazed a little." But with the way blood trickled yet from the wound, Valentina was probably right that he needed stitches. And maybe a tetanus shot. He didn't remember the last time he'd had one.

"What about Valentina and the kids?" Brennan asked, and his face was pale, too, with concern. "How are they doing?"

Cash's heart swelled with gratitude that his siblings cared about his family even though they had yet to meet the girls. "They didn't get hit with bullets—"

"What about the one with the fever?" Patrick interjected to ask.

After he took that call from Dave, he'd explained to

them he'd had to leave because his daughter was sick and Valentina was worried. He'd been scared, too, and then the shooting...

"Is she all right?" Brennan asked.

"Luci. She has the flu and is dehydrated. They gave her some medicine and have an IV in her now," Cash said. "And the doctor thinks that once her fever breaks, she'll be fine."

"Can we see them?" Ashlynn asked tentatively.

"I'll check with Valentina," he said. "And the doctor. While Luci's fever is starting to come down, they want to keep monitoring her and Ana to make sure that she isn't getting one. They're both really shaken up over what happened. And scared." His voice cracked as emotion overwhelmed him. "They shouldn't have been scared like that, from the shooting and from the thing with the car. They shouldn't be in danger like that..."

Because of him. He couldn't help but think this was all his fault. And Valentina undoubtedly blamed him, too. But his family, his siblings at least, all gathered around to comfort and embrace him and to make damn sure he got his bullet wound treated.

He was lucky that he had them, like he was lucky that he had the girls in his life now. But he couldn't help but worry that his luck wasn't going to last and that he would lose someone close to him again like they'd lost their dad.

HE KEPT INSISTING that he was fine, but Valentina had her doubts about him. Maybe he believed what he was saying or he was lying so that he didn't worry the girls, but either way he needed to be treated. He could have been in shock since the shooting.

She was. She'd known that car nearly running them down hadn't been an accident, not when the driver had turned around and tried again. But she hadn't thought that the person might know where she lived, might have gotten access to the parking garage and might have tried to kill them all just steps from their home.

Where she'd always felt so safe and protected and loved and happy with her grandparents and with her children. She'd been resenting Cash for keeping them inside this past week, but clearly his overprotectiveness had been the only thing keeping them safe.

She hadn't.

So when Cash asked if his siblings could come back and meet the girls, she didn't have the heart to say no. The girls were doing better now, health-wise, but they were still afraid and uneasy.

Thinking that maybe meeting their aunt and uncles would distract them, she had agreed to let them come back to meet the girls. When she saw how Brennan and Ashlynn and Patrick immediately fell for the little ones, her tension eased even as her guilt increased. She shouldn't have kept the girls from their family, from their Colton family of dad, uncles, aunt and all the many, many cousins that Cash had.

In comparison Valentina's family was small, especially since her grandparents had died. And her parents spent all their time traveling now, as if they were afraid to stop moving, afraid that if they did, they might stop living. It wasn't retirement that had killed her grandparents, though. It had been an illness.

Fortunately that wasn't the one that Luci had. She was going to be fine. The fever was gone and she was getting rehydrated. She was less sleepy, too, so she answered her uncles' and aunt's questions for both her and Ana, who was too shy to reply for herself.

Or maybe still too scared.

She'd been the one who'd seen the bad man first. Who'd seen the gun...

Valentina had seen him, too, with that cold gleam in his eyes. He had definitely intended to kill them. All of them? But why?

She could think of no reason but for Cash and the killers he hunted. He and his family. Maybe being with all of them put the girls in more danger.

But if Cash hadn't been there...then she and the girls wouldn't be here. They would have died for certain, if not from the car trying to run them down, then they would have died in the parking garage.

Once again Cash had saved their lives. And Valentina had yet to thank him. She felt guilty over that, too, and over how she'd treated him when he'd first shown up at the condo. All he'd wanted was to protect them.

So much so that he'd literally taken a bullet for them. He was lucky he hadn't died. No. She was lucky. She and the girls were lucky to have him as their protector.

But was that self-appointed position going to wind up costing him his life?

THE SON OF a bitch had hit him. Not the cop but the other guy. The one who'd stood in his way, who'd stopped him from eliminating the threat to his freedom.

The bullet had grazed his cheek even through the thick

mask, knocking it slightly askew so he hadn't been able to see clearly through the damn eyeholes. If he had been, he wouldn't have missed. At least he'd hit the guy.

He'd been bleeding, too, blood running down his arm and dripping from his hand. The blood left in the garage had to be all his.

He couldn't have left blood, couldn't have left any DNA that could get traced back to him. He was always so damn careful, until that day just before he'd tried running them down. Then he'd gotten sloppy, overconfident and everything had gone so damn wrong.

That wasn't like him; he was usually so careful. He always plotted everything out in advance, and he always made sure that he had insurance, too. A backup plan when things fell apart. A way to protect himself.

But now he'd gotten shot.

He pulled off the heavy ski mask he'd been wearing. It was heavy, saturated with his blood. But it must have caught most of it. And what had escaped from it had trickled down his neck and saturated his shirt. He hadn't left anything behind in that parking garage but the empty shells from his gun. A gun that could be traced to other crimes but not back to him.

He never registered a weapon. Never took any risks that could expose his identity or his culpability. Except that day...

He'd made a mistake then, and there was only one way to fix it: make sure that whole damn family died.

Chapter Fourteen

Cash would have felt uneasy driving back into the parking garage if it wasn't swarming with techs and officers. Some of the techs were from the FBI CSI. One of them being Patrick, who'd insisted on personally checking for evidence, no doubt hoping that he would find something to lead them to the man who'd shot Cash and who'd probably intended to shoot them all.

Fortunately the exhausted girls had fallen asleep in the back of the SUV, or they might have been afraid to return to the parking garage, like Valentina clearly was, her hands knotting in her lap as she sat next to Cash in the passenger seat.

"It's safe now," he assured her in a low whisper.

She nodded. "I know." But her long lashes fluttered as if she was blinking back tears, probably over the close call they'd had, over her babies being in the danger they'd been in because of him.

"I'm sorry," he said as the guilt weighed so heavily on him that his shoulders bowed with it.

She glanced across the console at him. "Why? For what? You saved our lives again."

"I can't help but think I'm the reason your lives have needed saving," he said.

Brennan was considering it even more of a possibility now that this was related to them and not Valentina. Even if it wasn't the Landmark Killer, it might be someone else they'd put away, or a fan of someone else they'd brought to justice.

Like the Landmark Killer was an obsessed fan of the Black Widow, Maeve O'Leary.

"You were right," she said.

He flinched.

"There is a lot of evil in the world," she said.

She had always been so bright and optimistic, so happy. He hated that the darkness of his world was casting a shadow over hers. And over the little girls.

A soft sigh emanated from the back seat and a little snore. She looked back at their daughters and smiled, love radiating from her. She was the good that was necessary in the world to balance out the bad.

She was too good for Cash. He'd figured that out too late, though.

"They need to get up to their beds," she said. And she opened her door, stepped out and opened the back door. She had Ana in her arms already when he picked up Luci. "Your arm!" she gasped with concern. "You're hurt. You shouldn't be trying to carry her."

"It's still numb," he lied. "From when they stitched it up." The local anesthesia had actually worn off before they'd left the urgent care, leaving his arm throbbing with a dull ache. But that pain was nothing compared to the ache in his heart when he thought of how close he'd come to losing them.

Even though he'd only had them in his life for a week, he couldn't imagine it without them now. Without her...

But he hadn't just had to imagine that; he'd lived that reality for the past three years when he'd lived without Valentina.

He held Luci close as they headed toward the elevator. Dave was there, holding open the doors for them. Valentina stepped inside first, and as Cash followed her, he told his old friend, "I'm glad you're okay."

Dave shook his head. "I wish I'd gotten him, but he was there and gone...like a ghost."

Luci tensed in his arms as if she'd heard them, as if their talk had scared her. "Shh..." Cash murmured to her. "It's okay. You're safe."

Dave shushed as well and stepped back so that the elevator doors could close. Valentina pushed the button for her floor, then leaned back against the wall as if exhausted.

She probably was. The girls woke up early every day and then this day...

So much had happened.

So much worse could have happened.

When the doors opened, Cash peered out first. There was an officer at the door to her apartment. Dave must have sent him up first to make sure the hallway was secure for their arrival. Could the shooter have gone inside the building?

Could he still be here?

"The area is secure, Agent Colton," the young officer

said as if she'd read Cash's mind. "We didn't have a key to the door, but the lock hasn't been tampered with. Unless they had a key to get inside, the unit should still be secure, too."

"Nobody else has a key," Valentina said as she fumbled hers from her bag and, juggling the child sleeping against her, managed to unlock the door.

Another door creaked open down the hall, and Cash caught sight of Blake Highland peering out of his unit. Highland had the code to the parking garage, the code Valentina had had to share with Cash for him to get in and out. "Hurry up," Cash said as Valentina pushed open her door.

When his gaze collided with Cash's, Blake shut the door again. But Cash was still on edge until Valentina stepped inside her condo. Even after he followed her in and she dead-bolted the door again, he wasn't totally at ease.

"Let's put them down in their beds," she whispered at him with a worried glance at his shoulder.

The stitches were starting to strain, but if the wound was bleeding again, it wouldn't be possible to tell as bloody as the sleeve of his shirt already was. He didn't want to get any of that on Luci, though. He just wanted to tuck her back into her little bed where she'd be safe and hopefully dream sweet dreams despite the scary incident in the parking garage.

That had been too damn close a call for all of them. Why would anyone want to hurt Valentina and the two little girls, though? It didn't make sense. But then evil seldom made sense to anyone but the evildoer.

Like the Landmark Killer.

Who really thought his killing in Maeve O'Leary's name was going to gain her release...

Especially if he worked in law enforcement at the 130th Precinct or at the FBI, he had to know better, had to know that wasn't how justice worked.

If justice worked...

Sometimes killers managed to escape it, to either never get caught or never serve time behind bars. That couldn't happen this time.

Valentina settled Ana into her bed and tucked her under her covers. Then she pulled back the blankets on Luci's bed. He hugged the little girl close for a moment before he settled her onto her pink sheets. Then Valentina pulled up the blankets again and kissed the little girl's forehead. She released a soft sigh that stirred Luci's curls.

"She's still cool," she said. "The fever hasn't come back. She's recovering from being sick."

But would they recover from the attempts on their lives? Valentina must have been worried because she stared at them both for a long moment, her brow furrowed with her concern, before she backed out of the room into the hall.

Cash followed her out and once again he whispered, "I'm sorry."

"You're not responsible for the evil," Valentina said. "It's not your fault that it exists."

"It's my job to stop it," he said.

"A job you work harder at than most people work in their lives," she said. "There's only so much you can do. You can't take responsibility for everything bad that happens."

"I take responsibility for us," he said. "For our divorce…"

Her lips curved into a slight smile. "Since you're the one who filed, you should."

"But you were the one who left," he said. "Because I couldn't give you what you wanted, the family…"

Her smile widened a bit and she glanced over her shoulder into the girls' room. "But you did…" Then she turned back to him and her smile slipped away. "And I'm sorry I didn't tell you about them. That I didn't share them with you and with your family."

"Their aunt and uncles are going to spoil them," he said, remembering how the little girls had charmed his siblings. Brennan, Patrick and Ashlynn had fallen for them nearly as quickly and hard as he had.

As he'd fallen for Valentina all those years ago…

And he felt himself tumbling now, so much so that he swayed on his feet and reached out to grasp the wall.

"Cash," she said with alarm, and she reached for him, sliding her arms around him. "You need to go to bed, too. You're injured and you've lost blood." But instead of guiding him toward the living room and the couch, she turned him toward her room.

"Valentina?" he asked when she guided him through the doorway toward her bed.

"You're injured. You can't sleep on the couch tonight," she said. "You can have my bed."

He shook his head. "I can't take it."

"You have to," she insisted. "You need your rest. You're barely able to stand right now you're so exhausted."

While her concern touched him, his male pride bristled and he pulled away from her. "I'm fine. Really. It was just…"

"What?" she asked.

"You," he admitted, "you still get to me, Valentina."

Her dark eyes widened with surprise. Then she sighed and said, "You still get to me, too, Cash."

A STUNNED SILENCE followed her admission. Cash didn't say anything for a long moment; then his throat moved as if he was struggling to swallow. Concern for him shot through her again. "Cash, you are not okay. Do you need painkillers? Sleep? A shower?"

He seemed to struggle to speak, his mouth open for a few moments before words rasped out of him. "I need you."

"Damn it," she murmured.

"What?" he asked, his body tense.

"I need you, too."

She didn't want to, but it was undeniable. And after how close she'd come to losing him in that parking garage, she couldn't waste another minute like she'd wasted the entire week fighting her desire for him.

He didn't move, stood frozen in place as if her admission had shocked him. She had kind of shocked herself with making it. But now that she'd admitted it, she couldn't take it back or take back the desire she felt for him.

So she stepped forward and reached for him again like she had in the hall. When she slid her arms around his waist, she turned and guided him toward the bathroom. "You need to clean up," she said as she closed the door and locked it behind them, just in case the girls woke up.

He grimaced. "The blood. I don't want to get any of it on you."

"And the bandage needs to stay dry," she reminded him. Once inside the bathroom, instead of starting the shower, she turned on the faucet and filled the tub.

"Join me," Cash implored her, his green eyes dark with desire, his pupils entirely dilated.

Despite his injured arm, he had no problem undressing. Once again he stashed his weapon where there was no way the girls could reach it on the top shelf of the linen closet. He loved them as much as she did and wanted to keep them safe, so much so that he'd stepped in front of a bullet for them.

It was no wonder she was falling for him all over again, even though she knew it wouldn't work out any differently than it had last time. She would always want more of him than he had left from his crusade against evil to give her. But now she wasn't going to worry about the future; she was only going to focus on the present.

And Cash…

Once he'd stripped off his clothes, leaving him bare but for that bandage on his arm, he reached for her.

But Valentina stepped back and pulled her dress over her head. Then she unclipped her bra and let it drop away before sliding down her panties.

He gasped as if he was in physical pain again. And maybe with the way his body was reacting, he was.

She was, her breasts aching for his touch. Her core throbbing, begging for release.

He stepped closer, but his arms stayed at his sides.

He didn't touch her. "Are you sure?" he asked, his voice raw with the desire that burned in his green-eyed gaze.

"Yes," she assured him.

But still he didn't reach for her. So she was the one who wrapped her arms around his neck and pulled his head down for her kiss. And it was as if her kiss gave him the permission he'd been waiting for, and he kissed her back passionately, his mouth making love to hers.

And finally he touched her, sliding his hands all over her body, caressing every inch of skin before he cupped her breasts and stroked his thumbs across her nipples.

She moaned in his mouth. And he moved one hand lower, between her legs, lightly touching her, stroking her. She parted her legs a little bit, and he slid a finger inside her.

And he groaned. Pulling back, he panted for breath and murmured, "You're so hot. So wet…"

So ready for him.

He lifted her up then, settling her onto the counter between the double vanities. And instead of joining their bodies, he dropped to his knees. "I have to taste you…"

His breath was hot between her legs, his tongue stroking over her clit before sliding inside her. And he made love to her with his mouth.

She arched her neck, and his hands cupped her breasts, teasing the nipples again. Pleasure shot through her, the pressure finally breaking in a climax that had her shuddering with release. She bit her lip to hold back the cry. And even though the orgasm left her limp with pleasure, it wasn't enough. She wanted him.

So she tugged on his shoulders, pulling him up from

the floor. And she slid her hand over his pulsating cock, down the length of it. He groaned and gritted his teeth, and muscles twitched along his jaw and one at the side of his neck.

"The water's going to get cold," she warned him, even as she tugged on his erection.

"Condom," he gritted.

She shook her head. "I had to regulate my periods, so I got another IUD. A better one. It's safe. You won't accidentally get me pregnant again."

He shook his head now. "They weren't an accident. They were a blessing."

And she fell even harder for him, tears stinging her eyes that he'd said that, that he clearly felt that way about his daughters. She'd been so worried.

He touched her cheek then. "Did you think I would be mad? Is that why you didn't tell me?"

"I didn't want you to think I was trying to trap you or get you back…"

"I wouldn't have thought that," he assured her.

She didn't want to talk anymore about the past. She'd made too many mistakes, cost him three years with his daughters that she couldn't give back to him. But she could give him the release he'd given her.

When she leaned over, though, to close her lips around his erection, he caught her shoulders and held her up. "I need to be inside you," he said. "I need to feel you…"

And then he was there, his erection filling her. He thrust in and out, and she wrapped her legs around him, holding him tight, matching his rhythm as the pressure built inside her again.

Despite the orgasm he'd already given her, she was frantic and desperate for release. She clutched at him, pulling him deep, using her inner muscles to squeeze him.

He gritted his teeth and groaned, sweat beading on his forehead. Then he reached between their bodies and stroked her, and she came apart in his arms.

His body shuddered as he joined her. But even after, he trembled a little. Probably with exhaustion and with pain from his injury. Blood seeped through that bandage, staining it.

And a pang of guilt struck her. "You need that bath," she said. "And rest."

"I needed you."

She'd needed him, too, not just now but the last three years. Honestly, she'd needed him before that, throughout the three years of their marriage, but she'd never quite had him. At least not enough of him...

His job had always been more important than their marriage. She didn't expect that to change now even with the girls in his life. In fact, having daughters to protect would probably make him even more determined to rid the world of evil...

She'd felt selfish for wanting more of him then. But now she wasn't thinking just of herself. She was thinking of Luci and Ana, too.

They deserved more.

So did she.

Chapter Fifteen

Cash would have suspected he'd dreamed the night before, the lovemaking with Valentina, if not for waking up in her bed where they'd made love again after the bathroom.

He wished he'd dreamed the rest of what had happened, of the masked man firing at them in the parking garage. But the bandage on his throbbing upper arm verified that it had really happened; it hadn't been just a nightmare.

And that bullet had come too damn close to them. He could hear the girls elsewhere in the condo, talking and giggling. They weren't sick and sleepy today. And they didn't sound scared, either.

That had been his biggest fear, that these attempts on their lives would change them. Would take away their innocence and trust like that serial killer had his when he'd taken his dad's life. Cash had to make sure nobody took *them* away from him. That they were safe...

Instead of leaving the bedroom, he stayed in it, making calls, checking his computer. Working. He had to focus on the case now, for everyone's sake.

The only blood Patrick had found in the garage was the blood Cash had shed. So neither he nor Dave had hit that son of a bitch. Was the man just that good? That much of a professional that Ashlynn suspected he was? Or was he just lucky?

He touched base with Dave, who'd interviewed other condo owners in the building. Everybody claimed that they hadn't been in the parking garage when the shots had been fired. They hadn't seen anything.

When Cash snorted, Dave reminded him, "We didn't see anything either, and we were there."

"Dark clothes, some kind of knit face mask this time..." Not the Mardi Gras one that the first theater victim, the one who'd survived, had said that the Landmark Killer had been wearing when he'd shot him.

What if this wasn't the Landmark Killer? Then they would have two killers to find.

"Did you check out that Blake Highland?" he asked.

"A couple DUIs," Dave said. Then he hesitated a moment before adding, "And a stalking charge..."

Cash cursed.

"Stalking charge was him following around an ex-girlfriend," Dave clarified. "Showing up at her work, at bars where she went and outside her apartment. There was no mention of firearms, and he doesn't have any registered to him."

"That doesn't mean he doesn't have them," Cash said.

"Yeah, but we don't have enough on him to get a search warrant for his place. Plus, I don't think a sloppy drunk would have been able to get the jump on us in that garage and then escape like he did."

"I would hope not," Cash said. But he'd been distracted ever since that text had come about his *sad ex-wife*.

She didn't sound sad now as her laughter drifted, like music, in from the living room. Then the little girls' giggles followed.

And such warmth flooded Cash's chest that he had to put his hand over it, had to feel if it was as warm on the outside as it was inside. Maybe he was getting Luci's fever.

Or maybe it was just love...

"This guy really does seem like a pro," Dave continued, "or maybe somebody in law enforcement."

Like the Landmark Killer. Cash couldn't share that suspicion with Dave, though. The fewer people who knew about their suspects the better. The Landmark Killer was already too close to the case and much too close to them.

Had that been him in the garage last night? Or someone else?

"Thanks for checking into Highland," Cash said. "I'm working on some angles myself. I'll let you know what I find out." After disconnecting that call, he turned his attention to his laptop and Jonathan Perkins's credit card invoices. The next calls he made were to the establishments where there were charges on the dates, around the times of the murders. The ones that retained customers' signatures on receipts agreed to scan and send them over to him. He had a feeling that the suspect he'd been assigned was not the killer.

That left five other suspects out there, and one of them was determined to kill again until all the letters of Maeve

O'Leary's name were spelled out with the first letter of the victims' names. Eleven victims.

Eleven lives that would be lost if they couldn't catch and stop this guy. And what about other lives he might take as collateral damage?

Like Valentina and Ana and Luci…

He didn't want them to be collateral damage in this crusade of his and his unit to stop the serial killer. He didn't want to lose them to anyone, but most especially not to an evil that he'd brought into their lives.

VALENTINA KNEW CASH was awake because she could hear the deep rumble of his voice coming from the bedroom. He was on the phone, as he had so often been during their marriage. Even when he hadn't been in the office, he had never been completely with her…unless they'd been making love.

She drew in a shaky breath and forced her mind from that, from what had happened between them. From how incredibly good it had felt…

And she thought of his work instead. She understood how important his job was, and she would never want to stop him from doing it. She'd just gotten tired of it consuming him 24/7. Of his professional life leaving no room for a personal life.

For her.

She'd had a professional life, too. She loved being a librarian, connecting people with the books they needed for enjoyment or research or escape. She missed her job, missed interacting with all the library patrons.

She wasn't the only one missing her life outside this

condo. The girls had been mentioning their day care friends this morning as well. They missed going to "school" as they called it. They needed to get their lives back. Their routine...

But she also remembered how she'd felt the day before with all the shooting in the parking garage. And she knew it wasn't safe for them to leave. Not yet.

Not until this person was caught, and she and the girls were no longer in danger.

Cash probably always would be, because he hunted down serial killers like they hunted their victims. Those brutal killers didn't want to be caught, to be stopped, so they would always turn on the ones trying to track them down.

Would they always come after the investigators' families, too? Would she and the girls always be in danger because of him? Maybe she should have never admitted that the girls were his. But there was no mistaking that they were with how much they acted and looked like him.

She needed to take her mind off the danger, and off what had happened the night before, of her making love with him. That might have been the most danger she'd been in, the danger of falling for him all over again, of thinking that they could make it work this time, of getting used to sleeping with him, curled up in his arms, her head on his chest, as she had every night they'd been married.

Or at least the nights he'd actually come home...

He'd pulled so many all-nighters at the office as well as doing overnight travel, tracking serial killers across the country. She'd been on her own a lot, so she hadn't thought moving out would feel that different than living with him. But it had. She'd missed him. And she'd grown to appreciate that even if they'd had just a little bit of time together, it had been better than nothing.

But then the divorce papers had arrived from his lawyer.

And she'd realized that even if she was willing to compromise to make their marriage work, he hadn't been willing or even interested. So she'd focused then on building her own life on Coney Island in the condo she'd inherited and loved. And when she'd finally realized that she had more than just a long case of the flu, she'd expanded that life to include the family she'd always wanted.

Her daughters.

She'd been so scared for their future yesterday. First with Luci and the fever that wouldn't go down, and then during the shooting...

But Cash had protected them, even taking a bullet for them. So it was no wonder she'd given in to her feelings for him, to the desire.

But she couldn't do that again; she had to protect her heart like he'd protected them. She couldn't trust him with it again, not after he'd already broken it once.

She drew in a shaky breath and reached for her cell phone. She'd checked in a couple of times with the library, answering any questions anyone might have had for her as well as making sure that her job would be there for her when it was safe for her return. The last thing she wanted to do was put any of her coworkers or library patrons in danger if someone tried to get to her there like they had on the street and in the parking garage.

She shivered despite the sunlight pouring through the

windows, warming the condo. Then she dialed work, wanting to stay connected to the life she'd put on hold.

"Coney Island Library Co-op," a male voice answered the phone.

"Randall," she greeted her coworker. "This is Valentina."

"Valentina, how are you?" he asked. "I saw on the news that there was a shooting in the parking garage of your building. Are you and the girls all right?"

"Yes, we are," she assured him. Thanks to Cash. "How are you doing? Everything okay at the library?"

"Yes, people missing you like crazy," he said. "Including me."

"That's sweet," she said. "I miss you all, too." And she wanted to get back to her own life before she got used to this life, the one with Cash home every day with her and the girls. She knew it would never be like that in real life. "How is Mrs. Miller?" she asked. "Did she pick up the memoir she wanted to read?"

"I left her a message when it came in on Monday, but she hasn't come by for it yet," he said.

She furrowed her brow, wondering why it would have taken her so long. The older woman didn't live far from the library and usually stopped by every couple of days even if she wasn't waiting for a book to come in.

"That's odd," she said. "Do you have her number? I can give her a call. No. Never mind, I think I have it." The woman had put her contact information into Valentina's phone a while ago with the offer of helping out with the girls if Valentina had ever needed it. She was such a sweet woman.

Valentina should have called her earlier, so that she wouldn't worry about her not being around the library. But then it sounded as if Mrs. Miller hadn't been there either, or for certain she would have picked up the book she'd been anxious to read.

Hoping that everything was okay with Mrs. Miller, she quickly ended her call with Randall, scrolled through her contacts until she found Mrs. Miller's and called. The cell went to an automated message that said the call could not go through at this time. But the woman also had a landline, so Valentina tried that next.

"Hello?" a man answered the phone.

Valentina froze for a moment. She'd thought the older woman was a widow living alone. "I'm sorry. I might have the wrong number. I'm looking for Mrs. Miller."

"So are we," the male voice replied.

"Why? What's happened?" she asked, fear and concern gripping her.

"Who are you?" the male voice asked.

"I'm—"

A big hand covered hers, pulling the cell away from her ear. "What's going on?" Cash asked her. "Who are you talking to?"

She shrugged. "I don't know. I'm trying to get hold of one of my library patrons but someone else answered her phone. I have a bad feeling..." It churned with nerves in her stomach now, making her feel sick. Had something happened to Mrs. Miller? Was that why she hadn't been around the library this past week?

Cash took the cell phone from her and lifted it to his ear. "This is Special Agent Cash Colton," he said. "Who are you?" He frowned, a line appearing between his eyebrows as he listened to the reply. "How long has she been missing?"

Valentina gasped and pressed a hand to her heart. "Mrs. Miller is missing?"

"How do you know her?" Cash asked, and now he held out the phone on speaker. "Detective Bentley, this is Valentina Acosta Colton. My wife."

Ex. But she didn't correct him. That wasn't as important as finding out what had happened to Mrs. Miller.

"I'm a librarian," she told the officer on the phone. "Mrs. Miller comes into the library every couple of days. I was just touching base with my work, and nobody has seen her all week and that is definitely unusual for her." Especially when she was waiting for a specific book.

"When is the last time you saw her?" the detective asked.

"I…" She drew in a shaky breath, remembering what day. "A week ago yesterday. A Friday…" The Friday that the vehicle had nearly run them down. She glanced up at Cash, wondering if he wanted her to mention that, but he shook his head.

Maybe he thought it had nothing to do with Mrs. Miller's disappearance. And hopefully it didn't.

"Surely someone's seen her since then?" she asked the detective.

"We're checking with her neighbors. It was her doorman who reported her missing. He said, like you did, that she was always out and about, going somewhere at least every couple of days. We're just checking now, trying to find family or where she might have gone."

"I don't think she had family. She'd been a widow for quite a while," Valentina said. "I am concerned..." She glanced at the girls, who were sitting on the couch watching cartoons. Hopefully they weren't paying their conversation any attention. "Mrs. Miller always wore a lot of expensive-looking jewelry. Maybe someone mugged her for it."

"Sparky..." Ana murmured.

And Valentina glanced over at her; she must have been referring to something on TV. But that was what they'd said when they'd seen Mrs. Miller the last time that Valentina had in the library and the sunlight had been reflecting off all the stones in her jewelry. Hopefully that hadn't been the last time anyone saw the older woman.

"It does look like someone's been in her apartment," the detective admitted. "Things have been gone through. Hard to know what's been taken, though. Have you been here before, Mrs. Colton?"

"A couple of times," she said. "I dropped off books for her when she wasn't feeling well last year, but I didn't pay much attention to her apartment. I wouldn't know what's missing or not." Except for Mrs. Miller. Why was she missing?

"What has been done to find Mrs. Miller so far?" Cash asked.

"The usual. We checked hospital and morgues," the detective replied. "But there were no unidentified females in her age range."

Valentina breathed a little sigh of relief then. That was good. That meant she was probably alive. Maybe she'd just gone on an impromptu trip somewhere. "She was writing her memoir," Valentina said. "She may have reached out to old friends." She'd wanted to write more about them than doing any kissing and telling of her own, as she'd put it to Valentina the last time they'd talked. "Maybe she has taken a trip somewhere…"

"Did she mention anyone in particular?" the detective asked.

"No, but she did have me find a memoir for her about a former Broadway star. I think they knew each other…" She shared the name of the star with the detective.

"She's been dead for a while," Bentley remarked. "She can't be visiting her."

"No," Valentina agreed. At least she hoped that wasn't the case; she hoped Mrs. Miller was still alive.

The detective and Cash talked for a little bit longer, but Valentina tuned out of the rest of their conversation as she kept thinking of the older woman, of how vibrant and full of life she was. She had to be okay.

She didn't even realize Cash had ended the conversation until he handed her cell back to her, its screen dark with the call ended.

"Sorry for interrupting," he said. "But when I heard what sounded like someone asking you intrusive questions—"

"Who I am is intrusive?" she teased him.

Cash had answered for her, calling her his wife. But she wasn't. Not anymore. And she wasn't sure if she ever could be again even if he asked.

"I'm sorry," he said again.

She wondered if he was referring to interrupting her call or last night. Or…

The divorce.

And with two little girls sneaking glances at them, she couldn't ask. So she focused on what mattered most at the moment. Besides the girls.

"Can you help find Mrs. Miller?" she asked. "I know you have a lot of other stuff going on, but I'm really worried about her."

"I doubt her disappearance has anything to do with what's happened recently." He glanced at the girls as well. "She's probably just gone out of town—"

"Without telling the doorman?" she asked. "She'd want him to hold her mail or packages. And she was waiting for that book, too. And if she was leaving, I really think she would have told me that day that the girls and I saw her." Tears stung her eyes as she worried about the older woman, worried about what might have happened to her. She was so sweet. And so alone.

Cash reached for her, closing his arms around her. "I will try to find her," he said. "I'll have Ashlynn do some digging, see if Mrs. Miller recently used her credit cards or booked airfare."

She released a sigh of relief. "Thank you," she said, and she wanted to hug him back, wanted to lay her head on his chest, but she saw the girls, standing now on the couch, staring at them.

She'd already been worried about their getting too attached to him being here, with them, but now she was worried about confusing them, about them thinking that they were that traditional family of mom and dad and kids all living together, all loving each other.

And she was worried that she was beginning to think that, too.

ELI SMITH. E. The last letter in *Maeve*. The perfect victim. Blond, blue-eyed and in his midthirties.

And now the Landmark Killer had the perfect location for the murder. Or at least the body drop, where that special team of FBI agents would be certain to find it and understand what it meant. How close he was to them.

Far closer than any of them realized…

Chapter Sixteen

"Ride horsey," Luci said, pointing out the living room window toward the bright lights on the rides at Luna Park. "Ride horsey."

Cash held the little girl in his arms, grateful that she was feeling better. Yesterday had been so scary for so many reasons. Her fever. The shooting.

And then last night and the feelings that kept overwhelming him after making love with Valentina. He wanted to do it again. So badly...

It was already past the girls' bedtime. But Valentina wasn't being as strict about it tonight, as if she was reluctant to be alone with him.

Did she regret what had happened between them?

He couldn't regret it, and he couldn't stop wanting to repeat it. He couldn't stop wanting her. He'd tried the past three years, and he'd failed dismally.

"Horsey," Ana echoed from Valentina's arms. She held up the other little girl to stare out the window while he held up Luci.

"They love Luna Park," Valentina said.

"Do you take them there a lot?" he asked.

She nodded. "Every weekend, but…"

Last weekend. When he'd come to stay with them after the incident with the car.

"Ride horsey?" Luci asked. And she touched his face, as if trying to get his attention.

"Soon," he said.

"School…" Ana murmured, and finally she was getting sleepy, her head dropping onto her mother's shoulder.

"School," Luci repeated.

They wanted their old lives back, their routines. He understood even as he realized he didn't want that for himself anymore. Not his usual routine of working around the clock. But how could he stop when there was a killer on the loose?

Especially if that killer was the one who was threatening and making those attempts on the lives of Valentina and the girls…

The Landmark Killer hadn't claimed another victim in over a week, as if he had been busy with something else.

With trying to kill Valentina and the girls?

It had to be him. Nothing else made sense to Cash. But then there was that woman missing. Valentina's friend.

Ashlynn had run down Mrs. Miller's credit card invoices and verified there had been no charges since she'd visited a salon on that Friday morning, the day that Valentina had seen her last at the library.

Could it have anything to do with…

Flashing lights on the street below caught his attention, fear gripping him that something had happened in the building again. But the lights continued on toward Luna Park.

"Sparky," Luci said.

Ana shook her head. "Not Sparky..."

"Flashing," Valentina clarified. "Those are flashing lights." She met Cash's gaze, and her dark eyes were full of concern.

He doubted those had anything to do with her friend, but he had a feeling in his gut, a churning of dread, that those lights had something to do with someone else.

His phone buzzed in his pocket. And he swung Luci down in order to take the call. As if Valentina didn't want the girls overhearing his conversation, she took Luci's hand and led her out of the room as she carried Ana toward their bedroom.

He probably didn't want them overhearing his conversation, either. "Hey," he answered Brennan's call.

"Sounds like another body might have just turned up," he said.

"Let me guess where..." Cash murmured. "Coney Island."

Brennan groaned with his frustration. "Yup, Luna Park."

"I just saw the lights heading that direction." And he'd instinctively known that something bad had happened. "He's messing with me. First the text about Valentina and then the other things and now this..."

"You don't have to come," Brennan said. "You were hurt last night—"

"I'm fine," he insisted. And the wound wasn't bothering him anymore except that the stitches were starting to itch.

"It might be a trap to get you out of the condo, get you away from Valentina and the girls," Brennan warned him.

"I don't think so," Cash said. "I think this is about Maeve O'Leary and his sick quest to free her."

Brennan groaned again. "Yeah, I'm on my way there. I told the local precinct not to touch anything. And I am sending a couple officers to Valentina's place, to make sure you're all safe."

"Make sure they're safe," Cash agreed. "I'm coming out to the scene, too."

"Patrick's heading up the team to process it," Brennan said. "I told Ashlynn to sit it out just in case it's a trap to bring her out, too."

"I don't think it's Jonathan Perkins," Cash said. "His alibis for the murders all checked out. I got the receipts to back it up."

Brennan released a ragged breath. "That's good. Hopefully it's not one of ours…"

"How else would he know so much about us, though?" Cash asked.

"Daddy! Daddy!" a little voice called out to him from the bedroom, pulling Cash's attention from his call while also pulling at his heart with yearning. He hated having to leave them.

"I don't know," Brennan was saying. "Want me to pick you up? I'm getting close to Valentina's building now."

"Yes, I'll meet you," Cash said.

"Daddy! Daddy!" another voice called out.

"Are you sure?" Brennan asked. Maybe he'd heard the girls calling for Cash.

Calling him Daddy…

He wondered if he would ever get used to it, if his heart would ever stop reacting to the sounds of their voices. He loved them. So much. And because he did, the best thing he could do for them right now was to find whoever was threatening them and stop him for once and for all. Then they could go back to their school during the week and the rides at Luna Park on their weekends.

"I'll be down in just a couple of minutes," he told Brennan. Then he disconnected the call and rushed through the living room to the girls' bedroom.

"Daddy!" Ana exclaimed.

"Daddy, read us the story," Luci said. "Mommy did it. Mommy did it a lot."

"They need new stories," she remarked with a smile that didn't reach her dark eyes. She was upset. Over all the things the girls were being denied? The park. Their books. Their school.

Or had she overheard his conversation with Brennan?

"I can't read to you right now," Cash said. "Uncle Brennan is coming to pick me up for work."

"It's dark out," Ana said, her little voice cracking with nerves.

"Some people have to work in the dark," he said. And on weekends and holidays and birthdays and anniversaries. He'd missed so much with Valentina even when they'd been married. He understood that was probably why she hadn't told him about the girls; she hadn't wanted him to disappoint them on all those days like he always had disappointed her.

"Why?" Luci asked, her bottom lip sticking out with the stubbornness she'd probably inherited from him.

"Because bad guys don't stop working when it gets dark." In fact, that was when some of them started, so that they could hide in the shadows and elude capture, just like the Landmark Killer had been doing.

"Get the bad guy, Daddy," Ana said as if imploring him. "Get 'im. Bang bang."

Valentina gasped as she stared at her daughter with concern. "Honey, we don't want anyone to get shot..."

"Bang bang," Ana repeated, her dark eyes filling with tears.

"I'll be safe," he promised her. "And you and your sister and Mommy are all very safe here at home."

And he had to do everything he could to keep them safe, to keep the evil away from them.

EVEN AS EXHAUSTED as they'd been, Valentina had struggled to get the girls to fall to sleep. Maybe that was because they had been overly tired and emotional. And there'd been so many tears when Cash left.

Some stung her eyes now as she stared out the living room window to where those lights still flashed at Luna Park. That serial killer, the Landmark Killer, had obviously claimed another victim or Cash wouldn't have been called out to the scene.

The girls had been so disappointed that he hadn't stayed to read to them, that he'd had to leave. And after seeing him get shot in the parking garage the day before, they were probably worried about him getting hurt again.

Like she was worried...

Maybe this murder was just to draw him out there, to where those lights flashed at the crime scene. Cash was with his brother and all those other law enforcement personnel, though. He should be safe.

Maybe safer than she and the girls were with him gone. A knock rattled her door, and her pulse quickened. There was supposed to be an officer out there. Cash had assured her of that as he'd left, that she and the girls would be safe even without him.

From the tortured look on his face, it hadn't been all that easy for him to leave the crying twins, either. Or maybe he'd thought that they would be safer without him there, that he was the reason they were in danger.

Valentina wasn't as convinced of that as he was, not since Mrs. Miller had gone missing the same day that car had nearly run them down. The coincidence just seemed too great to her.

The knock came again. And Valentina wasn't sure what to do, who to trust. If it had been Sergeant Percell, she would have felt more secure because she knew him, but it had been another officer out there. And Cash had told her not to open the dead bolt to anyone but him, not even that young female officer.

Valentina had given him the key so that he could unlock it himself when he returned. If he returned...

Even if he was safe at the crime scene, he was all caught up in the case, in catching the killer. She knew how cases like this in the past had consumed him, taking all his time and attention. And this killer was making it even more personal for him and his unit, taunting them with those texts and that article in the *New York Wire*.

"Valentina," a voice called through the door.

A voice she recognized. Ashlynn.

She hurried to the door and turned the dead bolt, pulling it open. "Did something happen? Is Cash all right?" she asked anxiously. He hadn't been gone long, but as the incident in the parking lot had proved, it only took a few seconds for someone to attack and for someone to get hurt.

"As far as I know, he's fine," Ashlynn said. "He and Brennan and Patrick didn't want me to show up at the scene..."

"Why not?" Valentina asked.

Ashlynn looked away.

And Valentina knew her concerns about Cash's safety were valid. "They're worried it could be a trap."

"And I'm a tech expert, not a special agent like they all are," she said with a sigh of frustration. "I don't carry a gun like they all do."

"I'm glad," Valentina said. "I don't want anything more to do with guns." She shuddered as she remembered what Ana had about Cash getting the bad guy. Bang bang...

Were they becoming so obsessed with guns because of Cash having to use his to protect them first with that car and then again last night?

"I'm actually here to see you," Ashlynn said. "I've been checking into your missing friend."

"Mrs. Miller," Valentina said, her heart fluttering with hope. "Have you found her?"

Ashlynn shook her head. "No, but I wish I had. From what I've been learning about her, she sounds like quite a character. She's known a lot of really interesting people, too."

Valentina nodded. "Yes. I keep telling her to write her memoir, and she said she was starting it."

"Yes, I think she was," Ashlynn said.

"You found notes or her laptop?" Valentina asked.

"So she did have a laptop," Ashlynn mused with a nod.

"Yes."

"That was missing from her apartment. Did she have it with her the day you saw her last?"

"She brought it to the library some days," Valentina said. "But I didn't see it that day. She always carried a big bag with her, though, so it could have been in that."

"I was able to find out who her internet carrier was, and I also tracked down her phone records. She used the same search engine on both," Ashlynn said. "She was looking up people and places and events that had happened in the past…" She shrugged. "Maybe it doesn't mean anything, but she sounds like an interesting woman."

"She is."

"I hope we find her," Ashlynn said.

"Thank you for helping look for her," Valentina said. "I know you have a lot going on with the Landmark Killer…" She glanced out the window toward where those lights flashed not that far away, not nearly far enough away. She and the girls walked there every weekend. Luna Park was closer than the library or day care even. Sometimes they could even hear the shrieks from the Cyclone, of the riders on the famous roller coaster.

She felt a bit like she was on it now with the way her feelings about Cash staying with them were all over the place. High and low.

"I should go," Ashlynn said, but she was peering around the condo. "Are the little ones asleep?"

Valentina nodded and flinched a bit as her head ached from their crying. The volume and the stress of it. "They were upset when Cash left."

"You're worried they're getting too used to him being around," Ashlynn surmised.

They weren't the only ones she was worried about, but she didn't admit that to Cash's sister.

"I've missed you," Ashlynn said. "It's so good to see you again."

Valentina hugged the other woman. "I missed you, too." And worse yet, she'd missed Cash. So damn much…

The past three years had been so hard, not knowing if she'd been doing the right thing, worried that she was cheating him and his daughters of the relationship they'd deserved to have. She hadn't considered all the other people she'd cheated, too. "I'm sorry," she said to Ashlynn. "I should have told you all about the girls."

"We would have been there for you," Ashlynn said. "Mom would probably have even moved back to New York to have a relationship with her grandbabies."

Valentina flinched as all the guilt and regret came over her.

"But we all understand," Ashlynn continued. "We know what Cash is like when he's working a case, how it consumes him. We know that you had your reasons for divorcing him."

"He was the one who served me," Valentina said. "I just wanted some space, moved in here to think…" She stared at the condo, remembering how empty it had felt without her grandparents here and especially without Cash here.

Ashlynn cursed. "Just goes to show what idiots guys are. I know he loved you. Loves you. I don't think he ever stopped. And when he got that text about you…" She shuddered. "From that sick serial killer…"

"After how you all lost your dad to one, I can understand how it would upset him."

"It upset him because it mentioned you," she said.

"Have you received one?" Valentina wondered.

Ashlynn shook her head. "And I sure as hell hope that I don't. But then it might give me another shot at tracing it back to the son of a bitch. He's good, though. He's smart."

Maybe too smart to get caught. Ashlynn didn't say it, but it was clear that the tech expert was worried about it. And she was worried about her brothers, too.

With another hug, she quickly left. And Valentina went back to the window to study those flashing lights and worry that it had been a trick, another way to draw Cash into danger.

Like the danger he'd been in the night before when that gunman had fired so many shots at him…

He'd gotten lucky in that only one had hit him and then only grazed him. Would his luck hold out if the killer came after him again?

If he was coming after him now?

Chapter Seventeen

He had his orders to follow. He'd carried out the first part of it. There was one body...

One he hoped would never be found. Then there was the rest of it. Dispose of all possible evidence and every possible witness.

Sure. He'd disposed of what he'd needed to protect himself, but part of that was holding on to some insurance, because he dealt with people he couldn't trust. And he'd learned how to protect himself.

He hadn't counted on the witnesses that there'd been to that first part of his order, and while nobody might take them seriously at the moment, when they got older...

They were an unknown, a threat he had to eliminate. It wasn't just his reputation on the line anymore. It was his life. The person who'd hired him wasn't someone you could let down without consequences, which was another reason for that insurance he'd taken out.

The person who'd hired him was a killer and would have no qualms about killing him. Hell, even if he finished his assignment, he was liable to die because just like those little witnesses to his crime, he was a threat.

He needed to act fast and go underground again. But he could only go underground after those kids were dead.

And that woman...

They had to die if he had any chance of living himself.

THE SOUNDS OF the rides and the flashing lights had Cash on edge. He wasn't worried about the killer standing out there somewhere beyond the lights and crime scene tape, hiding in the shadows. Cash *hoped* the Landmark Killer was there.

And not back at Valentina's building.

That was where Cash wanted to be. With the girls. Reading them the story they'd wanted him to read. Watching over them as they slept, keeping them safe.

And Valentina...

His pulse quickened just thinking about her. But that look on her face when he'd left her to deal on her own with the crying kids... He'd probably confirmed her every fear about him, about what kind of father he would be.

One who disappointed his kids.

Like, as a husband, he had disappointed her so many times. But if he didn't focus on his job, on stopping these serial killers, they would keep killing.

"He was shot to death," Patrick said.

"Will you run any ballistics from this scene against the ballistics from the parking garage?" Cash asked.

Patrick nodded, but his face was tense. So was Brennan's.

"You don't think he's the one who was shooting at me," Cash surmised.

"You don't match the profile," Patrick pointed out. And

he pulled the sheet back from the victim's face. His blue eyes stared blankly up at them, shocked, as if he'd had no idea the bullets were coming. As if he'd been taken totally by surprise...

And he probably had been.

It was as if the Landmark Killer was invisible to these people, like he just appeared out of nowhere and killed. Only one of his victims had survived, and even that victim had been unable to give them very much information. Just a vague description that could have been anyone.

But they had a detailed description of all the victims. They all looked the same. Blue eyes. Blond hair. Thirties.

"Along with his ID, for an Eli Smith, I found this in his pocket." Patrick held out a see-through evidence bag containing a note. The lights from the Cyclone flashed a myriad of colors across the words: *Until the brilliant and beautiful Maeve O'Leary is freed, I will kill in her honor and name. MAEVE down. O up.*

"But why here?" Cash asked. "Why so close to Valentina's?" He glanced over his shoulder, and he could see her high-rise building. He could probably even see which window was hers. Was she there? Watching for him?

Or was she still with the girls, trying to settle them down? Soothe their tears?

She'd had to do that alone for the past nearly three years. She knew what she was doing. Why did Cash feel so guilty about leaving her?

And not just now but for all the other times he'd left her during their marriage. When he'd gone out when someone else could have taken the trip or handled the assignment...

"He's messing with us," Brennan said, his voice gruff with irritation. "That article in the *New York Wire*. The texts. And these damn notes. He knows nobody is going to free Maeve O'Leary."

"So he's killing then for no real reason," Cash said. "Why couldn't he be the one going after Valentina and the girls?"

"The car, for one thing," Patrick said. "Stealing it right before using it to try to run them down. That felt like a heat of the moment thing." He pointed to the body lying on the ground. "This was thought out. The victim and the location specifically chosen. The guy going after you doesn't seem like a serial killer."

"But he's a professional of some sort," Cash said. "That's what you and Ashlynn thought after finding the vehicle burned up."

Patrick nodded.

And Brennan reminded him, "We all make enemies."

Even Valentina…

Or the girls?

He nearly laughed at the thought of any of those three making someone angry enough to want them killed. So it had to be about him.

Maybe he shouldn't go back to her. To them.

Maybe he should let other officers protect them. Or hire a bodyguard for them. Maybe they would be safer without him in their lives. But then he remembered the girls' tears, and he ached to be with them now, holding them, reading to them. And after they fell asleep, he could be with Valentina like he'd been the night before, in her bed, with her in his arms.

He'd been a fool to leave them, especially if that was what someone had been waiting for. For him to leave them alone and unprotected.

But they weren't. Officers were there. And Ashlynn had even texted him that she was stopping by to talk to Valentina about her missing friend.

They were safe.

He was the one in danger of falling so hard for his family that he wouldn't be able to leave them ever again. And then more people would die like poor Eli Smith who probably had a family of his own, kids and a wife that he would never see again, just as Cash's dad had never been able to see his family again.

So much time had passed since Cash had left for the crime scene at Luna Park, Valentina had begun to suspect he was never coming back.

That might be for the best, so the girls got over him, so she got over him…

But she didn't know if he'd decided that he wasn't coming back or if someone else had decided for him. She was so worried about him. Was he okay?

Had that killing happened so close to her place just to lure Cash out there? So that he could kill him?

Or were she and the girls the targets now? That was how it had felt that day on the street for certain. Nobody could have known that Cash would show up when he had, that he was coming out to check on them.

If he hadn't…

She shuddered to think about what could have happened. She hadn't noticed that car coming at them until she'd already pushed the stroller into the street. If not for Cash knocking them back, out of the way, they could have been seriously hurt or worse.

Just like in the parking garage.

Cash had been out that day, meeting with his team, and nobody had taken any shots at him when he'd left on his own. Or when he'd returned on his own.

It wasn't until she and the girls had been with him that the gunshots had been fired. And while Cash was the one who'd been hit, he had been standing in front of them. Protecting them...

That was when and how he'd been hurt. So hopefully he was safe now, out there with his team.

What about her and the girls?

Instead of trying to sleep in her bed, the bed in which she and Cash had made love what seemed such a short time ago, she'd curled up on the couch. Not that she could relax or fall asleep.

But it put her between the door and the girls' bedroom. No matter who stood outside in the hall guarding them, she was guarding them, too. She wouldn't let anything happen to her girls, wouldn't let the danger touch them any more than it already had, that had them talking about bad guys and guns.

She felt their innocence slipping away from them as the danger hovered over them. When would it be safe for them to go back to their normal lives? Their routine?

Or was she being naive to think that anything could ever be the same again? That she would ever be the same again?

The doorknob rattled as if someone was messing with

the lock, and she shot up from the couch, trembling with fear and anger. Anybody trying to get into the condo, to her girls, was going to have to go through her first.

She didn't have a gun, though. Thank God. With the girls' sudden fascination with them, she didn't like Cash even having his in the house, though he was good about keeping it out of their sight and reach.

Because she didn't have a gun, Valentina had to scramble to find another weapon, something to protect her and the girls from danger. To keep them safe.

She rushed toward the kitchen and reached for the knife block. But a knife could be easily wrested away from her, if the intruder was bigger, stronger.

So she grabbed the cast-iron frying pan that hung from the copper hook over the island. It was heavy, unlike the teal ones that had hung beside it. Clasping the handle, she hurried back toward the door. The knob had stopped rattling for a moment as if the person was struggling to unlock it.

Cash had a key, so he would have opened the door already if it was him. He probably would have called out to her first, too. So it wasn't Cash trying to get in.

Who was?

What had happened to the officer stationed outside the door? Valentina wished now that she had asked Ashlynn to stay at least until Cash got back, but the FBI tech didn't carry a gun. Ashlynn wouldn't have been able to protect them like Cash had that day.

Where was Cash now? When she needed him?

Was he still at work on this case, chasing a killer while that killer was out there in the hall, trying to get to her and the girls?

Chapter Eighteen

That damn neighbor was lurking around again. Despite how late it was, Blake Highland was the first thing Cash saw when he stepped off the elevator. As usual he was loitering outside Valentina's door.

When was he going to get the clue that she wasn't interested? That she didn't need him?

She hadn't even needed Cash the past three years. She'd gone through her pregnancy and the first few years of the twins' lives without any help from him. Financial or emotional.

She was strong and independent. So much so that Cash was surprised she'd let him stay this past week, that she hadn't tossed him out like she probably should have. But she loved their daughters more than she resented him, and she was willing to do anything to protect them.

Even put up with him.

But she'd done more than that the night before. They'd made love with all the passion they'd always had. Maybe even more because it had been so long. Too damn long since he'd been with her, inside her, part of her...

He had missed her so much these past three years

and, somehow just these past few hours that he'd spent at the crime scene with the rest of his unit, he'd missed her even more. Clearly he shouldn't have stayed away so long since Blake Highland had taken it upon himself to hover around outside again.

Thankfully the officer was still at the door. A young woman in uniform, and Cash realized what Blake was doing here, flirting with the female officer. Instead of getting rid of the guy, she was smiling at him and leaning back against the door, so distracted that she didn't notice Cash approaching until he cleared his throat.

Then she jerked away from the door while Blake turned and glared at him, as if he was the intruder. When he reached for his shield, showing his badge, the officer touched her holster but didn't draw her weapon. Cash would have felt better if she had pointed her gun at him, at least until she'd seen that he was pulling out a badge and not his own gun. She wasn't the officer who'd been here when he'd left for Luna Park. She must have replaced the other female officer.

"Special Agent Colton," she said as her face flushed. "I was sent here to relieve the other officer and guard the door, but I wasn't told anything else. I didn't realize the FBI was involved in whatever is going on here…"

"That's my family in there," he said, staring hard at Blake Highland.

The guy smirked, his glassy eyes glinting with resentment. "Wouldn't have known it these past few years. Never been around till now…"

Cash was not about to defend or explain himself to this

guy. "What are you doing around?" he asked Highland. "It's late. Why are you loitering outside my wife's door?"

The female officer's face flushed a deeper shade of red. She was young and inexperienced, so Cash wouldn't judge her too harshly for letting the guy distract her. But he also wouldn't trust her again to protect his family.

Hell, he really could only trust himself at this point. And Dave. Hell, maybe Dave was the better choice to keep them safe, but he'd been called out to Luna Park, too, since the body had been found in his precinct.

Basically in Valentina's backyard...

Why?

Cash turned toward Blake again. "What's your deal, Highland? You're hanging around all the time but you didn't notice that shooter in the garage last night?" Or had it been two nights ago? It was probably closer to morning than night right now.

"I wasn't in the garage," the man replied. "I asked you when you first turned up around here what was going on, if the rest of the building was in danger. You said we weren't and then that shooting happened in the garage. Innocent bystanders could have been hit. Killed. I'd say we are in danger. That having your family here is a risk to the rest of us."

"If you're so scared, what are you doing hanging around outside Valentina's door all the time?" Cash challenged his claim.

"I still care about her," Blake said, "I want to make sure she and those kids are safe."

The officer tensed even more, and now she glared at Blake, maybe realizing that his interest hadn't really been in her. The guy was pretty obsessed with Valentina. Obsessed enough to try to hurt her or the girls? For what reason? To scare her into *his* arms? Or out of anger and jealousy because she'd never given him a chance?

"I don't trust you, Highland," he admitted. "You have a stalking charge against you already. Want me to add another one to it?"

Now the officer gasped, probably realizing that she'd failed miserably at her job of guarding the door.

"You can leave now, Officer," he dismissed her.

"But, sir, I—"

"I've got this now," he assured her. "I will protect my family."

She glanced from him to Blake, who'd not slunk back to his apartment yet. Just how much had he had to drink? Enough to make him try something stupid?

Cash almost hoped he would, so that he would have a reason to arrest the guy and keep him away from Valentina.

The officer hurried off to the elevator, leaving Cash alone with the drunk neighbor.

"Your family," the guy said with a derisive snort. "You don't deserve or appreciate them."

Cash was tired. Tired from the shooting and then the long day and night, tired of chasing serial killers like the Landmark Killer who thought taking lives was some kind of sick game. And he was tired of this guy.

"Get the hell out of here," Cash advised him. "Before I arrest you."

"On what charge?" Blake asked. "And if you're going to do it without cause, I might just give you cause…"

And he tightened his hands into fists, as if he was going to lunge at Cash.

As if he was going to fight him for Valentina.

Because he wanted her or because he wanted to hurt her?

VALENTINA HAD BEEN standing against the wall for a while, listening to the deep rumble of voices in the hall. Was that Cash? Or someone else?

The officer?

She couldn't tell who was out there or what was going on. A tussle?

There were a few grunts. An expletive.

Then silence. Several long moments of silence. She should have grabbed her cell phone, should have called 9-1-1 for backup for the officer.

For herself...

But she didn't see her phone on the couch; it must have dropped between the cushions. And in the time she took to find it, the intruder could get through that door, could get inside and get to the girls.

Fury replaced her fear, coursing through her, making her strong. Making her brave.

For them.

She had to protect them. So she gripped the frying pan so tightly that her fingers tingled from the effort. And when the lock rattled again, the dead bolt turning, she was ready. She'd shut off the lights, so that the intruder wouldn't see her in the shadows. But light from the hallway outside the door spilled into the room, blinding her for a moment so that she couldn't see who stood in the doorway, just the height and broadness of the shadow looming over her.

She stepped away from the wall and swung. The frying pan connected with a hard body with such force that Valentina lost her grip on it, and the heavy cast-iron skillet dropped to the floor with a resounding clang. That clang echoed the curse and grunt of pain from the shadow.

And she recognized that voice...too late.

She'd hit Cash.

"Are you okay?" she asked with alarm. What if she'd hit his wounded arm?

Before he could answer her, screams rang out from the little girls' bedroom. Either they'd awakened with nightmares like they had a couple of times, or that loud clang and curse had awakened them.

And scared them.

All she'd wanted to do was protect them, but she'd made the situation worse, just as she had when she'd kept her pregnancy and their daughters secret from Cash and his family. Guilt and regret overwhelmed her.

"I'm coming," she called out to them. Then she turned back to Cash. "Are you okay?"

He closed the door behind him, shutting out the light from the hall, plunging them back into darkness.

And the girls screamed louder, as if they were closer or more frightened. Maybe they'd left their beds to find her, and they'd come into the living room just as it had gone dark again. They had been afraid of the dark even before all the bad things started happening.

The car nearly running them down.

The gunshots in the garage.

This, though, was her fault. And when the lights suddenly came on, she saw just how badly she'd screwed up when she saw the red mark on Cash's jaw. She had hurt him.

Chapter Nineteen

Cash had stepped out of the chaos in the hall, the altercation with that idiot Highland, into the chaos inside the
condo. The blow…

The screams.

And now the tears.

The little girls were crying, and tears glistened in Valentina's eyes, too. "I'm sorry," she said. "I didn't know
it was you."

"Are you sure?" he asked, but he was just teasing. "I
was gone longer than I thought I would be."

"I wouldn't hurt you," she said, and she reached out to
touch his jaw. "Not purposely…"

"You didn't do this," he assured her. Highland had
been drunk enough to hit him, and wanting a reason to
hit him back, Cash had let him. He regretted that now
since Valentina and the girls were so upset. He turned
toward their daughters. "Hey, hey, you two, what's with
all the tears? Everything's fine."

"Bang, bang," Ana sobbed. "Bang, bang…"

"It wasn't a gun," Valentina assured them. And she

picked up the frying pan that had dropped to the floor. "It was this. That's what the noise was that woke you up."

"Bang, bang," Ana insisted.

"No, nobody was shooting," she said.

But that wasn't true. Earlier tonight someone had been shooting: the Landmark Killer. And a man had lost his life because of that. His family had lost someone they'd loved just like Cash and his mom and siblings had lost his dad so long ago. It wasn't fair.

That was why he'd chosen the job he had, why Brennan had worked so hard to get their special unit established so that they could focus solely on serial killers.

And that was what Cash had done all these years to the exclusion of everything else. Even the woman he'd loved...

The woman he still loved, if he was honest with himself. While he could be honest with himself, he didn't dare be honest with her, not when he was probably the reason she and the girls were in danger.

Why the girls were so scared.

Now tears stung his eyes, tears of regret that the darkness of his world had touched the lightness and innocence of theirs. Maybe Valentina had been right to never tell him about them, to never want him to be part of their lives.

But it was too late now. He couldn't undo what had been done; all he could do was try to keep them safe from any more darkness and danger.

"You don't have any reason to be afraid," he told them as he scooped them both up in his arms. He flinched a little at the ache in his shoulder, the one Valentina had whacked with the frying pan.

She was so fierce. So unbelievably brave and protective. It was no wonder he'd fallen for her all over again. But just like before, he knew she deserved better than him as a husband and as a father for her kids.

"I will keep you safe," he promised, and he hoped it was a promise he could keep. He glanced at Valentina and saw how her brow furrowed with concern. Obviously she didn't think he could keep it any more than he'd kept the promises he'd made her on their wedding day.

While her lips pursed, as if she wanted to say something, she didn't. She just carried that frying pan into the kitchen and set it in the sink.

He focused on the little girls, who snuggled against him, sniffling and shaking yet. "Let's read that story you wanted me to read," he suggested, trying to distract them from their fears.

He wished he could distract himself from his fear that something would happen to them, and he wouldn't be able to protect them like he'd promised.

VALENTINA WAS A mess of guilt and concern and...love. She loved her daughters so much, but she was also falling hard all over again for the man who cuddled with them in their beds, beds which he'd pulled close enough together so he could span the distance and lie between them, reading the story to them that Valentina had read so many times before.

They needed new books. But after what had happened

in the garage the night before, she was afraid to take them out, afraid to put them in danger again.

Cash had vowed to keep them safe, but was that even a promise he could make, let alone keep? Finally they fell back to sleep, their eyes closed, their little bodies relaxed. They believed him, believed that he would protect them from the bad guys.

But Valentina saw how that red mark on his jaw was darkening to a bruise. If she hadn't done that with the frying pan, then someone else had. A bad guy from whom he hadn't protected himself?

He gently eased Ana from his right arm and then Luci from his left, and as he did, he flinched. Was he in pain from the bullet wound or from where she'd struck him?

"Are you okay?" she asked in a whisper.

He didn't answer her until he got away from their beds, squeezing sideways through the narrow space he'd left between them, and into the hall. "I'm fine," he said.

"Liar," she accused him, and she brushed her fingertips along his jaw. "You need an ice pack."

"It's fine."

"What happened?" she asked, her heart beating fast with concern. "Was it a trap? The crime scene at Luna Park?"

He released a heavy sigh. "Not for me. There was another victim, matching the description of the other ones, with a note from the Landmark Killer in his pocket."

She gasped.

"I shouldn't have shared that with you."

"I won't tell anyone," she assured him. She didn't want to think about a killer, much less talk about him. And she knew that psychopaths like that sometimes killed for the attention, for the fame.

He sighed again. "I'm sure it'll get out somehow, and if it doesn't, the Landmark Killer will make sure that it does, just like he got that article out about my dad." His voice cracked on that; the pain must have still been fresh all these years later.

Or maybe that article had made it fresh again. Even before she'd read that, Valentina had known that his dad was the reason that Cash did what he did, pursuing serial killers. And that was the reason that she had never asked him to leave his job, to quit doing what he felt he had to do; she'd just asked that he not let it consume him and destroy them.

He hadn't been able to keep that promise to her. She hoped he could keep the one he'd made to their daughters.

"If this didn't happen at the crime scene, where did it happen?" she asked, wondering about that mark on his jaw, hoping that she hadn't caused it with the frying pan despite his assurances that she hadn't.

"Hallway," he said.

She sucked in a breath. So she had been right to worry. "You were attacked in the hallway? Someone was out there trying to get in?"

"Your damn neighbor again," Cash said, his voice lowering to a growl.

"Blake Highland attacked you? He was the one trying to get inside?"

Cash sighed now. "I don't know if he was trying to get in or just trying to get a rise out of me."

"But you're the one who got hit," she said. "Did you have the officer arrest him?"

He shook his head. "I already let the young officer go," he said. "And Highland wasn't worth the paperwork. He's on notice now. He knows we've checked out his record."

"Record…"

"Couple driving under the influence convictions and a stalking charge," Cash said.

She shivered with the realization that her instincts about the guy had been right. She hadn't trusted him and apparently with good reason.

"You're cold," Cash said. "You need to go back to bed, too."

"I wasn't in bed yet," she said.

"It's late."

"I was scared," she admitted.

"It didn't show. You were fierce with that frying pan," he remarked, his mouth curving into a grin. And he touched his shoulder now and grimaced.

"I did hit you," she said. "I'm sorry. I didn't know it was you. I heard someone messing with the door, and I was worried."

"You gave me the keys when I left," he reminded her. "So I could let myself in without waking you up." He stepped closer now and touched her cheek, cupping it in his palm. "But I can see that you never went to sleep."

"I couldn't," she said. "I was worried about you, too, that it was a trap to get you out of here."

"I was worried about that, too," he said. "That it might have been a trick to lure me away from you, so someone could try to hurt you and the girls again."

"Why?" she asked. "Why come after us to get to you? And why would he even want to get to you? Are you that close to catching him?"

He grimaced again, but it seemed to be with frustration, not pain. "I wish. While we've narrowed it down to six possible suspects, the one I was assigned to investigate has alibis. It's not him. So I pose no threat to this killer. I have no idea why he threatened you."

"But did he?" she asked. "You showed me that text. He just mentioned me, just like he mentioned your dad. He didn't threaten to hurt me. He just called me sad." And he hadn't been wrong. Whenever she'd thought of Cash over the years, she had gotten sad.

But how had he known that?

Had he been watching her?

"Brennan doesn't think it's the Landmark Killer who's come after you. He thinks he just sends these texts to mess with us," Cash admitted.

"Is that what you think now?" she asked. "You don't believe anymore that he's the one who tried to run down me and the girls? Who shot at us in the parking garage?"

He shrugged and pushed a slightly shaky hand through his overly long hair. "I don't know…"

"I feel like it has something to do with Mrs. Miller," she admitted. "The timing of her disappearing and when all that started happening to me and the girls, it seems like too great a coincidence."

He released a soft breath and his shoulders sagged slightly. "I hope it's not because of me. I hope that I haven't brought this evil into your lives."

She could see how much that bothered him. She took

his hand and tugged him toward her bedroom. "It's not your fault that there's evil in the world, Cash," she said. "And it's not your responsibility to stop it all by yourself."

She'd told him that so many times during their marriage. That he didn't have to act as if he was the only one who could stop the serial killers. He had a team that all worked together toward that goal, and there were others in law enforcement who fought like they did, who enforced justice, who caught the killers.

"The girls shouldn't have been your responsibility all on your own either," he said. "I should have been helping you, financially and…"

"You said you didn't want a family," she said when he trailed off. What had he left unsaid? What had he thought she needed besides financial support? Him? Unfortunately she had, but she hadn't thought he wanted her. "You didn't want *this*. Didn't want them. I didn't want to force another responsibility onto you."

"Valentina," he murmured, his voice gruff with frustration and remorse. Then he reached out and pulled her into his arms, holding her close. His long body shuddered against hers. "There are so many things I want to ask you. So many promises I want to make."

"Don't," she said. "Don't make promises you can't keep. Not to me and not to the girls."

He flinched as if she'd hit him with that frying pan again. "I know I disappointed you before. And I don't want to disappoint them."

"I already told you that you can't take responsibility for everything," she reminded him. "You can't take complete responsibility for our safety. You can't be with us 24/7. I have to get back to work. The girls need to get back to their day care, back to their routine."

"I know. I just wish…"

"What?" she asked.

"That we could stay here in this little safe bubble, at least for a little while longer."

But it wasn't safe. Not for her. She was falling for him all over again, and that was putting her heart in danger. But for the moment, for what was left of the night, she didn't want to worry about it.

So she tugged him the rest of the way into her bedroom and closed the door behind them, locking it in case the girls woke up again. She would hear them if they tried to get in or if they called out from their room. But for the moment she didn't want to be just a mother.

She wanted to be a woman, too. And nobody had ever made her more aware of her sexuality than Cash. He must have realized what she wanted, because he began to undress her, slowly unbuttoning her blouse. And every inch of skin he bared, he kissed and caressed.

Her knees began to shake, threatening to fold beneath her. As if he knew, he lifted and carried her to the bed. Then he pulled off her yoga pants and underwear, and he stroked and touched her everywhere.

Heat streaked through her, and she throbbed as the tension built inside her. She needed a release. She needed Cash. She reached out toward him, trying to tug him down with her.

But he stepped back instead, and then he stripped off his clothes. Blood had seeped through the bandage on his right arm, as if his stitches had reopened.

She worried that she'd done that with the frying pan, but then she saw the angry red mark on his left shoulder. She could have hit his head or neck with as close as she'd come. She could have seriously injured him. Guilt gripped her.

Finally, naked, he joined her on the bed.

She reached out and touched his shoulder. "I'm so sorry."

"I'm not," he said. "I'm damn impressed. You're so strong, Valentina. So resourceful."

She'd had to be, loving him like she had and losing him, but she didn't want to make him feel any guiltier than he already did.

So instead of talking, she pushed him onto his back, and with her mouth and her hands, she showed him how resourceful she could be.

His body tensed and shuddered, sweat beading on his brow. "You're torturing me, Valentina. I need you." Then he lifted her up until she straddled him, and he eased inside her.

She was on top, in charge, so she set the pace, teasing him with slow rocking movements. He teased her back, cupping her breasts in his hands, rubbing her nipples between his thumbs and index fingers.

She arched her neck and swallowed the moan bubbling up the back of her throat. And that pressure that built inside her became unbearable. Then he moved his hands to her hips, clutching them as he thrust.

And the pressure broke as an orgasm shuddered through her. But he kept moving and she kept coming until finally his body tensed and pulsed beneath her. He came, and she dropped onto his chest, which heaved with his pants for breath. His heart pounded as fast and frantically as hers did and she melted against him, feeling boneless with satisfaction.

If only this could last...

If only they could stay in this bubble forever...that was what she wanted. But she knew they'd have to get back to the real world soon, the world that at the moment was filled with danger for all of them.

Chapter Twenty

He couldn't wait around for them to come out again. He had to finish up this assignment and get the hell out of Brooklyn before this assignment finished him.

He had to get rid of them because he figured it was only a matter of time before someone figured out what those girls had seen and what he'd done. And he was as much of a loose end to the man who'd hired him as those girls were to him...

At least he'd gotten some insurance. If he didn't make it out of this assignment alive, there would be consequences for a lot of other people. If the right person knew where to look...

Like he knew where to look for that damn loose end he'd left dangling. He had to pluck it off, had to burn them up like he had that car. And like he should have the body. But it wouldn't be found. At least he hoped, since he wasn't even sure where it was now himself.

But he knew where *they* were. He just had to figure out a way to get them out. So he could kill them all.

CASH HAD TO leave them again. He hated doing it, especially as it was getting close to night again, but when Valentina had learned that Ashlynn got one of those texts, she'd insisted he support his sister.

Before he left, Cash made sure that Dave was the one watching the door this time; he didn't trust anyone else to protect his family. His family...

He hadn't wanted one, just as Valentina kept reminding him, but now that he had them, he couldn't imagine his life without them.

That afternoon, before Ashlynn had let him and the others in the unit know about her text, Cash had been FaceTiming his mom in Florida, introducing her to his daughters, her granddaughters. Mom had cried, and Valentina had, too, with guilt for keeping their daughters from the Colton family.

He knew why she'd done it, though, because she hadn't trusted him not to hurt and disappoint the girls like he had her. His mother must have known as well, because she'd assured Valentina that she understood and that she just wished she could have been there for her and the girls. And she'd promised that she would be from now on.

Cash knew that his mother would keep her promise. She always did. Could he keep the promises he'd made to the girls, though?

Before disconnecting the call with his mom, he'd spoken to her alone for a moment. And she'd cried harder than she had over meeting her granddaughters. "This was what I wanted for you, Cash, for you and Valentina," she said. "I wanted you to build a future, to enjoy the present and to let go of the past."

"Mom—"

She'd interrupted him with a laugh, as if she'd known

what he was about to say. "I know that probably sounds hypocritical coming from me. But it's not like I didn't try to move on after your father died. I just never found anyone I loved like I loved him. He was my soulmate. Like I think Valentina is yours. Don't let her go a second time, Cash. Don't put your work before her again."

That was good advice, advice he'd had to ignore when just an hour or so after that call ended, he learned about Ashlynn's text.

"Go," Valentina had insisted.

And he'd felt a twinge uneasy, as if she wanted to get rid of him, as if she needed some space. They'd made love again the night before, but just like the last time, when he'd awakened, she was already up.

It wasn't because the girls had awakened her, either, because he'd found her alone in the kitchen, looking pensive as she sipped a cup of coffee. "You okay?" he had asked.

"I just keep thinking about Mrs. Miller." She was worried about her friend, and now she was worried about his sister. Valentina was such a caring person, such a loving protective mother.

And as a wife, she really hadn't asked for much from him. She hadn't wanted him to quit his job, just strike a better balance between his professional life and his personal life. He hadn't been able to figure out how to do that. Maybe if he'd tried harder...

But he'd always applied that attitude to cases. If they tried harder, they could catch the killer. They had to... because the Landmark Killer was too damn close now, to Valentina and the girls as well as the rest of Cash's family.

"You okay?" Brennan now asked the same question Cash had posed to Valentina that morning, drawing Cash out of his thoughts and back to the present and that small hotel suite he'd rented again.

Brennan and Patrick had been there when Cash had arrived. But Ashlynn...

"I'm just worried," Cash admitted. About all his family. Even though Dave was watching the door, he had a really bad feeling about leaving Valentina and the girls alone. After the attempt in the parking garage, there was no doubt that the shooter knew where they lived. How had he even gotten into the structure? Was he a resident?

"What happened to your face?" Patrick asked, pointing to the bruise on Cash's jaw. "You didn't have that last night at the crime scene."

"I had a small altercation with one of Valentina's neighbors," Cash admitted.

"A suspect in the parking garage shooting?" Patrick asked. "It would make sense to be someone in the building. Otherwise I don't know how he would have gotten in."

"It would make sense," Cash said. "But I don't think the guy would try to hurt her and the girls." Who would? Who was that big a monster? The Landmark Killer...

"He just wanted to hurt you?" Patrick asked with an arched eyebrow.

"He was drunk and goading me," Cash said. "Probably trying to get me banned from the building."

"So you let him hit you first," Brennan said.

He shrugged. "I don't want Valentina to get in trouble with the condo board." She loved that place, had had some of her happiest childhood moments in that condo with her grandparents. He didn't want to take that away from her, just as three years ago he hadn't wanted to take away her dream of having a family someday.

A knock rattled the door, and Brennan opened it to Ashlynn. "Where have you been?" he asked. "We've been worrying about you."

Ashlynn looked worried, too, her face a bit pale, and her hand trembled slightly as she reached out to close and lock the door behind her. "I'm just mad," she insisted. "I'm sick of this guy playing games with us."

"Show us the text," Patrick said.

She held out her cell, and they all passed it around. Brennan read it first and cursed, then handed the phone to Cash.

Your poor murdered daddy wouldn't be very proud of how little you've accomplished in HIS name. Should you even be alive yourself?

This wasn't as innocuous as the texts to Sinead and Brennan and him had been. This wasn't just a taunt; it was clearly a threat.

"Son of a bitch," he muttered, and as he passed the phone to Patrick, his hand shook a little with fury and fear for his sister.

Patrick read it and closed his eyes for a moment before focusing on Ashlynn again. "I assume this is also untraceable?"

She nodded. "I tried."

"Well, you're done," Brennan said. "You're off the case and off to a safe house. That is a blatant threat."

Ashlynn shook her head. "He's not scaring me off this case."

"We'll work harder, around the clock on it," Cash vowed. "We'll catch him." And once again he was making promises he might not be able to keep, promises that might make him break other promises...to his family.

But the Landmark Killer had blatantly threatened Ashlynn's life.

"You need to be in a safe house, protected," Brennan insisted. "Preferably a safe house far away from New York."

That was where Cash was going to have to put Valentina and the girls, somewhere the shooter wouldn't be able to find them. The Landmark Killer? Or someone else?

"I am leaving town," Ashlynn said. And she turned slightly to show the backpack she carried. "I've got my phones and my laptop. And I've a got a lead I need to follow."

"You're not a special agent," Brennan reminded her. "You're our tech expert."

"Yeah, so I know how to go completely off the grid," she assured him. "Nobody will be able to track me down. I'll be safe."

"What's the lead?" Cash asked. "Is it about Xander Washer?" He was the potential suspect she'd been assigned to investigate.

"I thought he had alibis for the murders," Patrick said.

She shrugged. "Yeah, but I don't know. There's something fishy about them."

"We need to tell the director," Brennan said with a sigh.

"Let me check this out first," Ashlynn said. "And I'll let you know what I find." She turned toward Cash. "Speaking of finds, I think Valentina's friend turned up."

"Alive?" He hoped that was the case, that the woman had simply gone on an impromptu trip.

She shook her head.

He cursed, and that feeling he'd had that he shouldn't have left Valentina and the girls intensified. They were definitely in danger, and even if it didn't have anything to do with the Landmark Killer, someone was obviously still very determined to kill them.

VALENTINA WAS WORRIED about a lot of things. One of them was that text that Ashlynn had received; she was worried about her. That was mainly why she'd encouraged Cash to go to that meeting with his siblings. She knew how close they all were, especially after their father's murder. Hopefully Ashlynn wasn't in danger.

Valentina was, of falling so hard for Cash that she wouldn't be able to get over him again. If she ever actually had.

That was another reason she'd been happy for Cash to leave for a while. So she could take a breath without inhaling the scent of him. So her pulse could slow to a normal rate. So she wasn't so aware of him that every nerve tingled.

But even with him gone, she couldn't stop thinking about him, about how they kept making love like they were making up for lost time. For three years…

Even though they'd been exhausted the past couple of nights, they hadn't been able to get enough. To love enough.

To feel enough.

But it wasn't just pleasure and attraction that she felt around him. There were so many other emotions.

That morning, while on that call with his mom, she'd felt so guilty about keeping the girls from the Colton side of their family. But his mom was right; she couldn't change the past. She could focus only on the future.

And she had to make sure that her girls had one. Cash had promised to keep them safe, but was that possible with all the dangers in the world?

She couldn't worry about all of them, though, just that man with the gun. The bad man...

That was what the girls called him. But they'd talked about him and that gun even before the shooting that day. "Bang bang," she murmured.

"Bang bang," Ana repeated, and then she shuddered. The girls were on the couch, watching cartoons. With the parental controls Valentina had on the TV, she doubted they'd seen anything violent on that.

That they'd seen anything violent until that day someone had tried running them down. Then Cash had taken shots at the car, making the driver speed away. Saving them...

So he wasn't the bad man they'd talked about, the bad man that went bang bang.

"Did you see a bad man with a gun before that day Luci was sick?" she asked Ana.

Ana turned toward her, and her dark eyes were wide with fear.

Oh, my God...

She had seen something.

"What was it, sweetheart?" Valentina asked. "You can tell me."

"Tell her bang bang," Luci advised her twin. "And Sparky falled down."

"Sparky..."

Oh, my God, Valentina repeated in her head. Sparky was what they'd called Mrs. Miller because of all her jewelry. "You saw the lady from the library?" she asked them both. "The one with all the pretty sparkling rings and necklaces?"

Luci shook her head and pointed at Ana. "She saw Sparky...by the garbage with the bad man."

Tears brimmed in Ana's dark eyes, and when she nodded, the tears spilled over and trailed down her face. "Bad man go bang bang and Sparky falled down..."

Her little girl had witnessed a mugging or worse yet, maybe a murder, since Mrs. Miller had gone missing. And then Valentina remembered their walk home from the library that day, how she'd been distracted, so distracted that she'd been startled when she'd heard a car backfire.

But what if it hadn't been a car?

What if it had been the bang bang that the girls kept talking about?

"Where Sparky at?" Ana asked. "In the garbage?"

Had the man thrown Mrs. Miller into a dumpster? Valentina's heart pounded heavy with dread and fear. And she hated that her baby girl had witnessed such an atrocity. She wrapped her arm around Ana, holding the little girl's trembling body close to her side as she reached for her cell.

She had to call Cash, had to let him know what Ana had said, what she had witnessed. Luci had been on the street side of the stroller, so Ana would have had just the view of buildings and...

Maybe an alley between them, where the dumpsters would have been. That had happened over a week ago, though, so the dumpster would have been emptied. And Mrs. Miller...

Tears stung her own eyes as she considered what might have happened to the older woman. She'd been so elegant, so glamorous, like old Hollywood royalty.

"Daddy," Ana murmured. "I want Daddy."

Valentina nodded. She wanted him, too, and wished now that she wouldn't have encouraged him to leave. Because she had a horrible feeling that the bad man had seen Ana, too, and that was why that car had come at them.

And then the shooter in the garage...

He must have followed them back here, or maybe he'd asked around about them and learned where they lived. Everybody at the library and the day care knew.

"I'm calling Daddy now," Valentina said. And she pulled up the contact for his cell but her call went directly to his voice mail. "Cash, I think we figured out what's going on. That Ana saw something..."

"The bad man!" the little girl cried. "The bad man!"

"He's not here," Valentina said. "You're safe." Then she turned her attention back to her cell. "She saw what happened to Mrs. Miller, Cash. And that man must have seen her, too."

An alarm pealed out, and the lights in the condo blinked before going out along with the TV. The girls screamed.

"It's just the smoke alarm," she assured them. "Probably just the super testing it—"

But then someone pounded at the door. "Mrs. Colton, Mrs. Colton," Sergeant Percell called out to her, "there's smoke, and the alarm is going off."

She heard that; it was ringing in her ears. And the girls were covering theirs.

"We need to evacuate."

Valentina clicked off her cell and shoved it in her pocket. But she would need money to go someplace else, stay someplace else. So she rushed to her bedroom to grab her purse. And the girls went to their rooms. "We have to leave," she told them from the doorway. "Just take your favorite stuffed animals. The bear and the bunny."

They didn't have time to pack up more, not if there was a fire. And if there was a fire, while Valentina would hate to lose the condo, she would always have her memories of being there. It was the girls she wouldn't be able to handle losing. They mattered most.

Keeping them safe...

But she couldn't help thinking as she opened the door that this was a trap. That the bad man was behind this just like he was apparently behind Mrs. Miller's disappearance.

Was he going to try to make Valentina and the girls disappear like Mrs. Miller had?

Forever.

Chapter Twenty-One

Valentina had been right to be worried about her missing friend. Adelaide Stewart Miller had been murdered. Shot to death, and her body tossed in a dumpster. If not for a homeless man rummaging through that dumpster, her body might not have been found before the trash was collected. But he'd pulled her out along with her bag and the jewelry that had been left on her body.

It hadn't been a mugging. It must have been a hired hit.

"The ballistics match what we recovered at the parking garage," Patrick said, his cell pressed to his ear as one of his CSIs told him what their tests had confirmed.

The same man who'd killed the library patron had come after Valentina and the girls. But why?

"We're going through her laptop and other things, too," Patrick assured him.

"Why did it take so long for her body to turn up?" Cash asked. She'd been missing for more than a week.

"The homeless guy took her to his hiding place in the sewer through a manhole right in that alley. He thought he could save her. He'd once been a med student," Ashlynn relayed. "Another homeless person that he asked to help him stole some of her jewelry and hocked it. When local police tracked him down and questioned him, he said where she could be found."

Cash shuddered at the gruesome details he didn't want to share with Valentina. She'd really liked the older woman. But that wasn't reason enough for someone to go after her and the girls. Unless...

Bang bang...

Had one of the girls witnessed the shooting?

"What dumpster?" Cash asked Ashlynn. "Where did the homeless person find her?"

"Not far from the library where Valentina works."

"On her route home?"

Ashlynn nodded.

And Cash's stomach plummeted. He reached for his cell, remembering just then that they'd shut them off and taken out their batteries just in case the Landmark Killer tried to trace them while they were at the hotel. He had to wait until he was out of here to reattach his battery. "I have to go. I have to make sure they're okay."

He hugged Ashlynn. "Take care of yourself and stay off the grid, so this sick bastard..."

She chuckled. "Though I know it's hard for my brothers to accept, I can take care of myself," she said. "I'll be fine."

"You don't carry a gun," Brennan reminded her.

She tapped her temple. "I don't need it. I can outsmart him."

Could they, though? So far it seemed like the Landmark Killer had been ahead of them, that he knew them too well. "You need to be careful," Cash insisted.

She nodded. "I will. You, too." She touched his jaw. "Looks like you're in more danger than I am."

He shook his head. "I don't think it's me who's in danger." It was his family, and he needed to get back to them.

"Go," Brennan said.

He was already opening the door, already rushing out. He waited until he was in the parking lot before he put the battery back into his phone, and when he did, his screen lit up with a voice mail.

And when he played it...

His blood chilled. The girls had witnessed that older woman's murder. The bang bang. The bad man. They knew who he was, had seen him kill the woman.

That was why the killer had gone after them. He must not have kids or know kids that well, or he wouldn't have considered them much of a threat. At less than three years old, even if the prosecutor considered them credible witnesses, they probably would have been too scared or shy to testify against him.

But the man had tried to kill them not once but twice. And then Cash heard the alarm...

And he knew that the guy was going to try again. Right now.

THE SMOKE WAS pungent and thick, so much so that it was hard for Valentina to see. It was thicker here in the stairwell that led down to the parking garage. The girls coughed and sputtered and burrowed their faces into her neck. She was carrying both of them while Sergeant Percell led the way down, his gun clasped in his hand.

Thankfully the girls couldn't see it, since he was ahead

of them and they were snuggled so closely against her. Even with their faces against her, she could feel the tears streaming from their eyes and from hers. She didn't know if that was because of the smoke or the fear.

"The fire must be in the parking garage," Sergeant Percell remarked, his voice raspy, and he coughed. "We should go back up. Or get out on one of these floors and head to another stairwell."

She knew that was what they needed to do, especially because of how she could hear someone coming down from above, and the way their footsteps sounded on the stairs, almost stealthy, as if they were stalking them.

Because she and the girls had taken time to grab her purse and their favorite stuffed animals, they'd been behind everyone else exiting the building. And nobody had been behind them, that she'd noticed, until this moment.

"Now," she shouted at Percell. "Open the door to that floor!"

The fourth. They'd come down seven, and her legs and arms burned from carrying the girls and her own weight down so many flights.

Dave must have heard the urgency in her voice because he stopped and pushed open that door, but he paused before passing through it. First he glanced out into the hall then he looked back at her and the girls. Then he raised his gaze and the barrel of his gun above her. "Go! Go!" he shouted, and she knew he'd noticed what she had.

That they were not alone.

She ran down the last couple of steps and through the door he held open for her. And as it swung shut, she heard the gunshots coming from behind her.

The exit light at the end of the hall was the only thing glowing in the darkness and the smoke. She ran toward that as the girls cried in her arms. She had to get out of here, had to get to the street. This stairwell would bring her there and to safety if she could get there before the shooter got past Sergeant Percell. Dave.

He'd told her to call him Dave. He would do his best to stop the shooter, to protect them, and hopefully he would save himself, too. She liked the man. He was like Cash, intent on protecting them. So she knew he would probably give his life for theirs. Tears stung her eyes, and she hoped that he wouldn't have to, that he would survive.

But she had to focus on the girls now, on getting them to safety. She ran down the hall to the opposite stairwell, where that sign glowed faintly through the smoke. It hadn't been as thick, but now that the door had opened onto the floor, so much had billowed into it that it stung her eyes here, too, making it harder to see. She blinked to clear her vision, but the smoke remained like fog. The exit light beckoned through it, and she reached the other stairwell door and turned around to push it open with her back.

She glanced back at the other end of the hall, to the other stairwell. While the smoke was thick, she could tell that it was still closed, the hallway still empty behind her. Nobody had come out of the stairwell yet. Maybe Dave had held the shooter off.

Maybe the officer was okay. She couldn't check on him, though. Her girls still weren't safe.

"Mommy..." Luci murmured, her soft voice raspy.

She had to get them out of the smoke, too. Legs and

arms burning, she started down the stairwell, keeping her balance by leaning against one wall, the handrail digging into her side. She'd made it down three flights when she heard the door slam open above them.

Dave would have called out, would have assured them that they were safe now. No assurances came. Just pounding footsteps...

He wasn't even trying to be stealthy anymore. He was just trying to catch them. To kill them...

She needed something. Some way to protect them, because she was worried that he would start shooting soon. And there was nowhere to hide in the stairwell.

She ran faster. Tripping on one step, she nearly dropped the girls. Pain shot through her ankle, and her arms ached. She had to let them go.

"Run," she told them. "Run to the bottom of the stairs and go out that door. Then run toward the lights. As fast as you can!"

"Mommy!" Luci protested.

She shook her head. "I'll be right behind you. Run toward the lights. Run to safety. Go!" And she gave them a little shove, propelling them ahead of her.

They looked back once. Then they grabbed each other's hands and ran ahead of her. She tried to run after them, ignoring the twinge in her ankle with every step she took. As she descended, she looked around, looking for something that could help her. That could protect her and the girls.

On the last landing, a fire extinguisher lay where someone had dropped it. She grabbed it up, and even though it was lighter than the girls, her arm hurt. She ached everywhere, but that discomfort was going to be nothing compared to the pain she would feel if something happened to her daughters. If she didn't do everything she could to try to save them, even give up her own life if she had to.

The door at the bottom of the stairs opened. And Ana must have hesitated, because she heard Luci say, "Mommy said to run. Run to the lights."

And the door slammed shut behind them. She had just a few more steps to go, a few more, but he was close now. So close that the gun fired, a bullet striking off the concrete wall of the stairwell, close to her head. She ran down the last flight and pushed open that door to darkness.

Where were the lights? Where were her girls?

The only lights she could see were the lights from Luna Park, from the roller coaster and the Ferris wheel. And she could hear the music from the carousel...

Where were the girls?

Would they realize that they had come out the back of the building and they needed to circle around to the front entrance to where the fire trucks and police had to be? Those were the lights she'd wanted them to find and the help and protection that they needed right now.

That she needed right now...

She held the fire extinguisher yet. And instead of running around to the front or toward the lights, she shrank into the shadows and clasped her weapon tightly, uncertain how to use it in her defense.

Throw it at him? Wait until the shooter was close enough that she could hit him over the head with it? But if he was close enough...

The door opened again, and a dark shadow stepped out of it, that gun pointed out. Maybe toward her daughters, whom she couldn't see in the dark. What if he could? What if he was aiming that barrel at them now?

A mother's instinct to protect her babies raging inside her, she swung the fire extinguisher at the arm holding the gun, whacking it harder than she had Cash with the frying pan. Or at least she hoped she had, because her life and her daughters' lives depended on it.

Chapter Twenty-Two

Lights flashed around the high-rise from the fire trucks and emergency vehicles pulled up next to the building. So close that Cash couldn't get near it. He had to abandon his SUV down the street and run the rest of the way.

Smoke billowed out from the parking garage, acrid with the smell of burning rubber. Someone must have set a car on fire in the parking garage. Someone...

He knew damn well who'd done it. That son of a bitch who was after his wife and kids. Cash could only hope that he'd arrived in time to protect them.

To save them...

Residents stood around the parking lot, staring up at the building. Cash scanned the crowd, looking for the beautiful dark-haired woman and the two curly-haired little girls. But he caught not even a glimpse of them. Or of Dave...

Where the hell was Dave? Cash had tried calling him on his way to the condo, but the call had gone straight to Dave's voice mail, like the call Valentina had made to Cash. If only he'd been here...

He never should have left them. But Ashlynn was in

danger, too. Ashlynn, while not a special agent, had been at the FBI so long that she knew how to take care of herself. Valentina was a librarian with such a soft, loving heart, unless she was protecting her children, like she had the night she'd hit him with the frying pan. Then she could be fierce.

But as fierce as she was, she couldn't stop someone with a gun, like the man who'd ambushed them in the parking garage a couple of nights ago. He must have come back through the parking garage, setting a car on fire first to flush out the residents. To flush out Cash's family.

He headed toward the parking garage now, but a crime scene was already set up, a tape stretching between two police vehicles, tied to their side mirrors. When he went to duck under the tape, an officer stepped up, hand on holster. "Sir, you have to stay back!"

He reached into his pocket, and the officer drew the weapon. "I'm FBI," he said. "Special Agent Cash Colton." He showed his shield. "What's going on?"

Because the officer wouldn't have been so on edge from just a fire…

"Shots fired," the officer said, then turned back as other officers and EMTs came out of the garage.

They carried a stretcher. Someone had been hurt. Or worse…

His heart pounding furiously with fear, Cash ducked under the tape and rushed over to the back of the ambulance where the EMTs were loading the stretcher. "Valentina?"

The body on the stretcher moved, but it was a male voice that called out to him. "Cash?"

"Dave!" Once the EMTs jumped into the ambulance, he could see his friend. The guy's face was pale and contorted with pain. Blood seeped from his shoulder and his leg. "You've been shot!"

"We have to get him to the hospital," a paramedic said as he reached for the doors, to pull them shut.

But Dave reached out, grasping the guy's arm. "Wait."

"Valentina? The girls?" Cash asked, his voice cracking with the fear overwhelming him.

"She heard him coming. She took the girls and ran toward the other stairwell."

But clearly Dave didn't know if they'd made it or not. "I tried..." He coughed and sputtered.

"We gotta go now," the paramedic said, and he pulled the doors closed on Cash.

Before the ambulance even pulled away, Cash was running toward the building. A fireman blocked the way. "You can't go inside. There's too much smoke."

He flashed his shield again. "My kids and wife are in there."

The firefighter shook his head. "Our team checked the building. The shooting victim was the only one still inside."

Because he'd been unable to get out...

So maybe the girls had managed to escape. From the building or from the killer, too?

"I checked the crowd," he said. "I didn't see them."

"There are two fire exits, here, through the parking garage and the other at the opposite end, back side of the building," the fire fighter said. "Some people came out that way, less smoke."

So maybe they were back there, safe.

Cash ran toward that opposite end of the building, and the air was clearer, less smoke, less light, especially when he turned the corner. The building, without power, was dark, casting a giant shadow over whatever was behind it. A parking lot? A field?

He couldn't see anything. But he could hear someone grunting, someone breathing heavily...

Pulling out his gun and a flashlight, he shone it around the area, which was overgrown with weeds. And he saw the man with that damn hoodie pulled tight around his face, which was covered in a mask.

Cash raised his gun and squeezed the trigger. But the man ducked and ran deeper into the shadows. Cash started to follow him until a moan in the dark brought his attention back to where he'd first seen the man.

And now he saw the body lying on the ground, in the weeds. Valentina...

IT HAD ALL happened so quickly. Her knocking that gun from the man's grasp, and when he'd crouched down to retrieve it, she had struck him again so hard that she'd lost her grip on the fire extinguisher. Then the man had reached out for her, closing his hands around her neck, cutting off her breath, her consciousness, her life...

No. She had to fight, had to stay alive to protect her babies. She kicked and punched and clawed until her hands were covered in blood.

Or was that because of a wound on the man?

Dave must have shot him. He was bleeding.

She could fight him off. But then he found the gun

and pressed it to her head. When he pulled the trigger, it clicked. He'd already emptied it.

She thrashed harder, fighting to get away from him before he could reload, and he grabbed her neck again. His grip tightened, and everything started to go black inside her head as her lungs burned for air.

Then she heard another gunshot blast, close but yet muffled. Had he managed to reload his weapon? How? She could feel both hands wrapped around her neck.

Then the hands left her throat, and she gasped for air and fought for consciousness. She had to stop him. But when she swung her arms around, she didn't feel anything.

As if she was floating, floating away...floating into oblivion. Then she actually *was* floating, because someone lifted her from the ground.

"Valentina? Valentina?" Cash called to her, and he sounded as if he was far away even though those were his arms holding her, carrying her. "Where are the girls?" he asked.

And his question jarred her back into consciousness with the sudden rush of fear. She tensed and tried to wriggle away from him. "Wh..." Her voice was raspy, her throat burning, and not from the smoke. "Where...?"

"Where are they?" he finished the question for her. "I checked in the front. They're not there. Were the firefighters wrong? Are they still in there? Hiding?"

She shook her head. "No. They ran ahead. They got out..." She'd heard the door. But she hadn't seen them. "I told them to go..." Her voice trailed off, and she fought to clear her throat, but it was swelling. She swallowed hard, finding more saliva to continue speaking, "...toward the lights..."

"What lights?" he asked, glancing around.

"I..." She struggled to get out the words. "Police. Fire trucks..."

"But you can't see them from here," he murmured, and then he turned, with her still in his arms, toward the lights of Luna Park. And he tensed.

And she knew. The man must have run off in that direction, where the girls had surely gone. With the oxygen filling her lungs again, her mind cleared, and some of her strength returned. "We have to try to find them."

Before he did.

The bad man who'd been haunting the girls' nightmares for over a week now. The bad man who was intent on killing them because he knew that at least one of them had seen him kill Mrs. Miller.

How THE HELL had what was supposed to be such a simple job gotten so damn screwed up? Kill an old lady...

How hard could that be?

Actually that hadn't been that bad at all. He'd intended to make it look like a mugging. Kill her in an alley. Get her keys and search her damn apartment for anything incriminating.

Not to him but to his client.

Get rid of that just like he'd gotten rid of her.

But he hadn't easily gotten rid of her because there'd been damn witnesses. So he'd stolen that car and had tried running them down, but he'd missed them then. And in the parking garage, after watching the building for a week, he'd figured out the code residents had been punching into the gate. But even in the parking garage he'd missed them.

He chased them now, through the weeds and brush of an abandoned field, toward those lights. That must have been where the kids had headed.

He would have caught up with their little legs already if not for their mother. She had to be dead. He had to have choked the life out of her. But damn, she'd fought him hard.

He hurt all over, from the gunshot wound she'd re-opened. And from that damn thing she'd hit him with.

His ears rang yet, but maybe that was because of firing his gun in that stairwell at the cop. Hell, that guy might have hit him, too.

He'd been so pumped, so impatient to catch those kids, that he might not have noticed the pain. Till now...

Now everything hurt. But he wasn't going to stop until he'd finished this. Until he'd gotten rid of those kids.

They'd seen his face. They were the only ones who had. He'd worn the mask after that, after his big mistake.

The closer he came to the park, the brighter the lights and the louder the music. It reverberated inside his head, making it ache even more than it had from her hitting him.

She damn well better be dead. But someone else had shown up, another guy with a gun. One that had had ammo in it. If only he'd had some in his...

Before getting any closer to the gates and risking anyone seeing him, he stopped, hiding in the relative shadows. He reached into his pocket and pulled out another clip and shoved it into his gun. This time he would be ready.

This time he would not miss.

He started forward, intent on finding his targets. And he nearly stumbled over a stuffed animal among the weeds. Maybe someone had won it in the park. He stooped to pick it up, thinking of using it to lure the girls out.

But he didn't need to do that. All he had to do was get close enough to get a good shot. Two good shots. He wasn't going to rest until those little mini witnesses were dead.

Chapter Twenty-Three

Cash hadn't wanted to bring Valentina with him, but he hadn't wanted to leave her alone and unprotected, either. In case the shooter hadn't left.

In case he hadn't gone after the girls.

But just like her, he was pretty damn sure that he had. As they neared the park, the darkness receded, illuminating the weeds and the stuffed bunny lying among them, blood staining its white fur.

Valentina grabbed it and gasped. "Oh, my God, he already found them…"

"We don't know that," Cash said, trying to give her hope even as his stomach lurched with dread. Those sweet little girls had to be all right. He couldn't have lost them just as he'd finally found them.

"Then why is there blood on Bunny?" she asked. "They weren't hurt."

Not like she was. Her neck was red, her voice raspy, and she limped beside him now that they weren't running like they had across the field.

She'd fought hard to protect them, to save them. She

hadn't failed them, not like he had. He should have been there.

"The blood could be his," Cash pointed out. "He could be hurt."

She raised her hands, which had red smears on them. "He is…"

Damn. She was fierce. A fighter. And maybe their daughters were, too.

"They know he's a bad man," Cash reminded her. "They would run from him. And he won't just shoot them in the middle of a crowd. He's trying to kill them because he thinks they're witnesses…"

"To Mrs. Miller's murder," she finished when he trailed off. "They were. At least Ana was."

"As tragic as that is, it's good at the moment," Cash said. "They'll be so scared of him that they'll run. They'll hide from him." The question was where.

They walked up to the gates, and as they did, they could hear a commotion inside, voices raised, some screaming.

"He's here," Valentina breathed.

Cash flashed his shield at the gatekeeper. "Did you call the police?" he asked.

The young woman nodded. "When I saw the man. He had a gun and is wearing a mask. And he's bleeding…"

Cash started inside, to track that blood like a hunter would track a wounded animal. But when Valentina followed him, he stopped. "You need to stay here, at the gate, wait for police."

She shook her head. "No. Those are my kids."

My.

Not *ours*. But then she had raised them alone until now. And even now…

She'd been the one with them tonight, the one getting them out of the burning building. The one fighting off a gunman to save them.

A professional killer…

Who didn't seem too damn professional right now, as if he'd lost his objectivity in his desperation. Or was he more afraid of whoever had hired him than he was of getting caught?

Either way, the guy had nothing left to lose at this point.

"Where would they go?" Cash asked her. Because she did know them best.

He barely knew them at all.

"They love the carousel."

"But they'd need tickets and they have no money."

"We come here so often, someone might let them on," she said, and she started limping toward that carousel.

Cash kept his gun steady in one hand while he slid his other arm around her, helping her, as they both hurried toward the ride with the music and lights. He didn't notice anyone standing around it but parents probably waiting for their kids. There was no bleeding man with a gun. Where the hell had he gone?

Had they gone?

"Where are they?" Valentina asked, her voice cracking with fear. "They would want to ride the horsey…"

"They would want to get away from the bad man," Cash said, hoping like hell that they had. "Where else? Where could they hide?"

"The bathrooms maybe…" Valentina murmured and she pulled away from him, heading toward the restrooms.

Maybe they would think they could hide from him in the woman's bathroom. Valentina pushed open the door and looked inside but shook her head. "They're not in there…"

They weren't the only ones who'd just disappeared. But then screams rang out again and people started running away from another attraction.

Valentina gasped. "The Fun House."

It made sense. Maybe they had been able to slip past the lines, to get inside, and hide. Hopefully Cash and Valentina would find them before the gunman did.

They ran toward the Fun House as other people ran from it, yelling, "Shooter! Shooter!"

He must have seen the kids go inside. He was already after them? Cash hadn't heard any gunshots yet.

People were still fleeing from the ride, running out the back. Then gunshots reverberated from somewhere inside it.

More people screamed and ran. Valentina was one of them, running toward the entrance instead of for the exit. Cash wanted to hold her back, but he knew that she would fight him as hard as she had the assassin if he tried. So he just stepped in front of her, entering first to the laughter of clowns and the flash of lights and the reflections of all the mirrors.

He moved ahead, keeping his body between her and the rest of the ride. "Ana! Luci!" he called out. "The bad man is in here so stay hidden!"

Gunfire rang out again, glass breaking around him. He ducked down and dragged Valentina down with him.

"Come out!" the guy yelled. "Come out or your mom and dad are dead, little girls!"

And in some of the unbroken mirrors, Cash caught the reflection of his daughters, their faces and bodies distorted and reflected back.

"No! Get down!" Valentina screamed. "Play dead!"

The man fired at those mirrors.

And Cash jumped up and fired back, striking him once. Twice. The guy dropped to the ground like Valentina had told their daughters to do. Had they done it in time?

Or had he hit them?

It was all over.

The bad man was dead. And the girls were not. That should have been all that mattered to Valentina. They should have been all that mattered as they had been for the last three years.

But too much had happened.

She'd fallen in love with her ex-husband all over again. But no matter how many times he'd called her his wife over the past week, she was definitely his ex.

And after they'd taken the girls out of the Fun House and back to a safe place, a hotel suite close to the beach, she felt that it was over between her and Cash.

He'd helped her settle the girls down in the bedroom, but even as he'd read to them, he'd been distracted, as if his mind was elsewhere. As if they weren't the focus anymore...

Probably because they were no longer in danger, they were no longer a priority or a responsibility to him.

The girls were safe and sleeping in the bedroom of the hotel suite. And as Cash closed the door on that room, he turned toward her. "Are you sure you're all right?" he asked, his gaze focused on her neck.

It was sore, like her ankle, but nothing was broken. Nothing had been fractured beyond repair but maybe their relationship. And she didn't know why...

He'd been so concerned back at the building and the park. But maybe that was why he was shutting down now.

"I'm fine," she insisted. "You can leave."

He sucked in a breath and quietly asked, "You want me to go?"

"I can tell you have one foot out the door, just like you did for most of our marriage." And she'd fought too hard tonight to fight anymore. That was why she'd just signed those divorce papers three years ago. She didn't want to be with someone who wasn't going to make time for her in his life, and she certainly didn't want that for her daughters, either.

"Valentina..."

She waited for him to go on, but it was clear he didn't know what to say. And she was too tired.

"I do need to go back to the scene," he said. "I have to finish giving my statement to the investigating officers. Make sure that this is really over. I'll have an officer posted at the door of the hotel until we know for sure."

"How about Dave?" she asked with concern. She'd asked earlier, but they'd had no news of his condition at that time. The sergeant had still been in surgery.

He released a ragged sigh. "He's going to be okay," he said.

She emitted a shaky breath of her own. "That's good. He saved our lives." Cash had, too, after Dave got hit. "And you, you killed the guy. We're safe now." There was no reason for him to go back to the scene, to leave, except that he clearly didn't want to stay.

"He was a professional, Valentina. That means someone hired him."

She would have glared at him, if she'd had the energy. "I realize that. Someone hired him to kill Mrs. Miller. Not us. The only reason the assassin came after us was because he thought Ana and Luci could identify him. Maybe he even thought I'd seen him..." She might have glanced into that alley when she'd heard what had sounded like a car backfiring. But she'd been so distracted thinking of Cash's call that she hadn't realized it had even been a gunshot and she hadn't noticed anything. Not like Ana had.

"It's over," she said, and maybe she was trying to convince herself now. "Ana won't need to testify or give a statement."

He tensed. "She won't have to testify, but I'll have to see about the statement. That's why I should go back there."

"You should go back there," she agreed. "Because you don't want to stay. You don't want to be with us. You don't want that family any more now than you did three years ago."

He flinched, but he didn't argue with her, just as he hadn't when she'd moved out three years ago. "You're exhausted, and we shouldn't be having this conversation right now." He glanced toward the bedroom where the girls slept.

She didn't want their children to overhear them, either. But they were so exhausted that she doubted anything could wake them up, not even another fire alarm. "You don't want to have a conversation with me," she said. "Just as you didn't want to talk three years ago. You don't want to talk. You don't want to compromise. When are you going to realize that it doesn't have to be all or nothing? I'm not asking you to leave your job."

"It's more important than ever that I focus on the job now," he said. "With the Landmark Killer making a threat against Ashlynn."

She was dubious. "A real threat? Or did he just mention her?"

"He said that maybe she shouldn't be alive."

She gasped and pressed a hand to her mouth. Why was there so much evil, so much violence in the world? She respected and understood Cash's need to fight it, just as she'd fought for her girls tonight.

She was too tired to fight for her and Cash, though. And maybe so was Cash, especially since he already had another fight on his hands. "You need to go to Ashlynn. Protect her," she said, and she reached for the door to the hall, intending to show him out. Then she would crawl into the empty double bed next to the one the girls shared in the bedroom, and she would probably cry into her pillow until exhaustion claimed her. She was exhausted physically and emotionally right now.

"I…don't know where Ashlynn is," he said.

And her pulse quickened. "Oh, no! I'm sorry. You need to find her—"

"No, I need to find the Landmark Killer," he said. "Ashlynn went into hiding."

Valentina's pulse slowed a little then. "So she's safe..."

"Unless the Landmark Killer finds her before we find him," he said.

When a short time ago he'd seemed antsy and desperate to leave, now it was almost as if he was stalling. "You don't have to explain yourself to me," she said. "I understand why you need to leave. I know why your job is so important to you, especially now, with Ashlynn in danger."

"I want to make sure that you and the girls aren't in danger anymore either," he said. "I don't want anything to happen to you." Then finally he stepped through the door she'd opened for him and out into the hall.

She closed it behind him and leaned back against it. She should have told him that he was too late. That it had already happened; she was already hurt. And it wasn't her ankle or her throat.

It was her heart.

He'd broken it again.

FURY COURSING THROUGH HIM, the Landmark Killer slammed his cell down onto the ground and barely resisted the urge to stomp on it, too. He'd been scrolling through the headlines, and all the local news, even some of the national news, was about the shooting at Coney Island's Luna Park but not *his* shooting.

Some nameless hired assassin was stealing all the news

headlines from him. Just because he'd gone after some helpless little girls...

That made the man a coward who shouldn't get any mention at all in the news.

The Landmark Killer was the *hero*.

He was the brave one.

The smart one.

Just like Maeve O'Leary.

She knew what he was doing for her, that he was trying to free her. That he appreciated her. Did anyone appreciate him?

Did the FBI's special team respect him? How smart he was? While they were desperately trying to profile and figure out everything about him, he already knew everything about *them*.

About their murdered daddy...

About Cash's sad ex-wife. She was certainly sad now because after the Landmark Killer had sent Ashlynn that text, they were all going to focus on him again. Which they should have been doing...

Instead, first Brennan and then Cash had gotten distracted with their personal lives. Cash should have realized the first time his marriage failed that he couldn't make it work. He couldn't do anything but his job if he had any hope of catching someone as smart as the Landmark Killer. Cash hadn't even realized that the Landmark Killer had been in the parking garage with him at Cash's apartment that night.

Cash had turned with his gun, on edge because of his text. The texts he loved sending them. He was having so much fun messing with them, letting them know that he was smarter than they were. Even Ashlynn...

Chapter Twenty-Four

Despite all his years in law enforcement, Cash had never been as scared as he'd been in that *Fun* House a week ago. He'd been so close to losing what mattered most to him. The gunman had been firing wildly, and Cash had had to take his shot, but in that moment, with all those mirrors reflecting back and contorting the killer's shadow and his daughters' images, he feared he might mistakenly shoot them instead of the bad man who'd been terrorizing them for more than a week.

And then he would be the bad man. Not just to them but to Valentina, too. But he'd wound up the bad man to her anyway because he hadn't known how to cope with the aftermath of that overwhelming fear he'd felt.

The fear that he would love and lose his family like he'd loved and lost his dad. To a serial killer…

And while the bad man hadn't been a serial killer, per se, he'd probably killed a lot of people. The FBI had already linked him to more murders than Maeve O'Leary and the Landmark Killer combined. But they hadn't yet linked him back to whoever had recently hired him to kill an old woman.

That made Cash uneasy. He wasn't entirely sure that his family was safe.

Not just Ashlynn, who'd gone so deeply underground that she couldn't be found, but his immediate family. The girls and Valentina.

She'd scared him nearly as much as that hired killer had. Because she'd just seemed so done with him, so tired. Of course, after what she'd been through, she'd had every reason to be. He was tired, too.

"Did you sleep here again?" Brennan asked as he walked into the conference room where Cash had been working. "You look like hell."

"I feel like hell," Cash admitted. He missed his girls. He missed his wife. He missed the family he'd vowed he'd never wanted. What a fool he'd been...

Not just three years ago but now as well. And he knew it; he just didn't know what to do about it.

"What are you doing?" Brennan asked.

"Working," he said. "We've got to find the Landmark Killer. He's threatened Ashlynn."

"And Ashlynn took measures to protect herself, which I suspect is what you're really doing."

"What do you mean?" Cash asked, his body tensing as his twin seemed to stare right inside him.

"Same thing I did for years, using you as my example, that there was no way to have a relationship while working this job, especially in this unit..." He gestured around the conference room where Cash had his laptop open and papers spread across the long table.

He glanced a little guiltily at those papers and the open files on his laptop. He was checking out Bradley

Jones, one of the many aliases of the man he'd killed a week ago. The man who'd been trying to kill his family.

Cash was the one who'd done that himself when he'd walked away from them, leaving them alone at the hotel when all he'd really wanted to do was hold them close and never let them go. But the reality of how close he'd come to losing them had shaken him so badly...

"I was wrong," Brennan said. "And you are, too. Stella and I are happy, are making our relationship work for both of us. You could do that, not just for you and Valentina but for those little girls, too. You've already missed too much of their lives. What the hell are you doing here?"

"Trying to make sure they stay safe," Cash insisted. "You know someone hired that killer—"

"Not to kill them," Brennan said.

"That's what Valentina said," he admitted. "But I can't help feeling that it's not over. That's why when Ashlynn checked in the last time, I asked her to do a deep dive, see what she could dig up on the assassin, see if he had some way of keeping track of who had hired him. Like a safe-deposit box or a file on the cloud. Something."

"You sound pretty desperate to find something," Brennan said. "To prove your point?"

"To make sure my *family* is safe," Cash insisted.

"I don't think it's the killer that you're worried about," Brennan said. "I think you're scared of losing them, so instead you're pushing them away first so it's on your terms, something you can control."

Cash sucked in a breath as he felt his twin's words like a sharp jab. He hadn't realized just how well Brennan knew him, maybe better than Cash knew himself.

"Losing Dad was so hard on us," Brennan said. "Made us feel so helpless. That's why we do what we do. To take back some control."

"And to take it away from the killers, to bring them to justice," Cash insisted.

"Yes, true. We're saving people, but at what cost? Losing ourselves?" Brennan asked. He pointed to Cash, who could imagine how bad he looked.

He hadn't trimmed his hair or beard in…he didn't remember how long, and he hadn't slept more than an hour at a time for over a week. "How can you back away? How can you keep the job manageable?" Cash asked, and he really wanted to know.

"Remember that you're not doing it alone," Brennan said. "We're all in it together, in this unit—"

"Unless one of us is the Landmark Killer." And that was looking more and more likely.

"You know who you can trust," Brennan said. "Me, Patrick, Ashlynn. Valentina."

Could he, though? She'd kept his daughters from him, but he knew why, because she'd been afraid that he would do exactly what he'd done. That he would get close to them and then back away, breaking their hearts.

Like he'd broken hers?

His heart ached in his chest, feeling hollow and empty without them, without his family. He'd broken his own heart, too.

God, he missed them so damn much. He'd reached out every other day over the past week, texting Valentina to ask if the girls could FaceTime him. He'd missed seeing them, holding them, reading to them. Instead of answering his text, she'd just had the girls call him. He hadn't even seen her, just their sweet little faces.

They'd kept asking him when he was coming home. As if he lived with them. He had for a week, but he didn't think Valentina would have ever asked him to move in with them. Maybe it was because he'd told her three years ago that he couldn't live on Coney Island, that he had to stay close to the office because of cases like this when he'd worked around the clock.

But his twin was right. He needed to stop doing that. He needed to take control of his life and make sure that he had one. That he didn't burn himself out with work and lose what mattered most to him.

His family.

He could only hope that it wasn't too late...

That he hadn't already lost them.

EVEN A WEEK after the threat against their lives was eliminated, Valentina was still exhausted. Since the fire had been confined to just that car in the parking garage, the smoke on the other levels of the high-rise had cleared and been cleaned up quickly. So she and the girls had been allowed to move back home a few days ago.

But it no longer felt like home to her or, she suspected, to the twins either, without their daddy there. They kept asking when he was coming home, and she didn't have the heart to tell them the truth.

Especially when she wasn't exactly sure what the truth was...

He'd been so strange after the shooting, so on edge,

that she'd thought he couldn't wait to get away from them, to leave them again.

That the only reason he'd been with them had been to protect them from that threat, that assassin.

She shivered as she thought of him and glanced around the library. After closing, it was eerily quiet. She was the only one here, working late to make up for all the time she'd missed. The girls were with her parents, who'd checked them all into a hotel with a swimming pool. After learning how much danger they'd been in, Mom and Dad had paused their travels to come home to see them. While Valentina was happy her parents were in town, she wasn't happy about all the questions they kept asking her about Cash.

Because she couldn't answer those questions.

She'd thought he was going to let them go just as he'd let her go those three years, with not a word of contact until he'd called when he'd gotten that text from the Landmark Killer. The text about his sad ex-wife. But over the past week, he kept reaching out, talking to the girls. He'd even read them a story over the phone the other night.

A book he'd had delivered to the condo.

And the sound of his voice…

The gentle, loving way he spoke to their daughters had her falling for him all over again. No. She'd never fallen out of love with him, not three years ago and certainly not when he'd moved in to protect them. She'd just fallen deeper and deeper. Her heart ached for missing him.

She was certainly sad now.

But she was more than sad.

She was also mad.

At herself and at him.

They'd fought so hard to save their daughters from danger. Why hadn't they fought for each other like that?

Why hadn't she?

He was busy trying to stop a serial killer and track down who'd hired that terrible man to murder Mrs. Miller. What was she doing?

She'd put away the last of the books that had come in. So she turned her attention back to the one that had never gone out...

She'd found it sitting on her desk when she came back, but she hadn't had the time or the wherewithal to look at it yet. It was the memoir she'd ordered for Mrs. Miller. Wanting a distraction from Cash, from the girls missing him, from her missing him, she picked up the book and began to read it.

The Broadway dancer hadn't just written about the famous people she'd met; she'd written about a powerful lover. A Mafia boss who'd treated her well while killing anyone else who'd crossed him. The memoir had been reprinted after the dancer's death and included a letter from the editor in the beginning that hinted at the dancer's death not being the mugging it had been made to look like but a cold-blooded murder. An act of revenge of that Mafia boss...

Valentina shivered at the similarity between that woman's death and the death of the woman who'd requested the copy of that memoir, who'd been writing her own. No. Mrs. Miller had been writing about people she'd known, more exciting and more famous people. She'd known the actress. Had she known her boyfriend, too? Suddenly Valentina knew who'd hired that assassin.

A very powerful man.

Of course she had no proof. Nobody had ever been able to get enough evidence or any willing witnesses to the man's crimes to put him in prison. He'd escaped justice for a long time, so long that he was an old man. He'd supposedly retired years ago, but the rumor around Brooklyn was that he was still in control behind the scenes.

She was suddenly very aware of how alone she was in the library, which was dark but for the light in her office. Rattled, she closed the memoir and grabbed her purse. Usually she would have no issue walking home, even at this hour, but tonight she thought about calling an Uber.

Or Cash…

She had the perfect excuse to initiate contact, to tell him she'd solved his case for him. Of course she'd had to work overtime to do it, just as he so often worked overtime. No. He worked all the time.

Could she find a way to accept that? To take whatever time he had left?

Didn't she and the girls deserve more from him?

Frustrated, with herself and with him, she figured the walk home would be good to clear her head, so she could come up with a plan to fix her broken heart. And she doubted that man who'd hired the assassin knew anything about her or her girls. The killer had just been trying to eliminate the witnesses to his crime.

She locked the door behind her, and then she turned around on the sidewalk. And immediately she realized the mistake she'd made in not calling Cash.

A limo idled at the curb, a couple big men leaning against the side of it. And when they opened the back door, she knew who was waiting inside for her.

That very old, very powerful, very murderous old man...

Chapter Twenty-Five

Cash wasn't sure if it was good luck or bad luck that he had a tendency to turn up just when Valentina needed him. Good luck on his part that he wasn't too late. Bad luck on hers that her life kept getting put in danger.

He knew he wasn't to blame this time, though. He knew who was; Ashlynn had found the evidence he was looking for. Then he'd tried to track down Valentina to tell her, and he found her just as she was coming out of the library to the men waiting for her.

As one of the big guys stepped forward to grab her, Valentina screamed and pulled a canister of pepper spray from her purse. While she raised that, Cash raised his gun.

"Stop!" he yelled, and he stepped out of the shadows into the light.

Valentina tensed as well as the men who reached beneath their jackets, as if they intended to pull their weapons and start firing at him.

"Special Agent Colton, FBI," he told them. "And I'm not alone. A warrant has been issued for your boss." Technically he wasn't alone since Valentina was there, armed with her pepper spray. But hopefully they would think that he wouldn't come by himself to serve a warrant to a Mafia boss. "We already have proof of one murder. I don't think he wants to add any more charges against him, especially of a federal agent."

The guys glanced from him through that open door to the man who sat in the back seat. Cash held his breath, hoping that he wouldn't be forced into another shoot-out. While he waited, he edged between that car and Valentina, using his body to protect her.

The guys took their hands from beneath their jackets and turned back around to face Cash. "We will be waiting for you at FBI headquarters with legal representation."

The old man said something, and one of the guys chuckled. "Unless you'd like a ride, Special Agent Colton."

God, he was brazen, but then he'd gotten away with his crimes for so many years that he probably didn't believe he would ever be prosecuted. And he probably wouldn't have been caught this time if he hadn't had to go after one little old lady. The assassin he'd hired to kill her had been confused about the old man's motive, too, confused enough that he'd gotten some more details out of him, details that Bradley Jones or whoever he really was had recorded and uploaded to the cloud.

He was actually going to go down for more than one murder.

But at least one of those would not be Valentina's. When the men got into the limo and it pulled away from the curb, Cash finally released that breath he'd been holding.

"Are you just going to let him drive off?" Valentina asked him as she gripped his arm, turning him around to face her. "He's probably heading straight to the airport to leave the country, to someplace with no extradition."

"Probably," he agreed. "But there will be agents at the airport to stop him. There really is a warrant for his arrest."

"You know?" she asked, her dark eyes wide with surprise.

"Obviously you do," he said.

She nodded. "I finally read the book Mrs. Miller had asked me to track down for her. She'd said it was about a friend of hers, and that she wanted to write about these friends. I think she intended to expose him in her own memoir for the murder of an actress she knew and that he had dated."

"Yes, that's exactly what she intended to do. Unfortunately she let that slip when she was talking to people about her memoir."

"The wrong people," Valentina said.

"But you didn't know before, did you?"

She shook her head now. "No. I would have told you." But her face flushed slightly.

And he pointed out, "You didn't call me when you found out."

She released a shaky sigh. "I thought about it. But lucky for me you have a habit of turning up when I'm in danger."

"That's not the only time I want to turn up, Valentina," he said, his heart overflowing with love for her. "I want to do more than protect you and the girls. I don't want to be with you just when you're in danger. I want to be with you always."

And now he held his breath again, waiting for *her* reply this time.

VALENTINA HADN'T INTENDED to keep Cash waiting for her answer, but his cell had started ringing. And then police and other FBI agents had shown up on the sidewalk as suddenly and unexpectedly as the limo and Cash had appeared. Apparently some agency or another had had the Mafia boss under surveillance and had reported what had happened.

And then she and Cash had had to give reports to those officers and agents. Sometime, during the course of those interviews, she'd lost track of him, and an officer had driven her back to the condo.

She hadn't had the chance to talk to him again, to answer that question, although it had actually been more of a statement than a question. *I want to be with you always.*

Instead of making her happy, the words filled with her sadness. It felt like another promise he couldn't keep, like the ones he'd made her when they got married.

He'd made promises to the girls, too, though, about keeping them safe, about protecting them from the bad man. And that promise he had kept.

He'd protected and saved them.

Could he keep this promise, too, if she gave him the chance?

Dare she give him a chance?

If she had the chance for that family she'd always wanted, the one she'd had that week that Cash had lived with them, was she selfish and cowardly not to take it just because she was afraid of getting hurt?

Pain and disappointment were parts of life, but so were joy and contentment. Without risking one, was the other possible? Probably not for her...

Not when love led her back to the man who'd hurt her before. But she would rather risk him hurting her again than live without him the way she had the past three years.

She would rather take whatever time he could give her and the girls around his work than never see him at all. Realizing that led her to another realization, that she had been as unwilling as he'd been to compromise before.

She'd wanted more instead of appreciating what she'd had, what he'd given her. The love. Their babies...

Tears rushed to fill her eyes, and she closed them. When she opened them, the elevator doors were opening to her floor. She was home, but it didn't feel like home right now, and that wasn't just because her girls were with her parents.

It was because Cash wasn't here.

She shouldn't have left with the officer. She should have waited for him. But she hadn't even known if he was still at the local police precinct or if he'd left without her.

Maybe he'd had to go back to the FBI office. Or maybe...

Maybe she hadn't answered him fast enough, and he'd thought she wasn't interested in a future with him.

She could call him once she got into her condo. She quickly unlocked her door to step inside, but once the door creaked open, she had a strange sensation that the place wasn't as empty as it was supposed to be.

That someone was here, waiting for her.

She reached into her bag again for that canister of pepper spray she was so glad she carried. But before she could pull it out, she heard a little giggle. Another one echoed it, and she smiled.

"Do I hear some mice?" she wondered aloud. "Or is that a robber?"

A light flickered on: a candle. Then another and another...

"We're not robbers, Mommy," Ana solemnly told her.

"We 'prising you," Luci said with a smile.

"You certainly are," Valentina assured them. But the biggest surprise of all wasn't their being here. She'd thought they might not want to spend the entire night away from home after just being able to come back a few days ago.

The biggest surprise was that it wasn't her mom and dad with them but Cash. He'd lit the candles on the dining room table and some on the kitchen counter and another on an end table.

Along with the candles were flowers and a couple of balloons that she suspected the girls had chosen since one said Happy Birthday and another Get Well Soon.

They really loved balloons.

"Wow," she said. "I definitely wasn't expecting this."

"Daddy planned it."

"That was quick," Valentina said.

"I was surprised earlier at the library," Cash said. "I wasn't expecting that. I thought I would be walking with you back here, once your mom and dad told me you were working late."

"You already had this planned?" she asked. "Before that...?" So his showing up when he had hadn't been just another coincidence. Maybe divine intervention. She shuddered thinking what might have happened.

"Definitely someone looking out for us," Cash said as if he'd read her mind. "Maybe your grandparents."

She smiled, thinking of how happy they'd been, how in love. She could see that. "But since you have a habit of turning up right when I need you, I think it could be your dad..."

He tensed for a moment, as he usually did when someone brought up his dad. But then he grinned and nodded. "Maybe it is. Then hopefully he's looking out for all of us, not just me."

Ashlynn was still in danger. Because the Landmark Killer hadn't been caught, a lot of people were still in danger. But yet Cash was here instead of at work, and apparently he'd been here before going to the library to see her.

"This is quite a surprise," she said, gazing around at the candles and flowers. There was even a pizza box sitting on the counter, from their favorite place. It wasn't even in Coney Island, so he must have picked it up earlier or paid extra to have it delivered here.

"A pleasant one?" Cash asked. "Could you get used to coming home to me every night?"

Her pulse quickened. "Is that what you meant when you said earlier that you want to be here always?"

He nodded. "I'm not quitting my job or anything—"

"I don't want you to," she assured him. "I know how important it is..."

"Catching bad guys," Ana finished for her when she trailed off.

She nodded. "Yes." He'd saved more lives than just hers and the girls with the bad people he and his unit had brought to justice. "I never wanted you to give it up," she told him. And maybe she hadn't made that clear enough; maybe she hadn't been understanding enough.

He stepped closer to her. "I know. You just wanted me to get my priorities straight. And they are now. You and our family, you're all my number one priority. And I'm just sorry I didn't realize that three years ago."

The tears rushed up on her again, making her nose wrinkle as she tried to hold them back. "I should have tried harder. Fought like I did for the girls and me that night..."

"Tonight, too," he said. "You're fierce and fearless."

"Not fearless enough to fight for what I want."

"What do you want, Valentina?"

"You. Our family."

He dropped to his knees then. And the little girls giggled and started climbing on him. He grinned. "Maybe I should have tackled this part alone..."

She shook her head. "No, this is perfect." And it was, even with the Happy Birthday and Get Well Soon balloons and all those flickering candles making her worry that the smoke alarm might go off again.

"Valentina Acosta Colton, I love you. I have always loved you and I always will. So will you have mercy on me and forgive me for not fighting for us three years ago? And will you give me a chance to spend the rest of our lives making that up to you? Will you marry me all over again?"

Her heart was beating so fast with excitement and love. "You have nothing to make up to me. I kept expecting you to compromise, and I wasn't willing to do that myself. I promise you now that I will always meet you at least halfway. That I will be the partner I promised to be six years ago, when we got married the first time."

"So is that a yes?" he asked, his green eyes shining with love and happiness.

"Yes, I love you!" She leaned down and pressed her lips to his.

And the girls danced around them both.

"She said yes!" Luci announced.

"She said yes!" Ana echoed.

And then Valentina's parents were there, too, and someone had a cell with Cash's mom FaceTiming on it, offering her congratulations as well.

But as quickly as they'd all shown up, they were gone again. His mom and her parents and the girls whom they'd whisked back to the hotel, leaving Valentina and Cash alone together again.

"I'm sorry," he said, his voice gruff with emotion.

"I am, too," she said. "I am as responsible as you are for what happened three years ago. More, maybe, because I didn't tell you when I found out I was pregnant. I'm surprised you've been able to forgive me for that." Surprised and blessed.

"I love you so much that I could forgive you anything," he said. "But I also understand why you did that. All

those times I told you that I didn't want to be a father..."
His voice cracked. "I can't believe what a fool I was. I
can't imagine a world without them in it. That was what
hit me so hard the night that hit man came after them in
the Fun House, after nearly choking you to death." He
shuddered. "I was so scared that I was going to lose the
people I love the most."

"But you withdrew..."

"To protect myself," he said. "To try to deny that feeling of helplessness and fear..."

And suddenly she understood him so well. He must
have felt so helpless when his dad died and then that horrible night in the Fun House...

She wrapped her arms around him, holding him close.
"I'm sorry."

"Let's put that all behind us from here on," he proposed. "We can't undo what we did or didn't do. Let's
move forward, if that's what you really want." He studied
her face now, his green eyes so intense. "That was what
I was just apologizing for, putting you on the spot, pro-
posing to you in front of them. I didn't give you a chance
to tell me, privately, how you really feel. I was fighting
for us, and that was fighting dirty."

"It was," she agreed.

And he flinched.

"But I'm happy that you care enough to fight right
now," she said.

"I love you so much," he said. "I always have, but how
do you really feel?"

"Like fighting," she said.

And he drew back as if he was expecting a blow.

"For us, too," she said. "I love you so much, Cash. I've missed you so much. I can't imagine my life without you in it. And because of that I will keep fighting. For us. For our family. For our love."

He lifted her up and spun around with her clasped tightly in his arms. "With as fierce as you are, I have no worries that we'll be together forever."

She wrapped her arms around his neck and pulled his head down for her kiss. "Forever," she promised him. And that was a promise she had every intention of keeping.

IT FELT LIKE FOREVER. Since Ashlynn had gone into hiding. Since he'd killed...

It had only been a little over a week. But it felt longer.

And he felt weaker, like his plan was beginning to fall apart. He had to claim the next life. An O to begin spelling out O'Leary. He couldn't wait much longer to take another life. Or to find her.

Ashlynn Colton was not smarter than him. She was not going to escape him...without one hell of a fight.

* * * * *

COMING SOON!

We really hope you enjoyed reading this book. If you're looking for more romance be sure to head to the shops when new books are available on

Thursday 12th October

To see which titles are coming soon, please visit

millsandboon.co.uk/nextmonth

MILLS & BOON

THE HEART OF ROMANCE

A ROMANCE FOR EVERY READER

MODERN

Prepare to be swept off your feet by sophisticated, sexy and seductive heroes, in some of the world's most glamourous and romantic locations, where power and passion collide.

HISTORICAL

Escape with historical heroes from time gone by. Whether your passion is for wicked Regency Rakes, muscled Vikings or rugged Highlanders, awaken the romance of the past.

MEDICAL

Set your pulse racing with dedicated, delectable doctors in the high-pressure world of medicine, where emotions run high and passion, comfort and love are the best medicine.

True Love

Celebrate true love with tender stories of heartfelt romance, from the rush of falling in love to the joy a new baby can bring, and a focus on the emotional heart of a relationship.

Desire

Indulge in secrets and scandal, intense drama and sizzling hot action with heroes who have it all: wealth, status, good looks…everything but the right woman.

HEROES

The excitement of a gripping thriller, with intense romance at its heart. Resourceful, true-to-life women and strong, fearless men face danger and desire - a killer combination!

To see which titles are coming soon, please visit

millsandboon.co.uk/nextmonth